The item should be returned or renewed by the last date stamped below.

Dylid dychwelyd neu adnewyddu'r eitem erbyn y dyddiad olaf sydd wedi'i stampio isod.

Newport
CITY COUNCIL
CYNGOR DINAS
Casnewydd

MALPAS

D0808892

To renew visit / Adnewyddwch ar
www.newport.gov.uk/libraries

'Five stars for a brilliant read which both
kept me guessing right to the end and whet
my appetite for more.'
Reader review

ABOUT THE AUTHOR

M.J. Ford lives with his wife and family on the edge of the Peak District in the north of England. He has worked as an editor and writer of children's fiction for many years. His debut novel, *Hold My Hand*, was published in 2018. *Watch Over You* is his third crime book. You can follow Michael @MJFordBooks.

watch
over you

M.J. FORD

Published by AVON
A division of HarperCollins*Publishers* Ltd
1 London Bridge Street
London SE1 9GF

www.harpercollins.co.uk

A Paperback Original 2020

First published in Great Britain by HarperCollins*Publishers* 2020
1

A catalogue copy of this book is available from the British Library.

ISBN: 978-0-00-832985-3

Set in Bembo Std 11.5/13.5 pt by Palimpsest Book Production Limited,
Falkirk, Stirlingshire

Printed and bound in UK by CPI Group (UK) Ltd, Croydon CR0 4YY

MIX
Paper from
responsible sources
FSC® C007454

This book is produced from independently certified FSC™ paper
to ensure responsible forest management.

For more information visit: www.harpercollins.co.uk/green

JAMES

FOUR MONTHS EARLIER

'We're just the same, you and me,' said Grady.

James looked at the shrivelled man sitting beside him, with his toothless gurn and beaten-up trainers that smelled of piss. He was eating a pasty one of the street pastors had bought him, and he didn't seem to care that there were baked beans dripping down the front of his coat.

No, we're not, James thought. *I'm* nothing *like you.*

'Resourceful, you know?' Grady went on. Beside him, his dog Biggles, wearing a set of fluffy reindeer antlers, lifted an eyebrow hopefully, as flakes of pastry fell on to Grady's legs. He brushed them off. 'Survivors, right?'

Just because you're still alive, doesn't mean you're not dying. James had no idea of Grady's age. He looked seventy, but he might have been thirty years younger. That's what decades on smack and dashed hopes would do to you.

A cold December wind whipped along the street where they sat, and James pushed his hands into his armpits, hugging the green field combat coat more tightly around him.

'Fuck, it's cold.'

Grady didn't seem bothered as he chewed. 'This is nothing, lad,' he said. 'When we was on the boats we had a warrant officer would get us out on deck in our undies on Christmas Day. Not a word of a lie.'

James didn't doubt it. For all his repulsive traits and crippling addiction, Grady was pretty honest. They'd met at a soup kitchen run by ex-servicemen a few weeks ago, and since that day he'd bumped into the old navy boy several times and couldn't shake him off. He quite liked Biggles, who attracted more than his fair share of kindness from the public – especially with the antlers – but Grady's endless tales of life on the high seas made James' blood boil.

'One fella got frostbite on his bloody cock!' Grady chuckled to himself at the memory, then offered the remains of the food to James. 'You want this?'

'No,' he said, taking in Grady's tattooed fingers and yellow nails. He stood and stamped his feet, trying to get the blood to flow into his freezing toes.

'Going somewhere?' asked Grady, handing the scraps to Biggles.

James spat on the ground. 'None of your fucking business.'

'Only asking,' said the old man. He looked afraid, his eyes watery under his woollen hat.

'I need to get warm.'

'If I were you, I'd head to the library then. They keep the heating on.'

'And if I were you, I'd do the world a favour and kill myself,' said James.

'Eh?'

'Go to the top of the multi-storey and throw yourself off.'

'What's got into you, lad?'

'You,' said James. He nodded. 'Give me that hat.'

'No,' said Grady.

'Give me the hat or I'll stamp your fucking dog's head in.'

Biggles, sensing the sudden animus, whined, the very tip of his tail wagging timidly.

Grady reached up slowly, and pulled the hat from his head. James realised he'd never seen him without it. Beneath, his hair was wispy and grey over a scalp scabby with eczema. He looked every day of seventy now. He offered the hat to James, who snatched it away.

'I thought we were mates, lad.'

James left the old man mashing his gums and wandered out into St Anne's Square, where the tourists milled about under the festive lights. He put on the hat, feeling instantly better. He'd never been good with the cold, and it was worse since he'd returned from abroad. The library wasn't a bad idea, but there were cameras everywhere, and he needed some cash urgently. So he went instead to one of the chain coffee shops. As usual in the middle of the day, it was filled with mums and their pushchairs, queuing for their skinny caps or whatever. It smelled of mulled spice. No one paid any attention to James, and after a show of looking at the menu board, he lifted the purse from a bag hanging over the handlebars of one of the buggies crammed in by a table of gossiping women. He was in and out in less than a minute.

Round the corner, he checked the contents beside the back door of a Chinese restaurant kitchen, air thick with rich, savoury smells of garlic and ginger. Sixty-five quid, bank cards and the like. There was a picture of a bloke and a baby, their noses touching. He kept the cash and dropped the rest in one of the restaurant's dumper bins. A guy in chef's whites stuck his head out of the door and shouted at him to clear off.

On exiting the alleyway at speed, tucking the money away, he almost collided with a couple walking arm in arm.

3

'Woah!' said one. 'Easy does it!'

James looked up. 'Go fuck your . . .' The words dried up in his mouth. The two strangers were both men, but that wasn't what caught his attention. 'I know you,' he said to the man on the right, tall and square-jawed, tanned, with short greying hair, maybe fifty. He wore a long navy coat that looked pricey.

The man's partner – smaller, boyish, with tight trousers and a tweed jacket – gave an amused smirk and glanced at his companion. 'I hope not, Chris.'

James swallowed thickly, unable to move. He couldn't place the face, but it was right there, like a word on the tip of his tongue.

'I don't think so,' said the older man. 'Sorry we bumped into you.'

They walked off and James stared after them. It was as they disappeared around a corner that his mind dug out the memory he was looking for. He remembered where he'd met the man before. Before he even stopped to think why, he followed.

The cold of the January evening suddenly meant nothing at all. Every inch of James' skin was hot, the atoms of his body vibrating on a higher frequency. New possibilities opened up ahead. If the man was who he thought, this changed *everything*. And even as the hope fired him, doubts set it. It *couldn't* be him, could it? What were the chances, after all these years? He walked around twenty paces behind them, and James' eyes bored into the back of the man's head. The face had been familiar, but as he tailed them, he became more certain. The ages would be about right, too. Even the man's gait, the way his upper body remained perfectly erect while his feet moved in small steps, aroused a deep-seated discomfort.

The men entered a restaurant on Deansgate, and James drifted past the front window, stationing himself beside a taxi rank. He watched as the men were shown to a table, took off their winter coats, and handed them to a maître d'. Then they sat opposite one another, reaching across the table to clutch hands. James felt a bit sick. Bracken, another private in his barracks, had once suggested he was a poof, solely on the basis that he didn't spend his free time poring over pornography like the rest of them. James had pinned him down and got a thumb into the soft flesh beside the top of his nose, threatening to scoop out his eye if he cared to make the insinuation again. Neither Bracken, nor any of the others, ever did.

James watched now, confident that the harsh light of the restaurant's interior and the relative darkness outside would keep him hidden. It was the guy all right – every mannerism rang true.

Falling right into my lap . . .

But there was still work to be done. He stood in place for a half-hour, observing the ebb and flow of customers from the restaurant, the waiting staff drifting from kitchen to table to bar. He saw their patterns of movement and the opportunities these allowed. The maître d' did the same for each new arrival, checking a computer, then leading the diners into the restaurant, before returning to the wall beyond the front desk to hang the coats. There was a twenty- or thirty-second window he could exploit.

So, as the next diners arrived – a party of five men and two women in business clothing – James timed his approach. If he was spotted, he could always run. But no one clocked him as he went to the coat-pegs and fished in the pockets of the navy longcoat, locating a card wallet inside. After a quick upward glance, he opened it, and found the driving licence. *Christopher Putman. 311 Victoria Tower, Salford.* He slipped the wallet back where he'd found it – best not to raise suspicion – and walked out feeling breathless.

The dark city seemed a different place entirely now, the

packed streets full of opportunity. He tried to maintain his composure, but it worked only for a few seconds at a time before his mind spiralled off into fantasies about what this could mean. A door into the past had opened just a fraction, and it could change everything.

Christopher Putman had claimed not to remember him, and fair enough. It had been over ten years, and their encounter had been brief. Probably just a few hours in the day of that bastard before he went back to his comfortable life. But for James it had turned his world upside down.

Soon the past would come back to Putman though. And when it did, he would be very sorry indeed.

Chapter 1

THURSDAY, 17TH APRIL

Jo Masters had attended dozens of dead bodies over the years and the majority of deaths – by far – weren't suspicious at all. Road traffic collisions, freakish workplace accidents, squalid drug overdoses, elderly people who died alone and weren't discovered until putrefaction set in and the neighbours raised the alarm. Death struck randomly, oblivious to notions of justice or moral standing, ready to snuff the lives of the living, and cast those left behind in darkness and misery. It was only when she became a mother that Jo realised quite how many threats lurked under her own roof.

The clock read 10.04, which meant her visitor was late. However, the extra minutes did give her the opportunity to do a final sweep of the house and make sure that it was, to all intents and purposes, completely death-proof for a six-month-old baby.

The magnetic strip that held the kitchen knives was way out of reach, so there was no danger there. The safety catches on the cupboards would keep any poisons safely stowed. All

7

plug sockets had protective covers to prevent the insertion of conductive metals by curious fingers. Curtain cords were looped and fastened a metre above the floor, so there could be no accidental self-garrotting. Stairgates were braced so tightly against their wall-mountings that even a rugby prop forward running at velocity would fail to dislodge them. Never mind that Theo could not yet crawl. Jo had vacuumed, swept, dusted, and anti-bac-sprayed to standards that would have impressed Vera Coyne, Thames Valley's forensic pathology supremo. Theo watched her with a mixture of smiles, squirms and frowning curiosity as she dashed about like a dervish trying to create the impression of parenting competence. He was probably wondering why all his stuffed animals were lined up on a shelf, as if awaiting a drill sergeant's inspection, and why his mother had suddenly deemed to disinfect his favourite teething ring when she'd never bothered before. He, thankfully, didn't understand the day's significance.

It was a little stuffy, so Jo pulled up a sash window. Would that look like a hazard, though? Maybe. She closed it again.

Passing the phone, she noticed for the first time that the message light was flashing. There was only one person who used the landline these days, apart from the ambulance chasers and the other cold-callers. She played the recording as she brushed a few specks of dust off the windowsill.

The message was two days old.

'Hello, Jo. It's been a while. Listen, there's something I need to talk with you about. I know you've got a lot on, but . . . it's delicate. Maybe you could give me a call back when you've got a minute. Oh, it's Harry, by the way.'

Harry Ferman. Former inspector with Thames Valley Police and her drinking buddy before life changed completely and she'd switched to gin-less tonics and early bedtimes. He hadn't cared, of course – it was her company he valued. But she hadn't seen him for, what, three months? *Too long.* She doubted he was busy that evening, and began to search for his number.

Before she could hit call, the doorbell rang. Jo pocketed the phone, and went to check her appearance in the hallway mirror. As so often these days, there was a moment of cognitive dissonance as she regarded the tired expression looking back at her. No amount of concealer could disguise the dark circles beneath her eyes, and she hadn't even bothered to dye the grey streaks multiplying around her temples. What was the point, really?

'Get a grip,' she muttered to herself. This wasn't a date, or an interview. It didn't, or shouldn't, matter how she looked. It was *her* house. Her turf. *I'm in control.*

She opened the door with the sincerest smile she could manage. Liz Merriman, the normal health visitor, was a diminutive five-foot-nothing, maybe thirty years old, with dreadlocks pulled back in a knot, and an easy, authentic expression that suggested she really did enjoy her job. She wore a blue nurse's tunic, sensible flats, and carried a satchel. But she wasn't alone today. The woman accompanying her was about ten years Jo's senior, dressed in a tailored navy skirt and a pale blouse buttoned up to her throat, with short-cropped grey hair. She reminded Jo of a Victorian governess, and the contrast between the two women on her doorstep couldn't have been more extreme.

'Hello, Jo,' said Merriman. 'Sorry we're late.'

Jo tore her gaze from Merriman's companion and waved her hand dismissively. 'Oh, you're not, are you? Time doesn't mean much to me these days!'

'I'm Annabelle Pritchard,' said the older woman, holding out a bony hand.

Jo took it. The woman's skin was cold, despite the heat of the day.

'Jo Masters,' she said.

'May we come in?' asked Pritchard.

'Have you got a warrant?' said Jo. Annabelle frowned. 'Just kidding. Occupational humour.' Jo tried to form a disarming grin.

'Of course,' said Annabelle, looking troubled rather than amused. 'I heard you were a police officer.' She said it with about the same level of distaste as if Jo had said she worked in a slaughterhouse.

Jo moved aside, and let her guests pass. Merriman slid off her shoes before Jo could tell her not to bother.

'How's the little man doing?' she asked.

I've managed to keep him alive, if that's what you mean.

'Fine, fine,' said Jo, leading the way through to the living room. 'He's just through here. Can I get you a tea or coffee?'

'Just a glass of water would be great,' said Merriman. 'Hotting up out there.'

'And for you?' Jo asked her companion.

'Nothing, thank you,' said Pritchard.

As Jo went to the sink in the kitchen to get the drink, she could hear Merriman cooing to Theo. A knot settled just under her heart. She'd known that this would be more than a routine visit, but the appearance of the other woman was still disconcerting. She carried the water into the other room. Merriman was already seated by Theo's bouncer, spinning the mobile that hung in front of it. Pritchard was looking out of the window into the street below, as if appraising the drop, and Jo was pleased with her decision regarding ventilation.

Jo placed the glass on the table.

'Thanks,' said Merriman. 'He looks a cheerful little chap.'

'He is in the daytime,' said Jo. 'The hair and claws sprout after dark.'

Merriman offered the briefest of smiles. 'And how are you coping with the lack of sleep?'

'Fine, actually,' Jo lied. She couldn't recall the last time she'd got more than two straight hours, and the night before had been hell; it had taken three strong coffees that morning to rouse her to anything like a functioning mind, and a ton of foundation to take away the zombie pallor. Theo had seemed like a dream sleeper at first, but in the last month the nights had become progressively more fractured by his wakefulness. There seemed no cause. Even when he was fed, dry and the room was a perfect temperature, he still woke frequently and it took forty-five minutes of rocking and singing to help him settle once more.

She threw a glance at the clock, and Merriman caught it.

'Don't worry. We won't keep you long.'

'It's not a problem,' said Jo. 'I just have to get to work by eleven.'

Pritchard looked surprised. 'Goodness. You're going back already? You're a super-woman.'

Again, perhaps the hint of criticism there. 'Thames Valley maternity pay isn't great,' Jo explained. It was a fib – they were rather generous - and Pritchard's eyebrow rose sceptically. Working in the public sector, Jo reasoned, she'd likely know such things.

Merriman leant across, and Jo flinched as her visitor laid a hand on her knee. 'I know it's hard to juggle things,' she said. 'Have you found a nursery?'

'Yes,' said Jo. 'Little Steps. They've got a good survival rate.'

Stop it, Jo. You're not helping.

'Parents nearby?' asked Pritchard from the window. Jo wondered if she'd had her sense of humour surgically removed, or if she'd left it in her crypt at home.

'Sadly my mum opted to pop her clogs rather than babysit,' said Jo.

'Oh, I am sorry,' said Pritchard, with a purse of her lips.

11

'Don't be – she wasn't particularly happy. In a home, you know. We weren't that close.'

Pritchard nodded, and moved across to the sofa. She opened her own bag and took out an ominous black file.

Jo knew how she came across when she talked about her mother. It was true what she'd said though. There'd not been much affection even before her mum went into Evergreen Lodge, and by the end there wasn't much of her mum there at all to love anyway. Jo hadn't even wanted to tell her about the surprise pregnancy – it would have involved too many awkward questions about the identity of the father. Plus, she really didn't feel she needed any advice on mothering at the time, especially from the woman who'd made her own child-hood so miserable.

In the end, the decision to tell her mum or not was taken out of her hands. The physical changes to her own body, un-deniable to anyone else, had coincided with her mum's sudden decline at the home, sleeping for longer and longer periods, barely eating, then eventually, on a Monday afternoon, not waking up at all. Paul, Jo's brother, had handled the arrange-ments, and she had been one of just seven at the Crematorium, her hips killing her as she waddled up to the lectern to read some cloyingly sentimental Victorian verse.

'How's feeding going?' asked Pritchard. 'Bottle or breast?'

'Bottle,' said Jo. 'I'd wanted to breastfeed, but there were medical issues. He's taken to solids though – loves pears!'

God, I sound deranged!

Pritchard wrote a few more words, then looked up. Her eyes moved around the room before settling on Theo. She smiled like an afterthought.

'And healing up well, I see?'

Jo tensed, internally at least. It hadn't taken long to get the pleasantries out of the way. The bruise across Theo's right cheekbone was a sickly yellow now. If only the memories that led to it would fade as quickly.

'I really don't think it bothers him at all,' said Jo.

'Probably not,' said Pritchard. 'Must have been frightening for you both though.'

A moment's silence. Jo heard the distinct sound of the kitchen clock.

Tick. Tock. Tick. Tock.

'Women drivers, eh?' she said at last.

'What's that?' said Pritchard.

'It was a woman who crashed into us. Silly cow was on her phone.'

'Us?' said Pritchard. 'My understanding was that you weren't in the car.'

This time, there was no accusation in the tone, but there didn't need to be. Facts were facts. 'Well, no,' said Jo. 'You know, it was just bad luck.'

'I understand,' said Pritchard, before returning to her notes.

'You don't need to write it down,' said Jo. 'I've already been over it twice at the hospital, and with the police.'

'We keep our own records,' said Pritchard, as she continued, infuriatingly, to scribble her notes. 'It's just a formality.'

Jo's throat felt tight, just from the memory.

'He's *fine*,' Jo insisted to the prim woman on her sofa.

'It does seem that way, yes,' said Pritchard.

'No,' said Jo. 'It *is* that way. The matter is closed.'

Merriman's mouth moved as if she was about to speak, but the older woman got there first.

'This is just a routine visit,' she said.

'Really?' said Jo. 'In the past, it's just been Liz.'

'There's nothing to worry about,' said Pritchard.

'I'm not worried,' said Jo, shaking her head. But as she spoke she felt a small tremble of her lip betraying her. She could

13

almost imagine how she was coming across. Defensive, unstable, neurotic. She was stuck in a downward spiral, drowning. What scared her most was that, though she could see the impression she was giving off, she felt powerless to stop it. She felt herself welling up, and clenched her jaw to stem the flow.

'Josie, it's okay,' said Merriman. She reached out again to touch Jo's leg, but this time Jo drew back.

Tick. Tock.

She took a deep breath, trying to regain some equilibrium. Then she leant down, unclipping Theo from the bouncer and holding him to her chest. 'I'm fine, thank you,' she said. '*We're* fine, as you can see.'

Merriman stood, as if ready to leave, but Pritchard remained seated. 'Is it okay if we go over a few more things, Jo?' she asked.

'I'm afraid I don't have time,' said Jo. 'You were late, you see?'

Merriman, to her credit, looked like she wanted to be out of there fast. After a couple of awkward seconds, Pritchard nodded too. 'If you need us, you know how to get in touch.'

The only thing I need is for you to get out of my fucking house.

'We can show ourselves out,' said Merriman softly.

Jo watched them go, then followed to the hallway. Neither of them spoke to each other, and the older woman led the way out of the front door. Merriman paused a moment, looking back to Jo. 'You're doing a great job,' she said. 'Hope the return to work goes well.'

Jo, already on edge, lost it then, and the first tear rolled down her cheek. She nodded. As the door closed behind her visitors, Theo squirmed a little in her grip, and she realised she was holding him tight enough to make his back clammy through his clothes. She loosened her grip, and kissed him on the head. Though her thoughts were an angry swirling mess on the surface – How could they march into her house? Ask her their stupid questions? – it was the pull of a deeper, more unsettling current beneath that was causing her legs to shake. Something Jo Masters rarely experienced. *Fear.* Theo was her child, and no one else was going to lecture her on how to look after him. No one was going to touch him, or talk to him, or ever take him away.

Chapter 2

Her first thought, in the aftermath of the visit, was to call and delay the return to work for another day, but after ten minutes giving Theo his bottle and spooning some mashed banana between his gums, she found a degree of calm. It wasn't even a proper day's work – she was only popping in for a catch-up. If she didn't show, it wouldn't look right. Her colleagues would make their own assumptions.

Having wiped Theo's face, and changed his nappy, she felt composed enough to search for Annabelle Pritchard online. She was listed as a 'welfare co-ordinator' with the Oxfordshire City Council Child Welfare Team. Jo preferred 'Child-Snatcher' – it seemed to fit Pritchard rather well. She didn't know why she had let herself be caught off guard like that, but told herself the visit was indeed a formality, a simple safeguarding procedure. After several incidents of neglect in the last few years, local authorities often erred on the side of caution. Better that than catch negative publicity later. And who could blame them? There really was nothing to worry about though. What had happened outside the shop was a freak accident – nothing more – and it certainly didn't reflect any cause for concern, or approach anything like the threshold for taking further action. She was, as everyone close to her said – and as she frequently tried to convince herself – a *good mum*.

The cottage she was renting was in the small village of Wolvercote, far enough from the city centre that she didn't feel tied to the station, but still walkable on a good day through Port Meadow. As she drove Theo to Little Steps, the nursery she'd found on the Woodstock Road, he gurgled happily from the rear seat. Though she tried to block out the memory of the accident eight days earlier, it was like a stubborn tune that wouldn't leave her, playing from the depths of her subconscious.

She'd heard the crash from the queue at the front of the minimarket – everyone had. She'd dropped the nappies and run out, seeing her own car at an angle, the front of an Audi TT buried in the rear wing. She hadn't even found her voice to scream; she could hardly breathe as she ran on unsteady legs to Theo's door. A young woman was climbing out of the Audi, her phone still in her hand. She looked up at Jo approaching and mumbled something about 'single yellows'. Jo rushed right past, and flung open the back door. Theo's cries were wild, like no sound he'd ever made before. She heard the woman say, 'Oh my God!'

Jo felt an echo of the same sinking feeling as she stopped at the lights. The pores of her skin prickled at the memory.

The only immediate sign of damage to Theo had been a graze across his cheekbone. The doctors said later that it could have been much worse, but the baby seat's headrest had done its job, cushioning the impact as the car jolted sideways. Still, they'd insisted on several different tests – keeping Jo in a purgatory of guilt and worry. Theo, amazingly, had stopped crying while they carried out the examinations, as if, even in his own distress, he'd recognised her emotional turmoil was greater. Though nothing turned up in the X-rays or brain images, they'd kept him in overnight as a precaution, with Jo curled up in a chair on the children's ward beside him, eyes gritty from tears and exhaustion.

She released a deep shuddering breath as she cruised down the Woodstock Road. What she'd told Pritchard about the matter being closed wasn't strictly true. Though the police had shown no interest in pursuing things, the insurers were still in a process of arbitration. Jo hadn't even noticed the parking restrictions when she pulled up directly outside the shop. She hadn't seen much at all, other than that the small car park was full. Theo was fast asleep; he *needed* to sleep after the broken night before, up every hour crying inexplicably. And if she parked near to the door, she'd practically be able to *see* him in his seat. It would be for two minutes, maybe less . . .

It had turned out to be more like seven − bloke at the damned checkout deciding he'd picked up the wrong hummus − and every second haunted her. Might she have made a different decision, if she hadn't been so fucking exhausted herself? If she hadn't been so desperate for him to get some decent sleep, and to wake up smiling rather than crying, eyes clear and shining rather than pink with fatigue? If she was a better mum, and not the sort who left her baby − her precious, defenceless, innocent, six-month-old baby − in the car while she dipped into a shop to buy nappies?

The car behind was honking its horn. The lights were green. Jo lifted a hand to apologise and drove on.

Theo had already had a couple of sessions to settle in at Little Steps and, despite some tearful protests, the staff had assured her he was perfectly happy as soon as she was out of sight. She wished she could have said the same for herself. As had so often happened in recent months, the extremes of her own emotions surprised her − the swings and lurches of her moods were not something she was used to at all. Tears came more easily, and mawkish films that would once have induced nausea now reduced her to sobbing. She'd actually had to turn off a nature programme a couple of nights earlier when it showed a lion cub being stalked by hyenas.

There was anger too, always there, like a Mr Hyde lurking and ready to attack. She really had come close to kicking the desiccated old bitch Pritchard up the arse on her way out of the door. But now, replaying the conversation from memory with her Dr Jekyll head, she wondered if actually she'd imagined the judgemental tone completely. For someone who so often had relied on calm intuition – on reading people and their motives – it was a little frightening to think so.

Today, there were no tears at all from Theo on drop-off, and so she took the nursery worker's advice and left without making a big deal of the goodbyes. Back in her car, she felt a sudden release, then immediately on its tail, guilt. Theo was still *so* young. The welfare officer wasn't the only person to express surprise at Jo going back to work so soon. Her sister-in-law Amelia, and Heidi Tan, the other mum in CID, had both suggested she needn't rush back. And it wasn't as though her financial position was particularly parlous even – with the inheritance, and her share of the sale of her mum's house, she could've easily prolonged her maternity leave for another six months.

So what was it, pulling her back in now? She was honest enough with herself to acknowledge that she missed the hustle of police work. Some women, she knew, never looked back once they started their families. Work took the back seat, and good luck to them. Amelia was like that, taking four years out for Emma, their first child. She'd been on the way to making deputy head at a good school prior to the birth, but she'd paid the price in terms of career progression, settling for a demotion in order to continue teaching when her former role was absorbed. She'd told Jo she really didn't mind the pressure being off, but Jo knew Amelia was no pushover, and she had always been ambitious; it must've stung.

Jo was luckier with her line of work. Once you had your rank, they weren't taking it away. She could have stayed out for a couple of years, and there'd have been few impediments to rejoining later. Maybe the odd training course to bring her up to speed on the latest rules and regs, but otherwise it would have been back into the thick of it. The only thing she'd had to fight for – and it was a quick and bloodless fight with the HR department – was a return to active duty rather than desk-work like Heidi had settled for. That had never been her thing.

It wasn't just the thrill of the chase she missed though. She'd been thinking about it a lot, and realised a large part of the job's appeal was that, at St Aldates, things were actually simpler. There were plenty of problems, obviously – mysteries to be solved, charges to be brought, wrongs to be righted, justice to be served. But at the end of the day, there was procedure, paperwork, and shared routine that everyone understood – shift patterns, briefings, pecking order. And results that spoke for themselves. No one had warned about the complexities of motherhood, and she'd never anticipated the psychological challenges it would bring. Not knowing the solutions to calm a crying child. The trial and error. Never being sure if you were doing the *right* thing, either in the moment or for the long term. The constant second-guessing. It had been a different proposition altogether, stirring up insecurities she'd thought she'd put behind her years ago, creating others she never knew she had, a rollercoaster of highs and lows, doubts and difficulties. Through the fog of sleeplessness, answers seemed less certain. Even the questions being asked weren't sometimes clear.

* * *

She pulled up in the St Aldates car park feeling a little like an adult revisiting her childhood school. In reality, it was only six months since she'd last been at the station, and she wasn't sure why she expected it to look different. Nevertheless, the complete *lack* of change came as a surprise. The same takeaway menus were pinned to the board in the hallway at the same angles. The same scuffs were on the floor. The same smells, even – whatever refrigerant was leaking in the break room, mixed with the stuff they used to clean the holding cells along the corridor. Plus George Dimitriou's strong, though admittedly very pleasant, aftershave.

As she entered the CID room, though, it was empty. Her own chair was under the desk, a woman's lightweight jacket slung over the back, and a nice-looking handbag perched on the edge of the desk. Heidi had mentioned a new DC had started, in her late twenties. Alice something. Jo heard the mumble of voices and laughter from the briefing room, so dropped her things on the desk and wandered over. The door opened before she'd reached it, and it was Dimitriou who ambled out. He was sporting a new, finely sculpted moustache, which unnerved her a little. She backed away, unable to take her eyes off it.

'Look what the cat dragged in,' he said. He smiled as he spoke, half-turning to a slim and attractive natural blonde behind him. 'Ali, meet the mighty Jo Masters.' As ever with Dimitriou, there was a hint of mockery. She was technically his superior, but he never spoke as though that occurred to him. Most of the time, she didn't mind, and the two of them had a lightly combative relationship that just about worked.

The woman shook Jo's hand firmly. 'Alice Reeves,' she said. 'Pleased to meet you at last.'

'Likewise,' said Jo. 'Looking forward to working together.'

Inside the briefing room, Heidi Tan and Andy Carrick were talking but broke apart when they saw Jo. Andy waved her in.

'We can catch up in a minute,' Jo said to Dimitriou. 'But don't try and tap me up for sponsorship.'

'Huh?' he said.

'For the novelty facial hair.'

Alice smiled, and Dimitriou blushed. 'Ha-bloody-ha.'

Leaving them, Jo walked across to the others. On the screen immediately behind them was a montage of several pictures of a young man in the front seat of a car – a white BMW. From one angle, he looked asleep, but another showed a significant wound that had mangled the left side of his face.

'Welcome back,' said Carrick. 'Theo okay?'

'I think I'm taking the separation worse,' said Jo. 'How are yours?'

'The older one's worked out how to bypass the parental controls on his phone,' said Carrick. 'I'm fighting a losing battle.'

Andy had two kids, on the way to being teenagers, and managed to carry off the balance of perfect family man and professional police officer with more grace and aplomb than she'd ever achieve.

'Got that to look forward to,' said Jo.

'I doubt it,' said Heidi. 'By the time ours hit ten, the phones will be implanted somewhere.'

Jo turned to the photos again. The man looked Japanese, or Korean. 'This the local shooting?' she said. It had been in the paper, and though she'd normally have taken great interest, it had coincided with the fallout from the accident outside the mini-market, and thus had made limited impact on her consciousness.

'Indeed,' said Carrick. 'Five days ago – the twelfth – at the old BT building.'

Jo knew the location – five floors of abandoned offices off the Cowley Road. Popular with graffiti artists. There wouldn't be any security cameras, because the building held nothing of value.

'Xan Do,' said Heidi. 'Twenty-one years old. Private school

educated, an undergrad here who dropped out after a year. He wasn't on our radar, but one of Dimi's informants seemed to think he was connected to the Matthis family.'

Jo nodded in acknowledgement. The surname was a common one from their case files. The Matthis family had been notorious, mid-level drug dealers in the South Oxford area since before she joined Thames Valley, though things had quietened down in recent times. 'They're inside, aren't they?'

'The dad is. Plus his eldest boy, Riley. There's another son, though – Blake. He's sixteen. Our theory is that Do was taking care of the dirty work, with Blake acting as a contact with his father.'

'So this was a deal that went south?' said Jo.

'Maybe,' said Heidi. She fished through a pile of papers and came up with a photo of several small baggies of pills. 'These were still under the seat though – a couple of grand's worth. Phone and wallet left untouched too. We're having the call and GPS data extracted.'

'Maybe a rival then,' said Jo. 'Or a third-party professional. Ballistics?'

'Single round, fired point blank through the window, which remained largely intact. It entered under his cheekbone and exited, well, all over the place. They're saying it's a Makarov, probably reactivated.'

'Xan Do's parents own a successful Asian food wholesaler on the edge of town,' said Carrick. 'They consented to a search, but it came up empty. George is pissed. He and Alice are about to head out to talk to Blake Matthis, see if we can shake the tree.'

'Great – I'll tag along.'

Carrick smiled. 'You don't want a cup of tea or something first? Catch up?'

'Maybe later,' said Jo. 'I need to get my sea legs back.'

*　*　*

Jo caught up with Reeves and Dimitriou as they were pulling out of the car park and waved them to stop. He wound down the window.

'Wait up,' she said. 'I'm coming too.'

Dimitriou flinched. 'We don't need hand-holding.'

'Don't be a spoilsport.'

The younger woman began to climb out of the passenger side to make room in the front.

'Don't worry about that,' said Jo, though the show of deference impressed her. 'I'm just observing.'

'Sure thing, ma'am,' said Reeves.

As they drove, Dimitriou filled Jo in on their suspect – Blake Matthis had been picked up numerous times in the last five years for possession, assault, and threatening behaviour. Currently registered as living at home with his mother, Tracy Grimshaw, he was known to visit his sibling and father in prison once a fortnight. Enough time to pass on info and receive instructions about the family business. He was also seventeen, as of that morning.

'You're going to ruin his birthday,' said Jo. Her eyes were still drawn to Dimitriou's moustache, and he seemed to realise.

'Can you stop that?' he said. 'You're making me self-conscious.'

'Sorry,' said Jo. 'It's . . . nice. You think Blake will give us anything?'

'Probably not, but no harm in rattling cages. If Xan was executed on their patch, they must have an idea who did it.'

'Might have been the Matthis family themselves. Maybe Xan was screwing them.'

'The thought had occurred,' said Dimitriou. 'Despite the low level trouble-making, Blake's managed to keep his nose clean so far. I doubt he pulled the trigger.'

Jo turned her attention to Reeves. 'So how are you finding it?'

'Good,' she said.

'Tell Jo about the OD,' said Dimi.

'What's that?' asked Jo.

'I'd rather forget it,' said Reeves.

'A squat in Abingdon,' said Dimitriou. 'Girl had been dead for a while. Let's just say they had a rodent problem. It was nasty. Mel Cropper was licking his lips.'

Jo smiled. Cropper headed up the crime scene team. He had a taste for the macabre and apparently no sense of smell.

'Carrick's a great gaffer,' said Reeves, as if keen to change the subject.

'A definite improvement on his predecessor,' Jo agreed.

'Yeah, I heard he gave you a hard time,' said Reeves.

Jo wondered what exactly Reeves had been told about her, by Dimitriou and the others. Since moving to Thames Valley, she'd worked two cases that yielded positive results, but made national headlines, and required some serious public relations handling. In both, lengthy inquiries had absolved her of wrongdoing, but the notoriety lingered. Phil Stratton, her former DCI, hadn't been so lucky. From her perspective, he'd hampered the investigations, refusing to listen to his officers, and she only guessed the rest of team had put the boot in too when giving their own evidence. In the end, just as she went on maternity leave, he'd been unceremoniously shown the door. Ostensibly it was an early retirement, but he and everyone else knew that was a weasel way of saying he was surplus to requirements. He was only forty-eight, and he hadn't even been given time to clear his desk and say farewell. Jo had actually bumped into him in the supermarket while pushing Theo around, about a fortnight after the C-section. He'd insisted, with slightly too much enthusiasm, that he was enjoying some time away. The microwave meals for one, and the two bottles of whisky in his basket, suggested otherwise.

* * *

The Matthis house, a sixties semi, was on the edge of Blackbird Leys Park, in the centre of a sprawling estate south of the city. Mostly built as social housing, it had had a reputation for many years as a high-crime area, but things were improving. It still accounted, however, for a significant proportion of low-level call-outs, like anti-social behaviour, petty theft, and domestics.

They parked a few doors down, and attracted a few sullen stares from some local teenagers hanging around outside a shopping parade opposite. One took out his phone. The fact Jo and her colleagues weren't wearing uniforms hardly mattered. Their sort could smell police a mile away.

As Dimitriou and Reeves led the way, Jo couldn't help but admire the latter's attire. It helped she had the confidence and shape to make it work, but the suit was no off-the-rail number like her own. Jo thought they were probably about the same height in socks, but Reeves' heels boosted her stature considerably. She obviously hadn't dressed expecting any sort of foot-chase, and Jo wondered how much beat work she'd done previously.

They reached the front of the house. The TV was on inside and Dimitriou rang the doorbell. A dog barked within, and through the marbled pane beside the door Jo saw it hurtling towards them, before its paws began clubbing and clawing at the inside.

They waited for half a minute before Dimitriou rang again, this time banging the door with the fleshy part of his fist as the dog continued to go nuts. 'Ms Grimshaw, it's the police. We'd like a word, please.'

Jo looked around, checking their surroundings. At the shops, one of the youths was still speaking into his phone, watching them.

Another shape appeared through the marbled pane, and the door opened. A morbidly obese woman, maybe not quite forty, stood there. She held the short lead of the equally rotund Staffordshire bull terrier, head like an anvil, tail held stiff as a car aerial. Dimitriou held his ground and Jo was glad to be a few steps back: she'd never got on with dogs.

'What do you want?' Tracy was breathing hard, and her cheeks were red, as if they'd interrupted a workout, though it seemed more likely it was just the exertion of getting to the door.

'We were hoping to speak to Blake,' said Dimitriou.

'He's not here,' she said.

'Any idea when he'll be back?'

'No.'

She began to shut the door, but Dimitriou put his foot over the threshold and blocked it. Tracy Grimshaw's features went from bored to lethal in a blink. 'Be careful where you put that,' she said. 'Niko here likes bacon.'

Dimitriou left his foot in place while he fished out a card, and offered it to her. 'If Blake puts in an appearance, we'd love to have a chat.'

Grimshaw looked at the card but didn't take it. After a second or two, Dimitriou withdrew his foot. The door slammed in their faces.

'I think that could be the start of something beautiful,' said Jo.

Dimitriou posted the card into the letterbox, where Niko promptly set about attacking it, and they turned back towards the car.

As they were getting in, Jo noticed that the boy who'd been on his phone outside the shops was slipping between parked cars towards an archway leading under the parade. He was still looking her way. *It might be nothing, but . . .*

'Hey, I'm just going to talk to those kids,' said Jo.

Reeves nodded. Dimitriou remained by his open door. 'Suit yourself.'

Jo crossed the street towards the shops. 'What's up?' said one of the kids – he looked about ten or eleven, slouched on an oversized mountain bike and sucking on a cigarette. Jo ignored him, and followed the route taken by the boy with the phone. The back of the shops opened up on a large block of flats, buttressed by external stairwells at intervals, leading up to three tiers of identical front doors. Jo couldn't see the kid at first and was thinking about turning back when she heard a metal screech coming from her left. It was another passageway, underneath the main block of flats, which she guessed led to the main estate artery, Brook Street, on the other side. She quickened her feet towards the opening, and stepped into a darker passage. It was about fifty metres long, with narrow garages, more like lock-ups, on either side. The boy she'd followed was standing by the door of one at the end. He clocked Jo at once, then turned and ran, shouting, 'Cops!'

Jo trotted a little more quickly, calling after him. 'Hey, I just want to talk!'

The lock-up door squealed open fully as she approached, and Jo heard the growl of an engine inside. As she drew level, a red and white dirt bike lurched out, carrying a young man wearing a baseball cap. She tried to leap out of the way, but the back end of the bike skidded around the slammed into her lower half. All she could do was throw out her arms as she was sent sprawling across the ground. The boy – and she was almost certain it was Blake Matthis – gave her a half-sympathetic look, before smoke clouded the air and he shot away in the same direction the other lad had fled.

Jo winced as she used the wall to haul herself to her feet. Her left leg was completely dead from the impact, but she managed to get on her radio.

'Dimi, he's here,' she said. 'Exited the flats on to Brook Street. He's on a bike.' She managed to stagger out too, but her leg still wasn't co-ordinating with the rest of her body, and it dragged behind her. The bike, which had no plates, was already a hundred metres away, and now the other boy was on the back of it as well. 'He's heading south.'

Dimitriou said they'd come to her, and they arrived on foot a minute later.

'You sure it was him?' asked her colleague.

Jo nodded, and pointed back to the lock-up. 'He was in there.'

'You get the tag?'

'Bike didn't have one,' said Jo. 'It was just a 50cc thing. Red and white.'

'Call it in.' It was practically an order, but she didn't quibble.

Dimi didn't seem to have noticed she was hobbling, but Reeves asked if she was okay. The feeling was coming back into her leg, in waves of a deep throbbing ache. Jo explained what had happened with the bike.

Dimitriou was peering into the lock-up. 'Looks like he's been holed up in here a while.' His face screwed up and he lifted his sleeve to his nose. 'Stinks.'

Jo, having come off the radio with Traffic, joined him inside. The interior of the garage looked like a delinquent's bedroom. Sleeping bag on a beat-up sofa, beer cans, a pizza box, as well as a small holdall. There was a mobile phone too. 'He left in a hurry,' said Reeves, picking it up. She sniffed at something unpleasant.

The smell reached Jo's nose too – it was like a public toilet, and sure enough, a bucket in the corner was a couple of inches deep with what looked like urine. The remains of several roll-ups floated on the surface.

'Why was he living in squalor when his family home is two hundred metres up the road?' asked Dimitriou.

'Maybe he was expecting us,' said Reeves.

30

Jo shrugged. 'Kids like Blake Matthis aren't scared of us,' she said. 'Probably learned his rights before he learned to read.' She thought of the bike. 'He was ready to run though.'

'All the more likely he had something to do with Xan Do,' said Dimitriou. He looked into the holdall, but all Jo could see were clothes. 'Let's do a search and take a look at the phone. He's not going to get far.'

★   ★   ★

There was no great urgency to bring Blake in, and for the remainder of the afternoon Jo settled back into work in a leisurely fashion, with briefings from Heidi on some of the latest stats, and an update from Andy Carrick on some of the personnel changes among the uniformed officers and operational frameworks. As the hours wore on though, she found her mind turning towards Theo with increasing regularity, like bursts of static. By four o'clock it was almost constant and she was struggling to concentrate on anything else. Dimitriou and Alice suggested an after-work drink to welcome her back, which she declined. George did not look terribly disappointed.

In the car, she flexed her leg before setting off. She didn't need to inspect under her trousers to know a hell of a bruise was coming through. Though she was pretty sure he hadn't ridden at her on purpose, an ABH charge would await Blake if Carrick was feeling vindictive.

Despite the pain, a glance in the rear-view mirror surprised Jo – she was practically beaming. And as she closed in on Little Steps, thoughts of seeing Theo and holding him made her almost giddy. Was this how it was going to be now, every time they were separated for a few hours?

She was driving past the university parks when a call came through on the emergency services network. Attendance required at a serious incident on Canterbury Road. An injured elderly IC1 male. Ambulance was already on its way. Jo suffered a moment of confusion.

That's Harry Ferman's road.

She wasn't far away. It would be a fifteen-minute detour, if that. Canterbury Road was maybe thirty houses, and she guessed most contained Caucasian residents over fifty. The chances of it being anything to do with Harry, at number 21, were slim.

A uniform responded they were en route, asking for more details.

'*Neighbour reported the sound of a disturbance,*' said the dispatcher, '*and found the elderly man next door with a head injury.*'

'*What house number?*'

A brief pause.

'*Twenty-one. That's two, one.*'

Jo swallowed, and pushed the respond button. 'DS Masters attending,' she said.

She checked her mirrors, indicated, and swung a U-turn.

Chapter 3

Harry Ferman's front door was open, and three civilians were standing on the pavement outside. There were no emergency vehicles yet. Jo pulled up, and climbed out, not bothering to close the door. 'Is Harry in there?'

An elderly woman – ashen-faced – nodded. 'I saw him through the window.'

Jo entered, struck by the familiarity of the place. The front door opened onto a narrow hallway, with a coat hanging from a peg, a small umbrella stand and a runner over a threadbare, heavily patterned carpet of faded russet and gold. She entered a lounge stuffed with plush furniture and an old cathode-ray TV. The walls were crowded with small paintings and photographs, and a dresser dominated one corner, lined with ornaments, including the paperweight she'd purchased for him the previous year in Edinburgh.

A young woman in what looked like a nurse's uniform was crouching beside Harry, who lay with his head propped up against a seat cushion. She was holding a towel to the back of his head and it was almost completely saturated with blood.

'Oh my God, Harry!' said Jo, kneeling down beside him.

His skin was grey and his eyes remained open just a fraction. A few tulips lay strewn on the carpet beside a broken vase.

The woman looked at her desperately. 'Who are you?'

'A friend. I'm a police officer.'

'Is the ambulance here?'

Jo shook her head. 'It will be soon.'

'He's not responding at all,' said the woman. 'I can't stop the bleeding.'

Jo had so many questions, but they could wait. 'Pulse?'

'I've not had chance.'

Wondering what sort of nurse didn't check for a pulse, Jo laid her fingers against his wrist. His skin was still warm, but she couldn't feel anything and his hand was completely limp. Heavy. She checked the carotid artery too, but there was nothing there either. She leant right over his face. 'Harry, can you hear me?'

Ferman's glassy eyes didn't so much as flicker.

'Okay, keep the pressure on,' said Jo.

She gently pulled back Ferman's chin, and bent her lips to his. Two breaths, ten compressions. She'd done resuscitation once before for real, off-duty, on a toddler pulled from a swimming pool, and it had worked. With children you had to be gentle – it was easy to break the breastbone. With adults, not so much. She put all her weight into the thrusts, driving the heel of her palm to get Harry's heart beating again. Nothing after the first round, so she tried again. Not good, but she was nowhere near ready to give up.

'Come on, Harry!' she said. The sound of competing sirens drifted from the distance.

The third round of breaths and compressions became the fourth, and she was aware of hope seeping out of the room. His body was so utterly inert – it already felt like she was pumping dead meat, not living flesh. A look in the eyes of the nurse confirmed her own pessimism. Then suddenly there were more people in the room wearing paramedic uniforms. Jo vaguely recognised faces from past scenarios, but her brain didn't have space to remember names. No time for pleasantries. She bent to deliver another set of breaths, but a hand gently and firmly pulled her back.

'I've given five sets of breaths and compressions,' she said.

'Okay, we'll continue.'

Jo watched, still seated on the ground, her fingers digging into the carpet as the paramedics took over, placing an oxygen mask on Harry's mouth. They spoke to each other in urgent, professional tones. The nurse originally on the scene stood beside Jo, eyes glued to their work.

Too quickly, after only a few attempts, the paramedics looked at each other. There was a shake of the head, a mumbled phrase, and a replying nod, then a checking of watches.

Harry lay completely still on his lounge floor, eyes still open and focused intently on the ceiling.

Jo buried her head in her hands.

★　★　★

'Josie, he's beautiful.'

'You have to say that.'

'True, but I mean it.'

She was rocking Theo up and down. He'd been crying since the moment she brought him inside.

'He's got your eyes too.'

'You need to stop with the clichés. You'll be telling me how well I look next.'

Harry smiled. 'Well, you do.'

'I'm desperate for the loo. Can I put him down on the floor?'

Harry held out his arms. 'It's all right. I can hold him.'

Jo hesitated. Not because she didn't trust Harry, but because the offer took her by surprise.

'Here, catch,' she said.

She moved closer to him, and with a little fumbling, he slid his arms between hers and lifted Theo to his chest.

'Don't take the crying personally. You sure you're okay?'

He stroked Theo's cheek with a large, nicotine-stained finger. 'It's been a while, but yes.'

'I won't be long.'

She went up the stairs to the only toilet in the house. The C-section had healed, but there was still a twinge as she reached the top of the steps. Strictly, she shouldn't even have been driving for another week, but she'd had to get out.

It was while she was washing her hands that she realised the crying had stopped. On the landing, she could hear Harry singing quietly, croakily, below.

'You are my sunshine, my only sunshine . . .'

For a few moments, she stood and listened, filled with an odd mix of emotions. It was a song her own dad had sung to her. She descended quietly so as not to break the spell.

Harry stopped abruptly as she stepped onto the bottom stair. She found him sitting in his armchair, cradling a sleeping Theo.

'Show off.'

'I have that effect on people.'

Her stomach rumbled. 'Excuse me,' she said. 'I missed breakfast.'

'Well sit yourself down, lass! I make a mean slice of toast.'

★　★　★

Time didn't exactly stand still inside number 21 Canterbury Road, but it felt like it was circling, not sure when to get involved again. Uniformed officers arrived, the familiar faces of PCs Oli Marquardt and Andrea Williams. Jo had drifted outside in a daze, and only recognised Andy Carrick when he was right in front of her on the pavement, talking.

'It's Harry,' she mumbled. 'He's dead.'

Carrick went straight inside. A crowd had gathered across the road, and another uniform was keeping them at a distance and answering questions. Jo walked back to her car. She hadn't cried – she felt too caught up in the moment still. Too confused. She'd made a call to Amelia, asking her to pick up Theo. As the minutes ticked by, the urge to rush away and hold him was becoming almost painful.

Her boss emerged from the house, making a beeline for where she sat in her car with the door open.

'I'm sorry, Jo,' he said. 'Can you tell me what happened?'

His voice seemed to be coming from somewhere distant, like she was hearing it on a time-lag.

'What happened?'

'Yes, from the moment you arrived.' He was speaking to her like a vulnerable witness, and his coddling tone pulled her out of her reverie. *I'm not a witness. I'm a police officer.* She went over the details as she remembered them. 'The nurse was the first on the scene, I think,' she said.

Carrick nodded. 'She's not a nurse. She's a dental assistant. Just happened to be passing by.'

That explained the reluctance to carry out CPR.

'Who called it in?' said Jo, mind still playing catch-up. She felt the burn of shame. *I shouldn't be sitting here. I should be helping.*

Carrick glanced back towards an elderly woman, being spoken to by a uniformed officer. 'The neighbour, Mrs Milner.'

'There was a report of a disturbance, wasn't there?'

'That's right,' said Carrick. 'Mrs Milner heard raised voices around three o'clock, but she didn't look in until four-thirty. Harry had already been assaulted. He was alone.' He paused. 'Jo, are you okay?'

She wasn't. Her feet and hands were like frozen blocks. Her brain was a mess of thoughts about Theo. What would he be thinking, picked up by his aunt? Would he be okay?

'Sorry, Andy. I'm back with it. You're sure he was assaulted?' She realised that she'd assumed a fall.

'We found the poker from the fire. There's blood and hair on the end.'

'Oh Christ.' A wave of nausea rose from her gut. Who on earth would hurt Harry? She'd sat by that fire and used that poker on a winter night during her pregnancy.

'Jo, I think you're in shock,' said Carrick. 'Do you want to go?'

He was giving her permission, but there was a hint of disapproval in his voice, so rare for Andy. He was finding this hard, too. He hadn't known Harry like her, but they weren't strangers. She knew she wasn't being herself, the Jo Masters he trusted and respected. *Snap out of it*, she told herself. *Do your job.*

'Of course not,' she said. She took out a bottle of water from beside her car seat, stood, and took a deep swig. 'Can we go in and look around?'

'Scene's secure. They won't move him until we've done.'

'Any more uniforms?'

'Four on the way.'

Jo looked up and down the street. It was a warren round here – old workers' terraces on a grid, ginnels between houses, and alleys running along the rear giving access to back yards. Whoever was responsible had a dozen ways to leave the area. If they lived close, they could have slipped away pretty quickly and easily, on foot or in a vehicle. 'Okay, let's get statements from everyone gawping. Every resident of the street, and any front door within fifty metres. There's CCTV outside the betting shop on the junction with Winchester Crescent – might be worth having a look, anything time-stamped between three and five. What about processing the scene?'

'Cropper and his team are on their way,' said Carrick.

'Already?' Jo knew the crime scene officers were normally very busy.

'Given Harry's ex-staff, we'll be pulling out all the stops.'

'You think this might have something to do with work? Revenge?'

'Could be,' said Carrick. 'Harry would have put a lot of people away in his time. Local folk too.'

The idea curdled in Jo's stomach. Harry Ferman was in his eighth decade, in poor health. If someone had wanted to hurt him, he couldn't have put up much of a fight.

'What about next of kin?' asked Carrick.

Jo had known Harry long enough to be pretty certain there. No kids since his daughter Lindsay had died years ago, an innocent victim in a drink-driving collision. 'There's an ex-wife, Jess. Lives in Derbyshire, I think he said.' From what Harry had told her, the split hadn't been anyone's fault – just a drifting apart after the tragedy with their daughter. 'I'll keep a look out – he might have an address book inside.'

'I can take care of that,' said Carrick. 'You get back to the station.'

'No,' she said firmly. 'I mean, I'd rather stay here. With him.'

It looked like Carrick was going to put his foot down, but instead he touched her shoulder. 'You sure you're up to this? What about Theo?'

Jo was grateful for the human contact, but the sudden mention of her son's name brought another spike of anxiety. Andy had been amazing at supporting her application for reduced hours. He knew what it was like as a parent, trying to assemble the jigsaw of work and childcare into something manageable. But in turn, she knew it wasn't just her personal life he was thinking of. He had to manage his team to ensure resources were available as and when needed for emergencies like this one. He was rightly nervous about making her the senior investigating officer on priority cases.

'That's sorted,' she said. 'You've got to let me take it, boss. You know I'll do a good job.'

He gave her a compassionate nod. 'I trust you completely but don't hesitate to let me know if it gets too much.'

'Of course.'

Carrick went across to speak with the uniform manning the tape. Jo texted Amelia, thanking her again, and telling her to call if there were any problems.

With a clearer head, she donned protective gear from the stash in her car, signed in with the officer now stationed at the door, and re-entered the crime scene like a different person entirely. In turn, the house itself seemed to have undergone a transformation from the familiar to the strange. Death could do that – change the complexion of everything. This wasn't Harry's house any more, a place she'd enjoyed cups of tea, and the occasional dram of something stronger – it was a crime scene, where every surface and fibre and object might yield evidence that would lead to his killer. Including, she thought, the body that lay, now covered in a sheet, where it had fallen. Grief threatened her resolve again, but she girded herself. She hadn't been here when it mattered, but she was here now, and there was a job to be done. She promised herself, and him: *no mistakes.*

Harry had lived in this house since his divorce – around twenty years. It had always been orderly when she visited, in keeping with its occupant's unwavering daily routine of walking to the newsagent's for a morning paper, then on to the pub sometime after lunch. Harry's only hobby had been watercolour painting. On one impromptu visit, she'd seen a picture of a city scene resting upright on his kitchen table, and he'd admitted, blushing, that it was one of his own.

As she looked around the living room, her first impression was that it looked almost identical to the last time she'd been here five months ago with Theo, yet there was *something* slightly uncanny. At first, she put it down to the fact that the brutal act with the poker had somehow changed the atmospherics, but on catching sight of herself in the gilt-edged mirror beside the mantelpiece she realised that wasn't it at all. Something *had* changed. She walked towards the mirror, and ran a finger along its upper frame. The glove came back clean.

Crouching to look at the floor, she examined the carpet near to the skirting board. Housekeeping had never been Harry's forte. He'd had a bad back, and arthritic hands, making any thorough cleaning hard. She'd surmised also that he simply didn't care, with only himself to please, but things had been getting worse. And the last few times she'd been here there had always been a considerable layer of dust in the hard to reach places, or anything out of direct eyesight. He had a vacuum cleaner, but it was as old-fashioned as the TV. Either he'd found a new pride in dusting and acquired a newer model, or he'd got a cleaner. Neither felt likely.

Behind the couch was the poker. As Carrick had said, there was an unmistakable coagulation on the hooked end, matting together a couple of Harry's grey hairs. Again, the questions throbbed in her head. *Who? Why?* The poker didn't answer, but it could well yield prints when Mel's team arrived. She looked away, surveying the room for any other signs of the struggle, and found what she was searching for across the light shade above. A foot-long string of blood droplets, each the shape of elongated tears. One didn't need to be an expert in blood spatter analysis to see what had happened as the assailant drew

41

back his arm from a blow. The ferocity of the attack lingered as Jo moved through into the kitchen.

It wasn't a large room, and the units appeared not to have been updated in all the time Harry had been a occupant. The cupboards were Formica, lined with aluminium trim. A free-standing gas hob. Harry had eaten his meals at a small square table tucked into the corner, with two chairs on the open sides. There were two mugs on the table-top now. *A guest then?* Jo went over, and saw the drink in one wasn't finished. She bent to sniff – coffee. Harry had told her he never touched the stuff. Jo laid the back of her hand against the side of the cups in turn, to test for any residual heat. Perhaps a little. Had Harry been sharing a cuppa with the person who killed him? Hard to see how a friendly chat, sitting just a foot apart, could descend to murder before a drink was even finished.

She examined the rest of the room, and her eyes took in the drying rack, stacked with two plates and several pieces of cutlery. A shared meal, too? She wondered if her old friend had met someone. She couldn't imagine him dating, but he'd always been good company, and kind, and the face of a once handsome man still lingered in his somewhat worn features. If he had found some romance, she was pleased for him.

There was a small dresser beside the table, displaying earth-enware ornaments, and a photo of Harry and his daughter. Lindsay had shared his pale, serious eyes, and his strong nose, but the rest of her face had been more vivacious and joyful. She was beaming in the photo, and strands of her long brown hair had blown across her father's face. Jo had once remarked on the picture, telling Harry that Lindsay had been a beautiful young woman. He'd surprised her by being only too happy to talk, and he'd told her the photo was taken on the beach in Hove on the south coast, on a trip the family had taken just prior to her first year at university. A year before she died. Even though Jo had never met the girl, it was almost heart-breaking to look at the image. What it must have felt like to her dad, to see her everyday, so *alive*, Jo couldn't grasp.

She tugged open the right-side dresser drawer. Inside was a collection of pens, keys, batteries, a small torch. The left side contained what she was looking for – a small leather-covered address book. She opened it, and flicked through the pages. Harry's handwriting was dreadful, and some parts were indecipherable. Several sections were crossed out, and Jo wondered if that meant the addressee had moved on, or was deceased. Many of the names had ranks attached in abbreviated code – old colleagues from Harry's thirty years on the job. He'd been in Oxford for all of it.

Jo found what she was looking for under G - Jessica Granger. He'd always called her 'Jess' in conversation, but the address was unlikely to be a coincidence – 'Ashbourne, Derbs'. The writing here was perceptibly neater too, as if he'd taken extra care inscribing it. There was no phone number, but a local officer could be sent to deliver the news. Hopefully Jessica was still at the same address. Jo made a note in her own copybook.

Directly beside where the address book had lain was a stack of paperwork, and she lifted it out to leaf through. The pile contained receipts, utilities correspondence, a recent bank statement, and the instruction booklet for the mobile phone she'd convinced him to purchase about a year ago. The second item down caught Jo's attention. It was an invoice sheet, signed by Harry himself, for £65, paid to a local glazier called PJ Adams Ltd, based on the Iffley Road. It was dated just over two weeks prior on March 29th. The work completed was handwritten – 'Single pane, rear door.'

Jo looked across the kitchen and saw the results. The back door had two panes of glass in its upper half. On closer inspection, she saw the lower one, just above the mortise keyhole, was new – with cleaner sealant around its rim. Jo remembered from the briefing notes Heidi had prepared for her return that there'd been a spate of opportunistic burglaries in the area, presumably addicts taking what they could. The warren of streets made the neighbourhood easy pickings. Mostly elderly residents, simple to sneak in from the back, hopping a fence, and nick what you could to flog elsewhere. It didn't take a leap of logic to work out the same might have happened here – someone could have knocked the glass through, then used the key in the lock to open the door. Pretty much a gift to a petty criminal. Jo pulled out her phone, and called the station, asking if there had been any recent reports from Harry's address about a break-in. The answer came back negative. Maybe she was jumping to conclusions. Harry didn't have much of value anyway. No computer, no jewellery. The TV would be more trouble than it was worth. And the key was in the lock still, which struck her as odd. If you'd been robbed in that way, why leave yourself open to exactly the same crime? Besides, she told herself, if the break-in happened two weeks ago, it seemed unlikely to be connected to the murder anyway.

She opened the door on to the small cobbled yard with a tiny outbuilding that would once have housed the toilet when the house was first built. There was a tall fence, but nothing that would keep out a determined burglar.

Jo retreated indoors and, on a hunch, she checked the fridge. It wasn't particularly well stocked, but there were two types of milk. More evidence that he was sharing the house with someone else. She opened the cupboards too, to find plenty of tins, but also a sweetened breakfast cereal alongside the porridge oats that seemed a better fit for her friend.

There was a noise from the living room, and she returned that way to find CSO Mel Cropper arriving, suited up, along with two technicians clad in similar white attire. One carried a digital camera on a loop around her neck.

'Jo,' he said in greeting.

She gave a nod rather than shaking hands, and filled him in on what she'd found so far, including the blood near the ceiling and the mugs in the kitchen. Mel showed no signs of acknowledgement that the victim was a friend of hers. The buffer of professionalism actually made things easier. Mel would do his job as thoroughly as always, gathering everything he needed with the corpse in situ before releasing the body to the morgue. There, the forensic pathologist would take over the evidence gathering.

Jo headed up the steep and narrow staircase. She'd never ventured this way other than to use the first-floor toilet. The house had once been a two-up, two-down, but the back bedroom had been split to accommodate an indoor shower room and WC. Harry's bedroom door, at the front of the house, had always been closed, and the rear bedroom door was shut now. She went first to the front. It felt strange, entering his private space like this. He'd usually presented himself carefully, in a suit and tie, even if the clothes were a bit shabby. But here, in his inner sanctum, hung a dressing gown, with a pair of slippers tucked neatly beside the double bed. A chest of drawers, and a solid-looking wardrobe; a beside table with a digital alarm clock, a pair of spectacles and a science fiction novel, splayed open to mark the page. There was no sign of another recent occupant. Indeed, there was only a single pillow on the right-hand side of the bed. Here though, Jo noticed, the signs of recent cleaning were absent. Dust coated the top of the bedside lamp, and the carpet's perimeter was discoloured with the same. The table where the book lay was marked with several rings where a mug or glass had overflowed its rim. Years of drinking had left Harry with a mild case of the shakes that he himself had joked about. She'd seen it in the pub herself a few times. It got to the stage where the barmaid at the Three Crowns would carry his drink over.

45

'*Table service!*'

'*Just looking out for my carpet, Harry.*'

She felt distinctly nosy opening up his wardrobe and drawers, but unsurprised to find a conservative collection of shirts and trousers, neatly folded and hung. Among the garments, wrapped in transparent plastic, was a police officer's uniform from the eighties, before he went into plain clothes.

Making her way back onto the small landing, she opened the door to the remaining bedroom. This one she'd entered before, by accident when looking for the toilet on her first visit, and she remembered it mostly being given to storage, with several cardboard boxes and plastic containers, as well as an old exercise bike. The bike was still there, but the boxes had gone, and a camp-bed was extended across the wall, with bedding made. A towel hung across the radiator too. Someone was staying here for sure. Jo moved the bedding aside carefully with a gloved hand, crouched down, and spotted a single long strand of blond hair beside the pillow. This was someone hastily accommodated, with little thought given to good impressions or comfort.

The room contained nothing else of interest, but as Jo put her head into the bathroom, she saw a floral washbag that looked completely out of place. Checking its contents, she found a toothbrush and toothpaste, a hairbrush with more blond locks, scrunchies, woman's deodorant, some foundation and blusher in a separate bag, plus half a dozen loose tampons. Jo's mind re-adjusted to the evidence. Not the possessions of an elderly friend, then, and the fact of the sleeping arrangements suggested this wasn't a romantic connection at all. A much younger woman. Was this the same person who'd wielded that poker so ruthlessly, felling Harry with what looked like a single blow? If she hadn't known the victim, she might have seen something creepy about the set-up, an old man giving shelter to a young woman, but that picture was so far out of keeping with what she knew of Harry Ferman, she couldn't countenance it.

Downstairs, Mel and his team were at work, and the body was uncovered once more while photos were gathered. With his spirit flown, Harry looked more like a mannequin than before, and she found she could inspect him with less painful emotion. Another tech was in the kitchen dusting surfaces.

'Looks like someone was staying here,' said Jo.

'Yes, a woman,' said Mel.

'You've worked that out?'

'There's lipstick on one of the glasses in the drying rack,' said the crime scene examiner. 'And there are several of these on the sofa.' He proffered a transparent evidence bag containing three wavy blond hairs, each at least eight inches long, matching the one Jo had found upstairs.

'Anything in his pockets?' she asked. 'Phone or wallet?'

Mel shook his head. 'You think they were stolen?'

'I've not come across anything,' she said. *Don't let all this be over a few quid, please . . .*

'If you find anything interesting, call me direct,' she said.

Mel turned away from her, to look down at the poker. 'Everything I find is interesting, sergeant, but I take your point.'

★ ★ ★

On the way back on to the street, Jo asked the constable signing her out of the premises where she could find Mrs Milner, the woman who'd reported the crime, and was given the address of the house two down. She knocked, and the door was opened by a young man of about thirty, dressed in a boiler suit, with a tool belt at his waist, and hands ingrained with some sort of white dust. 'What do you want?'

Jo showed her badge. 'I was hoping to speak with Mrs Milner.'

'Again?' said the man, making no move to shift his formidable bulk from the doorway. 'I reckon your lot have squeezed it all out of her already. Mum's had a shock, you know? She was the one who found the poor bloke.'

'We appreciate that,' said Jo. 'I'm the detective leading the investigation, and . . . well, Mr Ferman was also a good friend of mine.'

The hardness in the man's face softened. 'Mum, there's another copper,' he called back. There was no answer, but he stepped back. 'Go easy on her, all right?'

'Of course,' said Jo. Inside, the house had the same layout as Harry's, but the décor brightened it up considerably. The cast-iron fireplace was gone, replaced with a wood-burning stove, and the carpets were stripped back to reveal pale oak floorboards. An open-plan arrangement gave Jo a view through to a dining area, with a kitchen built into an extension at the rear of the house. Sitting at the dining table, nursing an oversized glass of white wine, was an elegant, bird-like fifty-something woman with short hair dyed to a reddish brown. Jo introduced herself.

'I know you've been through details with my colleagues,' she added, 'but I wonder if I could have a word too.'

The woman looked at her with a startled expression. 'I don't think I can help,' she said. 'I didn't see anybody.'

'But you heard a disturbance?'

The woman took a gulp of wine, holding it in her mouth for a few moments, before audibly swallowing. She nodded.

'Harry and a woman?'

'I think so,' she said.

'You *think* so?'

If there was accusation in her voice, she didn't intend it, but Mrs Milner's son bristled. He didn't understand how memory could degrade. This might be the last opportunity to glean vital information from his mother.

'Well, it was just raised voices for a few seconds as I came back from walking the dog. He had a girl staying with him. I assumed it was a relative.'

'Can you tell me what she looked like?'

'Young. Blonde hair.'

'Anything else? Height?'

'Not tall.'

Jo glanced at the minimalist clock on the wall. It was almost six. Theo would be getting really grizzly.

'But you didn't speak to Mr Ferman about her?'

'Why would I? It's not my business who he has to stay.'

'Shall we finish up here?' said the son.

'Almost done,' said Jo firmly. 'So you heard the raised voices about three? Did you see Harry or the woman after that?'

Mrs Milner shook her head, took another sip and continued. 'I went out a bit later – I had a doctor's appointment in Temple Cowley. That was when I saw Harry through the window. His next-door neighbour has a key, so I . . .'

She took a tissue and dabbed her eyes. Her son stepped protectively beside her, laying an arm over her shoulders.

'Happy, *detective*?' he said.

'Just a couple more questions,' said Jo. 'The woman – have you any idea how long she might have been staying with Mr Ferman?'

Mrs Milner dried her eyes with a piece of screwed-up tissue. 'Not exactly,' she said. 'But I did hear music coming from his house about a fortnight ago. He normally keeps himself to himself, but I was walking past and I heard one of those dreadful new pop songs, playing very loudly. Not like something a man of his age would listen to.'

Jo made a note. 'About a fortnight ago? Can you be more exact?'

The woman shook her head. 'I'm not . . . actually, yes! It was a Sunday morning, so what's that . . . eleven days ago?'

Jo checked the calendar in her notebook. 'The 6th. Thank you, that's very helpful. And one last question? Have you heard about any break-ins in the area?'

Mrs Milner's son made a scoffing sound. 'So now you lot give a monkeys about break-ins, do you? I reported it three weeks ago.'

'What's that?' said Jo.

'All my tools,' said the man. 'Nicked from my van while it was parked up the road. Broad-bloody-daylight.'

'I'm sorry to hear that. Nothing was recovered?'

'No one even came out to see me!' said the man. 'Just gave me a crime number for the insurance. And you wonder why people don't have time for the police . . .'

Jo didn't want to get into an argument in his mother's front room, and she understood his frustrations. She was glad Mel Cropper wasn't with her – he'd have wasted no time at all spelling out quite how far down their list of priorities petty burglaries sat.

'There were a couple of break-ins over on Chichester Road, too,' said Mrs Milner. 'It's the world we live in now. No one was hurt though. Not like this.'

Chapter 4

Thanking Mrs Milner for her time, and leaving her own details in case the witness remembered anything useful, Jo liaised with the officers outside, organising a door-to-door to glean any further information about the woman staying with Harry, the apparent argument, or the music heard by Mrs Milner. Mel's van was still parked up, and no doubt would be for several hours. The timeline was all too vague to be particularly useful at the moment. But someone must have seen something of this mystery woman's comings and goings. Each resident's front room looked directly out on to the street. In days gone by, before everyone had a car parked bumper to bumper on both sides of the road, it was the sort of place neighbours would have all known each other's business and kids would have kicked a ball up and down, smashing the occasional window but otherwise doing no harm. People like Mrs Milner would have known the name of her local bobby, and probably his kids' names too.

By the time she got to Paul and Amelia's, in the new development on the Abingdon Road, it was getting dark. Her nephew Will opened the door. Now almost nine, he'd shot up again in the last few months, and was looking more like her brother

Paul than ever. He had a pair of oversized headphones on his skinny shoulders.

'Shouldn't you be in bed?' she said, readjusting her face to a smile.

'It's only eight o'clock,' he replied. There were no hugs any more, and he peeled away, calling out to his mum.

Amelia came down the stairs, finger to her lips. 'I told you to keep it down!' she said to Will, who was putting headphones back on anyway.

'I'm so sorry!' said Jo. 'Emergency at work.' She didn't have the energy to tell them it was actually a friend of hers.

'It's not a problem,' said Amelia, warmly. 'I've put him down on a rug in Emma's bedroom. Forgotten how nice it is to have kids who can't speak.'

'You don't mean that!' said Jo. 'Will's a little gentleman!'

'Something like that,' said Amelia. 'You want a drink?'

'Actually, I'd better get home,' said Jo. 'But thanks. Another busy one tomorrow.'

Amelia frowned in concern. 'They're throwing you back in the deep end?'

'I'm not sure there's a shallow end in my line of work,' said Jo. She didn't really want to talk about what had happened – not until she'd had more time to process it herself. Amelia hadn't known Harry Ferman at all, so it wouldn't mean much to her anyway. She would no doubt read about it in the local paper within a few days.

Her sister-in-law looked like she wanted to say more, but Jo made her way towards the stairs. 'Do you mind if I get him?'

'Go ahead.'

Amelia followed her up. Jo found Theo looking angelic on an improvised bed in the middle of her niece's bedroom floor. She wondered if she'd be able to get him to the car without waking him.

'I'll ask Paul to get the old cot out of the attic,' whispered Amelia. 'Just in case.'

'I won't dump him on you again,' said Jo. 'It was just a funny day.'

'Honestly, it's fine,' said Amelia.

Jo knelt at Theo's side, and for a moment was reminded of earlier that day, crouching on Harry's floor. At both times, over someone completely helpless. She resisted asking if he'd missed her and kissed his cheek, then eased her hands under his warm body to lift him up. He was a dead weight, arms flopping.

'Emma not in?' she asked.

'At her boyfriend's,' said Amelia. 'We barely see her unless she wants a lift somewhere. Paul will be back from work soon though. You sure you don't want to stick around?'

'Better not,' said Jo. Now that she had Theo in her arms again, her energy drained. She just wanted to curl up and sleep herself.

With the sunset, the temperature had dipped outside. As she settled Theo into his car seat, he stirred only a little. Amelia followed Jo out, hugging herself against the cooling evening air. 'You know, Jo, I think it's amazing what you're doing. Going back to work so soon, especially as you're on your own.'

'Don't be daft,' said Jo. 'Loads of people do the same.'

'They don't have jobs like yours,' said Amelia. 'Dealing with criminals all day.'

Jo thought back to the incident with the motorbike earlier. 'I'm careful.'

'I'm sure you are . . .' Amelia wanted to say something else, Jo could see.

'Go on.'

Her sister-in-law smiled. 'Lucas was here, yesterday.'

Jo's hackles rose. 'Here? At your house?'

'I wasn't sure whether I should say anything.'

'He's got no right. What did he say?'

'He wanted to know how Theo was.'

'And what did you tell him?'

'Paul dealt with it. Sent him on his way. He'd been drinking.'

'Oh, Christ. I'm sorry,' said Jo. And she really was. Her brother's family didn't need her problems on their doorstep.

'It's not your fault,' said Amelia. 'I just thought you should know.'

'Well, thanks,' said Jo. 'I'll speak with the solicitor.'

'If you think that's best,' said Amelia. She sounded unsure though.

'He's got to get the message,' said Jo. She kissed Amelia on the cheek. 'And thanks again for stepping in today.'

They said farewell and Jo headed home. On the way, she called into the station. Reeves answered.

'Anything else on the girl?'

'A couple of the other neighbours thought they remembered her,' said Reeves. 'Nothing more concrete that a short blonde-haired girl between sixteen and twenty-five. Big coat. She'd been seen coming and going over the last two weeks, but always on her own.'

'Nationality?'

'No one ever spoke to her.'

It might be worth getting a composite drawn up, Jo thought, while memories were relatively fresh.

'We've managed to get in touch with Jessica Granger,' Alice Reeves continued. 'She's going to head over first thing tomorrow.'

'How did she take it?'

'Shocked, of course. She's not had any contact with Mr Ferman for years, but said she'd be happy to take care of arrangements.'

54

'That's something. You should finish up. Get some rest.'

'That's the plan,' said Reeves. 'See you tomorrow.'

Jo wished her a good night. Harry had spoken about his ex-wife a number of times, always fondly, if with a degree of wry detachment. From what she'd gathered, they'd separated on amicable enough terms, after soldiering on for a few years after Lindsay's death. By his own admission, Harry had coped badly, and sunken into a depression that made him hard to live with. She gripped the steering wheel tighter as she remembered the lines of grief etched on his face, sitting opposite her in the Three Crowns. To have overcome *that*, only for this, seemed so grossly unjust. His life had been a simple one, with few friends, and few comforts. Whoever had taken it from him was going to pay – she'd make sure of it.

Theo woke on the way inside, springing to sudden liveliness, all giggles and thrashing limbs. She'd been joking to the health visitors about claws and teeth, but there was something strange about the burst of energy just as the rest of the world was winding down. She gave him a bath, cupping water over his squirming pink body as he squealed. By the time he was wrapped in a towel, he was rubbing his eyes again. He lazily took a little milk, before settling into the cot beside her own bed. She lay down, watching him through the bars, as she sang a song of which she only half remembered the words.

Lucas returned to her thoughts unbidden as Theo dropped off, and she wandered downstairs, vaguely considering making a call. He no longer had her number, but she'd kept his just so she was forewarned if he called from that phone. In the end, she decided against speaking with him, just as the solicitor had recommended. If he was in bad patch, it was likely he'd have been drinking again today, so it would be pointless having a conversation anyway.

Their relationship, she reasoned from a position of hindsight, had been on rocky ground all along. First with the lies he had told her about his estranged family, and then later, even as they had tried to make it work, the truths *she* couldn't tell *him*. When she had informed him, soon after realising she was pregnant, that the baby might not be his, it had opened a wound. And she had let it fester, refusing for her own reasons to have any sort of paternity test. It didn't matter to her who the father was, Lucas or her former colleague Jack Pryce. Or rather, she simply didn't want to know. Lucas couldn't comprehend that at all.

Within a couple of months of sporadic contact, she'd realised he was back on the booze. She, and everyone close, especially his ex-wife, had tried to stop him, but the compulsion seemed too great, and soon she felt vindicated in cutting him out of her life and that of her unborn child. With her maternal hormones raging, she had found it easy to be brutally selfish, conscious that her capacity for compassion had shrunk. He needed support greater than anything she could provide. She'd suspected Paul and Amelia hadn't fully understood, and once or twice they'd made tentative queries to uncover what was going on. Harry had been the opposite. Non-judgmental, dependable, wise. A rock, whenever she needed to talk.

But when he had come to her, she hadn't been there.

Jo drank a glass of water on the couch, then leant across and listened to his voicemail again.

'Hello, Jo. It's been a while. Listen, there's something I need to talk with you about. I know you've got a lot on, but . . . it's delicate. Maybe you could give me a call back when you've got a minute. Oh, it's Harry, by the way.'

It was impossible not to interpret it differently now, and the guilt that had gnawed at her that morning came close to consuming her completely as she sat in the darkness. Whatever the 'delicate' matter was, it likely had something to do with the fate her old friend had met a few hours earlier. And if she had just picked up the phone to speak with him, who could say the route the day would have taken? He might have been sitting opposite her now, his big body sinking into the cushions of her couch, his gentle laughter filling the room as she filled him in on her first day back.

She pressed play again, torturing herself, searching for any hint in between the lines, any inflection in his voice that might be a clue. But there was nothing in his tone – no great anxiety or strain – that suggested he knew the fate that awaited him. He sounded pensive, a little confused and out of his depth, perhaps. Like he didn't want to cause trouble for her. Whoever this girl was who was staying in his upstairs room, eating cereal at his table and leaving hairs on his sofa, he'd had little inkling that she was going to do him harm.

JAMES

TWO MONTHS EARLIER

His watch read 07.33. He stamped his feet against the cold, and watched his breath spill out into the pre-dawn.

Where the fuck is he?

The stagnant water beneath James' feet reeked, blackly reflecting the arch of Victorian brickwork above. The underside of the bridge had grown a skin of moss over fading graffiti. This place hadn't been well frequented for a long time.

James was beginning to doubt himself.

Not that he could go through with it – there was never anything less than complete certainty on that count; the tools were ready in the holdall at his feet. But he was beginning to worry that Christopher Putman might not come at all. Perhaps tonight he hadn't felt like his regular Tuesday jog. Or maybe he'd decided to vary the route for the first time in eight weeks. Worse still, what if Putman had somehow spotted him over the course of his surveillance? Maybe he'd even recognised him and gone to the police . . .

No, that wasn't possible. For a start, there was no way Putman would remember him. James been a boy back then, a skinny thing who'd barely been able to look Putman in the eye. Nothing like the man he was now.

And James had been careful. So careful. Military precision was a cliché, but in his case, it was fairly applied. For the last two months, Putman had been his assigned target, and luckily that target was a man of routine. Every movement had been jotted down in James' little book. There was a fifteen-minute window during which Putman left his apartment building, walking the four hundred yards to the nearest tram stop, boarding the blue line, which took him on a nineteen-minute ride to Piccadilly Gardens in the middle of Manchester. From there it was a short stroll to his offices, via a coffee shop on Jewry Street, where he purchased a double espresso. Occasionally he dipped out between 12.30 and one, but more often it looked like a young female assistant or intern did a run to a nearby café on behalf of several employees. The office itself was accessed by a code at street level – 808080. James had thought about striking there, as Putman was normally last to leave the building. The problem was the cameras. Two across the street, each linked to different premises. If his plan had any hope of working, this first part had to go off without a hitch. There could be nothing linking him to what happened next.

Most nights, Putman went straight home, occasionally detouring via a supermarket to buy a few items he'd pack into a collapsible rucksack. He appeared, from the purchases James had seen, to be a vegetarian. One Thursday evening, he'd gone for a drink with colleagues, though he was first to leave after just a couple, heading out to meet his partner – a man he called Matt, and whose surname Putman hadn't been able to find out. There was no need. Matt was not important in the scheme of things. The two of them seemed to be married – at least they both wore rings – and from time to time James felt distantly sorry for the happiness he was going to shatter. But there was a debt to be paid, and Putman was the only one who could pay it.

At the weekends, the couple spent most of their time together – the exception was the running club on Sunday mornings, when Putman met a small group of Lycra-clad friends for a conversational hour around the Quays. He ran two other nights in the week as well. Friday's route was straight home from the office, through built-up urban areas that offered no opportunities for ambush. Tuesday morning was more promising: an early circuit from his apartment, along some of the more deserted and abandoned waterways of the old canal network. The run took forty minutes, give or take.

07.37.

But not today, it seemed. James took a deep breath, extinguishing his disappointment and frustration. It was no good guessing at a reason for the change of routine, and it didn't matter. His time would come.

He picked up the bag to leave, to head back to the hostel in the city centre, when the distant sound of slapping feet echoed along the path. Suddenly, it was back on. He moved briskly to the end of the tunnel, climbing the bank to a spot where he wouldn't be seen. He could hear Putman's heavy breathing, and slid out the crowbar.

Now came the glow of Putman's head-torch, rocking from side to side in time with his stride. James' hand tightened on the cold metal, and he jumped down into the path.

The light from the torch was too much, and James had to turn away dazzled.

'Sorry!' said Putman. He'd skidded to a halt, and as he hurriedly switched the beam off, James saw he had both arms raised in a gesture of apology. For a moment they stared at one another, then Putman caught sight of the crowbar. 'What do you . . .'

He didn't finish the sentence as the metal bar struck the side of his cheek with a dull thud. He staggered and hit the wall of the bridge, trying to support himself, but falling to his knees. Blood poured from his face down the front of his running vest and spattered in heavy droplets on to the towpath. He turned and began to crawl back the way he'd come, making a whining sound. James walked after him slowly, tossing the crowbar to the ground. Another blow to the head was too risky. He needed Putman alive.

His victim saw him coming and tried to crawl faster, but James placed his foot on the other man's back and pressed him to the ground. Putman made no effort to fight as James slid an arm under his neck, clasped his hands together, and used his body weight to push Putman's head forward against his own biceps and forearm, cutting off the flow of blood through the carotid arteries. There was a gurgling and then, after five or six seconds, he felt Putman's body go limp. He held the choke for a few seconds more, just to be sure Putman was out, then he rolled off, so they lay together side by side, Putman facing down, James looking towards the tunnel roof. He let his breathing calm, then stood to check no one was coming. Satisfied, he went to retrieve the crowbar, and put it back into the bag, where it rattled against the pliers and the hammer. He'd come back and clear up the blood later. He took out two zip-ties and a cloth, then returned to the body.

Christopher Putman was moving weakly. Muttering.

James fastened his ankles together, and tied his wrists behind his back, then forced Putman's teeth apart so he could insert the gag. Putman resisted weakly, his bloody face creasing in protest. Now for the hard bit. James took hold of Putman underneath the armpits and dragged him along the path, then hoisted him up onto the bank. Leaning his shoulder into Putman's waist, he managed to get him into a fireman's lift, and with great difficulty, to scoop up the holdall as well. He remembered doing similar drills in his army days, carrying a 'wounded' comrade and his pack half a mile over difficult terrain, with fake ordnance going off all around.

It was only a hundred and fifty metres to the abandoned rubber factory, concrete all the way, so no problem at all, but Putman was wriggling.

'Fucking give over,' said James.

He reached the building, kicked open the loose door, and went through to the old dark office at the back. All that remained were a couple of shelves, a desk, and a chair; a sports car calendar from 1993 on the wall. James dumped Putman on the floor. He was wide awake now, terror in his eyes. As James leant in towards his face, he flinched back, but James peeled the head-torch away, and placed it on his own forehead. The strap was still damp with sweat. He found the button and switched it on, illuminating the room and Putman's terrified expression. He was trying to shout, but the sound was muffled.

James brandished the crowbar. 'I'll let you talk, but if you scream I'll crack your skull open. Got it?'

Putman nodded.

'You sure?'

He nodded more vigorously.

James plucked the gag out, and Putman coughed up a mouthful of spit.

'I haven't got any money. You can take my phone . . .'

'I don't want your phone.'

'What do you want? I . . . I . . . ' He frowned, eyes widening. 'Wait . . . you're that man I . . . ?'

There was still defiance in Putman's tone, but there wouldn't be for long.

'You don't remember me, do you?' asked James.

'I saw you, in the city, the other day. Look, I'll give you whatever you want.'

That wasn't what James had meant.

He turned away and opened the bag again, and wondered where to start. Matt probably wouldn't even worry about his husband until half past eight. He'd come alone first, searching the route. There wasn't much time, but there was enough.

He fished for the hammer and when Putman saw it in his hand, he began to drag himself across the floor, trying to get out of reach.

Please!' he said. 'I haven't done anything!'

Hearing the words, James had to hold himself back. He couldn't let his anger get the better of him now.

'I need information,' said James, stalking closer.

'Okay, okay! I'll tell you anything I can. You won't need that!'

'If you lie to me, I'll hurt you.'

'I won't lie!'

I know you won't, thought James. Christopher Putman would give him everything he needed to know, because he thought it was the only way to survive.

Sadly, he was wrong.

Chapter 5

Each time she was woken in the night by Theo, the fact of Harry's death hit her afresh, bobbing to the surface of her thoughts. Each time she tried to get back to sleep, it took longer as the images lingered. She felt restless, energised and enervated at the same time, thinking she should be doing *something*, but knowing there was little she could do in the hours of darkness. By the fourth wake-up, just after five am, the sun was coming up. Theo resettled quickly, but she gave up on getting any more sleep herself. Pre-motherhood, she'd just have got into the car and headed to the office, but instead she poured regular cups of coffee down her throat and logged on from the desk in the corner of her living room. She was gritty-eyed as she wrote up her notes from the previous day, trying not to miss a single thing. Policework was about detail, and as SIO she would set the example others would follow. She then listened to Harry's message several times more, wondering whether she should include it in the official report. She decided, ultimately, not to record it. Her relationship to the victim was already a touch problematic; there was no need to highlight that further. Besides, it was too vague to have any useful meaning, and added nothing to the intelligence.

Theo woke just before eight in a good mood. His oblivious smile was just the tonic she needed, and though it couldn't chase away the demons entirely, feeding and dressing him and singing him songs kept them at bay for a while.

Reality stole back over her between home and the nursery, like a deadly tide encroaching unseen, but subtly felt, as she closed the front door, clipped his safety harness, and pulled out of the drive. By the time she handed him over, Theo was fractious, as if he too now sensed her disquiet.

'I don't know what's wrong with him,' she said. She lingered at the threshold of the nursery, giving him one last cuddle. Even then, he clung to her, and pulling his fingers from her sleeve to hand him across to his carer, Suzie, almost broke her heart.

'He'll be absolutely fine, won't you, little man?' said Suzie, looking down at him.

'I know he will,' said Jo with a smile. 'It's me I'm worried about.'

She fancied she could still hear him crying through the door as she walked back towards the car, and forced herself not to turn around and go back to peer through the window.

When she started the engine again, she looked in the mirror. *Game face, Jo. Get yourself together.*

★ ★ ★

She drove straight back out to Harry's place. The police tape had gone, and Canterbury Road had returned to normality, with no indication of the brutal act that had befallen an elderly man inside number 21. The curtains were drawn, and Jo allowed herself a moment's fantasy that she could knock

66

now, and he'd answer like yesterday had never happened. She scolded herself for wishful thinking, but it was in his no-nonsense tone: *That's not how we work, Josie. You play with the cards you've been dealt.*

She used her own key to enter the house again. The crime scene technicians hadn't made much effort to clean up – there were stray evidence bags on the floor, and various pencil mark-ings on the wall. The cushions from the sofa had been put back untidily. The house had lost any form of homeliness now its occupant was gone, and she wondered what would happen to it next. Even if he could never have anticipated his death in violent circumstances, Harry seemed the sort to put his affairs in order well in advance. There'd be a will, and it might be worth checking the beneficiary.

She checked the drawers of the dresser again, searching for anything that might look official, but found nothing. Out in the back yard, there was a plastic sheet laid out – it looked like Mel's team had emptied the contents of the kitchen bin over it, searching the detritus for any more clues. Jo didn't feel the need to inspect the rubbish in any detail, but something did catch her eye. Or rather, its absence did. She walked back to the kitchen cupboards, opened them all. Then the fridge. Now *that* was strange.

'No booze,' she muttered.

The Harry she'd known had been pretty much a functioning alcoholic. In addition to daily trips to the Three Crowns, the time she'd been here before the cupboards had contained both bottles of ale and an assortment of decent whiskys and brandies. She wondered if the crime scene team had removed them for some reason.

She headed upstairs and into the guest room. The bed had been stripped, but the other furniture in the room – the chair, storage containers and exercise bike – appeared to be untouched.

Jo opened some of the containers finding folded blankets, some tools, and a number of lever-arch files. Harry was indeed a man of order – he had payslips, bills, documents relating to conveyancing and car ownership, dentistry, insurance, and an expired life policy. It didn't take her long to find a slim folder marked Kitson and Partners, and inside that a last will and testament, signed and dated fifteen years earlier. Jo checked and saw that he had bequeathed his estate to one Jessica Granger, his ex-wife. She made a note of the details, then sealed the documents away.

★　★　★

By the time she got to the station, everyone was in, working quietly at their desks. The large incident board was separated into three columns: the first contained images of Harry Ferman's dead body, the murder weapon, and the house. Jo forced herself to walk up and take it in. Heidi Tan looked over, and offered a sympathetic smile.

'Morning, Jo. You okay?'

'Just want to find the culprit,' she replied. 'Did you find his phone or his wallet, by the way?'

'We got the phone,' said Heidi. 'It was in the pocket of a coat in the hall. Bagged in evidence. No sign of his wallet though. Safe to assume it was taken. We've notified his bank based on statement details.'

Jo recalled the hair on the sofa. There normally wasn't much DNA to be found, unless they had the follicles, but Mel's team would likely have scraped up skin cells too from the bedroom and shower upstairs. In the next twenty-four to forty-eight hours, they'd have a pretty strong biological profile for their suspect. Whether there'd be any match on the system was another question. Given the suspect's gender and age, chances were slim. The National DNA Database was almost five-to-one male to female.

'Did he have a thing for younger women?' asked Dimitriou, from his desk.

Jo shut him down. 'Don't be daft.'

Dimitriou pushed back his chair and spread his legs, hands behind his head. 'Is it though? We've established he doesn't have any kids. What other explanation is there for a seventy-year-old guy to hang around with a teenage girl?'

Jo knew he was trying to be provocative. Also, that he had a valid point. That was the annoying thing about George Dimitriou – he could be smug and right at the same time.

'She was sleeping in his spare room,' she countered.

'Some of the time,' said Dimitriou. 'Maybe he was lonely. It wouldn't be unheard of.'

Jo struggled to get her head around the idea. It wasn't beyond the realms of possibility that Harry might have used a sex-worker, but she couldn't see him finding a girl of that age attractive. Let alone inviting her to stay. And it was hard to see why she'd have attacked him if they were in a commercial, mutually beneficial relationship.

'I'll bear your thoughts in mind,' she said coldly. 'Anyway, we've got to locate her first. And speaking of finding people, any sign of young Matthis, or has the tyke eluded you?'

Dimitriou growled under his breath. 'Little shit's vanished off the face of the earth. But we're accessing his phone data. We'll soon see where he's been hanging around.'

Reeves came in from the AV suite. 'Ma'am,' she said. 'I've been on the CCTV from the betting shop at the end of Mr Ferman's road. The only young women I've got between three pm and five pm are in a group. And heading the wrong way. There was a bit of traffic too, but I can't get a good view of the drivers. Want me to widen the search window?' Jo was about to say it might be worth doing so, but Carrick came up behind her from the direction of the break room. 'No, leave it,' he said, before the words had left her mouth.

'You sure, boss?' asked Jo. 'It looks like this young woman might have been coming and going regularly.'

'Maybe later,' said Carrick. 'I've got to think of the best uses of manpower. He went to the pub a lot, didn't he?'

'Every day,' said Jo. In fact, she'd spent many an hour in there with him. 'The Three Crowns.'

'You want to head over at opening time, Alice?' said Carrick. 'Chat to the locals.'

'I could go,' said Jo. 'I know the place.'

Carrick and Reeves shared an awkward look. 'It's all right Jo – Alice has got it covered.'

Chastened, Jo nodded. She was the senior investigator, but Carrick, as DCI, ultimately called the shots. She must have looked ruffled, because he added, 'Harry's ex-wife will be here any minute. I'd like you to chat with her.'

'Sure, boss.' Now seemed as good a time as any to tell him about the will she'd found. It hardly crossed the threshold into being suspicious, but she didn't want him to think she'd been slacking on the case. 'By the way, I went by Harry's this morning, just for another scout . . .'

Carrick's phone rang, and he looked at the screen. 'Sorry, Jo – gotta take this.' He strode off to his office, and closed the door. She could see him pacing, rubbing his temples at whatever bad news he was hearing.

Jo didn't envy Carrick his new role. He'd always been her superior, but the fact he now sat separate from everyone in his own office underlined it. He wasn't quite one of the team any more. Pulling rank didn't suit his personality, but sadly it was part of the job. The least she could do was make things easy for him.

Alice Reeves was putting on her coat.

'Let me know as soon as you get anything,' said Jo. 'Anything at all.'

'Yes, ma'am,' said Reeves. Jo caught another, almost imperceptible glance at Carrick.

Or maybe it's me who's the odd one out these days.

★ ★ ★

While Jo waited, she went down into the bowels of the building to check Harry's phone in evidence. She signed in and found the relevant box. Sliding it into her hand from the transparent bag brought a stab of sadness. It had been her who had convinced Harry to get the thing, and they'd joked he'd at least joined the twentieth century, if not the twenty-first, because the model he'd selected was stubbornly basic – able to make calls, send messages and take poor-resolution pictures, but just about nothing else. She smiled as she remembered him unboxing it in the pub, and the struggles he'd had just pressing the buttons with his thick fingers.

It still had charge when she switched it on, at least, and she wasn't shocked to discover the access code was the same as when they'd selected it that day – 251200. 'The birthday even I can't forget,' Harry had joked.

The contents were a disappointment though. He clearly almost never used the thing, because the last call in the record was over a month ago. The messages were empty. She didn't hold great hope as she checked the photos. There were three, and to her astonishment they appeared to be selfies from the tiny thumbnails. She opened one. No, not a selfie. But it was Harry, in his dressing gown, and he appeared to be in his own kitchen, holding the kettle. In the next he'd put it down and was smiling, and in the third he seemed to be reaching for the phone, perhaps even laughing. He looked completely relaxed, happy.

She must have taken them. The girl . . .

Jo checked the dates. All three had been taken yesterday morning, less than eight hours before a violent blow had ended Harry's life. Jo tried to conjure the face of the person holding the phone, but it remained a stubborn blur of the paltry facts they had. Young, blonde-haired, female. Anonymous.

'Who are you?' she whispered.

★　★　★

Jessica Granger arrived at the station half an hour later, while Jo was sifting through a box of Harry's old case files in case there was anything that seemed promising on the revenge angle. As the largish woman was shown into the CID room by the front desk clerk, Jo threw a panicked look back at the main board. Thankfully, it appeared that Heidi had already taken the precaution of turning it around to conceal the images there.

'Mrs Granger,' said Jo, introducing herself.

Jessica Granger looked a good deal younger than Harry's seventy-something years, with barely a wrinkle on her face. She was a tall woman, with an imposing frame reminiscent of Harry's own. She'd taken time over her make-up, Jo thought. And she wasn't alone. At her side was a man of around thirty dressed in tailored jeans and a blue shirt, clean-shaven and well groomed, wearing fashionable thick-rimmed spectacles. Jo introduced herself and Heidi. Jessica shook her hand.

'I'm Richard,' said the man, shaking too. 'Jessica's step-son.'

'I can't believe it,' said Jessica. 'Why would anyone want to hurt Harry?'

'We're not sure at the moment,' said Jo. She invited them into the nicer of the two interview rooms, and went to make them a cup of tea. Carrick joined them as she was asking whether they minded her recording. Neither objected.

'I want to reassure you, Mrs Granger,' said Carrick from the off, 'we will find who did this. I've got the whole team working on it. Jo here is the best. You're in very good hands.'

Jo was grateful for the public vote of confidence, even if she felt Andy was slightly over-egging the pudding.

'I'm not sure Mum can help you much,' said Richard Granger. 'She's not seen or heard from Harry for almost twenty-five years.'

'I can speak for myself,' said Jessica, her tone lightly chiding. 'But Richard's right.'

'No contact at all?' said Jo.

Jessica shook her head.

'But he had your address?' She opened her pocket book to consult her notes from the day before. 'In Derbyshire.'

'I gave that to him,' she said. 'But I'd no idea he'd kept a record. For the first few years after we separated, I'd send him a card on the anniversary of our daughter's accident. Perhaps you didn't know about that?'

'We were aware,' said Jo. She almost mentioned then that she had been Harry's friend, but stopped herself. It felt wrong, like she was trying to insert herself into what was their story.

'Well, he never wrote back,' said Jessica, 'so eventually I stopped bothering.'

There was no anger in her voice. Just acceptance.

'And why do you think that was?' asked Andy.

Jessica gave him a very direct look. 'Harry was never very good at talking, or showing emotion. He dealt with things himself, his own way. Mostly through drinking. I think he felt guilty about Lindsay. God knows why. He couldn't have done anything.'

A silence fell over the room. Jo was no stranger to relationships failing, but the fact their daughter's death had pushed

73

them apart felt doubly tragic. Children were supposed to bring joy and togetherness. She even reflected briefly on her own situation with Lucas, and the brief time she'd naïvely imagined they could be a family despite everything stacked against that possibility. She realised that Carrick was waiting for her to continue.

'When did you separate?' Jo asked.

'In '96,' said Jessica. 'We struggled on for a few years after it happened, but it wasn't the same. We'd had her so young, before we were even married. Without her, we lost our connection, I suppose.'

Jo thought about the will, signed some ten years after the split. It wasn't her place to mention its contents now.

'It wasn't acrimonious?' asked Jo.

Richard leant forward. 'What are you getting at?'

'Calm down,' said Jessica. 'The sergeant is just doing her job. The answer is no. Not especially. Harry had an affair – a woman from work, as it happened. But we were already living separate lives by then. It actually made the divorce easier.'

She spoke frankly, and Jo took a second to let the information sink in. She'd only ever know Harry as an old gent, even-keeled and deliberate in all he did. To imagine him as a younger man, with the drives that younger men were prone to, was a leap she couldn't easily perform. In other circumstances, she might have probed more deeply. Was the infidelity really such a minor event as the matter-of-fact tone implied? There was no reason to doubt what Jessica was saying, and she sensed Carrick had no appetite to pursue it either.

The surprise of it did make her think though. Might there have been another child from this clandestine relationship? The maths were tantalising – any daughter from the late nineties would be in her early twenties. All they had so far about the mystery girl was that she was young.

'Do you know the name of the other woman?' said Jo.

'Annie,' said Jessica, and again Jo sensed no animosity. 'I can't recall her surname. But she was definitely a police officer.'

Jo made a note. They'd be able to track her down quickly enough through the personnel records.

Across the table, Jessica knotted her hands together and brought her gaze up to Jo's. For the first time since entering the station, she looked unsure of herself. Vulnerable, even. 'They couldn't tell me, the officers who came to my house . . . did Harry suffer much, at the end?'

The gory poker still in evidence not ten metres below flashed up in Jo's mind. The spatter of blood on the ceiling. There was no way of knowing if Harry had lost consciousness and never regained it, or if he had lain there, struggling, aware of his life ebbing away. The fact there wasn't more evidence of an attempt to move suggested it was probably the former.

'We don't think so, no,' said Jo. 'He was unconscious when we found him.' She let Jessica process for a moment, before continuing. 'I know that Harry and you weren't in regular communication, but back when you lived together, was there ever any trouble with threats? Perhaps something related to his work?'

'He barely spoke about work at all,' said Jessica. She shook her head. 'I'm sorry I can't be more helpful.'

'Would have to be a hell of a grudge to resurface now,' said Richard. 'You really you have no idea who might have done it?'

Before either she or Andy had time to answer, Jessica untangled her fingers. 'They keep their cards close to their chest,' she said, with a hint of wry amusement. 'And that's all right.'

'We're looking into one particular person of interest,' said Carrick. Jo was surprised, as they hadn't discussed disclosing the suspect. 'A girl who we believe was staying with Harry.'

'A girl*friend*?' asked Richard.

'We're not sure,' said Jo, taking the reins again. She really didn't feel comfortable speculating in front of them, especially given they didn't even have a proper description. 'Does that mean anything to you?'

Jessica wore a look of bafflement. 'It doesn't. Maybe it was a lodger?'

'Possibly,' said Jo. The thought had crossed her own mind, wondering if somehow an argument about rent or something more minor still had escalated to violence. She wasn't convinced though – either that Harry would have disrupted his life for a little extra cash, or that a young girl would ever choose 21 Canterbury Road as a suitable place to live, let alone seen Harry as a promising housemate. And the pictures on the phone had looked almost fond. She had a feeling it was something they weren't seeing at all. Maybe even the 'delicate situation' he'd mentioned in his message.

All the more reason to include it in the official report . . .

She blushed with guilt at the omission, but nobody in the room seemed to notice.

'Can I see him?' said Jessica, suddenly and forcefully.

'Mum!' cried her step-son. 'Why?'

Jessica shot him a piercing look. 'To say goodbye, of course.'

'I can ask someone to take you,' said Carrick.

'That would be much appreciated,' said Jessica.

'I'd be happy to,' said Jo. She smiled at the woman opposite. 'I knew Harry. He was a friend.'

There was a knock at the door, and Heidi looked in. She had an excited twinkle in her eyes. 'Andy, Jo, I need to borrow you urgently.'

Jo excused herself and Carrick, and once the door was closed, Heidi spoke in a rush. 'We've just been notified by the deceased's bank – his card has been used in a contactless transaction.'

'Holy shit,' said Jo. 'Where?'

'A supermarket. About three hours ago – just outside the city.'

Jo tempered her excitement. It was a lead, but the time frame was frustrating.

'How come it took so long to get to us?' asked Carrick.

Heidi gave Jo a furtive look, then held up her arms. 'Hey, don't shoot the messenger.'

'Jo,' said Carrick, 'go with Heidi and check it out. They'll have CCTV.'

Jo paused. 'What about Jessica? I promised I'd—'

'I'll find a uniform to do it.'

'But I—'

'Jo.' Carrick took a deep breath. 'You're my SIO. I know Harry and you were close, but you can't do everything. The potential footage is more important.'

'Got it, boss.'

Chapter 6

She didn't bother with the blues as they drove. There seemed little chance that their suspect was still anywhere in the vicinity of the supermarket where Harry's card had been used.

'Do you think the DCI's okay?' she asked Heidi. The contretemps with Andy bothered her. In the past they'd never even shared a cross word, yet now they seemed to be, if not in conflict, then at least not quite in sync.

'He's just stressed,' said her colleague. 'Ever since he took over from Stratton, he's been shoulder to the wheel. He had to fight to get Alice – HR wanted to trim CID back after the Pryce mess.'

Mess was putting it mildly, thought Jo. Jack Pryce had been the biggest embarrassment to Thames Valley Police in fifty years, and she herself had played no small part in the drama. She fact that she'd slept with him didn't help the overall look either – she'd undergone hours of cross-examination by the Police and Crime Commissioners afterwards, poring over their brief relationship in excruciating detail, reliving her shame before the incredulous faces of her inquisitors. She was convinced the only things that had saved her being pushed out was the potential

PR nightmare from sacking a pregnant woman, and the fact everyone else in the department had been duped by Pryce too.

'The Xan Do murder hasn't made things any easier,' Heidi continued. 'Chances of closing it look remote.'

'Thank God it's on George's plate,' said Jo.

'You should probably go easy on Dimi.'

'About the 'tache? No chance.'

'About the case,' said Heidi. 'He's feeling the heat a bit.'

Jo glanced across at her colleague to see if she was being serious. Tan's face showed no sign of irony. 'I think he can cope – he's a big boy.'

'Andy probably hasn't told you yet,' said Heidi. 'Dimi's being investigated over a complaint from Xan Do's parents.'

'How come?'

'Let's just say he didn't give them a lot of space to grieve. He went in hard on the search of their warehouse while Do was still on the slab. No warrant. Told them he'd get the place shut down. They allowed it, but it turns out they've got a good solicitor who's told them they have a case. They're pursuing a formal reprimand.'

'Dimi's methods were always going to catch up with him eventually,' said Jo. 'You're asking me to feel sorry for him?' She was still smarting from his earlier insinuations about Harry and the propriety of his relationship with his mystery house-guest.

'Maybe not,' said Heidi, 'but we all bend the rules from time to time, right?' She gave Jo a meaningful look.

It was true, in times gone by, that Jo hadn't exactly followed orders to the letter.

'Fair point,' said Jo. 'Alice looks like she'll keep him on the straight and narrow. What's her story?'

'She was on the beat in Cardiff before, scored top one per cent in her investigative exams. Her fiancé's a bit older – a doctor of some sort with a private practice in West London.'

'That explains the clobber,' said Jo.

'Miaow,' said Heidi.

Jo smiled. 'Sorry, I'm only just out of elasticated waists. The young offend me.'

'Don't be silly. You look great. You're doing great to be back at work.'

'My pelvic floor disagrees. Seriously, if I even sneeze hard—'

'Stop!' said Heidi, laughing. She pointed ahead, more serious. 'Take a left here – there's a short cut.'

As they closed in on the supermarket, the mood in the car grew perceptibly more tense. Even if the suspect who'd used Harry's card was long gone, in a matter of minutes they'd have a face. With the amount of resources that would be brought to focus on putting the case to bed, it wouldn't be long before they had someone in custody. She could look the person in the eye and tell them she'd do everything in her power to see them behind bars for a long time.

Jo tried to quell her anticipation. As her mind tracked forward, so came a gnawing sense of inevitable disappointment. If the motive for Harry's murder was simple greed – and often extreme violence was caused by nothing less banal – no conviction could bring satisfaction.

The supermarket was a small outlet attached to a petrol garage, with a twenty-four-hour gym beside and the beginnings of new housing estate behind a planted hedge opposite. It was at least two miles from Harry's house, right on the edge of town. It seemed unlikely their suspect had walked this far.

They found the manager quickly, and were taken through to the back office to review the footage with a security guard. With the exact time-stamp provided by Harry's bank, in a matter of minutes they were looking at colour images from the shop's CCTV. It was a busy time of day, morning rush-hour, with several people flowing through the self-service checkouts. But Jo knew at once when their girl came into shot. She was petite, wearing a padded jacket that looked a couple of sizes too big for her, and her legs were bare with clumpy boots on her feet. A few spirals of pale hair escaped from under a woolly hat. She moved with her head lowered, furtively, carrying a basket that was almost full. Jo made out bread, and what looked like a four-pack of beer, but the other items were harder to discern. The girl scanned them through, and a male clerk came over. There was a brief discussion, in which the young woman had evidently been asked to show some identification to prove her age. She appeared not to have any, and so after the clerk shook his head, she put it to one side without a fight. Then she paid with a flash of card, and left.

Jo rewound the footage, and turned to the manager. 'Who's the member of staff who ID'd her?' she asked.

The manager squinted at the screen. 'Anwar,' he said. 'He'll still be here if you want to talk to him?'

'We will,' said Jo. 'Do you have any other cameras?'

'Sure,' said the manager. He asked the security guard to help them, and went off to find Anwar.

It took a good forty-five minutes to sort through the various images taken of the young woman on the supermarket's cameras positioned in the other parts of the store. She had spent only three minutes or so inside the shop, moving up and down the aisles quickly. But on these, the resolution wasn't great. Jo had a sense of wide set eyes, and a wide jaw narrowing to a pointed chin. A small, button nose.

Anwar arrived as they were working, looking somewhat timid. Yes, he remembered the girl, he told them. She was pretty and nervous. She had a bandage on her hand – he couldn't remember which one but from scrutinising the footage it seemed to be her right. She had looked too young to purchase alcohol. She seemed in a hurry, and hadn't argued about the beer. Jo asked if he recalled anything else – any particular features or salient points. After struggling for a moment, Anwar said he could not, other than that the make of the beer was a super-strength lager. He'd thought it was an odd choice for a young girl like that. Normally they bought vodka, or maybe rum.

The most promising visual came from one of the supermarket's external cameras. It showed the young woman approaching across the small car park, and actually looking right into the lens. A baby face, almost – and surely under eighteen, given the lack of ID. That seemed to rule out her being the product of Ferman's affair with Annie. On her retreat, she headed the same way, but the frame lost her on the edge of the car park.

'We should check to the garage forecourt next door,' said Heidi. 'She might have got into a vehicle there.'

Jo worked with the security guard to send the necessary footage back to the station, then called Carrick to let him know they had a decent visual, and to ask Alice to cross-ref with faces seen near the betting shop at the end of Canterbury Road. They found the manager, and Jo asked if he could find out the exact items the woman had purchased. He pulled a face. 'We *can*,' he said, then paused, 'but it will take a while. I'll have to authorise it with head office. Privacy, you know?'

'Of course,' said Jo, though she didn't really understand the problem. She left her details, before she and Heidi headed over to the petrol station.

Sadly, the footage recovered was of even worse quality than that of the supermarket. It wasn't of no use at all though, as it showed the girl walking past the forecourt to an area behind, out of shot. When Jo and Heidi exited afterwards, to inspect the lie of the land in person, they saw it was waste ground with a derelict car wash.

'She must have had a vehicle here,' said Heidi as they stood beside a cracked concrete platform. 'You think she's with someone else? Someone who knew how to avoid the cameras?'

Jo turned to look in the opposite direction, away from the petrol station. Beyond, over a barrier, was dense scrubland, a copse of trees, and then, after around fifty metres or so, the dual carriageway. She could hear the arrhythmic thrum of passing traffic.

'Maybe,' said Jo. She headed towards the barrier and stepped over. Gorse bushes blocked the way, tendrils armed with thorns. 'Can't see her hiking through all this anyway.' Any lead was tenuous, and she felt deflated by the whole trip. *If only we'd got here a bit sooner . . .*

'I thought we had an alert with the bank,' she said, climbing back over. 'They should have called us straight away.' When Heidi didn't reply, Jo saw she looked uncomfortable. 'What's up?'

Heidi gave a thin smile. 'They said they had called your number and left a message – I didn't want to say anything in front of Andy before I'd spoken to you first.'

Jo felt herself colour again. 'I didn't get a call.' Her workphone was in her bag. She'd had it with her every second of the day. Except when she'd dipped into Little Steps. She did the maths – just over three hours ago.

Fuck.

She felt a heavy lump in the pit of her stomach. If she'd taken the call when it came in, she could have been making this journey just a few minutes behind their suspect.

Heidi must have sensed her discomfort. 'Hey, it's okay.'

But it really wasn't. They'd lost so much time. And all because she hadn't had her work head on. She'd just been thinking about Theo, lingering at the nursery door while the crucial call came in. It was an amateur mistake; one of the first things they taught you about tactical investigations. *Keep communications channels open.*

'It's all right,' she muttered. 'I'll let Andy know it was my responsibility.'

★   ★   ★

On the way back to the station, Jo struggled to shake the girl's image from her mind. And 'girl' was the right word. She couldn't have been much over five-two, and if she really was under eighteen, that only confused Jo more. Harry was old, but still a large man, and it looked like a single blow had felled him. Was the girl in those pictures really capable of such a feat? And it still begged the question – what had happened between them to precipitate such an act of extreme violence? She'd almost certainly been his *guest* for several days before the incident occurred.

'It doesn't make any sense,' she said aloud.

Heidi took a while to answer but appeared to be on the same wavelength. 'Sometimes these things don't,' she said. 'Or sometimes the answer is just too obvious. She's probably a user. She wanted his money.'

'There was no drug paraphernalia in the house,' said Jo. 'I think she might even have been doing his housework.'

'Let's just focus on finding her,' said Heidi. 'The *whys* can wait. Anyway, what about the theory she's his daughter?'

'It's a possibility,' said Jo. 'But Harry's ex said the affair happened twenty-four years ago.'

'Might not be connected to Annie at all,' said Heidi. 'Another relationship?'

'I'm not sure,' said Jo. 'Harry didn't seem the type to have an illegitimate child.'

Heidi looked at her like she'd just committed some cardinal sin of policing – assuming the best of someone. 'It's probably not the sort of thing he'd share.'

Granted, thought Jo.

Separating the Harry she knew from Harry the victim was no simple task, and it was a valid reason why Andy might question the wisdom of allocating her as SIO. She wondered how well she really did know him. They'd only met about two years ago, when he was drafted in from retirement to consult on a cold case, but since then they'd spent a good deal of time in each other's company. True, most was in the Three Crowns, mildly inebriated (not that *Harry* ever showed the effects of alcohol a great deal), but before and after Theo's birth she'd visited him at home several times, and he'd even come out to hers on the bus one time. She could acknowledge that it was a strange relationship from the outside – the gruff old pensioner and the single mum – but most of the time they talked shop, anecdotes of cases they'd worked on, the foibles of colleagues past and present. She'd probably shared a good deal more about herself and her family than he had, and she'd never pushed for more, though occasionally he'd mentioned Lindsay, and in those moments he'd come alive. He'd struck her as a private man, sad and stoic. But, above all, *good*. Decent, honest, and kind.

Despite her best efforts to keep a professional distance, she couldn't help comparing him with Xan Do, the other body on the books, a kid whose poor choices had caught up with him as inevitably as if he'd given the Grim Reaper a key to his front door. But Harry had just wanted to live his life out quietly, and the world, or fate, hadn't let that happen. The choices he'd made should never have led to this.

'Anyway, how's little Theo?' asked Heidi. *She wants to change the subject. And that's fine by me.*

'Still immobile, thank God,' said Jo. 'It looks like he wants to crawl, but he just flops.'

'Won't be long!' said Heidi, smiling warmly. 'He'll be climbing the bookshelves next. I found Spencer *on top of* our fishtank when he was fourteen months, I kid you not.'

Jo experienced a moment of shock when she realised Heidi had never mentioned the name of her child before, even though he must have been almost getting on for two. *And, more telling, I never even asked.* She concealed the surprise with laughter. 'At least you didn't have child services checking up on you.' She told Heidi about the visit of the previous morning.

'Oh God – because of the prang?' Heidi said.

'Yup,' said Jo.

Now, removed from the moment, it seemed a lot less disconcerting, and she was even able to inject some humour into her description of Annabelle Pritchard. 'I swear she was measuring Theo up for a cage.'

Heidi shook her head. 'You'd think they'd have better things to do.'

Jo was grateful for the solidarity, but already felt she'd overshared. Work was work, and family was family. There was no need to complicate things.

Chapter 7

Dimitriou was in Carrick's office, where they were both staring at a computer screen. The girl's face, blown up from the security footage, was already pinned to the board. Alice Reeves greeted Heidi and Jo, then said, 'You want the good news or the bad news?'

'Go with the good,' said Heidi.

'I found Annie Connelly,' said Reeves, reading from a file. 'Constable on secondment here for training between February and November 1995. Logs show she worked closely with Harold Ferman. However' – she flipped around an image of a redhead in uniform – 'she's also deceased, in distinctly unsuspicious circumstances. Ovarian cancer. You want the sister's details?'

'Why not?' said Jo. 'Looks like a dead end though. Anything from the Three Crowns?'

'Nope,' said Reeves. 'Place was like God's waiting room.'

'That's my regular you're talking about,' said Jo.

'Sorry, ma'am' said Reeves quickly, her pale skin reddening. 'But none of them had seen Harry with a young woman, or at all over the last few days. They thought he might have been ill. You said he used to go in most days?'

'Religiously,' said Jo. She recalled the missing booze at the house. Had Harry actually quit the drink for some reason? She couldn't see him following a doctor's advice on that score.

'However,' said Reeves. 'We got a call from a window cleaner who was working on a house across the street. He called to say a girl entered number 21 with her own key. He thought she might have been a cleaner, because she was carrying a mop and a plastic bag.'

Jo glanced at the image on the board again. *Who the hell are you? The same person who vacuumed the place?*

Dimitriou emerged from Carrick's office, on the phone. 'Yes, I need the image circulated to staff at the prison in case he's stupid enough to make contract in person. I'll be along within a couple of hours to speak to both of them.'

He hung up. 'We're closing in on the little bastard,' he said.

'Matthis?' said Jo.

Dimitriou sat at his desk and began typing as he spoke. 'Triangulation puts his phone in the vicinity of the old telephone exchange in the half-hour before Xan Do's shooting, then back at home an hour after. First call was to Xan himself, and the second one corresponds to HMP Long Lartin. Can you guess who's a resident?'

'Matthis Senior?'

'Full marks to the head girl,' said Dimi.

'So where'd he get a firearm?' asked Jo, ignoring the jibe.

'Not my problem,' said Dimitriou. 'You're the one who said he might be responsible in the first place, remember?'

'I thought the family might be involved,' said Jo, 'but it sounds like he knew Xan. Maybe they were friends.'

'Friends fall out.' Dimitriou shrugged. 'You sound like you're on Blake's defence team.'

Jo held up her hands. 'I dunno. When I saw him, I thought

he looked sort of scared. He was pissing in a bucket. Hiding in that lock-up.'

'Yeah, from us,' said Dimitriou. 'Don't look a gift-horse in the mouth. This is open and shut.'

'Got to catch him first. Any other clues in the phone?'

Dimitriou was typing without looking at her. 'Calls mostly from his home, or the estate. One stood out though – right in the middle of Stanton St John.'

Jo felt her eyebrows drift up. She knew the village. Well, a hamlet really. It was a collection of thatched cottages and country houses a few miles from the city. Distinctly wealthy, and literally the last place she'd expect to find a kid from Blake Matthis' side of the tracks.

'You think he was dealing to someone out there?' asked Heidi.

'Unlikely,' said Dimitriou. 'But I'm going to swing by. One way or another, we're going to track him down.'

★ ★ ★

Once Dimitriou and Alice had gone, Jo returned to her own case. She consulted the forensic pathologist's notes on Ferman's body. Here were the essentials of her friend's life, boiled down to bare figures and scientific terminology, and signed off by pathologist Vera Coyne. Male. Caucasian. Age seventy-three. Five feet eleven inches in height. Grey hair. Dentures. A tattoo of a heart she'd never known about on his left biceps, and an appendectomy scar on his abdomen. A full autopsy had been carried out, as the death was clearly suspicious in nature. They revealed severely clogged aortic arteries and stage three cirrhosis of the liver.

The cause of death was listed as cerebral haemorrhage as a

result of a depressed skull fracture just above the victim's right ear. Vera Coyne had opened part of the skull to confirm. The speculation, supported by the crime scene examination, was blunt force trauma. There was a second injury though, supporting the same hypothesis – a lateral fracture of the ulna in Harry's right forearm – plus bruising to the skin. It was listed as a likely defensive injury, and the fact there was subdermal haematoma confirmed one thing: Harry's heart hadn't stopped pumping blood around his body for a good while after the arm injury was inflicted. He'd not died quickly. Whether or not he'd been conscious was a question that couldn't be answered.

A diagram noted the spot the poker had impacted upon Harry's skull, and Jo didn't feel the need to open any of the photographic images to be reminded in high definition or full colour how the wound looked. She noted the fact his blood alcohol level was zero, which led credence to the theory he'd gone teetotal. On any normal day, Harry would have had a least a couple of drinks by the early afternoon.

She guessed that Vera, having been in her post for several years, would likely have known Harry too. She wondered how it would have felt to have him laid out on the slab in front of her. Though macabre, that speculation brought an odd comfort. Harry would be looked after, at least in death. Seeing that the coroner's office were happy to release the body, she sent an email to the funeral director appointed by Jessica Granger to pass on the details.

She next made a call to Mel Cropper. He sounded like he had his mouth full as he answered the phone.

'Jo,' he said.

'No pressure, but have you got anything for me?'

'We didn't get any prints from the poker,' he said, 'but there were some on the fireplace surround, right beside the poker stand. They're not a match for the victim. And we've hoovered up some skin cells from bedding upstairs. It's going to be at least another twenty-four hours until we have anything concrete for you. Anything to share your end?'

Jo filled him in on the evolving picture of the young woman, and Vera Coyne's observations, before asking about the removal of any alcohol-related evidence. There wasn't any, Mel confirmed. Looking again at the injuries listed, Jo added: 'Something's bothering me, Mel. This girl – she's tiny. It's hard to see she'd have the strength to take Harry on. Especially if he saw her coming.'

'He was over seventy, wasn't he?' said Mel.

'Even so,' Jo replied. She couldn't square the ferocity of the attack with the waif-like girl in the supermarket footage. There were two blows, and both had broken bone. 'Maybe there was someone with her. An accomplice.'

Mel was silent for a few seconds, and she imagined him chewing thoughtfully. 'That might make sense of some of the prints we found.'

'Go on.'

'There are two other sets besides Harry's – one set on a mug in the kitchen and the fireplace surround, and another distinct set in various locations, including the back-door handle. Did Harry have many visitors?'

'Not that I know of. Maybe it's a boyfriend of the mystery girl?' *Someone who was waiting behind the petrol station. Someone who wanted our girl to buy him some lager.*

'I'll leave the detective work to you,' said Mel.

★　★　★

Jo consulted with Carrick on the public appeal for the as yet nameless girl at the supermarket. On the latest findings, they decided between them to name her as a person of interest, rather than a suspect. It would go out on Thames Valley's social media feeds, as well as the evening news. Jo was confident they'd have a name before the day was out. In this day and age, people couldn't stay hidden for long.

She was writing up her notes when the front desk clerk came through. 'Sorry, ma'am,' he said. 'There's a gentleman just walked in. He wants to speak to you personally.'

'Me? What's it about?'

'I'm afraid he's intoxicated.'

Just then Jo heard an angry shout drifting through the station. 'I just want to *talk* to her, for Christ's sake!'

Lucas.

'Great,' she said.

Carrick had heard the shout too, and came out of his office. 'Problem?'

Jo didn't see much point in lying, and anyway, her boss deserved the truth. Her colleagues were too polite to display any curiosity about her private life, but given the past public nature of some of her relationship catastrophes, they might have guessed at the basics and why there was no father in Theo's life. 'My ex,' she explained. 'I can handle him.'

'You sure? We can deal with it, if you want.'

Jo stood from her desk. 'Let's see how it goes,' she said.

Carrick nodded, still looking doubtful, and Jo followed the front desk clerk through booking, and out into the reception area. At first she thought it was deserted, that Lucas had done a runner, and she'd breathed half a sigh of relief before she saw him. He was standing in one corner, leafing through the pamphlets on a stand. As he turned towards her, she was shocked. The top of his nose was cut, with an angry-looking scab, and one eye was surrounded by a dark bruise, the white a mess of broken capillaries. His hair, the thick golden locks that had always smelled of a sun-kissed beach, were straggly and unwashed. One hand was wrapped in a dirty bandage.

'What *happened*?' she said. Some vestigial affection made her move closer, and reach out.

'So there you are!' he said. Even though he was several feet away, she could smell the booze.

Jo was aware of the stocky front desk clerk moving from her back to her side. Nigel wasn't a tall man, but she knew he was ex-services, and perfectly capable of dealing with any problems that might arise.

'Your face,' she said.

'Just a bash,' said Lucas, with a dismissive wave. 'Anyway, how are *you*?'

His speech was slurred, his gestures theatrical. It was as if some alien personality had taken over. He'd been honest with her about his historic problems with alcohol, but the reality of it had always been comfortingly remote while he'd remained dry. Confronted now with this version of the man she'd known was almost heart-breaking. He looked a shrunken version of himself. Like his lights had gone out.

'I'm fine, Lucas,' she said gently, 'but I'm working.'

'Aren't you always?' he said. He tried to slot the leaflet back into the stand, and ended up dropping it to the floor.

'You can't come here like this,' she said. 'Not when you've been drinking.' He nodded slowly, pouting like a child, and his body sagged further. 'It's all right Nigel,' she said. 'I've got this.'

'If you're sure, ma'am,' said the clerk. He stepped back through the gate, walking to his counter. He didn't take his eyes off Lucas though.

Jo approached. Lucas was wearing workclothes, and she hoped that meant he still had a job to go to. He'd been a gardener, at several of the colleges. One of his shoelaces was undone, which added to the overall effect of vagrancy, but she happened to know it wasn't a symptom of inebriation at all. Even back when they were a couple, it had been a frequent occurrence.

'Lucas, we can talk later,' she said.

'Can we?' he said. 'I don't have your number. And no one will give it to me. I don't even know where you live.'

'We can arrange to meet somewhere,' she said.

He gave her a suspicious glance. 'You won't show up.'

'I will,' she said. 'I promise. How about . . .' She thought for a moment. She wanted somewhere neutral, but nowhere near her home. 'What about the Botanical Gardens? You can tell me about the plants.'

'Don't patronise me,' he said, and his eyes flashed with bitterness.

'I'm sorry. If you want to go somewhere else, that's fine.'

As she said it, he nodded, taking it in. The tension seemed to dip a fraction, and she was hopeful the episode was coming to an end. Then he asked, 'How's Theo?'

'He's fine,' said Jo. 'Really good actually.'

'Can I see him?'

Jo reached out, and touched Lucas's shoulder. She spoke softly. 'Not when you're like this. You understand why, don't you?'

He looked at her, very directly, and in his eyes, even the damaged one, she saw the man she'd once loved. 'Yes,' he said. 'I just wanted to see you.'

'I know that,' she said. 'And we'll talk properly. I can't do today, but Saturday is good.'

Jo heard the gate open behind her. It wasn't Nigel though. Andy Carrick was holding a phone. 'Sergeant, I need you,' he said. From his tone, she didn't think this was just a ploy to rescue her.

'Lucas, I've got to go,' she said. 'What time shall I see you on Saturday?'

But her ex was already pulling open the door, and half stumbling on to the street outside. She took a half step after him.

'Jo, it's George,' said Carrick. 'We've got something serious in Stanton. More bodies.'

Chapter 8

Stanton St John was a quintessentially English postcard village. Houses of thatch and pale Cotswold stone, many over three hundred years old, lay spread along a crossroads surrounding a grand Norman church, and across the road, a low-ceilinged public house – the sort of place hung with pictures of the area's rural past, polished horseshoes and old farming equipment on display. There wasn't a soul around as they drove through, in convoy with another squad car.

The house called Copse View was situated a couple of hundred metres from the church, its private drive branching from the country road and overhung with ancient trees. Dimitriou's car was parked up outside the Tudor cottage of twisted timbers and small mullioned windows, alongside a Land Rover. Jo spotted Alice Reeves standing on the doorstep, sucking on a vape pen, which she hastily put away as they came to a halt on the gravel. She looked pale.

'Boss,' she said, on seeing Carrick.

'George still downstairs?' he asked.

Reeves nodded. 'Through the kitchen.'

They all donned protective footwear and entered. The house

might once have been beautiful – expensive-looking classic furniture was placed with an eye to interior design, modern art on the walls rubbed shoulders with the occasional sculpture – but someone had ransacked the place, throwing open dressers and cupboards, leaving the contents strewn across the rugs and stone floors. Jo saw two staircases leading to the upper floor, the balustrades hand-crafted from oak. They passed into a surprisingly expansive country kitchen opening on one side to a view across a tiered garden and woodland beyond. Like the rooms they'd already seen, the kitchen had been torn apart, leaving smashed crockery and glass everywhere. One door opened to a boot room, but a second one, ajar, led down a set of steps. 'Oh Jesus,' said Heidi.

A split-second later, Jo's nose caught the familiar smell – like the worst bin truck you'd ever walked behind, rotten and pungent. Her eyes watered, and Carrick clutched his tie to his mouth.

Dimitriou appeared at the top of the stairs. He'd removed his jacket, and a sheen of sweat covered his face and made his moustache glisten. 'It's not pretty,' he said.

Jo was no stranger to dead bodies, yet still felt a deep trepidation as they approached the door, doing their best to avoid the detritus strewn across the kitchen floor. They descended in single file. The foetid air was uncomfortably warm, and Jo knew if she breathed it in too deeply, she'd probably pass out. The cellar was lit by a strip light with a tiny flicker, and revealed well-ordered shelves containing DIY equipment, paint pots, and the like. There was a large, oil-fired boiler, which explained the temperature.

The air was thick with flies, buzzing in a concentrated mass around two bodies lying on the stone-cobbled floor. Large puddles of dried blood radiated beneath their throats. Their hands, tied behind their backs, were grey and bloated, and the cords used to tie them had disappeared into the sloughing flesh of their wrists. From her angle Jo could see their faces had leaked considerable fluids through the orifices, making them unrecognisable, and if it weren't for the fact that they were in their underwear, sex would have been indeterminable. Her stomach protested, but she held in the nausea as she stepped over a spillage from what looked like a can of engine oil at the bottom of the steps.

'Going by the mail on the doormat upstairs, this is Mr and Mrs Bailey,' said Dimitriou quietly.

Jo glanced at Carrick, who was shaking his head as if genuinely distraught. His eyes lingered on the prone corpses, then he turned back to the stairs. 'Heidi, call in another uniform car, and get in touch with SOCO. Dimi, get two cordons up. One at the end of the drive, one around the house, then speak to the neighbours either side. See what we can find out about Mr and Mrs Bailey.'

'Can't Alice take care of that?' said Dimitriou. 'I'd rather—'

'Just do as you're told,' said Carrick.

Dimitriou looked a little taken aback. 'Sir, this has got to be Matthis. We need to get the word out.'

'Not necessarily,' said Jo.

'We've got his phone pinging right here,' said Dimitriou. 'He's prime suspect in another murder. I'd say on the balance of probabilities, we need to treat him as a credible and serious threat to life.'

'The phone call from here was three days ago,' said Jo, recalling the file. 'Those flies wouldn't have had time to hatch.'

'Maybe he killed them and came back later to look for something,' said Dimi. 'They didn't slit their own throats.'

She resented the condescending tone. 'You think a sixteen-year-old dealer from Blackbird Leys ties people up and does that?' she said.

'So you're a profiler now?' said Dimitriou.

'Enough, you two,' said Andy. 'Leave the CSI to Mel and his team. They'll give us facts not speculation. Jo, grab Alice from outside. Make sure she's okay, then see what you can find in the house. I want to know what these two possibly did to warrant being butchered in cold blood.'

Jo was glad to leave the confines of the cellar. Upstairs, she went out through a boot room hung with jackets and hats, a stand holding umbrellas, and what looked like a long walking stick, the embossed end in the shape of a bird of prey's head. She opened the unlocked back door, then walked around the side of the house. There was another car parked there – a brand new Mini Countryman. Whoever had killed Mr and Mrs Bailey could have taken one of the two cars, but had left them both. Maybe the Blake Matthis hypothesis was right after all – she doubted very much he was legally permitted to drive, or that car theft was his thing.

Back at the front, Alive Reeves was seated on a stone bench, head bowed.

'You okay?' asked Jo.

Reeves looked up, breathed heavily through her nose, and shook her head. 'Not really.'

'First one?' said Jo.

'First one like that.'

'They're all different,' said Jo. 'If it makes you feel better, I almost puked.'

Reeves offered the thinnest of smiles.

'Listen, the gaffer wants us to recce the house.' She relayed Carrick's instructions, and offered Reeves a hand. 'You up to it?' The younger woman took her hand, and got to her feet.

While Dimitriou stalked past to speak to the uniforms, Jo and Reeves entered the house once more. The smell was still in the air, but Jo was already getting used to it.

'You take upstairs,' said Jo. 'Holler if you find anything.'

There was post on the dresser inside the front door, and more paperwork in the drawers. The Baileys' names were indeed on several items. Rachael and Mark. She was listed on several items as 'Dr', but Jo couldn't find any evidence of a specialism. The lounge was ripped apart – furniture looked like it had been attacked with a blade, the cushions' innards exposed. An enormous TV remained untouched. At the rear was a study, and Jo flinched back as she entered. A dead dog lay on the ground. *Fuck*. No, it wasn't a dog. What the hell was it?

Relief flooded her veins as she realised the corpse was a toppled piece of taxidermy – a badger. She moved it aside with her toe. The filing cabinets and drawers had been turned out, and a whole bookshelf toppled, contents spilled across the floor. A number of bound editions caught Jo's eye, titled *European Journal of Paediatrics*. There were a number of other titles on children's health and psychology. Certificates on the wall showed that Dr Bailey was well regarded in the field of paediatric oncology. Hanging over the computer was a large crucifix, complete with a dying Christ. Jo wasn't a religious person by any means, but the irony of the so-called saviour looking on was still upsetting. One of the drawers contained two passports, and she took a moment to absorb their faces. Mr Bailey, whose age was fifty-two, was slight of face, clean-shaven, with neatly parted fair hair. His wife, the doctor, was a couple of years older, and looked rather elegant. The contrast between the photos and their mortal remains couldn't have been more striking.

She left the room, and headed for the stairs. A cupboard beneath had been rifled through, and among the board games were items of sporting equipment. A cricket glove and bat, tennis rackets, a yoga mat. For the first time since arriving, Jo realised Mr and Dr Bailey likely had children, maybe even grandchildren. In her mind, she constructed images of their contented middle-class life – Sunday lunches *en famille*, skiing holidays, good school results. On the stairs hung several pages that looked to be from some fishing almanac – the various species of freshwater fish, accompanied by vivid illustrations and their Latin names. Halfway along was a smeared bloody handprint, as if someone had steadied themselves on the way down. There were a few drops on the stair carpet too.

The first floor was a different story to the carnage below. Here, the house seemed undisturbed aside from a few more drops of blood on the landing. The first bedroom she entered evidently belonged to a young man with a passion for rugby, if the shelf of trophies, and the signed and framed British Lions shirt on the wall were anything to go by. There was a team photo – all young men – and it read 'St Cuthbert's First XV, 2018'. The bed was neatly made.

'Ma'am,' called Reeves. 'In here.'

Jo came out and saw the younger woman at the far end of the landing, standing in a doorway. 'I think it's where he cornered them.'

'Let's see,' said Jo. She hurried past three other doors.

Reeves was in the master bedroom. A simple bolt lock had been smashed off the inside of the door, and there was significant splintering in the architrave around the frame. 'Someone kicked this in,' said Alice. The room beyond, which overlooked the back of the house, hadn't been thoroughly searched, but there were signs of a struggle, and bloodstains on the floor – several heavy spatters thoroughly soaked into the shaggy pale blue carpet. A tiltable full-length mirror was at an almost horizontal angle, as though something had knocked into it. A telephone cradle on a dressing table lay empty. Jo found the receiver in the corner of the room, and gingerly picked it up. The battery had run down.

In the en-suite, a razor lay beside the sink, still crusty with shaving foam, and the sink itself was soiled with short hairs. It looked like Mr Bailey had been in the process of shaving when he was interrupted.

Coming out again, Jo noticed that there was a shelf beside a small window overlooking the west side of the house. It contained half a dozen striking porcelain plates, and corresponded to six more on the opposite side of the room. The bright glaze showed semi-figurative versions of the Stations of the Cross. Two of the plates though were broken – one split in two, and the other in several pieces on the floor.

Jo pointed to the one still on the shelf. 'How do you think that happened?'

'I'm not sure I understand.'

'Unlikely that someone broke a plate and put it back, isn't it?'

Now she was closer she saw the wallpaper behind the plate was pocked in places with small black marks like smudges. She pulled across a spindle-backed antique chair, and climbed up carefully. As her eyes came level with the shelf, she saw there were a number of lead pellets on top.

'Bingo,' she said, showing one to Reeves. 'Someone let off a round in here.' She pointed to the blood. 'My guess is that it found a target, at least partially. The rest of the blast hit the plates and the wall.' Glancing sideways, she saw some had shredded the curtain. Jo dropped to the ground – there were more pellets scattered in the thick shag of the carpet. She stood and turned over the tilted mirror. As she did so, shattered fragments of glass spilled onto the floor.

Reeves moved across the room, past the blood on the floor, until she was facing Jo from the doorway. She mimicked a shotgun held at the hip. 'About here?'

Jo nodded. The range and trajectory fit perfectly with the blood and the damage. 'Any sign of a spent shell?'

Reeves got on her hands and knees, and it was only a few seconds before she moved to reach under the bed. 'Got it.'

'Leave it in place for Mel,' said Jo. She looked too. Sure enough, the shell had come to rest a few inches under the divan. She reflected on the taxidermy, and fishing equipment. It appeared that Mr Bailey was a country sports enthusiast. 'I suppose it's plausible Mr Bailey had a licence, and kept the gun in here for security. Someone broke in, and they took shelter in the safest place. He breaks down the door, but Mr Bailey's waiting for him, and gets a shot off. The intruder is injured, but not critically. He then overpowered them and got the gun.'

'But didn't shoot them?' said Alice.

'Maybe he was worried about the noise,' said Jo, though as she theorised she felt uneasy. The thing that had happened in the cellar seemed more than a panicked response.

Next along the hall was a guest room, completely undisturbed by all appearances, but the bedroom between it and the boy's belonged to a girl for sure. Even if the shades of pink and purple bedding didn't make it obvious, there was a dressing table, its surface covered in brightly coloured cosmetics bottles, with powder stains around the feet too, plus what might have been a lick of red nail polish or dye of some sort. Music posters on the walls, and several pairs of shoes ranging from pumps to heels lined up along the floor. The area around the bed's headboard was entirely given to a collage of photos, stuck at angles. As Jo moved into the room, it was like stepping back into her own past. Here, the mess was entirely organic, the product of a scattergun life rather than criminal rifling.

'I don't get it,' said Alice. 'Where are the kids?'

Jo had been thinking the same thing, and she was trying to stay positive. Maybe they were away on holiday, or didn't live here any more. The alternatives didn't bear consideration. She scanned the photos.

'As long as they're not here, I'm happ—'

What the fuck?

'Found something?'

Jo's voice was somewhere way in the back of her throat, her eyes glued to the wall of photos, darting between different points, and the same face. Most were group shots, or selfies with a friend or two. Some pictures were in school uniform, others appeared to be a park, or at various gatherings. But there was a single set, taken in a photo booth, showing a girl pulling a succession of funny faces, before ending in a sultry, over-the-top pout. The hairstyle changed a little in some of the photos, and sometimes it was tied up, but in this row of poses, she wore it loose. Shoulder length, springy curls. It couldn't be . . . but it was.

'It's her,' said Jo. 'The girl from Harry's.'

This is her bedroom.

Chapter 9

Within five minutes, the rest of the investigative team were staring at the same wall. Jo had found the girl's name – Megan Bailey – written on a few schoolbooks in a drawer, and the name of her school, Marsh Hill Secondary. Reeves came back up from downstairs, where she'd found a photo of the whole family together. It looked like a professional portrait – a studio background – and a sticker on the reverse confirmed it came from MX Studio Photography, based in central Oxford. The image showed Dr and Mr Bailey on the flanks, with the two siblings – Megan and a broad-shouldered young man – in the centre, arms looped around one another. Though Megan was smiling, it wasn't the same full-beam as on the faces of the others. Or perhaps that was simply Jo's imagination running away. Certainly though, compared with the other pictures of her, the ones taken on her own terms, there was *something* guarded in her eyes in that family shot.

Jo dipped into the boy's room and cross-referenced with the rugby team listings beneath the photo. His name was Gregory. After consulting with Carrick, she found a number for St Cuthbert's, which was apparently a boarding school thirty miles away. It came as a relief to think he was probably somewhere safe, but the last thing they needed was for the boy to arrive at the door and find a police cordon. She got through to the school secretary, and explained she was a police officer enquiring after the whereabouts of a student called Gregory Bailey.

'We can't give out any information about students,' came the reply.

Jo had anticipated as much. Tied by what exactly she herself wanted to disclose, she said simply, 'I'm afraid to say I've got some upsetting news about his parents. If you like, you could call the Thames Valley switchboard to confirm my identity. They'll put you through to me.'

That seemed to soften the secretary's defences. 'I'm sure that's unnecessary,' she said. 'Would you mind holding the line for a moment?'

'Of course.'

As Jo waited, she wandered back into the master bedroom. Mel Cropper would get the blood processed for DNA, and the handprint analysed for any matches; they'd bring in a ballistics expert to draw up likely scenarios, as well as identifying the relevant details on the shotgun used. The whole of Thames Valley normally dealt with less than a hundred shootings a year, so two in a week, within the same geographical area, was highly irregular. She had to assume the shotgun was now in the possession of whoever had killed the Baileys. If Dimitriou was right, and that individual was Blake Matthis, it would be a priority to get both boy and firearm off the streets.

'Hello?' said a man's voice on the phone. 'Has something happened to Mark?'

'Sorry, who is this?'

'My name is Dai Armitage,' said the man. 'I'm the head of the sixth form at St Cuthbert's. You're a police officer, I'm told.'

Jo introduced herself. 'I'm looking for Gregory Bailey.'

'Has something happened to Mark?' repeated Armitage.

'You know Mr Bailey?'

'Very well, yes – we served together. What's happened exactly?'

Jo saw no reason to keep him in the dark.

'I'm sure you can appreciate the need for discretion, and I'm very sorry to be the bearer of bad news, but it appears both Mark and his wife have died in suspicious circumstances.' Here, Armitage muttered something indecipherable under his breath. 'We're trying to get hold of Gregory to determine his safety, and to inform him in the most tactful way.'

'Greg's no longer at St Cuthbert's,' said Armitage. 'He finished last summer and took a place at Cambridge reading Natural Sciences. My God – this will *finish* him.'

'Do you have any contact details?' said Jo.

In a subdued tone that suggested he was still reeling from the news, Armitage said he hadn't, but that Greg was at Pembroke College. 'Do you need me to pass on their number? Or I could call them myself?'

'It's best if you leave it to us, sir,' said Jo.

'You mentioned suspicious circumstances,' said Armitage. 'You mean they were murdered?'

The scene two floors down hardly left room for any other hypothesis, but Jo said simply, 'We're working on that assumption, yes, but we need to keep that under wraps until we've spoken to next of kin. I assume we can rely on your discretion.'

'Of course, of course,' murmured Armitage. 'My God. He was a good man, you know. And Rachael too – a wonderful woman. I can't imagine why anyone would hurt them.'

'So you can't think of any enemies they might have had?'

'Not at all. Mark was a management consultant – retired now, but he still did a bit of pro bono for a missionary charity. Rachael was a celebrated figure in child medicine. Cancer.'

'And what about their daughter, Megan. Do you know her?'

A pause. 'Not really. She was a bit younger than Greg, and only here for a couple of terms.'

Jo recalled the other school name listed in the text book. 'She was at St Cuthbert's too?'

Another long pause, as if the line was suffering a delay. 'Er . . . yes. She left.'

'Do you know why?' He didn't answer. 'Mr Armitage, I'm sure you appreciate we're concerned for Megan's safety. She's missing. If you can help us, at all . . .'

'She was here, about four years ago. She was expelled.'

'For what?'

'It's really a private matter. I'd rather not—'

'You're assisting a murder inquiry,' said Jo. 'It's not the time for being coy. Drugs, I'm assuming?'

Armitage lowered his voice. 'If you must know, there were issues regarding sexual propriety.'

Jo looked at the image of the girl on the wall. She looked like any other teenager, but that didn't mean a thing. She thought again of Dimitriou's insinuations about Harry. 'Go on.'

'Mark's daughter attempted to seduce a member of staff.'

Jo's lips curled into a wry, sceptical smile. She'd dealt with a number of cases when an older man claimed his young victim was the instigator. 'Seduce how?'

'She sent images of herself.'

'And how old was she at this stage?'

'She would have been around twelve.'

'And this teacher – he reported it at once?' said Jo.

'Actually, the teacher was female,' said Armitage. 'But it wasn't an isolated incident.'

'And was any of this reported to the police?'

'Look, we did what Mark wanted,' said Armitage defensively. 'We agreed that Megan would leave. It was for her own good, and her brother's.'

'I see,' said Jo.

'I mean, why drag Mark's family through the dirt?' said Armitage.

Or the school's reputation, thought Jo. 'You've been very helpful,' she said. 'We may need to talk to you more though.'

'Of course,' said Armitage, but his voice failed to disguise his burning antipathy for the idea. Having swapped numbers, Jo ended the call with a distinctly uneasy sensation in her gut. It was hard to deduce much at all from Armitage's vague accusations. Though twelve was at the more extreme end, a promiscuous girl was hardly a rare thing. The thought of one staying with Harry didn't look at all good though.

Heidi Tan was waiting in the hallway. 'We spoke to Marsh Hill,' she said. 'Megan Bailey's in the final year of her GCSEs, but hasn't been in school for the last week. From what we can gather, her truancy is not uncommon and her parents were well aware of the issue.'

Jo shared her own intelligence from St Cuthbert's.

'Sounds like a troubled kid,' said Heidi. 'How the hell did she end up at Harry's?'

'I've no idea,' said Jo.

And things aren't going to get better for her any time soon.

JAMES

SEVEN WEEKS EARLIER

The train was rammed, all seats occupied and people standing in the aisles. He'd managed to get a seat on a table of four, beside a mum trying her best to control her two young kids. The girl and boy were arguing over what to watch on an iPad, sharing the ear-buds between them. It was doing his head in.

Getting out of Manchester felt like a release. Since Christopher Putman's death, he'd stayed well clear of the Salford area, lying low in the hostel. He'd sunken his own bloody clothes further up in the canal. And though he'd heard of a few members of the homeless community being questioned, it was clearly a last resort, just to see if any of them had heard anything suspicious. The police had no leads. The papers, he noticed, had kept the worst details out of the reporting.

He could have hitched to Oxford, but he knew he didn't look particularly approachable, and the thought of two days or more thumbing at the road-side had filled him with despair. He'd run out of cash too. Jumping the barriers at Manchester Piccadilly would have been too risky – too likely to draw attention – so he'd taken a train in from a local station further out, then walked across the platform to get to the Oxford train, deliberately choosing a busy Saturday service.

With his hood up, James rested his head on the window, and watched the countryside of middle England flash by.

'Give it to me! Mum said it was my turn to choose!'

The girl was trying to wrest the tablet from her brother, but her hand slipped and she hit herself in the mouth. Her face screwed up and she began to cry. James smiled.

'Charlie – give it to her,' said the mum.

'But she snatched—'

'I don't care,' said his mother. 'The rest of the people on this train don't want to hear you two fighting.'

The boy – Charlie – handed over the iPad, sulkily. 'I'm hungry.'

'Well I've got some fruit in the bag.'

'I don't want fruit.'

'Well you're not hungry then.'

James tried to switch off, to focus on the task ahead. They'd be in Oxford in half an hour. It wasn't a city he knew at all, but he was pretty good at finding his way around a place.

'All tickets please!'

He heard the voice above the carriage's general hubbub and chatter. Glancing up the aisle, he saw the red-jacketed inspector at the far end, leaning over a table to speak to a passenger. *Shit.*

'Excuse me, please?' he said to the woman beside him, half-standing.

'Of course,' she replied, shuffling from her seat.

James climbed out of his, plucked his bag from above, and without a backward glance walked to his end of the carriage, through into a vestibule. There was a toilet, and he slipped inside, locking the door. All he had to do was wait for the inspector to pass.

He checked his reflection in the mirror. His hair had grown out in the last six months, and needed a trim. His beard too. Maybe when he arrived at his destination, he could find somewhere to clean himself up. Didn't want to make a bad impression when he made contact. His heart sped up at the thought.

After about five minutes, he figured it would be all clear. All he had to do now was head to the far end of the train and he was home and dry. He pressed the door button. It slid open to reveal the ticket inspector standing right there in front of him, wearing a smile. He was a big guy, bald-headed, belly pushing out the shirt over his belt.

'Ticket, please, sir.'

James made a show of feeling his pockets, and saw the look on the inspector's face. Not convinced.

'Having trouble finding it, are we?'

'I think someone must have taken my wallet.'

'Oh dear. Without a valid ticket, I'll have to charge you the full price for the journey.' He began to tap at a machine on his waist.

'I said, someone's had my wallet. I've got no money.'

'Right,' said the inspector, with no sympathy at all. 'Name, please.'

'James Munro,' he lied.

The bald twat noted it down.

'Address?'

'12 Cardiff Road, Manchester.'

'Got any ID to prove that?'

James looked left and right. They were alone. 'I told you . . .'

'Oh, yeah, the disappearing wallet. So you've no way to show me that the address or the name you've given is genuine?'

'I suppose you'll have to trust me.'

He tried to side-step, to head back towards his seat, but the big man shifted his body too. 'It doesn't work like that, sonny.'

He reached for the radio on his lapel. 'Station security will meet us at Oxford. If they can't verify your details, the police will—'

James' forehead met the man's nose in a crunch, sending him staggering backwards into the wall behind. As he reached for his face, blood pouring through his fingers, James drove a fist into his lower abdomen, doubling him up. Then he grabbed the back of the man's collar, and the underside of his chin, and pulled him hard into the toilet cubicle. The guard sprawled on the floor. James lifted a foot and stamped on the back of his head. Once, and he was still moaning. The second one silenced him. James glanced around. No one had seen.

He pushed the guard's stray foot inside the cubicle, then stepped in himself, closing the door behind them and locking it.

Fuck. Fuck. Fuck.

'You couldn't just leave it, could you?' he said to the motionless man at his feet. What other choice had there been? The cunt had made his bed – let him lie in it. He didn't think he was dead, but he didn't care either.

He took a deep breath to calm himself. Now what? He could remain in here until they reached the station, but there was no guarantee of getting far before the body was discovered. That's if they even got to Oxford at all. Chances were the inspector would be expected to check in via the radio or in person with the driver. And when he didn't, it would draw attention. No, he had to act now. First, he felt inside the man's jacket and found a wallet with forty quid. He left the rest, but took his watch, and a wedding ring. Then he unlocked the door, and peered out to check the corridor. The coast was clear. He slipped through, closing the door again to conceal the body.

An inter-carriage door swished open, and a woman approached. He held his ground as she checked to see if the toilet was occupied.

'You don't want to go in there,' said James. 'Some animal's smeared shit everywhere.'

The woman's mouth took a downturn of disgust, and she went on her way. James looked out of the window. They were passing through a village. A platform blurred past. It couldn't be far to Oxford now. He didn't fancy trying to convince everyone who needed a piss to keep on walking.

It was time to get off.

He found the emergency stop by the door, and slid the plastic cover up. There was a button inside, with a number of warning notices. He pressed it. The change in speed threw him against the wall, and a screeching noise filled the vestibule, followed by screams and yells from the carriages on either side. In five or ten seconds it was over, and they came to a halt. They were in a cutting, scrubby trees with litter-flecked branches growing up the bank on either side.

The door release was behind another panel. This one he smashed with his elbow, then yanked the lever. The doors on one sides opened outwards a fraction with a dull clunk, as the locking mechanisms disengaged, and James heaved it across, hopping down onto the tracks. Pulling his hood over his head, he scrambled up the bank and reached the top. There were fields, with a row of pylons, and in the distance, a small village. He struck off in that direction.

It might be two miles to Oxford, or it could be twenty.

A small delay, but it hardly mattered now.

Chapter 10

George Dimitriou appeared to still be reeling from the news that Jo's investigation and his own were connected, and the common link was Blake Matthis. Three of them – Jo, Alice and Dimitriou himself – were standing at the side of the house to escape the smell. 'Blake and Megan must be about the same age,' he said. 'What school is she at?'

'Marsh Hill,' said Jo. 'Catholic school.'

He frowned. 'Blake's at Isaac Newton Academy.'

'Doesn't mean they didn't know each other,' said Reeves. 'They might have had a thing? Sounds like she wasn't picky.'

Dimitriou nodded in agreement. 'Doesn't explain why he went after her folks though.'

'*If* he did,' said Jo. She wasn't ready to drop the mismatched time-scales. Those bodies were more than three days old, and that meant they were dead for some time before Matthis was confirmed in the vicinity.

'Maybe he was robbing the place,' said Reeves. 'They caught him at it, and things . . . escalated.'

'It looks like it was first thing in the morning,' said Jo. 'Mr Bailey was shaving. They hadn't even got dressed.'

'That's all speculation,' said Dimitriou. 'They could have been getting ready for bed. Or he made them strip.'

'And why in God's name would he do *that*?' said Jo. 'Is he a pervert as well as a murderer and a drug dealer and a schoolboy?'

Dimitriou rubbed his temples for a few seconds, eyes closed. She was sorry she'd snapped; they were all in the dark here, and struggling to process the discovery.

A uniform at the outer cordon came over to say there was someone who wanted to speak with them.

'A priest,' he added.

They went around to the front, just as Andy and Heidi came out through the front door. True to the constable's word, the visitor wore a floor-length cassock and dog-collar. He looked unwell – perhaps recovering from an illness. He might have been in his mid-forties, his painfully thin physique accentuating his long face and aquiline nose, his Adam's apple protruding. He wore small, wire-rimmed spectacles.

'I'm Father Tremayne,' he said, looking past them to the house. 'Are the family all right?'

'You know them well?' asked Carrick, deflecting.

'Very,' said Tremayne. 'They're parishioners at St Peters. Rachael is a bell-ringer.'

'The church in the village?' said Carrick.

Tremayne nodded eagerly.

'I'm sorry to inform you Mr and Mrs Bailey have been killed,' said Jo's boss.

Tremayne stared at Carrick for second, his mouth moving but no sound coming out. Then he looked at Jo, before crossing himself. 'God have mercy on their souls. And the children?'

'We aren't sure at the moment,' said Carrick. 'But they aren't in the house.'

'Father,' said Jo. 'Can I ask when you last saw the Baileys?'

'Not for many weeks,' said Tremayne. 'They've been on a

cruise to celebrate their thirtieth anniversary. They were due to return this week.'

'Any idea which day?' asked Dimitriou, before Jo could say anything.

'No,' said Tremayne, 'but I don't think they were back on Sunday, as they would have come to the service.'

'And do you know if the Baileys had any enemies?' asked Carrick.

'In the village?' said Tremayne. 'I doubt it.'

'Anywhere?' said Jo. 'Did either of them mention anything to you? However small.'

'What my parishioners entrust to me is sacrosanct,' said Tremayne, straightening his shoulders. It struck Jo as an odd thing to say, almost mealy-mouthed. And not in the least helpful. The priest himself seemed to realise how he'd come across, and quickly went on. 'I wish I could help, really. Mr and Mrs Bailey were upstanding members of the community. I can't think why anyone would want to harm them.'

'It's puzzling us too,' said Carrick.

Dimitriou fished in his pocket, and handed the priest a card. 'If anything springs to mind, do let us know.'

Tremayne took the card, and his eyes went to the house again. 'Is there anything else I can do?'

'Keep it to yourself,' said Jo. 'We need to inform the next of kin.'

'And pray for their souls,' added Carrick, without a hint of irony.

★ ★ ★

Dimitriou announced he had a new theory.

'All ears,' said Jo.

'So the parents come back from their boat trip. One way or

another, they come across Blake in the house – this kid they don't know. All hell breaks loose – they try to shoot him. Afterwards he tries to make it look like a burglary that went wrong.'

'By cutting their throats?'

'He did what he had to in order to cover his tracks. Couldn't risk the gun going off again in case it alerted the neighbours.'

'Sorry, George,' said Reeves. 'I'm with Jo here. The facts on the ground don't fit. Someone broke through the door of their room.'

'And it looks like the culprit lost some blood. I don't remember seeing any sign of an injury when Matthis fled on the bike.'

Jo's mind went back to what the shop assistant had said he'd noticed when he asked Megan for ID, the day after Harry's murder. She had a bandaged right hand. Going by the position of the bloody print on the stairs, it belonged to someone's right hand also. Could she have been here too, when all of this happened?

Dimitriou didn't look ready to drop his latest idea though, and Jo had a feeling why. Blake was his case, Megan hers. Now this scene linked them, it made sense to fold the cases together, pooling their resources, with her as SIO.

'We're missing something,' she said, in her most conciliatory tone. 'Blake and Megan are into something bigger than either of them.'

* * *

Heidi left shortly afterwards, along with Alice Reeves. The latter looked happy just to be getting away. On the way out, Jo overheard Heidi and Carrick talking about Greg Bailey. They'd confirmed he was indeed at Pembroke College in Cambridge, and Carrick asked Heidi to get in touch with Cambridgeshire Police to organise a liaison to inform Greg of the murder and to offer him transport to St Aldates. Jo didn't envy the poor bastard who got that job. It looked like Greg Bailey was twenty years old at most. Dealing with the practicalities of a parent's death was hard enough at the best of times, when the end was anticipated and natural. To do so in these circumstances was quite a different story.

While Carrick spoke to the Chief Constable on the latest developments, Jo took a turn around the garden. Through mature trees she could see the house next door about a hundred and fifty metres away. Close enough, probably, to have heard a shotgun blast. Her immediate, optimistic thought was that the suspect might have dumped a murder weapon somewhere in the vicinity. The garden was well manicured – the work, she assumed, of a gardener, given the scope of it. In the far corner, concealed from the main home through a pergola, was a substantial summer house, perhaps four metres by three, with mostly glazed walls. It sat on a raised wooden platform. As she approached, her stomach dropped. There were more flies inside, and they were buzzing against the panes.

Oh, Christ . . .

Jo considered called for the others, but her legs moved her close of their own accord. Her shoes made a hollow knocking on the decking steps up to the glass door. Inside were a few pieces of garden furniture stacked up, presumably as the previous summer had ended, lying in wait for the next to begin. There was also what looked like a folded badminton or volleyball net, and a covered barbecue. She could easily imagine the two siblings knocking a shuttlecock back and forth while the smell of cooking meat drifted across the lawn. The flies that weren't at the window seemed to be concentrated towards the rear of the room within, buzzing around under a collapsible table.

'Found something?' came Dimitriou's voice. She turned. He was upstairs, leaning from a window.

'Maybe,' she called back. 'See if you can find a key for this door?'

After a search through the kitchen, no key was forthcoming, but Andy gave them the okay to break the glass, and Dimitriou used a mallet found in the property's shed. The smell wasn't anything like back in the main house, and Jo's heart slowed a little. She went in first, crouching with Dimitriou to look beneath the table. 'How disappointing.' he said.

There, against the wall, were the decomposing bodies of two rats, and what looked like several poison pellets.

'At least we won't need Mel,' said Jo.

Dimitriou reached in, and Jo thought for a moment he was going to grab one of the rodent corpses, but instead he picked up one of the pink pellets. On his palm, Jo saw it had a heart motif on its surface.

'Looks like these guys OD'd,' said Dimitriou. 'This ain't rat poison.'

Between them, they removed the furniture and other equipment onto the grass, until all that was left were the bodies of the rodents and the pills, and a torn blue polythene bag that still contained a couple of dozen more. There was a small hole in the raised floor platform that looked like it was for wiring. As far as Jo could see, it was the only way the rats could have squeezed in.

Dimitriou, leaning over it, shone a torch inside. 'Jackpot.'

They couldn't see a way to get under the raised floor, but checking the perimeter of the platform outside, a long panel at the rear was found to be loose. Prising it aside by hand, they revealed a cavity with the same footprint as the structure, filled with packages. Dimitriou began to pass them out. It was almost entirely pills – thousands of them, in a variety of colours. Jo tried doing some mental calculations, and her conservative estimate was north of a hundred and fifty grand in street value.

'So this is what Blake was looking for,' said Dimitriou. He stood, with mud on the knees of his suit.

'You think the Baileys knew this was here?' said Carrick.

Dimitriou shrugged. 'I can't see it. They were away, right? And they went to their deaths rather than spilling the beans.'

'We're getting ahead of ourselves,' said Jo. 'Blake's a suspect, but the question is why these drugs are even here.' She looked at Carrick. 'Better tell Cambridgeshire Police to keep a close eye on Greg Bailey in case he tries to run.'

Dimitriou laughed. 'I'll put money on it being the girl and Blake,' he said.

Jo had her doubts about his modern-day Bonnie and Clyde theory, but they were ill-formed, and she wouldn't have staked much on Dimitriou being wrong. The St Cuthbert's tutor hadn't mentioned drugs at all, but it wasn't a stretch to think Megan, with all her other issues, might have taken that path too. The murder sat in a different category entirely though. Violent, cold-blooded, and remorseless killing was a long way from truancy and sex. On the other hand you didn't have to look far to see what otherwise normal people could do under the influence of drug-induced psychosis, especially those predisposed to sociopathy. Human compassion and empathy were often the first things to be stripped away.

She looked at her watch – just after five. If she was going to make it to Little Steps, she'd have to leave now or the traffic would be too heavy. Carrick caught her expression.

'You should be off,' he said. 'We can take care of things here.'

'No way,' she said, reflexively. 'I'll call someone.'

'Like yesterday?' said Carrick.

Jo hesitated. The old, proud part of her wanted to tell him, 'Yes', and to mind his own business about how she organised her affairs. Amelia would understand, at least partly. She couldn't walk away now; there was still so much to do. But she didn't say it. She needed to be with Theo, and even the twenty minutes it would take to reach the nursery seemed an unbearable delay.

'It's all right,' said Dimitriou. 'Go and see your son.'

There was a surprising warmth to his voice. Jo had no doubt he'd rather work the scene without her – it was still as much his case as hers, after all – but she didn't think it was as simple as him wanting her out of the way. He had no kids himself, and she knew from hints he'd dropped in the past that both of his parents had died when he was still at school.

'Honestly, I can make arrangements.' Even to her own ears, the protest wasn't convincing.

Carrick motioned with his head for her to join him, then wandered back towards the house. When she fell alongside, he stopped and turned to her.

'Go home,' he said. 'That's an order.'

'But . . .'

'No buts,' said Carrick. 'Trust me, I've seen enough idiotic blokes mess up their families over the years by not leaving work on time. I won't see someone I respect doing the same. Those bodies aren't going anywhere soon, and this scene is going to take an age to clear. I'd rather you were well rested.'

Jo could see it wasn't worth arguing further, and gave her boss a nod of understanding. 'Okay, but if you need me, or if anything happens, you've got to call. I've got family who can step in as and when.'

'Noted,' said Carrick. 'See you Monday otherwise.'

Jo signed out of the scene, then drove away, though every professional instinct in her body told her it was wrong. How could she be leaving work when Harry's killer was still on the loose, and the bodies were stacking up? Along with the guilt, she knew herself well enough to register that it was her ego as much as her conscience. In her forced absence, there was every chance Dimi would be assigned as the lead. It wasn't that

128

he was a bad investigator. Though he gave the appearance of idleness within the office, when it came to gathering evidence, he actually got stuck in, if not with enthusiasm, with a certain dogged and single-minded energy. *He*'d certainly never leave the office just because his shift was up. And while he jumped to conclusions, his results spoke for themselves: in most cases, the simplest answer *was* the correct one.

Something told Jo, however, that this case was different, and nothing was as it appeared.

Chapter 11

Andy Carrick's words of wisdom were in Jo's mind throughout the following day as she concentrated on being Jo Masters the mum, and she regretted forcing him to couch his advice as an order. He was quite right either way about the importance of family. Though she couldn't go as far as leaving her work-phone off, she put the ringer on silent.

There were periods in the day when the machinations of St Aldates faded very much into the background. The morning took her to swimming the local pool, and a session designed for babies where she and the other new mothers cooed and splashed in the shallows with their little ones. She recognised a few of them from the antenatal group she'd attended, though their names escaped her.

She'd taken the doctor's advice to sign up, planning to make friends, but from the outset she'd felt out of place. All the other first-time mothers-to-be were accompanied by partners, practising breathing exercise together, talking hospital advocacy, and laughing over the many shades of baby effluence. She'd been on her own, even though Amelia had once offered to come with her for moral support. She'd swapped numbers with everyone at the end, almost through a sense of duty, but made no effort afterwards to keep in touch.

By the end of the swimming session, a mere twenty minutes, Theo's lips were showing a slightly purple tinge and he howled the place down in the changing rooms, only to fall asleep as soon as he was in his car seat. Jo grabbed a coffee at a drive-through, and read a text from her brother asking if she'd like to come over the following day for some lunch. She was going to call to accept, but instead she found her fingers dialling the station's number almost as instinctively as a nicotine addict lighting up a cigarette. Alice Reeves answered.

'Oh, hello you,' she said.

'Just wondering what the latest was,' said Jo.

'Well, we got hold of the son, Greg. He's halfway through his first year in Cambridge. Obviously a shock. He's coming over, and the family solicitor is going to organise an interview.'

Jo's detective antennae tingled.

'How come there's a solicitor involved already?'

'I don't think it's anything untoward. It's a family friend of some sort. Hang on, let me put you through to the gaffer.'

'Oh, no need for—' But the call was already transferred.

'Jo,' said Carrick after a few seconds. 'How *surprising* to hear from you.' His voice, she was pleased to hear, had an edge of mockery.

'Theo's asleep,' she said, looking briefly at his reflection in the rear-view. Once again, she wondered why she felt the need to explain herself. 'You can't expect me to switch off completely.'

'Mel's team are still at the house,' said Carrick. 'We found the shotgun licence, and a case in the wardrobe, but no sign of the weapon itself or any ammunition. Mel is going to check for residue on Mr Bailey's hands to confirm he fired the shot. They've taken hundreds of prints, but so far there's nothing that matches Blake Matthis on preliminary examination. And certainly not the blood-print on the stairs. I suppose it doesn't mean much. He'd have to be pretty stupid not to wear gloves, and he may well have been accompanied.'

'Did Mel mention the time-frames with the flies?'

'Give him time, Jo. There was a lot to look at.'

'It's just, I looked into last night. Really, there's no way fly eggs could hatch, then go through a larval phase before—'

'You're an entomologist too?'

'It's not only that,' said Jo. 'The phone records had Matthis there less than eighty hours ago. Those bodies were *seriously* decayed. I'd guess a week or more.'

'I wouldn't go that far. There are margins of error.'

'You don't have to tell me that, but if we can find out when they returned from holiday, it might give us a clearer window. There should be travel documents in the house somewhere. Failing that, local airport taxi firms might have a record . . .'

'We're on it,' said Andy. 'Don't worry.'

'Okay – but seriously, gut instinct, do you think Blake did it? A barely seventeen-year-old boy?'

'A young man from a criminal home with a record of violence and theft,' said Carrick. She could almost imagine him pinching the bridge of his nose against a tension headache as he spoke. 'There's a narrative. They were using the house to store the drugs while the parents were away. He went to get them, maybe with an older accomplice. Things went pear-shaped when the Baileys fought back.'

'Anything about a gunshot wound from the hospitals?'

'No.'

'Going from the volume of blood in the bedroom carpet, it wasn't an insignificant wound.'

'And we'll know soon if it belonged to Blake,' said Carrick. 'Believe it or not, we've got things in hand here.'

'Fine,' said Jo. 'One more thing.'

'I hope it's a question about teething and not work-related,' said Carrick.

'Do you trust the priest?'

Carrick gave a joyless laugh. 'You think he did it?'

Jo grinned. 'I thought he was hiding something. About the Baileys. He got defensive pretty quickly.'

'Because he didn't want to share things about their private lives? Jo, I think you've misunderstood the nature of the confessional. Even if he knew they were rural Oxford's answer to Pablo Escobar, he wouldn't be in a position to tell us. Look, I've got to go. We'll be putting out the appeal we discussed on the evening news for Megan – officially she's a person of interest and potential witness in the murder of Harry Ferman, rather than a suspect – and we're not releasing any details about Stanton St John before we've had time to inform her directly.'

'She can't be in the dark about it, surely?'

'As far as that girl goes, I'm not sure about anything,' said Carrick. 'All I know for certain is that there are a trail of dead bodies in her wake, and I'd like to find her before we come across any more.'

In the back of the car, Theo stirred with a high-pitched wail.

'Hey, hey, it's okay,' said Jo, reaching back to stroke his face.

'I'll let you go,' said Carrick.

'No, it's fine,' said Jo. 'He's just grizzling.'

Carrick had already hung up.

★　★　★

A steady downpour set in for the rest of the day, keeping Jo indoors. She wondered how Lucas was faring, and if he would even remember her suggestion that they should talk. She certainly had no stomach for it now, and he'd vanished before they could arrange a time. Towards the final days of their relationship, though he'd appeared relatively sober, she'd soon realised he suffered from complete and regular blackouts, not remembering their increasingly fractious arguments. At the very end, as she grew increasingly gravid with Theo, it had been easier to sever contact completely than deal with Lucas. In the grip of impending motherhood, with the weight of responsibility, she'd banished all uncertainty and unsafety from her life. And that included him. Occasionally, and painfully, she blamed herself for what had happened, or at least the way she'd dealt with things. She'd tried to put herself in his shoes, but never quite succeeded. She'd told herself he had his other family, his ex-wife and children, to care for him; even fantasising in the intervening period that he had found happiness with them. Yet she'd known, somewhere, that she was lying to herself, and his dishevelled appearance at the station confirmed the worst.

She looked into Theo's face as he contorted his lower body, tugging at the toe of his bodysuit in an effort to chew it. He had blonde hair, but there was no sign of Lucas's curls there yet. His eyes were dark and owlish like Jack Pryce's. The small dimple in his chin might well vanish as his face slimmed, but Jo fancied it would mature into the same cleft that her own father had possessed. He hiccupped as he lost his balance and rolled over.

'Oopsie!' she said, leaning across to right him. He came up looking surprised, but smiled as she held him straight, head bobbing. Whatever the composition of his genetics, she told herself, he was neither of his potential fathers, and innocent of their flaws. He was her little boy, and deserved to live unburdened of her chequered romantic past. She owed him that at least.

Periodically, as she went through the motions of mothering – encouraging Theo to sit up and reach out for his favourite toys, tickling him until his laughter turned on a sixpence to anger – she also thought about logging on to the police network to see what had been added to the files. Until around three o'clock, she resisted, but as he settled down for his afternoon nap, the urge became too great. Carrick could keep her out of the station, but not out of the loop completely.

The Harry Ferman case file was a disappointment. It had barely advanced in the last twenty-four hours, what with all the attention suddenly switching to Stanton St John. Jo had hoped something might have come through on the DNA, or at least some further door-to-door work, but there was nothing recorded. She was well aware of the paucity of resources, and that things necessarily slowed down at the weekends, but she couldn't help thinking that Harry was simply being forgotten. As SIO, it was her job to rectify that, even if her hands were partially tied.

She looked again at the crime scene photos, forcing herself to linger on the most upsetting, of her friend's body in situ, body temperature dipping after his spirit had flown. She still hadn't mentioned to anyone the message he'd left on her phone, and listened to it again. He certainly didn't sound scared, or in danger. Simply curious. To reveal it now would look a lot like professional negligence. After all, what were they always saying to potential witnesses? *If you remember anything amiss, however small . . .*

Theo was beginning to stir through the baby monitor as she skimmed the photos faster, moving on from his body, past the close-ups, on to the murder weapon. There was definitely a commonality between Harry's death and that of Megan's parents – an efficient, uncaring brutality. What made it worse was the premeditation. In both cases, there would have been plenty of opportunity to walk away. It was hard to imagine that either victim was a physical threat to the person who killed them.

She was about to close down the image files when a final one caught her eye – the repair to the glass in the back door. Mel had found prints on the inside door handle, matching others in the house. It seemed likely those were Megan's. But they were no closer to identifying who had drunk from the coffee mug – those prints were entirely distinct. However, it was the door that interested her, as it presented one other avenue of enquiry she could explore without alerting Carrick, or treading on anyone's toes. She closed the files, then walked through to the bedroom where Theo was writhing in his cot. 'You fancy some fresh air, mister?'

★ ★ ★

The rain outside had eased a little, and Jo didn't bother with her umbrella as she walked from her car along the parade of shops where the Iffley and Cowley Roads intersected. Theo was happy in the sling she wore, his face nestled against her chest.

The doorbell of PJ Adams tinkled as she entered. The glazier also sold door and window framing in a variety of materials, plus mirrors and decorative coloured-glass inlays. There was one other customer in the shop, a woman inspecting a catalogue of conservatory designs. The man behind the counter was a small, broad-shouldered, grey gentleman, with a significant hunch in his back, and he wore a long black apron over a checked shirt. He was leaning over a machine, wearing goggles and moving a cutting guide. He ceased work as she approached, held up a key in dirty fingers and blew away metal dust.

'Can I help you?'

'Are you Mr Adams?' asked Jo.

'The one and only,' he replied. He cleaned his hands on a rag. 'Looking for something in particular?'

'Actually, I wanted to talk to you about some work you've done. Number 21 Canterbury Road.'

Mr Adams took the unusual request in his stride. 'Chap who had the break-in? That's right. About a fortnight back.'

So it was a burglary . . .

'I'm a friend of Mr Ferman, the man who lives there,' said Jo. 'I wondered – did he tell you anything about it?'

'Only that he caught her at it,' said the shopkeeper. 'Came back from the pub, he said, and found her right there.'

'A girl?'

'So he said. You know what druggies are like. Steal anything to feed a habit.'

'Did he say what she looked like?'

Mr Adams wiped his knotted fingers on his apron. 'I can't recall that he did. No, I tell a lie. He said she was just a slip of thing.' He frowned. 'Sorry, what's this about? The replacement was top notch. Twenty-year guarantee.'

'Oh, I'm sure the work was very good,' said Jo. The other woman had left by then, so she explained that she was in fact a police officer as well as a friend, and that she was investigating the murder of Mr Ferman. The shopkeeper's face fell at the disclosure; he obviously hadn't made the connection, until that point, between the death on the news and the job he'd done recently.

'That's just awful,' he said. 'What a world we live in. He was a real gent, that fella.'

'Yes, he was,' said Jo. She thanked him for his time. 'You've been very helpful.'

As she was leaving, he called after her. 'Do you think it was this girl who did it?'

'We really don't know,' said Jo, and she meant it.

Back in her car, Theo safely buckled, she pulled out into traffic, trying to digest the new information. It seemed almost certain, then, that Megan Bailey had broken into Harry's house, two weeks before he was killed. And following that, instead of reporting her to the police, he had let her stay. And for some bizarre reason, she had agreed. Nothing made sense about Megan Bailey at all. Sexually promiscuous, possibly drug addicted, a school dropout, but was she really a murderer too?

★   ★   ★

As if he'd picked up on own troubled thoughts, Theo chose that night to sleep fitfully. At three in the morning, having ascertained he was both well-fed and dry, a period of wretched tiredness ensued, in which nothing would quiet him and every effort at comfort was met with angry cries. If she picked him up, his legs curled and his fists clenched as if he was in pain. If she set him down he would reach out to be held. In the end, she found a compromise, opening the side of the cot and placing one hand beneath his back, the other on his stomach, massaging gently. Though his protests dimmed, occasional eruptions at a higher pitcher were enough to jolt her frequently to wakefulness.

Eventually, sheer fatigue must have overwhelmed her, because she woke to what she sensed were the early hours in almost utter darkness and a sound she couldn't place. Wolvercote had no streetlighting, so the only illumination through the curtains was the ambience from distant houses. Theo was sound asleep, and the side of the cot was raised, so it seemed fair to assume she had closed it in some semi-sleeping state. She was about to roll over when she heard another noise – some sort of rattling from downstairs. For a few seconds, she remained under the duvet, ears pricked. Sure enough, she heard the noise once more. It sounded very much like someone's hand on the back door, testing it.

Jo's throat was dry, and her heart felt solid, and small, like a golf-ball knocking back and forth inside the walls of her ribcage. She looked for her phone, but couldn't see it. As she rose from the bed, she felt curiously disembodied, and before she knew it she was descending the stairs. There was that sound again. She told herself there was no danger. The back door was sturdy, secured with a deadlock, the key inside, and bolts at the top and bottom.

Reaching the bottom of the stairs, she entered the kitchen. It was cast in shadow, and the windows were black. She reached up to find the lightswitch, but when she pressed it, nothing happened. She tried again. With a sudden spike of terror, she saw the key missing, and as she watched the door handle turn slowly downward, registered that the bolts were in fact drawn across. She moved in a flash as the door eased ajar, slamming her arms against it in an attempt to drive it closed, but whatever was on the other side resisted. 'Go away!' she cried, because it was the only thing she could think to say. Whoever was there made no sound at all, but even as Jo leant all her weight to the door, the pressure on the outside increased. She was losing the battle. Whoever it was on the other side, he was stronger. Upstairs, Theo was crying, and she knew, in the deepest part of herself, that if she didn't close this door and lock it, a sequence of events would follow that would leave him defenceless. 'Please, leave me alone!' she begged.

It was no use. She had no strength left. In a sudden thrust, the door slammed open, snatching her up like a wave and hurling her backwards . . .

Jo woke with a gasp, covered in sweat. Theo was crying in anger, and as the reality of the dream subsided, she looked across to see why. Her arm was right across his chest, pinning him. When she tried to move it, it wouldn't respond. The angle had left it dead and bloodless, and only by rolling over did she succeed in dragging the lifeless limb from the cot. She sat up, and for a few seconds, there was nothing she could do but wait for the circulation to return. Then she picked Theo up, and cradled him against her as the air of the bedroom cooled her damp nightdress against her skin. 'I'm sorry, baby boy,' she said. 'I'm so sorry.'

Chapter 12

The night's disturbances meant Jo was in a daze as she prepared Theo's milk in the hour before sunrise, and thankfully they both managed to sleep a little more afterwards. When Jo woke properly, she was surprised to find it was past nine am. She had a message on her phone from Paul, suggesting she come over early – at ten – in order to sort through some of their mum's possessions prior to disposing of anything unwanted. It didn't give her much time to get ready, but she replied that she'd be over shortly.

The horrors of the dream stayed with her as she prepared a nappy bag, milk and the other assorted items she now took everywhere. She couldn't recall the last time she'd dreamt at all, let alone a nightmare so close to the bone. As she carried Theo to the car, her phone beeped again. Probably Paul telling her not to bring cheap wine. But on checking, she saw it was actually Dimitriou: 'Someone paid Blake a visit . . .'

The text was accompanied by an image, taken in the twilight, of a fire engine outside the house where they'd visited Tracy

Grimshaw in Blackbird Leys. The front door was off its hinges and the downstairs windows were just twisted frames with black soot marks climbing the outside of the walls up to the second floor. She got on the phone at once, and Dimitriou answered.

'Thought that might pique your interest.'

'Is everyone okay?'

'How sweet of you. Tracy's recovering in hospital from smoke inhalation. She was asleep upstairs when someone poured petrol through her front door. Luckily the dog woke her.'

'You think someone was sending a message?'

'Seems likely, doesn't it? Those drugs have been out of circulation for maybe a week. My guess is someone hasn't been paid and this is a warning. Anyway, enjoy your Sunday!'

'Wait!' she said. 'What are you doing next?'

'I'm going to talk to Ms Matthis once she's stopped wheezing,' said Dimitriou. 'Convince her that it's her darling angel who's got her into this mess, and it's in everyone's interest for him to hand himself in.'

'Think she'll bite?'

'Probably not,' said Dimitriou.

Jo heard wild barking in the background. 'Where are you?'

'At the fucking vet,' he said. 'Someone had to bring the dog in, and let's just say I'm a softie.'

'And a man of many surprises,' said Jo.

★ ★ ★

Jo didn't think she'd be able to tear her thoughts from the case, but the process of sifting through her mother's possessions was actually more emotional than she had anticipated. Most of it had been in boxes since the time Madeleine Masters had gone into care a few years ago, and Jo hadn't anticipated finding a single item she might want to keep. Her mother's taste in jewellery was distinctly Victorian, and Jo rarely wore anything more than a bracelet and a silver band she'd bought years ago at a flea-market in Prague. Some of the contents of the boxes were their father's, though, and the smell of the old suits, as well as the styles, brought back hints of memories that were more a vague nostalgia than actual moments. As well as jewellery, clothes, records, old pictures and ornaments, there were bundles of photos, letters and birthday cards dating back forty years and more. Time flew past for a while as she and her brother sat on the floor of Paul's spare bedroom, sorting things into piles depending of their destination. By far the most would go to charity shops or to a refuse site, but there was a surprisingly large collection of items neither of them had the heart to throw out. These bits they repackaged and began to stow back in the attic.

'So how is it being back at work?' asked Paul from the top of the ladder, as she handed him the last of the boxes.

'Harder than I expected,' said Jo, honestly. She watched him disappear into the gloomy interior of the loft.

'Because of the hours?' he called to her from within.

'The lack of them,' Jo replied. She thought about the grinding gears and cogs of the current case. She'd rarely shared anything about the machinations of St Aldates with her brother, even before having Theo. And she was grateful he didn't bore her with *his* work, which, as far as she could gather, involved making money from currency speculations. 'It's hard to switch off.'

'I bet,' said Paul. He climbed down and folded the ladder into the loft-space. 'Criminals don't respect the nine-'til-five right?'

'Correct. The DCI's been great,' she said brightly. 'He could have insisted I stay on office duty.'

'And wouldn't you rather that?' asked Paul.

'A desk job? I can't think of anything worse.' She caught herself. 'No offence.'

Paul brushed some dust off his shirt. 'None taken. Anyway, my job isn't without drama. The old duffer in charge managed to break his hip this week when his chair collapsed. There's talk that it was sabotage.'

'You want me to send someone over?' Jo said, edging towards the stairs. Paul smiled, but his heart wasn't in it. He remained where he stood. 'What's up?' she said.

He gripped the banister. 'I wondered if you wanted to talk about Lucas?'

Jo felt herself colour. 'Not really. There's nothing to say. He came to the station a couple of days ago.'

'And?'

'I tried to talk to him, but he was a mess.'

Paul looked pained. 'That's not going to stop, you know?

'It will when he gets the message.'

Paul's eyebrows rose theatrically. 'And what message is that?'

Jo didn't like her brother's presumption, but this was his house and there was still the prospect of a long and painful lunch if they fell out. 'That he can't be part of Theo's life.'

'Ever?' said Paul. Jo's rising anger must have been obvious in her face, because her brother softened his tone. 'It's not my business, I know. But people can change. They can get over their problems.'

'He doesn't strike me as the sort of man who's moving in that direction,' said Jo, remembering the sorry figure stumbling around the police station reception. 'And to be frank, I haven't got the energy to help him. I've got to look after Theo's best interests, and a drunk, occasional father isn't one of them.' She almost added, *Have you any idea how hard it is at the moment?* But instead turned and headed for the stairs. Sometimes it was easiest just to walk away. And it would give her bother a chance to take a hint.

In the kitchen Amelia was setting the table. The house had a hatch, leading to the living room, where Emma was sending

Theo into giggles of delight by lifting him into the air repeatedly. Will, in contrast, showed no interest at all in the baby, and was playing some game on his phone. 'She's a natural,' Jo muttered to Amelia in the kitchen.

'Don't say that!' her sister-in-law replied. 'I'm barely getting used to the idea of her having a proper boyfriend.'

Jo recalled Amelia had mentioned it the other day too. 'Serious?'

'As far as we can tell. His name is Jacob, though Paul insists on pretending he can't remember it. You're about to meet him actually.'

Sure enough, the doorbell rang a few minutes later, and a gangly young man stood on the doorstep. He greeted both Paul and Amelia shyly, but before Jo had chance to be introduced, Emma had whisked him off upstairs.

'You and Jack keep that door open!' shouted Paul.

Jo manoeuvred Theo into the high-chair Paul had dug out from the depths of their garage. Will had agreed, under some duress, to set down his game and feed his baby cousin when, while Jo was washing some glasswear in the sink, her phone rang on the table. Will leaned over and read the caller id. 'Who's HT?'

Jo hurriedly extracted her hands, and wiped the soap suds off in time to answer the call.

'We've got Blake Matthis,' said Heidi.

'Where?'

'He's at the hospital. Visiting his mother, bless him. They called us.'

'So he's in custody?'

'That's right. He tried to do a runner, but an orderly got in the way. Dimi's chomping at the bit.'

'I can imagine,' said Jo. 'Any sign of an injury consistent with a shotgun?'

'Sadly not, though we'll be making a more thorough assessment when he arrives.'

'You don't think it's a little odd that he'd come up for air like that? Hardly the behaviour of a killer.'

'He's not the sharpest knife in the drawer,' said Heidi. 'And anyway, boys love their mums, don't they?'

'I hope so,' said Jo, tickling Theo under his chin. 'Keep me in the loop.'

★ ★ ★

As lunch began, Jo attended intermittently to the various conversations at the table, surreptitiously checking her phone beneath the table at intervals, but by the time they reached dessert, she was at breaking point. No news had come through. Excusing herself to use the bathroom, she sent Heidi a message asking what was going on.

She replied almost at once: '*Still waiting for his chaperone.*'

Jo guessed she was referring to whichever 'appropriate adult' Blake had nominated. Given he was under eighteen, he was entitled to have an adult of his choosing present while he was questioned. Normally it would have been a parent, but with mum in hospital and dad inside, he'd have to nominate someone else, or use a Duty Solicitor. On a Sunday, it could be hours before they managed to bring in the latter.

She emerged from the toilet with her phone still in her hand, to find Paul waiting. 'Something wrong?' he asked.

Jo slipped the phone into the pocket of her jeans. 'Er . . . no.'

'I know my stories can be boring, but you've hardly been off that thing.' Before she had time to make an excuse, Paul added, 'Is it about Harry Ferman?'

'You heard?'

'It was on the news last night,' said her brother. 'You knew him, didn't you? From the clown case.'

She felt her guard sliding up. 'A little, yes.'

'And you're involved in this investigation?'

'Of course,' said Jo. 'I want to find out what happened.'

Paul nodded doubtfully. 'Are you in danger?'

'Me? No! What makes you think that?'

'You do have a habit of putting yourself in harm's way.'

'I'm a police officer,' said Jo. 'I catch harmful people.' She could tell her frivolous tone had pissed him off. 'I told you, desk-work doesn't interest me.'

'But it's not *only* you, is it? Not any more.'

'What's that supposed to mean?' Against her better judgement, she felt the by-now familiar sting of tears. Her body betraying her in a way it never had in the past. Her brother must have seen it too, because he backed half a step away.

'Look, I shouldn't have said anything . . .'

'Why not?' snapped Jo, swallowing. 'You seem *very* interested in my job. And my love-life. I'd rather know *exactly* what you've been saying about me.'

Paul glanced back at the kitchen, and Jo realised her voice had likely carried. 'I'm sorry,' he said. 'We just worry about you.'

'And about Theo?' said Jo coldly. 'You think the car accident was my fault too, I suppose.'

Paul raised both palms. 'No! Of course not!'

'Because you've never let either of your kids out of sight for two minutes?' she asked sarcastically.

'Jo, please,' said Paul. 'Come and sit down. This is my fault.'

She wanted to do as he said. She wanted to wind back the clock and try the last minute over again, but the reset button kept jamming in her head. Failing that, it was fight or flight. 'I'd better leave,' she said.

'You don't have to do that,' said Paul. 'Honestly.'

But she really just wanted to be out the door. Gathering Theo's things, she wiped his face, removed him from his chair, and thanked Amelia for lunch. Emma looked particularly perplexed, Jacob embarrassed, and Will largely oblivious.

'I'm sorry,' she said, before muttering her farewells, and heading for the door.

★ ★ ★

She drove, not home, but to the station, and with every metre she put between herself and the argument, the stupidity of it grew more obvious in her mind. Paul was her brother, and though they weren't as close as some siblings, his concern for her wasn't unreasonable. Past cases *had* endangered her life, and even those of her nephew and niece. She'd come out on top, but not without skirting very close to tragedy. By the time she'd pulled into the car park at St Aldates, she'd reached a state of utter dismay at her behaviour. She thought about calling him then, but as she turned the key to switch off the engine, her mental turmoil calmed. She needed space to think.

From the other vehicles parked up, she saw that Andy Carrick was in the building, as well as Heidi, Dimitriou, and Reeves. The whole squad, bar her. She placed Theo back in his sling. 'You want to see where mummy works?' she asked, then strode in like it was the most normal thing in the world.

Heidi was the only person in the squad room and she did a double-take.

'Hello, little guy!' she said, standing up. She peered at Theo's face, stroked his cheek, then added, 'Didn't think you'd be in today.'

'I was in the area,' said Jo lightly. 'Wanted to make sure you guys weren't slacking in my absence.' She threw a glance at the empty workstations. 'Which, it appears, you are.'

'Au contraire,' said Heidi. 'Andy and George are in with Matthis now. Ali's watching from the AV suite. I'm guessing you might want to have a peep too?' Her eyes flashed with mischief.

'Well, it can't hurt,' said Jo. 'Anything from the appeal?'

'We got Megan's phone number from a schoolfriend, but it was a dead end. Ceased emitting a signal three days ago.'

Jo mulled it over. 'Bit odd, no?'

'Maybe she didn't pack a charger.'

Jo thought of her niece Emma, forever glued to her phone. 'I think keeping your phone on as a sixteen year old comes slightly higher than food and shelter in the priority list.'

'You think she's deliberately keeping off the grid then?'

'Could be.' Though even that seemed not quite to fit.

Theo was thankfully quiet as she made her way down the short corridor, past the interview rooms, and tapped her code to access the AV suite. Reeves looked up with a start.

'Ma'am!' she said.

Jo pulled up a seat in front of the screen. 'Constable, meet Theo. Theo, Constable Reeves.'

Reeves stared at Theo as if she'd never seen a baby before in her life, but Jo ignored her and focused on the screen, where Dimitriou and Carrick were sitting opposite Blake Matthis and a smartly dressed young man of about thirty. 'So what's happening? Is that guy a legal rep?'

'Jordan Tomasz. "Family friend", apparently,' said Reeves.

'Looks like dad's keeping an eye on junior,' said Jo.

'Not a lot we can do about that,' said Reeves.

'Think he'll talk?'

'Not usefully,' said Reeves. 'He's a cocky little bastard.'

On the screen, the body language said it all. Blake Matthis was practically reclined in his chair, hands over his crotch, and an angled baseball cap on his head. There were already a large number of papers on the table between himself and his interrogators.

'And how it make you feel when you heard?' asked Dimitriou.

'I dunno,' Blake replied. 'Bad, I s'pose'

Then Dimitriou again: 'And how well did you know Xan?'

'A bit.'

'You had his phone number though.'

'Got lots of numbers.'

'And the nature of your friendship?'

'We weren't friends.'

'So it was strictly business?' Dimitriou stated.

Blake didn't respond.

'You rang him four times the day he was killed. Seems like more than a passing acquaintance. From our data, it looks like you were the last person to speak to him, in the late hours of April 12th.'

'If you say so.'

'It's not me who says so – it's the triangulation data. Which is admissible in court, by the way.'

Matthis played with the waist elastic on his tracksuit bottoms.

'Did you have an argument?' asked Dimitriou.

'Nah – we were good,' said Blake.

'About drugs maybe?'

Blake didn't answer.

'When did you find out he was dead?'

'Can't remember.'

'You made a call straight after he was shot. Then another the next day. Both to the same number. Remember what they were about?'

'Nope.'

'The number you rang wasn't registered, but the phone was located at HMP Long Lartin. Telling daddy you'd done what he wanted?'

Matthis laughed, and to Jo it seemed a comfortable gesture rather than a bluff. *Dimi's off here . . .*

'Our ballistics guy says Xan was shot with a nine mm bullet that came from a Makarov. That's exactly the sort of gun your father once threatened an undercover officer with.'

'Better talk to my old man then.'

'Your old man won't be in the dock with you,' said Dimitriou. 'It'll be you, on your own, and what you say in here today can and will be used in evidence against you. But if he told you to do it, that changes things. If he's keeping an eye on you now' – Dimitriou turned a pointed gaze on the strange man beside Blake – 'well, that changes things a lot. You wouldn't be as culpable.'

Blake was switching off, looking at the floor to one side.

'Okay, let's move on,' said Dimitriou. 'Do you remember what you were up to the next day, April 13th, Blake?'

'No.'

'See, the same set of triangulation data puts the same phone – your phone – somewhere else at 19.40 that night. Can you guess where?' Blake didn't answer. 'No?' said Dimitriou. 'It tells us you were in the village of Stanton St John – specifically at the house of a Mr and Dr Bailey. Do you remember anything about that maybe?'

'Never heard of them.'

And it's not the day they were killed, thought Jo. *Dimi's fishing here . . .*

'Gosh,' said Dimitriou, sorting through a file. 'That's odd. Here's a refresher.'

Jo couldn't see the pictures well through the feed, but she saw Blake recoil. At the same time, Carrick looked sideways at Dimitriou. She knew what he was thinking – there'd be a procedural question mark over the legitimacy of sharing the images with a juvenile, however streetwise he was.

'They'd been there a while by this stage,' said Dimitriou, covering the images again. 'We know you were at the house. The phone data doesn't lie.'

'Someone must've nicked me phone,' said Blake.

'And gave it back again?' said Dimitriou. 'How civil.'

Tomasz puffed up his chest. 'You don't have to say anything at all, Blake.'

'No, he doesn't,' said Carrick. He leant forward. 'Blake, you're not helping yourself. The phone data puts you near Xan on the twelfth, just before he was killed, and at the house of the Baileys, who were also, coincidentally, murdered. That alone will be enough for us to hold you for seventy-two hours while we gather more evidence. When we find your fingerprints and DNA at the Baileys' house, it'll be enough to charge you. And you're not going to end up somewhere your old man can look after you. The only way you make things easier for yourself now is to tell us what you know about all this, because I'm having a hard time believing you did it single-handedly.'

Matthis rubbed the side of his face as if there was dirt there. 'No comment.'

Dimitriou moved his gaze to Tomasz, but when he spoke, it was addressed to Matthis. 'You know, Blake, the decisions you make in here will have repercussions. The prosecution service look very kindly on people who help investigations rather than hinder.'

'He's telling you everything he knows,' said Tomasz. 'Do you need a break, Blake? This is very stressful for him. His mum's in hospital.'

Silence ensued, until Carrick intervened. 'Let's take ten.'

As he was suspending the interview, Alice Reeves turned to Jo and said solicitously, 'I meant to talk to you, the other day . . .'

'Yes?' said Jo.

'When I went to the Three Crowns, asking about Harry – they said your ex had been in looking for you. Caused a scene, and broke some glasses.'

154

'Lucas?' Jo did her best to retain her composure. 'Why didn't you mention it?'

'I didn't know if it was private.'

Jo knew she should have been grateful for the discretion, but she couldn't help being embarrassed that the new kid on the block was covering for her.

'I appreciate your dilemma,' she said, 'but you really should have brought it up. We can't afford to have secrets around here.'

Reeves looked chastened. 'I'm sorry, ma'am. It had nothing to do with the case, so I thought it was better to keep it out of my report.'

Carrick and Dimitriou were leaving the interview room.

'I understand. Have you any idea what day this was?'

'They just said a few days before.' Reeves looked a little afraid. 'Did I do the wrong thing?'

'I'm sure it's fine,' said Jo. 'Like you said, it's just an unfortunate coincidence.'

Outside, in the corridor, Dimitriou was standing with his hands on his hips, and a face like thunder. When he saw Jo, he acknowledged her and the baby with just a nod, before stalking off in the direction of the break room. Carrick, exiting behind him, caught sight of Theo strapped to her chest and his eyes widened theatrically. 'You shouldn't be here,' he said. 'And *he* definitely shouldn't.'

'I won't be for long,' she said, offering no explanation.

Carrick sighed. 'Seems you might have been right about the level of decay,' he said. 'Crime scene analysis says the Baileys were dead for at least five days, so Blake's appearance at their house doesn't tally by around forty-eight hours. At least not when he made the call. Plus, he's left-handed, and Cropper's certain the blade was drawn across the Baileys' throats by a right-handed assailant, left to right.'

'But we can hold him for seventy-two hours?' said Reeves.

'Without one of the murder weapons, probably not,' said Carrick. 'Especially given his minor status. There's no indication he's suffering any injuries either. Whoever got clipped with that shotgun is still out there.'

'But he knows *a lot more* than he's letting on,' said Jo. 'Want me to have a crack at him?'

Carrick shook his head. 'It's Dimi's suspect.' He nodded at Theo. 'And I hardly think a cute baby's going to make him open up.'

'We need to ask him about Megan,' said Jo. 'He might know where she is.'

'And we will,' said Carrick. 'But you're not on duty, remember?'

'Does it matter?' said Jo. 'I'm here. Heidi can take Theo for a minute.'

'Jo, this isn't a crèche,' said Carrick.

'But, boss, Harry was one of us . . .'

'Don't you think I bloody know that?' shouted Carrick, turning on her. Alice Reeves looked startled. In all the time Jo had known him, he'd never raised his voice, and 'bloody' was as close as Andy Carrick ever got to swearing.

'Just go home,' he added, more quietly.

Chapter 13

Jo had never been much of a text-messager. It was one of the things her friends had always remarked on. She'd half-heartedly blamed her thumbs – writing long missives made them ache – but the truth was that there was just too much room for error and she always seemed to get it wrong. Texting was just about fine for arranging a meet-up, but for difficult discussions, it was almost always wiser to pick up the phone, or better still, deal with things face to face.

That's if you wanted to deal with things at all.

She'd had messages from both her brother and Amelia. She guessed they themselves weren't quite on the same page because the sentiments expressed by each were different. Her brother said that he was just worried about his little sister, while his wife apologised 'for whichever foot Paul put in his mouth'. Jo had no energy to speak to them directly, so broke her own rule. She'd spent a good half-hour composing a response to both, intermittently cheering on Theo's attempts at crawling on the living room floor, repositioning cushions so he could flop without injuring himself.

In the end, she gave up on trying to explain herself and

what had led to her fit of temper, partly because she couldn't order the thoughts, even to herself. They didn't need to know about how this case was different, because she couldn't expect them to get it.

She could completely see where Paul and Amelia were coming from. Putting herself in their shoes, it was understandable. Here she was, a single mum going back to work too soon. They hadn't known Harry, the bond he and she had shared. And they could never truly know what her job meant to her, and what it meant to her at this precise moment. How it felt like a junction in her life, with no road map telling her which way to go.

She'd tried therapy before, under duress, and hated every minute. The problem was, once you tugged one thread, the whole bloody mess of her life became unstuck. Lucas was only the latest chapter, but it went right back. Mum and dad, Ben . . . oh yeah, and Jack Pryce. And how could she ever tell them *that*? *'By the way, I slept with my psychopathic colleague twelve hours before a police marksman blew out his brains. He might actually be Theo's dad, and one day I'm going to have to explain all this to my son, and how will he not hate me fucking up his life as well as my own . . .'*

She held down her thumb and deleted the latest missive she'd written. She wrote instead to Paul apologising for leaving early, and saying she'd see them soon. To Amelia, she said simply, 'He's not the *worst* brother.' Only afterwards did she realise she'd sent each message to the wrong recipient.

Oh well, they were in the same house. They'd get the message.

As soon as the texts were sent, she felt a little better – not about clearing the air, or about life in general. Just because she'd bought herself some time to think. As she was putting Theo down for the night, her phone rang. It was Andy Carrick. She answered with trepidation, anticipating the worst. *Jo – this isn't working out . . .*

'I want to apologise for earlier,' he said.

'No need,' she said, secretly relieved. 'I was out of line.'

'You were, but I get it,' he said. 'Can we move on?'

'Christ, let's,' she said. She would have hugged him if he'd been in the room.

'All right,' he continued. 'One of the neighbours in Stanton thought they heard the shotgun go off, and it fits your theory. Pre-dawn on Sunday 13th. They assumed it was an engine back-firing.'

'So it can't have been Blake Matthis?'

'Looking more unlikely. We also discovered the Baileys' flight from Auckland came into Heathrow later than planned at around four am that day, so it all matches. They get home in the early hours. A burglar arrives expecting no one around.'

Jo felt a flicker of triumph. The flies fit the timeline perfectly too. Motive was still a mystery though. 'Can't help thinking there's more to it, Andy. A burglar just runs – he doesn't kick in a bedroom door and take on someone wielding a shotgun.'

'Not unless he really can't afford witnesses.'

'Or they knew him,' muttered Jo. 'Maybe we should talk to the priest again?'

'He didn't look the type,' said Andy.

'You know I didn't mean that. But if there was someone in the community . . . Who's the neighbour?'

'Single woman, living alone, and fairly infirm. I think that's a non-starter. Listen, I'm not buying Blake's responsible, but he knows *something* he's not letting on. Someone was looking for those drugs, and I think the Baileys were just caught in the crossfire.'

'Megan's the key,' Jo muttered, half to herself.

'We've got the next best thing,' said Carrick. 'Can you meet me at an address tomorrow? We've got an appointment with Greg Bailey.'

'Doesn't Dimi want it?'

'Extension was denied for Blake, so we've only got him until eleven am. Dimi thinks he can get something after the lad's sweated some more.'

Recalling Blake's demeanour, Jo seriously doubted it.

Carrick said he'd text Jo the address where they'd be meeting the Baileys' son.

She couldn't help but ask. 'Has he given us anything about his sister?'

'All communication's come through the solicitor,' said Carrick. 'I get the impression she may have been a black sheep of the family.'

Andy often had a way with understatement.

'That's one way of putting it, boss.'

MONDAY, 21ST APRIL

'Have you found her?'

Greg Bailey looked like a banker in waiting. Clean-shaven, locks a glossy blond Jo once would have envied, with an athlete's physique. He was six-three at least, and every inch of him looked fine-tooled for a graduate job in the City. He wore a pink polo-shirt and blue jeans, with a pair of loafers. She tried to put first impressions aside, and remind herself he was a grieving son, though the only sign of grief that Jo could detect was a slight rawness to his eyes, which looked almost pink under pale lashes.

'We're still looking,' said Jo. The other man in the room, the Baileys' solicitor, was a rotund and florid fifty-something. He introduced himself as Aiden Chalmers, and invited them, having all shaken hands, to be seated on two facing Chesterfield sofas.

'Would you mind if we record the interview?' asked Carrick. 'It's just for our records.'

Greg looked to Chalmers, who shook his head. 'Of course not.'

'First of all,' said Carrick. 'We're very sorry for your loss, Mr Bailey. Can I ask when you last had contact with your parents?'

'A week or so ago,' said Bailey. 'They'd just landed in Singapore on the stopover. Their flight was delayed.'

'And when did you last see them in person?'

He shrugged. 'It would have been the very end of January, just before I went back to uni. I gave them a lift to the airport.'

'And what is it you study?'

'Economics and Management,' he said, before glancing at Chalmers. 'Sorry, how is my course relevant to what's happened to Mum and Dad?'

'Please rest assured we're doing everything we can to find your parents' killer,' said Carrick.

'Then your best bet is to start with my sister.'

'What makes you say that?' asked Jo.

Bailey looked at her with something close to contempt. 'She's a fuck-up, that's why. It's pretty obvious what's happened. I just wish Mum and Dad hadn't been so naïve.'

'Please, enlighten us,' said Carrick.

Greg leant back, and the sofa creaked. 'Megan was nicking stuff from the age of about eight,' he said. 'Just little things, like my toys, or biscuits from the cupboards. It seemed funny at the time, because she'd always deny it, and kids are crap at lying. But it got worse. She took a neighbour's bike, and when they came to get it back, she dumped it in the river to avoid getting caught. Dad thought that my school would sort her out, but if anything, being away from home sent her the other way.'

'We know she was expelled,' said Jo.

Greg blinked and settled his gaze on her. 'I believe *asked to leave* is the term they prefer.'

'It was something to do with sex,' said Jo. 'Could you clarify for us?'

'Certainly,' said Greg. 'She sent her maths teacher, Miss Estevez, a picture taken between her legs.'

'She's gay?' said Jo.

'I think the point is that she was twelve,' said Bailey. He let it hang, before adding. 'Actually, Megan would fuck anything if it meant she could get what she wanted.'

'And what was that?' asked Jo.

'Back then, I don't know. Affection? Later, it was all about drugs though. Well, money anyway, which equals drugs if you're wired that way. If she could fuck for drugs direct, I'm sure she would.'

Jo's mind went back to what the glazier had said. *You know what druggies are like. Steal anything to feed a habit.*

'She stole from Mum and Dad, repeatedly.'

'And they never tried to do anything about it?'

'Like what?' said Bailey. 'Report her to the police?'

'Perhaps counselling?' said Jo.

Bailey shook his head, and looked sincere for a moment. 'They believed in a higher power,' he said. 'Dragged both of us to church every Sunday, watched us toddle into the confessional to be absolved of our sins. Fuck, I've no idea what the priest must have made of Megan. She probably quite enjoyed tormenting him. Anyway, none of it seemed to help. I'm sure Mum and Dad prayed themselves hoarse asking for divine intervention.' He seemed to be looking inward, staring at the table between them. 'My parents weren't saints, but they always tried to do the right thing.' He glanced up, almost a snarl on his lips. 'Kind of ironic, isn't it?'

'Ironic how?' asked Carrick.

'Well, they took Megan in, and this is the reward they get.'

Jo was momentarily confused, and Andy's face told a similar story. 'Sorry,' she said. 'What do you mean?'

Bailey sat up, suddenly more animated, and threw a smirk across to his solicitor, before answering incredulously. 'You didn't even know she was adopted. Christ on a unicycle! I'm glad we've got Thames Valley's finest on the case.'

The blood rushed to Jo's face, and she was glad that Carrick spoke first.

'We weren't aware of that, Greg. You'll appreciate that there is a lot of evidence to process at your parents' house, and our immediate concern is intelligence gathering related to the murder itself.'

'Still!' said the solicitor, chiming in with some obvious delight, but apparently nothing to add.

Jo had gathered her composure. 'And if you'd spoken to us more promptly, this fact would have been in the open sooner.'

'I'm sorry I inconvenienced you,' said Bailey acidly.

He's actually enjoying this, thought Jo.

'Is it fair to say that your relationship with your sister wasn't a good one?' said Carrick.

Chalmers, now seemingly invigorated, intervened. 'I'm not sure how Gregory's feelings about his sister are important at all,' he said.

'No, it's all right,' said Bailey. 'To be honest, I had very little to do with her. I was a boarder, and she was at school in Oxford. Now I'm at university. Unlike my parents, I'd written off any good ever coming of Megan. And it looks, regrettably, like I was right.'

'Do you know of someone called Blake Matthis?' asked Carrick.

Bailey frowned. 'I don't. Is he the one you think killed my parents?'

'We think he might be connected somehow,' said Jo's boss. 'What about Xan Do?'

Bailey sighed and shook his head. 'Gosh, are these all of Megan's boyfriends? She's been busy.'

'We think Megan was staying with someone recently,' said Jo. 'A man called Harry Ferman.'

'The old man who was killed?'

Jo nodded. 'Have you any idea how she might have known him?'

'I imagine he was giving her money and she was giving him something in return.'

'Did your parents know where she was?'

'Unlikely. Megan did her own thing most of the time. Staying with friends, nearer town. She treated the house like an occasional pit-stop.' He folded his arms. 'Would you like my view?'

'Go on,' said Carrick.

'Megan's got herself mixed up with some drug dealers. Maybe she owes them money, or maybe she stole something from them. But she couldn't fuck her way out of the problem, and it's getting people killed.'

It didn't seem a bad summation, but Jo kept her face impassive.

'So you see why we need to find her?' said Carrick.

Bailey slapped his hands down onto his knees with relish, then looked from Carrick to Jo and back again. 'I'm afraid I can't do *all* your job for you.'

Chapter 14

'Well, he was obnoxious,' said Carrick, as they made their way back to their respective vehicles.

Jo had a rather choicer epithet in mind, but kept it to herself.

'Grief affects people differently,' she said. 'The day my mum died, I bit the head off a woman in Boots when she bumped into me in the queue. And I didn't even particularly like my mother.'

Carrick chuckled, and Jo sensed their relationship was getting back on to an even keel.

'Greg Bailey certainly wasn't fond of his sister, was he?' said Carrick.

'She sounds hard to love,' Jo replied. 'If she was adopted, there'll be a record of monitoring with child services. I'll get in touch and see if they can shed any light.'

'Good thinking.'

Jo knew she might not get another chance, so she asked. 'I'd love a few minutes with Blake too. If Megan was involved with the trafficking of narcotics and using her parents' house to store them, it could be one of the numbers he was calling belonged to her. He might give it up.'

They'd reached the cars and Carrick paused with the door open. 'Talk to Heidi about the phone data,' he said. 'And let me talk to Dimi about the other thing. He was looking pretty burnt out by the end of yesterday. Blake had clammed up completely.'

'Got it,' said Jo. 'See you back at the station.'

As she was climbing into her car, she noticed Greg Bailey across the street, to one side of the building that housed Chalmers' offices, climbing into a racing-green Jaguar. She wondered absently if it was a gift from his parents, or if he'd somehow bought it himself.

Either way, she wasn't sure why it left an odd taste in her mouth. The boy had lost his mum and dad – having a flash car was hardly compensation.

* * *

The clock in her car read 10.19 as she pulled up at St Aldates. They had Blake Matthis in their custody for another forty-one minutes. Carrick took George Dimitriou aside immediately and closed his office door. Alice Reeves was on the phone, but when she saw Jo she beckoned her over. 'The inspector on the case has just walked in, let me transfer you.' She put the call on hold. 'Ma'am, got a teacher of Megan Bailey on the phone. She saw the appeal.'

Jo's heart quickened a fraction. A lead – any lead – would be something.

'Put her through,' said Jo, taking off her coat. She didn't have long if she still wanted to talk to Blake, but she could ascertain quickly enough if the caller had useful information.

'Hello,' she said, picking up the phone and sliding into a chair. With her free hand, she opened her notebook. 'My name is Jo Masters – I'm the lead investigator.'

The woman, who sounded timid, introduced herself as Claire Arnold.

'You're a teacher, my colleague told me?'

'Used to be,' said the woman. 'I'm a SEN coordinator at Marsh Hill now.'

'And you know Megan Bailey?'

'I *think* I do, yes. And I don't think she killed that man.'

'Megan is just a person of interest,' said Jo.

'Yes, I saw the appeal,' said the woman on the other end of the phone, 'but there's a rumour going round the kids here this morning that she killed him. Is that what you think?'

News travels fast, thought Jo. *Wait until they hear what happened to her parents . . .*

'We're not really sure what happened,' said Jo honestly. 'Can you tell me a little about Megan? What is she like?'

'She was always troubled,' said the educational needs officer. 'Angry too, at times. She didn't really make friends for long, and she definitely had problems with authority figures. She ended up in my office on a number of occasions, mainly when she was disruptive. It was fairly obvious she had an addiction, but we're strict here, and she was never found with anything on site. If she had, it would have been an immediate exclusion. She used to bunk off a lot. Days at a time, or she'd just disappear in the middle of the day.'

'Was she ever violent?'

'Not to my knowledge,' said Arnold. 'She was brighter than that. I know it sounds silly, but she wasn't a bad person. She just . . . wore a lot of armour.'

'And you said she *used* to be truant?'

'Well, that's why I'm calling,' said Arnold. 'I felt things had changed. Recently. She came to school the week before last, for the first time in a fortnight or so. She was like a different person. She actually looked happy. Healthy.'

'You think she'd kicked her habit?'

'I'm not an expert, but I believe so, yes.'

'That's very interesting,' said Jo, though it was hardly conclusive. Her eyes drifted to the clock. She was thinking about winding up the call.

'There was an incident though,' continued Arnold, 'that afternoon after school, right at the gates. There was some sort of fight. Megan had an argument with a couple of men. One ended up hitting the other.'

Now she had Jo's attention. 'Could you describe either of them?'

'I didn't see it first-hand, only the aftermath. One of the men got into his car and drove off. I think he was Japanese.'

Jo's hand tightened on the phone.

'Might he have been Korean?'

'I suppose so. Sorry, I know it's probably not very helpful.'

'Did anyone report it to the police?'

'I tried to speak to Megan. She just said he was her ex-boyfriend. She didn't want a fuss, and she insisted she didn't want her parents involved.'

Jo looked up at the clock. 10.25. Blake was almost home free.

'Thank you very much, Claire,' she said. Oxford's East Asian population wasn't huge – a few hundred people at most – and it was tempting to jump to conclusions. 'This is very important – can you recall anything about the vehicle?'

As she spoke, she accessed the Xan Do files and brought up a wide shot of the crime scene, with Xan sitting back in the white BMW.

'Only that it was white,' said Arnold. 'I'm afraid I'm not really a car person.'

'That's perfect,' said Jo. 'Just perfect.'

★ ★ ★

'Hi, Blake. Do you remember me?'

He looked up sullenly. 'Should I?' The kid was tired, she could see. Beside him, his minder Jordan Tomasz looked angry.

'You almost flattened me on your bike three days ago.'

The flicker of a smile crossed Blake's features. 'Nah. I'd remember.'

Jo smiled back. 'Listen, Blake – I had to beg my boss to let me talk to you. And we don't have long, because they're going to cut you loose in about' – she looked at her watch – 'twenty-six minutes.'

Blake shared an incredulous glance with Tomasz, as if to say, *What the fuck is this bitch on?*

'Do you have anything to ask the lad?' said his companion.

Jo turned to him. 'You're a family friend, right?'

'Just here to serve Blake's interests,' said Tomasz. 'Make sure you don't stitch him up.'

'Only Blake's interests?' said Jo.

Tomasz looked at his watch. 'The fella with the lip-fluff thrown himself in front of a bus, has he?'

'My colleague thinks you're a killer, Blake.'

'And you don't?'

'Believe it or not, I want to help you,' said Jo. 'And your mother.'

'This has got nothing to do with Trace,' said Tomasz.

'I think we all know that's not true,' said Jo. 'Ms Grimshaw could easily have been killed last night.'

Blake was silent.

'I need to talk to you about Megan Bailey,' said Jo.

'Oh yeah?'

'How well do you know her?'

'Who?'

'You were at her house. She's the daughter of Mr and Mrs Bailey, who were killed.'

Tomasz shook his head. 'His phone was at her house.'

Jo blew out her cheeks. 'We're still going with that line, are we? Okay, you've heard of the food chain, right? Little things eaten by bigger things, et cetera?'

Blake nodded. 'Sure.'

'Well Megan Bailey is what we call the bottom of the food chain. She's the smallest fish in the sea. There are loads like her, but they get eaten in their thousands. In the narcotics trade, they're the addicts. No one gives a shit about addicts, but without them, the whole thing falls apart, just like the food chain collapses without the little fish.'

Blake waited for her to continue.

'Xan knew Megan. It looks like he was her dealer and maybe her boyfriend too. Slightly higher up the food chain. We were watching Xan. And he must have had a feeling, because he moved a substantial stash of narcotics from his parents' warehouse to Megan's house. They were away and the place they lived, well, it's the *last* place the police look for drugs, isn't it? This ringing any bells?'

Blake stuck out his bottom lip, just like Theo when she held a toy out of reach, though the teen was considerably less endearing. Jo tried not to think about her son – he'd been fractious again that morning, clinging to her at the nursery.

'You know what I couldn't work out? Why you were so thorough in your search downstairs, but upstairs was practically untouched. And you didn't even think about the summer house, which is where the stash actually was.'

Tomasz was shaking his head and smirking, but Blake, she sensed, was actually listening.

'Sorry,' said Jo. 'I sometimes think aloud. My colleague, Sergeant Dimitriou, thinks that you killed Mr and Dr Bailey. For what it's worth, I don't agree. It takes serious *commitment* to cut somebody's throat. It's not like in the movies – you have to go *deep*. There are tendons to get through, you know? People think it's just a quick slit and all that spray, but it's not like that at all. It's more like sawing, and you need a sharp blade. They'd have been wriggling too, screaming for mercy. Especially after the first one was done.'

Now she had both their attention.

'Can I give you my theory?'

Blake looked at his watch.

'Xan fucked up somehow. Either he told someone about the drugs he was selling for your dad, or more likely Megan did. They killed Xan and went to get the drugs, but they didn't know exactly where to find them. In the meantime, you panicked, rang your dad, and he told you to get there and find them first. You did what he said, but you got a lot more than you bargained for. You searched downstairs, and went into that cellar. Two dead bodies, probably already beginning to stink. And you did what any of us would. You got the hell out. And though you'd taken the precaution of wearing gloves, you were still dumb enough to use your phone again, right then and there. If you hadn't, you wouldn't be here now.'

Blake's eyes became a stare of dead malice. 'I don't know what you're talking about.'

'Fair enough,' said Jo. 'But if you didn't do it, you need to worry about who did. Everyone thinks they're the big fish, untouchable. Xan thought *he* was, but there's always someone higher up the food chain, swimming in darker waters. Someone who's okay with screaming, and tendons, and blood. A big shark that eats little fish like Xan. And like you. And, going by last night's events, your mum too. You thought you could hide, but you can't.'

'I can look after my mum.'

'How, Blake? You can hardly put her on the back of your

dirt bike and ride off into the sunset. You can't go home. Whoever your dad owes money to, they know where you live.'

'His dad will make sure nothing bad happens to Blake or Trace,' said Tomasz.

'I beg to differ,' said Jo. 'Blake's father wasn't there last night putting out the fire, was he? If it hadn't been for that poor dog . . .'

Blake looked up. 'Niko?'

'You didn't know?' said Jo. 'I'm afraid Niko didn't pull through. Brave little thing though. Loyal.'

'It's just a dog,' said Tomasz. Blake looked across at his companion, who must have caught something in the teenager's expression. 'You can get another one.'

Blake continued to stare at the older man, then said quietly. 'I want a few minutes on my own.'

'No way,' said Tomasz. 'I'm staying here.'

Jo stood. 'Mr Tomasz, give Blake some space please.'

The guy remained seated, as if considering his options. Really, though, there weren't any. An interviewee, even a juvenile one, could dismiss an appropriate adult at any time.

'Blake?' he said.

'Fuck off,' said Blake sullenly.

Tomasz stood. 'You can't trust her, Blake. Bitch'll do anything she can to make you talk.'

'I can turn off the recording Blake,' said Jo. 'Nothing you say will be admissible in court. It's just a chat.'

'Bullshit,' said Tomasz. 'In ten minutes, you're free to leave Blake. Don't say *anything* else.'

'In ten minutes, I'll walk Blake out the door myself,' said Jo. 'That's a promise.'

★   ★   ★

172

Jo had turned off the recording. Not just because she needed Blake to trust her, but because he wasn't the fish she was trying to catch.

'I need my mum to be safe,' said Blake. His demeanour had changed considerably since Tomasz had left the room.

'We can arrange that,' said Jo. 'But you have to help us. Do you know who might have carried out the arson attack?'

'I've got a good idea, yeah,' said Blake.

'Who?'

'I've never met him personally. Xan made all the payments.' He paused. before adding. 'Dad didn't want me involved.'

'And do you think it was the same individual who killed the Baileys?'

'I don't fucking know,' said Blake. 'Can't see why they'd try to nick their own drugs. If that fucking slag went behind . . .' He trailed off, venom spent.

'Megan was Xan's girlfriend, we heard,' said Jo.

'She used to fuck him, yeah. I told him not to. It wasn't good business. You could see she wasn't right.'

'In what way?'

'I dunno. Just sort of dead inside.'

'Did you ever have sexual relations with her?' asked Jo.

'No way. She's not my type.'

She's missed out there, thought Jo.

'Do you know where she is now?'

Blake shook his head. 'I aint seen her for a while.' He gave Jo a forceful stare. 'That's the truth. I told Xan not to use her place, but he said we could trust her. And it was empty.'

'But she was there.'

'No. Her folks were away. She was with friends or something.'

With Harry.

'So what went wrong?'

For a moment, he gnashed his teeth and screwed up his fists,

173

like he could see Megan Bailey in front of him and wanted to tear her to pieces. 'She *said* she was finished with him, and the drugs. She wanted him to get rid of the stash at her house. We were supposed to be going to get them, me and Xan, that night.'

'The night he was shot?'

Blake nodded briskly. 'Fucking bitch sold us out. Put someone onto us.'

'It appears so,' said Jo. *And they seemed such a sweet couple.*

'So when you found Xan's body, you ran?'

'What was I supposed to do? He was dead.'

'And you really think Megan knew Xan was going to be killed?'

'She was fucking cold, innit? She was fucked up.'

'It doesn't sound like that,' said Jo. 'It's sounds like she was getting clean.'

'I dunno,' said Blake, distantly. 'Reckon that fucked her up worse.'

JAMES

The small café was directly opposite the school gates. On the table in front of him, a cold cup of coffee and a folded newspaper showing a crossword half finished. The paper he'd found in a bin. He wasn't interested in puzzles. His eyes were on the gates as the kids in their blue uniforms poured out.

He'd been in Oxford for two weeks, putting together the pieces of a temporary life. The first couple of nights had been spent on the street, until a bit of intelligence had sent him to a squat in the Headington area of the city. Six or seven drunks in a two-bedroom house that had been condemned. No heating, but at least a supply of running water. In the day he begged outside one of the colleges, and it was better money than he'd ever made in Manchester. It had provided him with enough money to purchase some of the materials he needed. The rest, when it was safe, he'd stolen. Hardware stores were often easy pickings. Local places, tight aisles packed with stock, one guy running things, no cameras, and no suspicion of a slightly scruffy customer carrying a bag. Buy the cheapest pack of nails, and

175

load the rest of the ingredients into the sack. Putting it all together back at the house wouldn't be a problem. Most of the residents couldn't recognise their own parents, let alone an explosive device. That was all a last resort, of course. If things went south. First things first, he had to find her.

A little research back at the Manchester library had given him the locations of all nine Oxford secondary schools, and they were circled on the streetmap he'd stolen from the local charity shop. One day at each, morning and afternoon, positioned close enough to see the kids as they entered and left. Boring as hell, but necessary. It wasn't a perfect system. Some kids arrived by bus, carried straight into the school grounds. Sometimes there was an influx and he struggled to catch every face. And if that day she was ill or absent . . . Still, it was the only system he had. Any other method was apt to draw attention.

Marsh Hill was the sixth school he'd cased out, and one of the easier ones. A couple had been tricky even to get close, stuck out in residential areas where the sight of a lone man would have sent a dozen eagle-eyed parents reaching for their phones to ring the police. He'd taken more care there, armed with alibis – that his car had run out of petrol nearby and he was looking for a garage, that he'd lost his dog, or his keys. Most of the time, though, he went unchallenged except for the occasional odd look. There'd been a more direct confrontation about a week ago, a fleshy-faced dad in sports gear demanding, 'What exactly do you think you're doing, hanging around here?' In that case, he'd resisted the urge to break the man's jaw, and said he was a former student, arrived early to visit an old teacher, Mrs Edwards. He figured the name and his age were vague enough to allay suspicion. Luckily for both of them, it didn't escalate, and the man actually apologised.

He barely remembered his own school days, but Mrs Edwards had been a real teacher of his, back in Manchester. One of the few who'd treated him with respect. Not a busybody, or a bully – just someone who knew not to push his buttons.

'Can I get you anything else?'

The waitress smiled.

You could leave me the fuck alone, he thought. Eyes back on the school.

'No, thank you.'

And then, just like that, there she was. His heart felt like a balloon, suddenly inflated, rising under his ribcage. He couldn't breathe. He stood, leg catching the table and rattling the empty cup in its saucer.

'Are you all right?' said the waitress. He picked up his bag and walked towards the door, eyes fixed on the girl leaving the school gates on her own. 'Hey, you need to pay!'

James fished in his pocket for a couple of quid, and tossed them on the table.

She had changed, of course. Changed almost completely. Her hair was blond. Her face thinner. But it was her. He knew it.

He rushed to the door, and went out into the street, walking parallel to the girl. He wanted to call out, but not to scare her. She looked to be in her own world, walking fast, bag slung over her shoulder.

He quickened his steps, drawing level, looking for a gap in traffic so he could cross. Then she stopped, and shouted across the road.

'Why the fuck are you following me?'

Thankfully there was no one in earshot. There was no recognition in her eyes at all. 'I need to talk to you,' he called back. As he began to cross the road, she turned and walked away. He'd anticipated this part, but he forgot what he was supposed to say, so instead he ran, his rucksack bouncing uncomfortably. He caught her though, and grabbed an arm. 'Wait! Hear me out! I'm your . . .'

She turned, and her foot flashed out, catching him in the groin. His legs gave out at once, crumpling him to the ground. The pain was all-consuming, and he fought back a wave of bile. 'Fuck off!' she said.

She kept on walking, leaving him curled into a ball. With difficulty, he scooted to the edge of the pavement, using a low wall to help him stand. He checked under his tracksuit bottoms, fearing he might see blood, but he was still intact. She had vanished out of sight.

That hadn't gone according to plan at all. Fuck, she'd kicked him hard!

It didn't matter though. He'd found her now, and one way or another, he was never letting her go again.

Chapter 15

A clearly enraged Jordan Tomasz had to be escorted from the police station, and Jo wondered how soon he would report back to Blake's father. Blake himself was still in the interview room where Jo had left him. Perhaps he felt pleased to get things off his chest, but it wouldn't be long before he began to reassess the wisdom of the information he'd given her. They hadn't charged him with anything, and it would be an arduous and detailed conversation with the Crown Prosecution Service, taking into account the assistance that he'd offered, before they decided how to take things forward. In the meantime, he would likely be released. She doubted it would be long before he was hooked again though – some fish, she knew, were like that. If they did press charges, Jo was under no illusions. Any half-decent legal brief would argue that Blake was under the powerful influence of his hardened criminal father. The chances of him doing time were minute.

Jo's boss had given her a clap on the back as soon as she left the interview room. Dimitriou approached her with smile and a shake of the head. 'I can't believe you used the dog. So cold.'

That was as close to congratulations as she'd get from Dimi.

'Not as cold as Matthis family Christmases from now on,' she replied.

Their first priority at this point was the safety of both Blake and his mother. Carrick had already instructed Heidi to get in touch with the youth offender team, and to have a uniformed officer stationed at the hospital.

As Jo sat back at her desk, Reeves said, 'That was amazing, ma'am.'

It had been a gamble, but it had paid off. And she knew she should feel better than she did. The fact was though, a couple of pieces might have come together, but the big picture was more than a little hazy. There was no leads for the arson attack. They still had no murder suspect in custody for the deaths of Xan Do, or the Baileys, and why Harry had paid the ultimate price was a deeper mystery still. He wasn't involved in the drug trade at all, other than historically, when he'd done his best to stem its flow into Oxford in the nineties. She was struck, suddenly, by a vivid memory from the Three Crowns – one of the times he'd spoken about his work in some detail. It had been the night of the work Christmas party, but he was on duty, and called to a suspected overdose at an illegal rave. When he got there he had discovered the boy was the son of a colleague. He'd had to deliver the news himself, while *White Christmas* played in the background.

If the killings had been carried out by someone higher up the narcotics food chain, the chances of bringing them in without hard forensics was tiny. They could try talking to Matthis Senior, but he wasn't likely to offer them the name of his supplier even if they had almost killed Blake's mother. Grasses in prison tended not to fare well. He would have to find a way to make good on whatever profits the police seizure had diminished.

The only other person who might have been able to pass on useful information was Xan himself.

Carrick gave her a tap on the shoulder. 'Can I have a word?'

She followed him into his office and shut the door.

'None of this makes sense, does it?' he said.

'I was thinking the same thing,' said Jo. 'Xan's killing looks like a drug hit, but the Baileys is something different altogether. Whoever killed them took their time.'

'And a good amount of buckshot in the process,' said Carrick.

'Any word on the DNA in the blood on the carpet?'

'Samples went to the lab Saturday for extraction. They'll be sent to the national database for comparison any time now. Until then, the priority is still to find Megan Bailey. She's a dangerous person to get close to, it seems. God knows how Harry got mixed up with her.'

'I had a thought about that,' said Jo.

'I'm listening.'

'What if he was looking after her?' said Jo. 'It looks like she tried to rob him, probably for a bit of cash or valuables. For some reason, he didn't turn her in. Instead, she started living with him.'

'It's a nice theory,' said Carrick, 'but why?'

'Maybe he was lonely,' said Jo, and she remembered Dimitriou had said the same thing, back at the start of the investigation. He'd been implying a sexual connection, of course, and she still couldn't wrap her head around anything like that. In her heart it made some sense that he would want to help. Harry had had no one, other than the drinkers at the Three Crowns. And in the last few months, he'd not even had Jo herself to talk to. 'Perhaps he thought he could help her get clean.'

Carrick stroked his chin. 'I suppose it's academic for now.'

'I also think we have to assume there's another male on the scene.'

'Someone who took an exception to Harry?' added Carrick.

'And who drove Megan across town to the supermarket where we saw her later. She's definitely not on her own in all this. I want to take another look at the CCTV from the betting shop on the corner of Canterbury Road. We only looked at the window immediately around the attack, but maybe this individual had been hanging around a while.'

'Go for it,' said Carrick, 'but unsavoury types and betting shops are hardly uncommon bedfellows.'

*　*　*

The youth offender team took Blake Matthis away just before midday, while Dimitriou finally went home after twenty-eight hours on duty. Jo went over the footage Reeves had sourced from the bookies. After so much time focused on Blake Matthis and the Baileys, it felt good to be returning her attention to the case of her deceased friend.

She hadn't told Carrick the full reason for wanting to access the recordings. What Alice Reeves had confided about Lucas being in the Three Crowns had never fully left her mind over the last twenty-four hours. The fact he'd been in the area in and around the time of Harry's death didn't necessarily mean anything – and indeed, the thought of Lucas being involved in violence of any sort seemed daft – but she had to remind herself that Lucas had known where Harry lived, and he had been particularly determined to track her down recently. He was also no stranger to being black-out drunk. She wouldn't be doing her job if she didn't check it out.

With a strong coffee to prepare her reserves of patience, she plugged in the hard-drive in the AV suite, winding back to approximately the time of the murder. She watched in reverse – the police cars and the ambulance retreating across the screen, the punters staggering back into the front of the building. Her own car, just a blur. Order restoring itself as the clock ticked back.

With a notebook open at her side, Jo made meticulous notes of the comings and goings, each accompanied with precise time-stamps. They'd estimated the time of the attack at 16.30, and the hours prior were busy ones at the bookies. More than nine in ten of the people who entered were men. She disregarded anyone who went inside – figuring that she was looking, specifically, for outsiders coming to the area and thus simply walking or driving by. She ignored women, of whom there were few, and anyone she recognised specifically from the Three Crowns. There were plenty of others whom she could safely cross off the list. The very old, or the infirm – there were two on motorised scooters, and one visually impaired man with his guide dog. Of possible male suspects in the two hours prior to the murder, there were six. But none of them seemed to be in a hurry as they passed the bookies walking away from Ferman's. And winding back further, none had approached from the same direction.

It was the day before the murder – Wednesday 16th – that she spotted Megan Bailey. She played the footage forward and saw the girl, dressed in the same voluminous coat as at the supermarket. For a few dozen frames, she crossed the camera angle moving towards Harry's. She was carrying a bag of shop-ping in one hand and a bunch of flowers in the other. The same flowers that had been on the floor beside Harry while he breathed his last. Jo made a note, and rewound, discovering shortly after that Megan had left the house twenty-seven minutes before she returned. Just nipping out to the shops, it seemed.

The day before there was no sign of Megan, but Jo did see the same man passing the front of the bookies on four occasions, two times back and forth. The gap between his journeys to and fro were only a couple of minutes, suggesting a destination somewhere on Harry's road or close. He wore a hooded top, and walked with purpose. Jo tried zooming in the picture to get a better idea of distinguishing features, but it was frustratingly unclear. He was white, she thought, wearing boots of some sort, black tracksuit bottoms, and a dark hoodie. He carried a rucksack that looked almost military issue. She guessed he was around five-foot-ten, with a stocky build, which hardly narrowed things down. Still, she printed out several of the images, before rubbing her eyes and continuing.

At 8.28 pm on Tuesday 15th she saw Lucas. He was stumbling from the direction of the Three Crowns, along Canterbury Road, towards Harry's place.

'Shit.'

She paused the recording, sinking back in her chair, trying to work out the implications.

On the surface, it didn't *mean* anything. It wasn't even on the day that Harry had been attacked, so there was nothing specifically incriminating. But it would still have to be written up as a line of enquiry, and as soon as Carrick realised her personal connections were further elbowing into the investigation, as surely as Lucas had staggered into the station the other day, her boss would be back to thinking about damage limitation. And she could hardly blame him. The last thing Thames Valley needed was *another* case with her name front and centre.

At the same time, a thought occurred. The 15th was the day of Harry's message, regarding a 'delicate situation'. Now it was all too easy to see what he'd meant. If Lucas had come to his door, drunk, demanding to know where she was, he wouldn't have known what to do other than call her.

She made her notes and continued. It was important, now more than ever, not to get side-tracked. The rest of the day followed a similar pattern – the bookies were busiest between eleven am and four pm, with many of the same sad faces as on days she'd already looked over. With long periods of little pedestrian traffic, she could get through the footage at a decent lick, but with the frequent stops to make jottings, it took a couple of hours to get through the first couple of days prior to Harry's murder. Her eyes were stinging from the intense focus, and she was about ready to give up.

Heidi knocked and stuck her head around the door just after two pm, handing Jo a sandwich. 'We've got hold of the Oxfordshire City Council Child Welfare Team – they're going to organise a liaison tomorrow with a member of staff who knows the file.'

'Good of them to rush,' said Jo, rolling her eyes.

'We offered to send someone over today, but apparently it's not as simple as that. Needs to be signed off through their legal department.'

'Of course it does,' said Jo. 'They live for crossed T's and dotted I's. Cheers for the sarnie.' Alone again, she moved her search into the previous day – Monday 14th – and the time-stamp ticked backwards from midnight. Then, a few minutes short of nine pm, something made her stop. She blinked and paused, then slowly brought the car back into shot. It had been the distinctive shape of the front fender that caught her eye, and it was hard to see from the few frames if the colour was a match. But one thing was certain – the man in the driving seat was Greg Bailey.

He was driving straight down Harry Ferman's road. It wasn't the only surprise.

Jo zoomed in closer to be sure, focusing on the person in the passenger seat.

'What the actual fuck?' she muttered.

It was almost certainly Greg's sister, Megan.

Chapter 16

When Greg Bailey didn't answer his phone, they contacted his solicitor's office directly. Aiden Chalmers did his best to deflect their enquiry, saying that his client was grieving and should be left alone.

'Mr Chalmers,' said Jo, the call on speaker in Carrick's office. 'We've got some important lines of enquiry that only Greg can answer. There were some inconsistencies in his previous statements.'

'I'm sure there's a perfectly reasonable explanation for any anomalies,' said Chalmers, remaining unflustered. 'Let me see what I can do and get back to you.'

He ended the call.

'He's a slippery one,' said Carrick.

'You think he'll find Bailey?' asked Heidi.

'He'd better do,' said Jo, 'because if I get to him first, it won't be pretty.'

Bailey hadn't strictly denied being in Oxford recently, but the impression he gave to the contrary had been a strong one. Jo listened back to the recording of their conversation in Chalmers' office. He said he'd last seen his parents at the 'very end of January, just before *I went back* to uni'.

That was a long way from *I was in Oxford a week ago with my sister* and as far as Jo was concerned, he'd lied.

While they waited, Jo opened up the notes on the Ferman case, looking through the fingerprint record. If they could put Greg Bailey in the house, on the day of the murder, it would be more than a promising lead. Her brain searched for a motive but struggled to identify anything remotely credible. Bailey apparently despised his sister, but how that led to Ferman being bludgeoned was anyone's guess. Perhaps Greg and his sister had argued, and Harry had somehow got in the way. In that case, it wasn't beyond the realms of possibility that Bailey would get off with a manslaughter charge.

But the revelation threw up all sorts of other possibilities. If Greg was involved in Harry's death, if he'd been in Oxford when he claimed to be in Cambridge, did that mean he was somehow caught up in Stanton St John too? In the murders of his own parents? If that bloody print on the stairs was a match, this was open and shut and the motive hardly mattered. But Jo's immediate thought was the drugs. For all his avowed distaste for the world of narcotics, if ever there was a vice that turned family members against one another, made people do unspeakable things . . .

And he'd been so keen to pin it all on Megan. If that was a deflection, it was as good a ruse as Jo had ever seen. But she had to admit, her own prejudices hadn't helped. Everything about him had screamed privilege – a walking stereotype of the private school to Oxbridge conveyor belt leading to an easy life in the one per cent. A million miles from someone like Blake Matthis.

But maybe not so far from Xan Do . . .

It was only the spark of an idea, but it took hold.

'Heidi,' Jo said across the desks. 'I think Dimi mentioned Xan Do was privately educated. Any idea where?'

'No. You want me to speak to the parents and find out? Might not be wise, given the complaint they're bringing.'

'Hold off, then,' said Jo. *It's probably nothing anyway.* She turned instead to the search engine on her computer and typed in 'Xan Do St Cuthbert's.'

The hunch she'd had was a good one.

'You need to see this,' she said, as the results came up.

Heidi came around, and Jo opened the top link. It was a report from four years earlier, detailing the results of an orchestral competition held in London. Xan Do was mentioned as one member of a string quartet that took the second prize, and the school he represented was none other than St Cuthbert's.

'Oh my,' said Heidi. 'He knew Greg Bailey.'

'They're two years apart, but it's probable.'

'We need to tell the gaffer.'

'Tell him what?' said Carrick, appearing at the door.

Jo spelled out the link. 'Whatever's going on, Bailey's got a lot of questions to answer.'

'Lucky for you, he's on his way,' said Carrick. 'Chalmers just called. They're both coming in.'

*   *   *

Andy Carrick joined her in the interview room. Jo was in no mood to pussyfoot as she cautioned Bailey, and read him his rights. Neither he, nor Chalmers, looked terribly alarmed.

'You lied to us, Greg. You said you hadn't seen Megan.'

Bailey crossed his long legs, revealing five inches of naked ankle above the loafers. 'I didn't lie,' he said. 'I said I hadn't seen my parents. That was true.'

'You lied by omission. You knew we were looking for your sister.'

'It was family business,' he said. 'Really none of yours.'

'In case you hadn't noticed, fifty per cent of your family are dead,' said Jo.

'Oh, come on!' scoffed Chalmers. 'That is grossly inappropriate. If you can't be civil, I'll have no alternative but to advise my client to terminate this *voluntary* interview.'

Jo was pretty sure the threat was empty, but if he did try to get Bailey out of the station, she was perfectly willing to arrest him in order to continue the conversation. She kept her focus on Megan's brother. 'I appreciate that privacy is important,' said Jo, 'but this is a murder enquiry. Is there anything you *can* tell me about the reason for your visit to Oxford.'

'She wanted money,' he said with a shrug.

'And you gave her some?'

'Not at first,' he said. 'She'd called me in Cambridge. Claimed she was off the drugs and promised to get out of our lives for good if I helped. I said I wanted to see her, face to face.'

'So you came to Oxford?'

'That's right. We met in town – I can give you the name of the café if you want. Afterwards, I dropped her off at a place she was staying with the old chap.'

Canterbury Road.

'And did you believe her? About the drugs?'

'To an extent,' said Greg. 'She looked different to when I'd last seen her. But looks can be deceiving, as I'm sure you know.'

'That isn't what I meant,' said Jo. 'Why did you believe her? Addicts are always saying they're clean, and they're almost always lying. Yet you drove all the way from Cambridge.'

Bailey shrugged. 'I'm an optimist,' he said.

'But you did give her money?'

Greg shook his head. 'I'm not stupid,' he said. 'I gave her fifty quid and told her I'd send her more, when I was sure she'd gone.'

'Have you any idea where she might have disappeared to?'

'She mentioned up north, but as long as it was far from Oxford, I didn't care.'

'So why on earth didn't you tell us this before?' said Carrick.

Greg paused, eyes lowered for a moment. 'It's her mess. When I saw the stuff about the murder of the old chap, I didn't want to be connected to any of it, to be honest.'

'You can understand that, surely?' said Chalmers.

'Not really,' said Jo, though in fact it wasn't beyond the realms of possibility. People lied in interview rooms all the time, even when they had nothing major to hide. It was an instinct – a way of maintaining some control in an encounter where no one was sure who they could trust. She thought of the message on her answerphone, still separate from the official police record. Was that a lie by omission too? Perhaps she wasn't so different from Greg Bailey, if his fib turned out to be as innocent as he claimed.

'You weren't worried about her?' asked Jo, ignoring Bailey's solicitor. 'You might not be related by blood, but she's still your sister.'

Now Greg's blue eyes latched onto hers. 'Those are lovely sentiments, sergeant, but with all due respect, you haven't lived with her. She made my parents' life hell, and almost wrecked our family. If there was a chance she'd just disappear, it would be better for everyone. With any luck, she's already overdosed in a train station toilet somewhere.'

There was plenty of spite in his words, but his eyes contained a degree of sadness as he spoke. He looked and sounded convincing enough, but Jo remembered plainly that she'd thought the same the first time she'd met him. There was something of the chameleon about Greg Bailey, adapting himself, and his persona, to the situation.

'Tell me, Greg – do you know anything about a young man called Xan Do?'

Bailey's brow creased. She looked for guilt, but couldn't see any hint. 'Should I?'

'He was a drug dealer here in Oxford. We think he had something to do with the narcotics found at your parents' house. He was having a relationship with Megan.'

'The name doesn't mean anything to me at all,' he said. 'And I imagine her relationships are many.'

'That's odd,' said Jo. 'Xan Do was at St Cuthberts at the same time as you.' She showed Bailey the picture she'd printed of the string quartet.

Bailey gave it a once-over, seemingly unfazed. 'Sorry, I was more into sports. We didn't mix with the musical lot.'

'You don't think the connection's interesting?'

'What exactly are you getting at?' said Chalmers. 'Are you implying Gregory has something to do with the drugs?'

'Do you, Greg?' Jo asked.

Bailey looked at Chalmers. 'Do we have to be here?'

'Yes, you do,' said Jo. 'You lied to us before.'

'We were speaking informally,' said Chalmers, 'and Greg was not under caution then. It's kind of him to help with your enquiries at all at such a difficult time.'

'Spare me the sanctimony,' said Jo. She pointed at the picture of Xan Do clutching his violin. 'You're denying knowing him?'

'I am. I'm pretty sure he wasn't in my year, or the one above.'

'Isn't it possible that Megan knew Xan from her own time at the school?' said Chalmers. 'It seems she attracted the wrong sorts of people.'

Jo had thought of it, but there were five years between Megan and Xan Do, and just two between him and Greg Bailey. It was hard to see them interacting a great deal in the brief time Megan had been at St Cuthberts. She spoke to Bailey once more.

'If we were to look at your phone, we wouldn't find any evidence of contact between you and Xan?'

192

Greg slipped his hand into his pocket, took out his phone and put it on the table between them. 'Go ahead.'

'Now wait a minute,' said Chalmers, reaching out and placing his own hand over the phone. 'There's no need to do that, Greg. They're speculating here and frankly it's a little desperate.'

His client shrugged. 'I've nothing to hide. Go on, sergeant, take it.'

It was a power-play, and he thought he had won. 'We may want to later,' said Jo, ignoring the phone. She paused the recording. 'Give us a minute, please.'

'Take all the time you need,' said Bailey.

Outside the room, she and Carrick consulted.

'You believe him?' said Carrick.

'No,' said Jo. 'He played us the first time at his brief's office, and I think he's doing the same now. There might be some truth in what he's saying, but I don't buy that he wouldn't mention this when we questioned him before. He's not ashamed that he wanted his sister out of life – in fact, he rather seems to revel in the animosity. So why lie about it the first time?'

'What do you want to do?'

'Let's get his prints and a swab – that'll keep him on his toes. Then release him, I suppose. Can't see him doing a runner.'

★   ★   ★

She wasn't surprised when Greg submitted to the tests without protest, but her heart was still in her mouth while she made a visual comparison between the thumbprints from the mug in Ferman's kitchen, and those of both Greg Bailey's hands, double-checking with Heidi and Carrick also. They all agreed there was nothing close to a match. The partial bloody handprint at his parents' house would take a more specialist analysis, but it looked distinctly unlikely. Greg certainly had no visible injuries that might correspond to a shotgun blast.

'It was worth a shot,' said Carrick flatly. 'We'll get the swab processed asap and run it through the database.'

Jo didn't hold much hope of a match. Didn't hold much hope full stop.

If Greg Bailey was telling even half the truth, Megan could be long gone by now. It wasn't hard for a girl to disappear, especially if she was resourceful and had some help. Jo saw her own growing despair mirrored in the faces of the others. They had four unsolved murders on the books, and until Megan came out of the woodwork chances of closing any of them were slim.

Jo had an awful feeling that Bailey's prediction might well turn out to be true, and his sister would be found, weeks or months from now, and what had really happened to Harry Ferman, and her parents, and Xan Do, might die a secret with her.

Chapter 17

With little else to follow up on, Jo left to fetch Theo. She considered popping around to her brother's house with some sort of peace offering, then changed her mind. Funny enough, it wasn't the thought of facing either Paul or Amelia that made her decide against it, but the kids. They'd never seen her behave the way she had after lunch the day before. She wasn't a 'cool aunt', but she'd always prided herself on projecting to them her best side – the capable, professional woman the public and they could rely on. She remembered fondly that between the ages of seven and eight, Will had said he wanted to join the police himself to be like her – he even had a pretend uniform that he asked his parents to iron, complete with plastic hand-cuffs. And Emma, just last year, had come to Jo rather than her own mother to ask for advice about the pill. But as they became more worldly, that sort of façade couldn't last. And her own behaviour hadn't maintained it terribly well. Now she was the struggling mum who lost her shit and stormed out over the smallest thing. *Auntie Jo the fuck-up.*

At home, she ran a bath for Theo, donned her dressing gown, and spent a happy quarter-hour entertaining him, topping up the water as it cooled. He loved bath-time, and watched her intently as she blew soap bubbles for him to swat and burst. She wondered though, when the time would come that his needs became more complex than simple games, than food and warmth, and even love. A time when he too came to see her for what she really was, rather than just what he needed her to be? A day when she ceased to be infallible and became a source of embarrassment, or even pain? It would come, and she doubted she'd be ready. As soon as he realised what fathers were, or shortly after, he'd ask about his own. And how could she ever be ready with an answer that wasn't just another lie, by omission or otherwise?

The bubble mixture ran out. She pulled the plug, and wrapped Theo in a towel as the water sucked through the drain. In the bedroom, his eyes were owlish and wide, like a nocturnal creature entering its element. But as she massaged coconut oil into his perfect skin, his comically long lashes began to flutter. She had to cajole him from sleep to make him finish his milk.

Afterwards, as he slept, she called a number she had avoided for months.

'Didn't expect to hear from you,' Lucas said. His voice wasn't slurred, but it was utterly without brightness.

'I'm afraid it's a professional call,' she said. 'I need to ask you about your visit to the Three Crowns last week.'

'Oh,' he said. 'You heard.'

'I heard.'

'I think I may have broken a glass or something,' said Lucas. 'Cut my hand.'

'It's not that I'm worried about,' said Jo. 'Did you go to Harry's house, too?'

'Did he tell you?' He sounded morose. 'I should go and apologise.'

He doesn't know. How can he not know? Jo's voice cracked. 'He's dead, Luke.'

There was a pause on the line. 'What?'

'He was murdered, a few days ago.'

'I don't watch the news,' said Luke. 'What happened?'

Jo hardly had the energy to explain it all. 'We don't know. Someone attacked him in his home.'

Again, it seemed to take him a few seconds to process. 'He didn't answer the door,' said Lucas. 'I guessed you'd told him not to.'

'I didn't even think you'd go around there,' said Jo. 'Maybe he wasn't in.'

'He was,' said Lucas. 'I saw someone moving inside.' He paused. 'Are *you* okay?'

He said it in the way he always had, and she could almost feel the comfort of his thumbs kneading the knots from her neck, as he had on many an evening when they were together.

'I'm fine,' she said.

'Are you in trouble because of me?'

'No,' she said. 'It's just bad luck.'

'If you want, I could come by the station tomorrow,' he said. 'Clear things up. Maybe we could grab a coffee afterwards.'

There was no mistaking the vain hope in his voice – she knew him too well. On the baby monitor, Theo made a brief distressed cry from his cot. She wondered briefly if babies dreamed, and if so, what neuroses could possibly haunt their sleep?

'I don't think that would be a good idea,' she said.

TUESDAY, 22ND APRIL

'We've got a DNA match, Jo,' said Carrick. Though he looked shattered, a week's worth of stubble across his jaw, her boss's eyes were gleaming. He and Heidi were in the DCI's office, but there was no sign of Dimitriou or Reeves.

'For Bailey?'

'For an unknown,' said Carrick. 'The blood from the bedroom floor in Stanton St John matches a profile from an unsolved murder a couple of months ago in Manchester.'

Up north . . . Jo made the link to where Bailey claimed Megan was heading, then disregarded any significance. *Too vague.*

'Another gruesome one,' said Heidi. 'Fifty-eight-year-old male, throat cut, but with signs of torture first.'

Jo went to the desk, and looked at the open file where a crime scene photo was displayed. A man, in shorts and a charity sports vest, lying on his side in what looked like a warehouse. His head was curled against his chest, which was soaked through with blood, and it appeared his hands were tied behind his back.

'Who was he?'

'Christopher Putman,' said Carrick. 'Educational charity worker from Salford. Gay. He went out jogging and never came back. Partner reported him missing.'

'Where was the body?'

'In an abandoned industrial building a mile from his house. We've been in touch with Greater Manchester Police and the DI on the case is going to brief us.'

'You want me to head up and speak to him?'

Carrick glanced at her. 'George and Alice have already set off,' he said.

Jo felt the news like a punch to the gut. 'Don't you want a DS there too?'

'It's just intelligence gathering,' said Carrick. 'I'd rather you stayed here.' *You mean because I'm tied here*, thought Jo.

'We've got someone from child services coming in shortly,' said Heidi. 'They're bringing the files on Megan Bailey.'

Jo tried to put her disappointment aside. Carrick was probably right – the reconnaissance trip was unlikely to reveal anything new. Plus, the Stanton St John murders were Dimi's chance to prove himself.

'We should look into drug networks with links between Manchester and Oxford,' she said to Heidi. 'Maybe start with known associates of the Matthis family.'

'Got it,' said Heidi.

At her desk, Jo opened the files from Greater Manchester Police, as well as an online search. The first result appeared to be a follow-up piece in the *Manchester Evening News*. It was accompanied by an image of Christopher Putman, sitting astride a bike with a number on his chest. The headline was 'Killing Continues To Mystify Cops'. She read the text below.

Police are appealing again for information relating to the brutal murder of local man Christopher Putman. Mr Putman, 58, from Lark Street, Salford, was found dead by a disused section of the Stretford Canal. According to Mr Matthew Benn, the partner of the deceased, Mr Putman left the home they shared in the early hours of April 16th for a run, but did not return. A search was carried out along Mr Putman's known running route, yielding nothing, but police dogs working with surveyors on the site found his body the following day in an abandoned building near the channel. Police are keeping an open mind about the motive for the attack, but believe it might have been premeditated, and possibly a homophobic hate crime. They have advised the public to be cautious.

The article ended with a number the public could call anonymously.

Jo turned her attention towards the police files themselves, beginning by watching a recording of an interview with Putman's partner. It made for harrowing viewing. He was being supported by a woman identified as his sister, and there were frequent pauses as he broke down. They'd been together for seventeen years, and he knew of no reason why anyone would harm his beloved. A keen amateur triathlete, Chris was 'the kindest man in the world', who'd never even been in a fight. He had no addiction issues, though suffered from bouts of depression. There were no long-standing grudges, and they were planning to marry that September. There were, Benn said, no money problems – Putman was soon to have retired, having spent the later part of his career as a special needs teacher and then a consultant for an educational advisory charity. Benn himself was still a working paramedic.

The rest of the files, showing DI Sue Southam's investigation, seemed thorough, and concurred with the picture painted by Benn. Financial records revealed no anomalies, toxicology no adverse findings. The coroner listed death due to blood loss from the carotid artery, but two of the fingers on Putman's right hand showed nail injuries consistent with a tool like pliers, and one of his kneecaps was shattered. It appeared from bruising on the neck that he might have been partially strangled too.

Jo knew there were some sick people out there, but she found it tough to ascribe the attack to a drug-induced rage, or a mugging gone wrong. The killer hadn't even taken the watch from Putman's wrist. A hate crime, or sexual motive was a possibility, but as Heidi pointed out, the victim's genitals had been untouched. It felt to Jo that there was some method to the torture. The killer had wanted to extract something from his victim.

Her phone rang. An internal call.

'Jo, you've got a visitor,' said Nigel from the front desk.

God. Not Lucas. Not now. She'd been feeling guilty about the way she'd ended the call the night before.

'It's someone from the council,' added Nigel.

Jo rolled her eyes with relief.

'Thanks, Nige. Show them through.'

When, shortly after, she saw the face of the woman coming

towards her, it took her a moment to place it from five days before, on her own doorstep. She composed herself.

'Mrs Pritchard, wasn't it?' she said.

'Please, call me Annabelle.'

The handshake was even colder and more limp than the last time. Pritchard looked apprehensive, and Jo guessed she'd recognised her too. She kept hold of the hand. 'I'm Sergeant Masters. Please, follow me.'

Jo had been planning to carry out the meeting in the comfort of the briefing room, but changed her mind, and led Pritchard instead through to the starkest of the interview rooms at the end of the corridor. She asked her visitor to take a seat, then offered her a drink. Pritchard opted quietly for water.

Shoe is on the other foot now, isn't it? thought Jo.

'Do you want a wingman?' asked Heidi, as Jo filled a glass with lukewarm water from the tap.

'Don't worry,' said Jo, with a grim smile. 'I can handle this solo.'

★　★　★

Pritchard had come armed with paperwork – all hard copy – in the same large document case that she'd carried at their previous meeting. Jo switched on the microphone device on the table, and introduced them both for the recording. Pritchard swallowed.

'Thank you for coming,' said Jo. 'As part of one of our investigations, we're trying to find Megan Bailey. We've been told, by her brother, that she was adopted into the Bailey family. Can you confirm that?'

Pritchard sifted through the case, and brought out some bound sheets.

'Megan was fostered by the Bailey family from the age of four, and formally adopted at the age of seven, in 2011.'

Jo made a note slowly, letting the silence stretch.

'And since that time, what level of contact have you had with Megan and the Bailey family?'

'Once the child is legally adopted, we're not required to monitor them for safeguarding,' said Pritchard. 'However, in Megan's case, she came to our attention again in 2016, when she was discovered to be pregnant.'

Jo, momentarily taken aback, did the calculations. 'At twelve.'

Pritchard tilted her head. 'Indeed. We interviewed her at the time, both in the presence of her parents, and separately. She couldn't disclose the identity of the father, claiming the sexual intercourse had happened at school when she had been drunk.'

When she was at St Cuthbert's. Xan Do?

'And the pregnancy was terminated?'

'It ended naturally before such steps had been fully considered.'

It was an odd choice of words, Jo thought. 'What would there be to consider? She was twelve.'

'I believe the family may have had certain religious convictions,' said Pritchard.

Jo recalled the solicitous priest. 'Poor girl,' she said. 'It must have been hard for her.'

'For the whole family, I imagine,' said Pritchard, entirely missing her point.

'Was anything reported to the police at the time?' said Jo.

'It was decided between the family, their legal team, and child services, to keep the matter confidential.'

'And did Megan have a say in that either?'

Pritchard looked taken aback. 'As I said, it was the family's wishes.'

'But did you carry out any sort of investigation into who the father might be?' asked Jo.

'It wasn't deemed an appropriate use of resources,' said Pritchard. 'Our concern was looking after Megan.'

'But it was *deemed* she was best served by remaining with the Bailey family?'

'Oh, yes. The most important thing for a girl like Megan is stability. And besides, she left the school, so the immediate welfare issue was resolved.'

'Tell me, what is a *girl like Megan?*' asked Jo. 'In your professional opinion.'

'From the reports and psychological profiles, very damaged,' said Pritchard. 'Sexually precocious and manipulative from a young age. Anger management problems, pathologies of demand avoidance, low scores on empathetic testing. Sadly, if the child comes into our care after three or four, the harm to their psychological wiring is already done.' She paused. 'That's why good parenting in the first couple of years is so important.'

Touché, thought Jo.

'So after the pregnancy, you began to monitor her again?'

'Yes,' said Pritchard. 'On a six-monthly basis. The family weren't happy, as you can imagine, and nor was Megan. She missed several of the appointments.'

'And what did you do in those circumstances?'

'There isn't much we can do.'

'But they were rescheduled?'

Pritchard coloured. 'In most cases, no. We don't have those sorts of resources. We're only obliged to make reasonable efforts at contact.'

'Surely a case like Megan's is a priority. Vulnerable girl, problems with alcohol and later drugs. Sexually precocious. Doesn't something like that come top of the list when it comes to dishing out "resources".' *As opposed to struggling mums who leave their baby in the car for seven minutes.*

'We're battling cuts, just like the police,' said Pritchard. 'And I'm sorry to say there are much more extreme cases to deal with, in which lives are in immediate danger.'

Jo nodded. 'Oh, I understand. We're dealing with four lives that have been quite severely endangered in the last week. And Megan links them all. I can't help wonder, if you'd been doing your job differently, less box-ticking and buck-passing . . . might they still be alive?'

The temperature in Pritchard's glare was sub-zero. 'It's easy to point the finger of blame,' she said. 'I suppose all we can do now is try to find her.'

Jo could have tormented Pritchard a little more, but she'd made the woman squirm for long enough. For all her weasel words about resources, Jo knew she wasn't lying about the cuts. Taking kids into care and looking after them was always fraught, always rushed and subject to reversals, and rarely straightforward. She'd had to hold back a drunk and screaming mother herself once, as a constable, while an emergency duty team lifted a baby from a cot and took it away to what they deemed a safer environment. She also knew the outcomes for kids taken into care. The prison, substance abuse, and suicide statistics were grim reading.

'Have you any idea where she might be?' asked Pritchard.

'The only lead at the moment – and it's tenuous – is "up north",' said Jo.

'Interesting you should say that,' said Pritchard, sifting through her piles of paperwork again. 'I'm pretty sure she was originally from the Manchester area.'

Jo felt a tingle of electricity up her spine. It might be nothing, but first the DNA link to the gruesome murder, and now Megan's own origins – both pointing to the same city. 'Would Megan have known that herself?'

'She's still too young to have access to any of her files, and it's unlikely Mr and Mrs Bailey would have been told any pertinent details about her past – not formally, anyway. They may have gleaned it from her accent, though the file notes she was still barely verbal when they first took her in. Her name, if it helps, was Megan Brown when she came to us.'

'Not a rare surname,' said Jo. 'How usual is it to move a child across the country?'

'It depends on the reasons for the removal from the bio-logical parents,' said Pritchard. 'Normally we try to rehome with close relatives, but if there aren't any, or if there's a safe-guarding issue, it's often decided a fresh start is best.'

'And do you have those details?' said Jo. 'About Megan's early years?'

Pritchard shook her head. 'We don't. It's dealt with at a regional level. You'd have to talk to child services in Manchester.'

'I will,' said Jo, standing up. 'Would you mind waiting here a few moments?'

Out of the interview room, she went to Heidi. 'Have you got a number for the inspector on the Putman case?'

Carrick overheard. 'For what, exactly?'

'Might be nothing, but it looks like Megan Bailey was taken into care in Manchester originally. Didn't Putman work with children? He might have known her.'

'It's a long shot. Twelve years ago. She was three when she went into care.'

'Worth checking out though,' said Jo.

Carrick checked his watch. 'Dimi will be there in half an hour . . .'

Jo understood where he was coming from. She knew full well that George wouldn't appreciate her sliding into his case again.

'Sir, it'll take two minutes. One question.'

'I agree, sir,' said Heidi. She passed the number across on a Post-it.

'One question,' said Carrick, sternly.

* * *

205

Two minutes later, Jo put the call on hold, struggling to control her breathing. DI Southam had been very helpful indeed. Carrick, alerted by her increasingly excited speech patterns through the course of the brief conversation, was standing right beside her desk, and Heidi was looking on intently from the other side of the work station.

'Well?' said Carrick.

Jo managed to her words out. 'I think it's a member of the family,' she said.

'Megan's family?'

Jo nodded. Was she jumping to conclusions? 'Christopher Putman worked at a fostering agency in Manchester before being a teacher.'

Carrick and Heidi linked eyes, confirming they too knew this was as significant as Jo did. She was speaking to herself as much as to them.

'Has to be her dad,' she said. 'The real one. He found out the agency responsible for Megan's rehoming, and then extracted the information. He travelled to Oxford . . . it wouldn't be *that* hard to find her if he knew her exact age. Just trawl the schools, social media. Even if it was twelve years, a dad would hardly forget his daughter's face.'

'Maybe,' said Carrick. 'Can we find out a list of the kids Putman rehomed?'

Jo got back on the phone with the Manchester inspector, who listened patiently to Jo's theory and said she'd find out more details and send them straight away. 'Do you want me to relay all this to your colleagues?' she asked.

Jo had forgotten about Dimitriou and Reeves in her rush of excitement. It was looking like a wasted trip for them. She told Southam not to worry, it was better coming from St Aldates. They agreed to keep the channels open, and Jo hung up.

Her mind was still reeling as she sank into her chair. The

implications, disordered and random, were cascading through her brain. *Harry, Xan Do, the Baileys, Putman* . . . Was this all the work of one person, trying to find his daughter?

'Who the fuck are we dealing with?'

Seeing the faces of the others across the squad room, she reckoned she was speaking for everyone.

Chapter 18

'You can do a lot of damage with one question,' joked Heidi.

Carrick was on the phone to Reeves and Dimitriou, filling them in on the latest. From the slightly strained pauses, Jo could imagine that George was having trouble following just how fast things were moving during his enforced absence on the M6.

She went back in to Annabelle Pritchard. There was no need to take her through the developing theory, so instead she simply thanked her for her time and offered to show her out. Pritchard seemed relieved to be dismissed. At the front desk, as she signed out on the register, Jo told her they'd be in touch if they needed anything else.

Pritchard shook her hand, and Jo was sure her skin was warmer to the touch.

'I hope you find her,' she said.

'We will,' said Jo, though quite what it was they *would* find, she had no idea. In all of this, Megan's own thought processes were still a stubborn mystery.

Time to find dad.

Jo logged on to the national computer, searching records pertaining to Manchester and the surrounding counties and the surname 'Brown' between the years 2002, twelve months prior to Megan Brown's birth, and 2006, for all cautions and convictions of males between the ages of fifteen and fifty. There were 3,014 entries.

Jo let out an 'Ugh!'

'Hard luck,' said Heidi, placing a cup of tea on her desk. 'Maybe narrow it down by violent crime. If you're right that this guy's responsible, he's not squeamish.'

It did seem justified given the nature of the recent spate of crimes in Oxford. Jo filtered again for crimes ranging from common assault to murder. The number dropped to seventy-four.

'Better.' Looking down the list, a number of names appeared several times, but there was no way to see quickly and easily the parental status of the suspect.

Leaving the window open, she went through to the Home Office's prisoner register. 'If it's the dad, and it's only happening now, maybe he was inside until recently.'

She searched for Browns between the ages of thirty and sixty released in the last twelve months, nationally, for any sentence length or conviction type. The records weren't always terribly reliable, so she didn't get her hopes up. There were forty hits. She copied the results, listed alphabetically, then compared them to the violent offenders from the Manchester area. There were several matching names, but many of the first names were common ones – John, David, Mark, Simon and William. After several minutes of jumping between both sets of records, she ascertained there were only two actual shared identities by date of birth: Simon Brown and Aljamain Brown.

Aljamain, arrested several times for aggravated burglary, was forty-six years old, released from Berwyn, a category C prison, in February. Arrested several times in Liverpool between 1995 and 2001, and then in Manchester in 2003, 2004, and then for the last time in 2012. Convicted of armed robbery and sentenced to sixteen years, but released after serving eight. On checking the arrest records, he had three known children. Sadly, the mugshot showed a black man, so that counted him out as Megan's biological father.

Simon looked more promising. He'd come out of Frankland, a notorious Category A, meant to house some of the UK's most dangerous inmates, all of whom were kept in single cells. Jo recalled a particularly nasty case a few years ago when two prisoners had disembowelled a third who'd been convicted of raping a child. Simon had a long list of drug offences to his name, culminating in the beating to death of another man in a fight in Bolton, in 2002. The sustained nature of the assault and the lack of remorse had led to a life sentence, with no chance of parole for fifteen years. He had served three more than that – his file saying he was had spent the final years of his time in prison dealing with addiction problems. Satisfied he was clean, he had been released on probation. There was, however, no record of any offspring.

Jo found the number for Simon Brown's probation officer at once, and made the call with middling hopes. The short conversation dashed them. Simon Brown had died two days after being released. Cause of death – an overdose of heroin leading to heart failure.

Jo sagged in her chair – ninety minutes of her day wasted. She could have gone back and expanded both searches, but it seemed pretty hopeless – conjecture built on conjecture, a house of cards ready to collapse. Maybe the biological father of Megan Bailey had never been arrested or imprisoned at all. Maybe he'd never even known about, or met, his daughter.

There was a good chance she was barking up the wrong tree altogether, and Megan Bailey's father had nothing to do with any of this.

* * *

DI Southam of Greater Manchester Police rang back less than quarter of an hour later.

'I spoke with Mr Putman's partner. The fostering agency Christopher Putman worked for is no longer functioning. It closed its doors six years ago.'

Another dead end.

'There must be records though.'

'Yes, they were subsumed by the city council. I've been in touch and they're digging out the relevant details. They said it might take a day or two, but I've impressed upon them that that won't be acceptable. I'll go down there myself if I have to.'

Jo was beginning to like Sue Southam.

'By the way, your colleagues have arrived. Sergeant Dimitriou wants to talk with you.'

'Put him on.'

'Jo,' said Dimitriou. 'You've been busy.' He spoke the final word as if it implied any number of unsavoury activities quite distinct from straightforward policework.

'It might go nowhere,' she replied, 'but if it's someone from Megan's past . . .'

'Some sort of avenging angel?' said Dimitriou.

He clearly wasn't convinced, but she was ready to fight her corner.

'I can't see any other link between a charity worker in Salford and the Baileys in a quiet Oxfordshire village. Can you?'

He was silent for a moment. 'We're going to look into possible drug links too,' he said. 'Check out the financials of Putman and his partner. Can't hurt to cover all bases, given we've made the trip.'

Again, a certain bitterness in his voice wasn't well disguised.

'Sure,' said Jo, though she thought the theory that Putman was involved in the drug trade sounded rather more fantastical than her own.

Heidi was on another call when she came off the phone, and she wore a puzzled look. 'And how old was the girl, roughly . . . uh-huh. Okay, keep her there. We'll send someone . . . maybe half an hour.' She ended the call. 'Jo, we might have something.'

'You've not found her?'

'Hard to tell. A woman's just been car-jacked at gunpoint near Woodstock. We've got officers from Kidlington on the scene. But get this – the victim said her attacker was with a teenage girl.'

Chapter 19

They reached the scene in less than twelve minutes after Heidi had put down the phone. Jo had done the talking while Andy Carrick drove, slicing through the Oxford traffic with the blues on, then opening up the Toyota as they hit the Woodstock Road. By the time they reached the A44 dual carriageway, he was doing close to a hundred and ten miles per hour. Jo trusted his auto skills, but did her best not to look at the road as she co-ordinated a response on the phone. First and foremost was to share the details of the victim's vehicle, a black Audi A3, this year's reg, with neighbouring forces, and to set the ANPR network to automatically alert them in the car passed one of the cameras in the area. A helicopter had already been scrambled to search from the air and an armed response from Thames Valley was on standby.

Two squad vehicles were parked at the side of the B-road and a single uniformed officer who Jo didn't recognise was directing traffic around the obstruction they were causing. Carrick followed the signals and parked in front of the other cars. Jo got out. A young Asian woman in smart work attire, maybe only late twenties, was standing by the side of the road on her phone, gesticulating and occasionally pulling at her brown hair as she spoke. Two more officers – Marquardt and Williams from St Aldates – were standing nearby. Jo approached, stepping over what looked like part of a car bumper lying at the edge of the tarmac.

'Ms Patel is speaking to her partner,' said Williams, a formidable female constable from St Aldates who towered a good five inches over Jo.

'Anything else on the description?'

'She's pretty shaken up,' replied Williams. 'You should speak to her directly.'

The woman had seen them and finished on her phone with an 'I love you too', then walked over.

Jo introduced herself and Carrick. 'Ms Patel?'

'Call me Saskia,' said the woman.

'Would you like to come and sit in the car?'

'My husband's coming to get me,' said Patel. 'He'll be here in about fifteen minutes.'

'That's fine,' said Jo. 'We won't keep you long.'

In the car, Andy took the back seat, while Jo spoke to Patel in the front, offering her a bottle of water. She looked very composed given her ordeal.

'Can you tell me exactly what happened?' said Jo.

The young woman took a gulp. 'I've already told the others. It all happened very fast.'

'If you wouldn't mind telling me,' said Jo gently.

'Okay.' Saskia's hand was shaking as she screwed the lid back on the bottle. 'I was driving along, and there was a man came running into the middle of the road. I slammed on the brakes. I knew there was something wrong straight away – he was wearing a balaclava. I put the car into reverse, but he just came charging forward, with a gun. I lost control and went into the hedge back there. He was screaming at me to get out. I froze.

216

I couldn't move at all. I tried to lock the door but he was quicker, and . . .' Patel put her hand to her mouth as her eyes moistened. 'I thought he was going to . . . I didn't know what he wanted . . .'

'Take your time,' said Jo. 'You're safe now.'

'He . . . he tried to drag me out, but I still had my seatbelt on. He was just screaming and screaming. I managed to get the seatbelt off, and I begged him not to hurt me. As soon as I was out of the car, he waved the gun, beckoning someone else, and this girl in a baggy coat came out from over there.' She pointed a little further along the street where there was a dusty layby.

'Can you describe her?' said Jo.

'Short, dirty blonde hair. They both looked like they hadn't washed for a while and the guy really stank. I offered them money, my phone, but he pointed the gun at me, and told her to get in.'

'How did she look?'

'A bit scared, to be honest. She was carrying a rucksack, like the sort of thing hikers have. It looked way too big for her. She said she was sorry.'

'To you?'

Patel nodded. 'I got the impression she really didn't want to be there.'

'But she got into the car?'

'Yes. So did he. They drove off really quickly.'

'In which direction?'

Patel pointed ahead on the road. 'That way.'

Away from the city.

On her phone, Jo fetched up the image of Megan Bailey from the family portrait at her parents' house. 'Look closely – do you think this was her?

Saskia squinted. 'Yes, that's her!'

'You're sure?'

'Absolutely. She's the girl from the news, isn't she? I can't believe I didn't recognise her before.'

'It's not that surprising given the stressful circumstances,' said Jo. 'And what about the man? Any distinguishing features?'

'He was wearing the balaclava,' said Patel. 'He wasn't particularly tall though.'

'Build?'

'Medium – I guess. Not skinny. Not fat.'

'Accent?'

'Northern, I think. English though.'

'Could you be more specific?'

'Not really. I've got family in Bradford. Maybe a bit like that? It all happened so fast.'

'You're doing brilliantly,' said Jo. 'What about his clothes?'

'Dark,' said Patel. 'Black, maybe. His trousers were cargo pants or jogging trousers. A dark hoodie. Big boots, like army boots. Oh, he had a bandage or something on his neck, right here.' She touched the side of her own neck.

Jo immediately thought of the blood from the shotgun blast, in the Baileys' bedroom.

'Okay, Saskia, we're nearly done. Can you tell us about the gun?'

'I don't know. A black one.'

'A handgun?' When Saskia looked confused, she clarified, 'As opposed to a shotgun?'

'Oh yes,' said Patel. She held her fingers about eight inches apart. 'Maybe like this.'

'Great,' said Jo. 'One more thing.' Patel nodded. 'I know you couldn't see the man's face, but did you get any idea of how old he might have been?'

Patel sighed thoughtfully. 'Young,' she said.

'What makes you say that?' asked Jo.

'I don't really know. People just move a certain way, don't they?'

'I suppose so,' said Jo. 'But when you say young, what do you mean?'

'I think he was younger than me. A grown-up though. Older than the girl.'

Jo, concealing her disappointment, looked at Carrick. 'Anything to add, boss?'

Carrick shook his head. 'Saskia, that was incredibly helpful. I'll talk to my colleagues and they'll stay with you until your husband arrives. It might be that we need to talk to you again, just to go over a few details, if that's all right?'

'Of course,' said Patel. 'I just want to go home.'

'Perfectly understandable. But if you remember anything else, even if it seems completely uninteresting, can you let us know? Sometimes little things come to mind later.'

'That girl?' said Patel. 'Wasn't she wanted in connection with a murder?'

Jo saw no reason to lie. 'Yes.'

Patel looked like she was going to be sick. 'So that man – the one with the gun . . .'

Jo put her hand across to touch Patel's. 'Don't worry. No one's going to hurt you now.'

* * *

The husband arrived a few minutes later, and they clung to each other for a good thirty seconds, before beginning a whispered conversation, with their foreheads pressed close together. As Carrick went to tell the uniforms that they could disperse, Jo walked further along the road to the layby from which Patel claimed Megan Bailey had emerged. Over a stile, there was a footpath, leading into woodland overgrown with nettles. Was this where Megan and the mystery man had been hiding? It was hard to imagine they'd walked along the side of the road itself, given there was no pavement and the many blind turns would make it a potentially hazardous place for pedestrians.

She was thinking of the description Saskia had given them. The rucksack and the boots sounded just like the hooded man she'd seen multiple times on the bookies' CCTV footage. Plus the fact it was a handgun that superficially matched the Xan Do murder weapon. It looked more than ever as if one person had carried out all of the killings.

Saskia's age estimate undermined the idea this was Megan's father, but Jo wasn't ready to jettison the theory just yet.

The more puzzling thing was Megan's behaviour. Maybe she wasn't such a willing participant to the unfolding carnage as they'd first believed. Or perhaps she was beginning to get cold feet in whatever larger game was being played.

Carrick called over to her. He was crossing the road towards her, pointing at the sky, where the helicopter was hovering in the distance. 'Chopper says they've found an abandoned car over there. We'll have to go this way.'

They climbed the stile and pushed their way through the undergrowth on the other side. The path led through a strip of woodland just a few metres wide. The air was thick with the smell of leaf mulch, and insects danced around them. She and Carrick emerged on the far side of the trees, crossing another stile at the edge of a field planted with willow saplings that reached to her eyeline. The path led straight along the side of the field, but they entered the willow, using the helicopter's position as a guide. There was no indication that anyone had come this way before.

After about thirty seconds, and what she guessed was eighty metres or so, they emerged from the wall of trees to find the car parked right in the middle of the crop, like it had been

220

dropped from above. It was a slightly battered Ford Focus with mud flecked up both wings.

'Odd place to park,' said Carrick, with typical understatement.

They passed around opposite sides of the car, peering inside. There was rubbish in the footwells – sweet wrappers, crisp packets, and empty beer cans, and the rear seat had a balled-up sleeping bag across it. The key remained in the ignition. Jo took a handkerchief from her pocket, leant through the open window and started the engine. It turned over a couple of times, but the fuel gauge was bottomed out.

'Empty,' she said. 'They had to dump it.'

Towards the rear, Jo could see now the route by which the car had reached its current resting place, cutting a six-foot-wide swathe through the willow. Maybe they'd made the decision quickly, pulling off the main road and ending up here. Carrick, at the back, said, 'Rear plate's gone.'

Jo checked the front and found it was the same.

Carrick popped the boot open.

'Anything?' she asked.

'Ammo box,' he said. Jo joined him and saw an empty card-board box with the name of a well-known sport-shooting manufacturer.

'Must've taken them from the Baileys' house,' she said.

'So he's still got the shotgun,' Carrick added.

He closed the boot and waved to the helicopter above, shielding his eyes from the sun with his free hand. The chopper turned and wheeled away.

'They won't get far,' he said.

Jo wanted to agree with him. If the road cameras didn't locate them in the stolen Audi soon, every force within thirty miles would be out looking. The question was, what were they planning? Keeping the shotgun set alarm bells ringing. Most murder weapons were dumped, because they were obvious hard evidence linking suspect to crime. If their guy was holding on to his, that spoke volumes about his mindset. Either he was supremely confident of not getting caught, or he wasn't intending on ever coming quietly.

Jo turned from the sun, blinking away bright spots, and was about to follow Andy Carrick back in the direction of the road when something caught her eye.

'Boss . . .'

He turned back towards her, and she pointed at the car's chassis, just beneath the rear windscreen.

Someone had written, likely using a fingertip, in the thick dust and dirt than covered the blue paint. The letters spelled, very clearly, a message.

HELP GREG. HE'S COMING.

JAMES

TWO WEEKS EARLIER

He arrived back at the squat just after eight am, entering through the back door. The house would once have been grand, but just about everything had been stripped away over time, even the carpets. He went up to his room on the third floor, passing a couple of open doors where familiar faces were going about the business of blocking out their wretched lives and slowly poisoning their bodies.

At the top of the stairs, the first thing he noticed was the padlock on his door was hanging loose. *What the fuck?* He considered turning and leaving, getting as far away as possible, but couldn't. All his stuff was in there.

So instead he crept to the door and looked inside. Dasha, or Desha, or whatever her fucking name was – a stick-thin junkie bitch he'd passed once or twice – was crouching over one of his bags. She must've heard his foot on a creaking floorboard, because she stood quickly, staggering a little for balance.

'What are you doing?' he asked.

He saw her pathetic brain ticking away, trying to find an excuse. Her mouth worked silently. He stepped into the room, and she backed away.

'It's all right,' he said. 'I don't mind.'

'What you making?' she said, nodding nervously at a pile of stuff in the corner. Wires, some tools, a circuit board, nails.

'Just a little project,' he said.

'I wasn't nicking.'

'Go on, off you trot, eh?'

He stood aside so she could leave. She looked at the gap he'd left for her.

'I promise I wasn't nicking. Really.'

'I know,' said James, with a smile. 'It's fine.'

She nodded, wringing her hands, and made for the door. On the way through, he caught her by the hair and yanked her backwards. With a foot behind her leg, he tripped her and dragged her to the ground in the middle of the room, straddling her body. She managed a single squeal before he had a blanket over her head. She tried to claw at his face, but he swatted the arm away, maintaining pressure over her mouth and nose with his other hand. She couldn't have weighed more than six stone, and it was like manhandling a child.

When she finally went limp, he lifted the blanket, tossing it to one side. Her eyes were still open, in a slightly confused stare. 'Your own fault, sweetheart,' he said. He was sweating, despite the cold in the room.

This hadn't been part of the plan.

But it wasn't as bad as it could have been. He lifted one of her brittle hands to check the nails. He didn't think she'd actually managed to scratch him, so there shouldn't be any of his DNA. He tried to think straight. An autopsy would likely be done – even on a worthless specimen like her – but they wouldn't rush. And judging by the traffic of waifs and strays coming through this place, there'd be a dozen other suspects when they eventually found her. Besides, no one here knew *his* name. One of two might give a description, but he couldn't imagine them getting anything resembling a true likeness.

He hauled the girl to the corner of the room, behind an old set of shelves, and sat her up out of sight of the door. Under her empty gaze, James loaded his things into his two bags – a holdall and a rucksack. He made sure he took every scrap of wire, every nail, every piece of gaffer tape. He rolled the blanket. On the way out, he fastened the padlock again and wiped off any prints. It would be a few days before the decomposition of Desha or Dasha began to penetrate the scrambled consciousnesses of those downstairs.

★　★　★

He tossed the blanket in a skip half a mile away, and the key to the lock in a bin outside a newsagent at the end of Canterbury Road, the place Megan appeared to be staying.

Her life was still a bit of a mystery to him. After their first encounter, he'd stayed well clear for a full two weeks. Getting close was too risky after that reaction. But for the last seven days he'd been back to Marsh Hill. For the first couple of days she didn't make an appearance at all, and the panic that gripped him was like nothing he'd felt before. To have come all this way, after all this time, only to have her slip through his fingers . . .

But on the third day she'd shown up, and since that time he'd worked out her movements, to and from 21 Canterbury Road each day. James still wasn't sure who the old guy was who lived there too, but he guessed it was her grandfather. He'd never met either of *his* grandparents, and presumed they were as fucked up as his mum and dad, so probably long dead.

The problem was getting Megan alone. He'd acquired a vehicle and if it came to it, he could probably grab her without too much fuss, but that might get them off on the wrong foot. And he *really* didn't need an audience. Ideally he'd have waited a few more days, but Desha or Dasha's unfortunate interference had complicated things. Getting out of Oxford was a priority. He had to speed things up.

She passed him on her normal route at 8.40, and he tracked her from the other side of the street. He'd rehearsed what to say, of course. Hundreds of times. As long as she didn't scream, or run – if she just looked long enough at his face, surely it would click into place.

She crossed a park – well, more of a grassy square – on the way to school. He watched her through the hedge, then matched his steps to her, planning to intercept her at the gate on the far side.

He was thirty metres away when a white car pulled up, loud hip hop playing through the open window. Megan clocked it, and stopped.

The car window rolled down.

'Not now,' said Megan. 'I'm busy.'

The door opened and a stringy Chinese guy climbed out. 'I asked nicely. Come on.'

'I'm going to school.'

The man laughed. 'So?'

'You heard her – she's busy,' said James, approaching.

She saw him, and looked suddenly alarmed.

The kid smiled. 'Who's this?'

'I . . . I don't know,' said Megan.

'Something funny?' James added.

The guy looked back to Megan, as if he'd dismissed James completely from his thoughts. 'You haven't been answering your phone.'

'And you can't take a hint,' said Megan.

James set down the rucksack, and walked towards the car. Now the kid reached inside to pick up something. James was quicker, and grabbed him by the shoulder and hauled him into the street, where he fell. Megan said 'No!'

James drove a boot into the kid's kidney, and he howled in pain. He thought about finishing it then, just kicking the guy's head in, but he forced himself to back away. His prone victim scrambled towards the car. Across the street, a couple of boys in school uniform were watching them.

'What the fuck are you looking at?'

They turned and walked away. The young man had started the engine. James managed to get one kick on the rear light as the car sped off.

'You shouldn't have done that,' said Megan.

James laughed. 'I'm not frightened of kids.'

'He's got dangerous friends.'

'Good for him.' Megan studied him. 'You don't remember me, do you?'

'I kicked you in the bollocks,' she said.

'Before that,' he said. 'From Manchester.'

In a second, her expression changed completely – he'd never seen the blood run from someone's face, but it did in that moment, like a white veil falling down her skin.

Chapter 20

Jo called the number Bailey had left them as they made their way back through the field, but he didn't answer. Next they tried Aiden Chalmers.

'We're looking for Greg,' said Jo.

'Sorry, detective – don't you think he deserves a little personal time?'

'We think he might be in danger.'

'Really? How so?'

She didn't think it wise to explain exactly the nature of the scrawled message on the back of the car in the field. 'All I can say is that it's a credible threat. Please, where is he?'

'He's staying with a friend,' said Chalmers. 'Have you tried calling him?'

'Of course. There was no answer. Do you have the friend's number?'

'No, but I have the address. Look, this is highly irregular . . .'

'He's probably ignoring our calls,' said Jo. 'Can you ring him now, right now? Tell him to stay where he is. And tell me the address. We'll send someone.'

Chalmers said he would, and gave her the address in Cumnor,

a village south-west of the city. It would probably take them twenty minutes to get there, but a squad car might be closer, so Jo called it in. She tried Greg again, and this time left a message.

'Greg, it's DS Jo Masters. Listen, it might be nothing, but we'd like you to stay where you are. Megan is still in the area, but she's with a dangerous individual who we think might intend to hurt you. Just hold tight.'

★ ★ ★

They drove with the sirens again, taking the back roads. She told herself, several times, that it was probably nothing. For Megan's companion to stay in the area seemed crazy, almost unhinged – he must have known half of Thames Valley would be out looking for him. Yet, she had to remind herself, he might be exactly that. Megan was clearly wary of him, going by the fact she was leaving messages in secret. Was she with him against her will somehow?

'What's he got against the son?' said Carrick.

'Greg was lying to us about something,' said Jo. 'All that stuff about giving her money to go away – it never made sense. No one hates their sibling that much.'

'And Megan cares about *him* enough to leave a warning.'

They crossed the A40, the main road running west out of Oxford. Still ten minutes out from Cumnor.

'You think he's kidnapped her?' said Jo.

'Would make sense if he was the estranged father,' said Carrick, 'but Saskia seemed to think he was young.'

He concentrated on the road, overtaking the car in front with a lurching manoeuvre that had Jo gripping the handle above the door.

'He was wearing a balaclava. She might have misjudged. Especially given the fear factor.'

At a crossroads, they met a squad car coming the other way, who waved Carrick ahead.

Cumnor was a country village bigger than Stanton St John, but much the same in terms of its inhabitants. They shot past the village pub, then the cricket club, before bouncing up a private track towards a clutch of four or five grand-looking Georgian houses. The one they were looking for was called 'Heron's Perch' and straight away Jo noticed Greg's Jaguar wasn't anywhere in sight. She was out of the car before the engine stopped, and strode towards the front door, where she knocked loudly.

A middle-aged woman in pearls and a cardigan came to the door, and behind her was a young man of about the same age as Bailey.

Jo showed her warrant card. 'I'm looking for Greg,' she said.

'I'm afraid he left about ninety minutes ago,' said the young man.

'Do you know where he went?'

'No. He didn't say.'

Jo didn't think he was lying, but pushed anyway, 'Are you sure? He's not in any trouble.'

The man shook his head. 'He got a call, and said he had to go.'

'How did he seem?'

'In a rush,' said the friend.

'Agitated?'

'I suppose so.'

That call must have come through about the same time as Saskia Patel was being dragged out of her car. 'Can you ring him now?' said Jo. 'We think he might be in some danger.'

The man nodded briskly, and took the phone from his pocket. After holding it to his ear for twenty seconds, he shook his head. 'He's not picking up.'

231

'Shit,' said Jo, earning a look of reproach from the boy's mother. 'If he calls back, tell him to go to the nearest police station.'

'God! Is everything all right?'

'I hope so,' said Jo. She jogged back towards the car to share the news with Carrick.

They sat for a few minutes side by side, going through the options. The most precise method would be to trace his phone via either the sim's GPS or the phone's own triangulation, but both would require a warrant. With the best will in the world, even if they invoked the emergency protocols, it would take twenty minutes. Carrick made the call anyway to the telecoms liaison unit, in order to put the wheels in motion. Jo meanwhile got in touch with Heidi to find Greg's vehicle details and to put an alert on the ANPR network in case his car turned up. It wouldn't give them a real-time location, but it would narrow things down considerably. To her surprise, Heidi rang back almost at once, and Jo put her on speaker.

'You've found him?'

'No, we've got a possible visual on the stolen Audi.'

'Fuck, where?'

'Ten minutes ago, outskirts of Banbury, northern carriageway.'

Banbury was about twenty miles from the car-jacking site. The time-frames added up.

'Why "possible"?' said Carrick. 'Didn't the cameras pick it up?'

'No, member of the public. Driver was behaving erratically. Mentioned the missing rear bumper.'

'That's our guy,' said Jo. 'We'll head that way now.'

'Heidi,' said Carrick. 'Send all available units in pursuit. And get surveillance units set up north of Banbury on the major routes. He's not getting far. We'll need a tactical firearms squad too.'

They drove at speed north, overtaking a couple of other

police vehicles on the way. *If he's making a run for it, he's got no chance*, thought Jo. With the whole of Thames Valley activated, there'd be close to a hundred patrol cars and several unmarked vehicles scouring the Banbury area like a giant net closing in. Her only hope was that they could take him alive, and no one else would get hurt.

They slowed as they reached the outskirts of the city. Jo kept checking her phone, and watching the in-car radio, expecting a call at any moment with a location. When none came, and the minutes ticked by, the adrenalin in her blood began to dull, only to be spiked again with the sudden realisation that it was almost five pm. She was due to pick Theo up in an hour. *Shit! Shit! Shit!* She went through a range of emotions, from panic to anger at her own stupidity, settling into a queasy sense of embarrassment and guilt. She asked Andy to stop the car so she could make a private call. He pulled over, beside a mobile burger van at the side of the road.

With the smell of grease hovering in the air, she called her sister-in-law. It was Paul who picked up the phone. 'Hey, sis. Amelia's in the shower. What's up?'

She took a deep breath. 'I know I said I'd never ask again, but I really need your help . . .'

He spoke quickly, before she had time to continue. 'You want us to get Theo?'

'Can you? Please? I'm in the middle of something really important.'

Her brother hesitated. 'Of course we will, but, Jo – this is what I was talking about. You'll always be in—' he stopped mid-flow. 'Look, forget it. It's not the time. Don't worry about Theo. Just do what you need to.'

'Thank you,' said Jo. 'It's been a crazy day, but it's going to be over soon.'

'I know it will,' said Paul. 'Be careful, all right?'

'You need to be somewhere else, don't you?' said Carrick, as she got back into the car. 'I'll drive you back.'

'Nope. All sorted.' She spoke brightly, but inside she felt torn apart. Twice in a week she wouldn't be there to hold her son.

'Jo, I spot liars for a living,' said Carrick. 'Talk to me.'

She dug her fingernails into her palms to stop herself welling up, and changed the subject. 'I bet he's ditched the vehicle somewhere.'

'I give the orders, remember,' said Carrick.

She really couldn't stop the tears, however hard she tried, so she just let them come. 'I can't fucking do this,' she said. 'I thought I could, but I can't.'

Carrick unbuckled his seatbelt, and reached across to the glove box, taking out a packet of tissues.

'You're doing a great job,' he said, handing her one.

She snatched at it, and rolled her eyes. 'How is *this* a great job? Look at me!'

'You're crying, for the first time since I've known you. Are you seriously ashamed of that?'

She wiped her nose. 'I'm not ashamed of crying. I'm ashamed of why I'm crying.'

'Which is?'

'Because I miss my son, Andy,' she said, and with the admission came another, uncontrollable flood of tears. 'And when I don't miss him, that's even worse, because I *should*. It's like I can't help fucking up his life, and he's only six months old. Because every time I try and do the right thing – to buy a fucking nappy, for fuck's sake – it turns out to be wrong.'

Carrick touched her hand. 'You're not . . . effing up anybody's life, apart from maybe your own. Give yourself a break.'

'You don't know what it's like,' she said. 'I'm on my own with him, and I know that's *my* fault, which makes it a real kick in the gut. There aren't enough hours in the day.'

234

'Actually,' said Carrick softly. 'I do know what it's like. Sort of, anyway.' Jo sniffed. His voice, she realised, was close to breaking, and if she wasn't mistaken, there were tears brewing in his own eyes.

'Andy?'

He breathed out a slow, shuddering breath. 'I haven't told anyone at the station, because . . . well, what's the flipping point? But Jasmillah left me, about five months ago, when you were on maternity leave.'

'Christ, Andy, why didn't you say?'

'There isn't much to say, is there? She's met someone else – I think she met him a long time ago and she was just waiting until the kids got older.'

She couldn't believe it. Jasmillah and Andy were as strong as couples came. At least they were going by the photographs Andy posted on social media. Lucas and she had even used to joke about it – they and their kids looked like something out a lifestyle catalogue.

'Where are they now?'

'The oldest with me, the youngest with her. It's a mess to be honest, but amicable enough.' He smiled briskly. 'I didn't even see it coming.'

Was this where Andy's anger had come from, when he'd kicked her out of the station? When he'd spoken of *idiotic* cops messing up their families? Jo had resented him shutting her out, but now it took on a quite different complexion.

He still had his hand on hers, and she folded it in hers. 'Look at us,' she said. 'So much for the thin blue line.'

The radio crackled and they pulled their hands apart.

'*Firearms crime in progress. Walton Street Cafe, Walton Street, Jericho. Tactical unit, please respond.*'

'*This is ARU Alpha. We're in Banbury. Confirm Walton Street, Oxford?*'

235

The dispatcher confirmed, and Jo and Carrick listened to the unfolding drama in a series of radio traffic broadcasts between patrol cars, the tactical unit, and the control centre.

'It's got to be him,' said Carrick. He swung the car out and turned one-eighty at the next roundabout. The armed response van shot past them.

'Why would he head back to Oxford?' said Jo.

'I've no idea.'

Carrick spoke to the control centre as he drove, instructing them to keep half a dozen vehicles in the Banbury area. They began to hit denser rush-hour traffic a couple of kilometres outside Oxford. Carrick pulled across on to the hard shoulder, wheels close to the ditch, still travelling at seventy.

Another call came in to Carrick's phone. It was Heidi.

'We've pinged Bailey's phone,' she said on speaker. 'It looks like he's at the site of the shooting in Jericho. Waiting for confirmation from the ground.'

Carrick slammed a hand on the wheel. 'Dammit!'

Chapter 21

By the time they reached Jericho, a quarter of an hour later, they couldn't even get close to the site of the shooting. Walton Street was busy at the best of times, but at 17.30 it was completely clogged with traffic. Ahead, a couple of hundred metres up the road, the competing lights of several squad cars looked like a rave in progress. Carrick parked his own vehicle and they went on foot, passing many people who'd got out of their vehicles to complain, or those who'd emerged from nearby houses and businesses to see what was going on. A cordon was being set up twenty metres from the front of the café. Several officers, some armed, were keeping people back. Dozens of mobile phones were raised, recording the scene for kicks and posterity.

Jo took it in. An entire front window of the café had been shattered. Chairs and tables lay on their sides inside and out. Among the glass fragments were several pools of blood, the largest of which had trailed down the pavement, and was trickling into a drain. Inside the café, a paramedic was tending to an elderly man who was bleeding from his head, while two uniformed officers were chatting to a shaken waitress, her white apron covered in more blood.

Jo and Carrick made their way through the cordon, showing their ID.

'Is that the casualty?' she asked.

'No,' said the officer. 'He got hit with broken glass.' He pointed up the road. 'Ambulance managed to get the other guy out already. Didn't look good.'

'Do you have an ID on the victim.'

'No, ma'am. Young fella.'

Jo walked towards the café entrance, stepping over the channel of blood, still shockingly fresh and red. She counted three spent cartridges on the ground.

Inside, the café tables were still covered with half-eaten plates and glasses, of which several had spilled. Jo had actually come here once, she remembered, with Lucas in happier times. They'd sat just inside the window that lay in pieces on the ground. She pushed the memory away as a Middle Eastern man, bald and moustachioed, came towards them, his white shirt filthy and sweat-stained. He was carrying a broom, gripping it like a weapon with both hands.

'Are you the owner?' asked Jo.

He nodded. 'What am I going to do?'

'Can you tell me what happened?'

'I was in the back. I hear the shots, then yelling and screams. By the time I come through, it is done. Everybody running. But the boy, he is lying there.' He threw out a hand, theatrically, towards the blood.

'Did you see the shooter?'

'No, no – but Aylin did. My daughter.'

Jo nodded towards the girl in the apron. 'That's her?'

'Yes. She was so close! Praise be to God she is okay!'

Jo walked to where the officer – Constable Paulo Bianchi – was talking to the witness and taking notes.

'Ma'am,' he said.

'What've we got?'

Bianchi, who Jo had always liked, consulted his pocket book. 'Miss Yilidrim was serving outside when a man in black clothes and a balaclava pulled up in a black car, climbed out, and fired five or six shots at the man sitting at one of the tables. He then took a bag from the victim and drove away, heading north. She tried to administer first aid until the ambulance arrived. Before he lost consciousness, he said his name was Greg.'

Not that there had ever been much doubt.

Jo turned to the waitress. 'Aylin, did you see anyone else in the car with the gunman?'

'I didn't see. I think he was on his own.'

'And did the gunman speak to the victim at all?'

She shook her head. 'Not that I heard. He just started shooting.'

Jo thanked her. Back in front of the café, she was aware more than ever of the camera-phones pointed in her direction. It wouldn't be long until Emma and Will, and all her extended family, saw the images. She should text as soon as possible, and let them know she was okay.

'It had to be a planned meeting if he knew where to find Bailey,' Carrick muttered to her.

'So why shoot him? It doesn't sound like they even argued.'

'Can you go to the hospital?' said Carrick. 'We need to speak to Greg if he pulls through.'

'Sure. Doesn't sound positive though. Christ, Andy – what sort of person just opens fire in the middle of town? It's insane.'

'I agree it's brazen,' said Andy, 'but I don't think we're dealing with someone out of control. Think about it. He must have switched the plates on the Audi, or avoided the cameras on a circuitous route. There are a half a dozen between here and . . .' He turned to one side, and laughed bitterly. 'You know what? I wouldn't even be surprised if he made the call about Banbury in the first place.'

Jo caught his meaning. 'To distract us?'

Carrick nodded, and rubbed his brow. 'And we fell for it hook, line and sinker. Emptied Oxford of personnel, and the armed response.'

It was only conjecture, but it had the ring of truth. *We left Greg Bailey like a sitting duck.*

'I'll report back from the hospital,' she said.

Carrick offered his car, given it was furthest from the mad congestion around the scene. As she was walking past the scene again, Bianchi approached.

'Ma'am – you'll want this. Pretty sure it's the vic's phone.' He offered her a mobile, a new model with a cracked screen. 'We found it on the ground.'

She took it, and hit the home button. An image appeared of Greg Bailey, mid-charge, with a rugby ball under his arm. Despite her antipathy towards him, the sight of him very much alive and untroubled made her unexpectedly sad. 'Yeah, it's his. Thanks.'

★ ★ ★

Jo's most recent visits to the Radcliffe Infirmary had been with Theo after the accident, but she'd spent a lot of time in hospitals professionally. They were part of the job. Either to speak to the victims of violence, or those who perpetrated it. Drunk-drivers who'd crashed, neighbours whose disagreements had escalated into physical conflict, kids who'd thought it was a good idea to take a knife into school and had ended up on the receiving end of the blade. There was a lot of waiting around, drinking bad coffee and watching that day's unfortunates being confronted with their vulnerability and mortality.

The reception desk found someone to talk to her quickly, and she was directed to a family liaison room. The greying man who met her there, dressed in an open white coat over a suit, was of East Asian heritage and introduced himself as Dr Wilson Kim.

'How is he?' asked Jo, straight away.

'Still in surgery,' said Kim. 'He's stable at the moment. Does he have family?'

Jo hesitated. *Talk about complicated!* 'Not really.'

'There may be difficult decisions to be made,' said Kim. 'It looks like he's been shot three times. Once in the forearm, a second clipped the femoral artery near his groin. We've pretty much controlled the bleeding there. But there was a third entry wound . . .' Here, Kim pointed to his lower abdomen, halfway to the right hip. 'It looks like the bullet hit his pelvis and sheared, with fragments shredding part of his lower intestine and spinal column. He's got some significant internal bleeding.'

'Do you think he'll pull through?'

'I'd say he's got a good chance, but it'll be a long road to recovery. Is there anyone close to him? We can have someone ready to explain things when he wakes up, but it sometimes helps to see a familiar face.'

Jo thought of Chalmers, and of the friend from Cumnor, whose name she didn't even know.

'I can find someone,' she said. 'How long until he's out of surgery?'

'I'm going to guess four hours at least, but it could be longer. We'll keep him under afterwards though.'

'So there's no chance of speaking to him today?'

'You might never speak to him at all,' said Kim bluntly. 'Check in with us in the morning.'

★　★　★

By the time Jo returned to pick up Carrick the police had drawn in the cordon and got the traffic moving again on a single lane outside the café, and the unfortunate owner and his daughter had begun the clean-up. Nothing had come through on the radio about the black Audi, or the shooter, and though Jo told herself it couldn't be long, she didn't really believe it any more. Whoever was doing this was making careful calculations. If the killing spree had been entirely the work of one man – and one of the firearms guys had confirmed the shells were indeed nine mm just like those used to kill Xan Do – their suspect had been on the run for over a week already and by best guesses hadn't been more than ten miles from the St Aldates police station at any point. Worse still, they didn't even have an ID to start the search other than a youngish, average height man. *We're working blind here..*

As she and Andy drove back towards the station, she looked at the faces of the men in the street. He could be any one of hundreds and she wouldn't know. Of course, the likelihood was that he, and Megan, were far away by now. If they were sensible, they would have abandoned the Audi somewhere and switched vehicles, making the possibility of finding them soon even slimmer.

Heidi was getting ready to leave for the day. She told them that Dimitriou and Reeves were staying up in Manchester for the night, hoping to speak to someone from the council the following day about Megan Bailey's past prior to Oxford. Otherwise, they faced the same frustrations as Jo and the team at St Aldates.

Just waiting for his next move . . .

On walking past Heidi's desk, Jo noticed a copy of the warrant for Bailey's phone. It reminded her of the phone that she had failed to leave at the hospital, and an idea suddenly occurred. She picked up the paper.

'What level of tap have we got on Bailey's phone?'

Heidi was slipping on her coat. 'The emergency warrant gives us full access.'

Jo fished out the phone. 'Bianchi found it at the scene.' She explained that she had meant to give it to Greg.

'But you forgot?' said Carrick, joining them.

'Genuinely, I did,' said Jo. 'But now we have it . . .'

Carrick picked up his own phone and Jo heard him speaking with the telecoms support team.

Ten minutes later, the access code of Greg Bailey's phone had been remotely altered to four zeros and they were in. Jo went straight to the messages. She got the impression Carrick was holding his breath just like her.

The top message was from Chalmers, and read: **'Greg, the police want to talk to you. Where are you? Call me.'** It was the only message from the solicitor.

Then, below, from Rohan Kirk: **'Mate, the police were here! They're worried about you!'** Other messages in the chain above seemed to pertain to the practicalities of coming to stay at his friend's place in Cumnor.

But below that, waiting like a treasure chest to be opened, was a series of messages from an unknown number.

Jo opened the chain. There were only three messages, and they were all from Greg himself, that day.

'I'm going to leave in five minutes.'

Nine minutes before: **'I'm here. Where are you?'**

And half an hour prior: **'I've got it.'**

'You think those are to his sister?' said Carrick.

'Or the man who shot him,' said Jo. 'They'd arranged to meet.'

'But no messages from the other party,' noted her boss, 'unless he deleted them.'

'But we can get them, right?' said Jo.

'Telecoms can tell us,' said Carrick.

'If he deleted them, he's got something to hide' said Jo.

'What was in the bag the shooter took?' said Carrick, as he redialled. 'Money? Drugs?'

'Could be,' said Jo. 'Blake said the drugs at the Baileys' house were put there by Xan with Megan's knowledge. But if Greg knew Xan, it could have been the three of them involved.'

'And then they fell out somehow?' said Carrick.

'Sounds plausible. Until he wakes up we're guessing.'

Carrick began to speak to the telecoms team once more, but from his face and disappointed questions, she knew the answer wasn't what they wanted. He finished the call. 'They don't hold the information at the service provider,' he said, 'but they might be able to extract deleted messages from the physical phone. It'll take time.'

'Doesn't everything?' said Jo. 'We can get the phone couriered over to the tech lot.'

'I'll handle it,' said Carrick. He looked deflated. 'You should get out of here. It's going to be a busy one tomorrow.'

This time, Jo didn't put up a fight. Unless there was a sighting of the gunman or Megan, there was nothing else to be done. But more importantly, she needed to get to Theo. She gathered her things.

'Hey, Andy,' she said. 'Thanks for earlier. It meant a lot.'

'No problem,' he said. She noticed that his eyes lingered for a split-second on the family photo on his desk, so she looked away.

Chapter 22

Jo was expecting an inquisition when she got to her brother's, but instead Paul gave her a hug that caught her completely by surprise. 'We saw the news,' he said.

'We saw *you*!' called Emma, from behind him. She emerged from the living room with Theo in her arms. He reached out when he saw Jo, and she took him and buried her nose in the wispy hairs on top of his head. For a few seconds, with her eyes closed, lips against his warmth and the scent of him in her nostrils, she was in her own world, completely untouchable.

'Is someone dead?' said Will.

The moment passed. Her nephew was wide-eyed.

'Will!' snapped Paul. 'That's not appropriate.'

Jo bounced Theo up and down, shared a look with her brother, and said, 'The man who was shot is in hospital, and he's very ill.'

'Have you caught the person who did it?' said Will.

'No, but we will.'

'Kids, give us a minute,' said Paul.

'I hope you're not talking to *me*,' said Emma, glaring in mock outrage.

'Sorry,' said Jo's brother, shooting her a hard stare in return. 'Kids, and any other financial dependants – please go somewhere else for a moment.'

As Emma and Will retreated, Paul looked serious, and ready to embark on a lecture, so Jo got in first.

'I can't face an argument,' she said, 'but I want you to know I'm going to make changes. I really am. As soon as this case is cleared, I'm going to sit down with HR—'

'Jo, stop,' said Paul. 'That's not what I was going to say.'

'Oh . . . right,' she replied.

Paul put his hands in his pockets, and looked at her with a contrite expression. 'I know I gave you a hard time earlier, and on Sunday. That was wrong. Amelia and I spoke afterwards, and we get it.'

'Get what?'

'You. Your job. How hard it must be, *all the time*. And, well . . . we wanted to run something by you.'

Jo felt uneasy. She had no idea what was coming, but she was scared Paul was about the ask her to come and live with them.

'We didn't want to say anything before, but Amelia's quit her job.'

'No way!' said Jo. Amelia had only recently returned to working as a teacher. 'Why?'

'The politics, the workload, the pay . . . you name it. About the only thing she does like are the kids, and they sound dreadful, in my opinion. '

'What's she going to do instead? Yoga and long lunches?'

'That's just it – she's going to retrain as a childminder.'

'Are you serious. You're going to run a crèche?'

Paul laughed. 'Hey! No! If I had my way, they'd all be contained in the garage.'

Jo suddenly understood what he was getting at, and found herself lost for words.

'You wouldn't have to use her,' continued her brother, 'but we want you to consider it as an option. Obviously, no mates rates would apply, and Theo would have to pull his weight like all the others . . .'

'I couldn't . . .' said Jo, managing to speak, but still flummoxed.

'Yes, you *really* could,' said Paul. 'Amelia would love it, obviously. And it would great for Emma and Will too. And me. I love the little guy. Plus, we could be more flexible than a nursery.'

'I know,' said Jo, 'but it's such a big thing. A big decision. We're family, and—'

'Exactly,' said Paul. 'We *are* family, and sometimes we don't act like it. Don't take this the wrong way, but I don't feel I know you any more.'

'Sadly, I'm just the same as always,' said Jo. 'Just more hormonal.'

'Promise me you'll think about it.'

'Of course I will,' said Jo, emotions threatening to get the better of her again. 'I'm not going to cry, you know.'

'I wouldn't expect anything less from my tough sister,' said Paul.

WEDNESDAY, 23RD APRIL

The evening brought no developments. Megan and her mystery companion had simply disappeared off the face of the earth. Whoever he was, the man in the balaclava seemed able to step onto centre stage in an explosion of sparks and noise, then vanish into the smoke.

But somehow, despite the day's drama, repeated on the evening news, and despite the fact their chief suspect was armed and dangerous and on the run, Jo slept like she hadn't slept in months. It was as if some magic spell had been cast over her bedroom, enveloping both herself and Theo in an enchanted slumber. She woke a few minutes before her alarm, and watched him sleeping through the cot bars beside her, a picture of perfect innocence, until his eyelids began to flicker with whatever dreams a baby was capable of having. She clung to the moment as long as she could, but as he surfaced to consciousness, the realities of life outside crept into their cocoon as surely as the light seeping around the edges of the blackout blind.

'Morning, sweetheart,' she whispered.

He answered with a beaming smile, and kicked violently inside his sleeping suit like he wanted to burst free and face the day.

'Let's go get 'em,' said Jo.

She checked her phone. No updates. She fired off messages to both Andy and Heidi. While she prepared Theo's porridge, they both replied that there was nothing to report.

Fighting her frustration and impatience, Jo was still considering her brother and sister-in-law's offer as she dropped Theo at nursery. On the face of it, it seemed too good to be true, but still her mind naturally went to the negatives. Why complicate their personal relationship by introducing a professional one? What if, like this very week, she imposed upon them too much? And she was honest enough to acknowledge there was a third, deeper concern. Theo would be spending many, many hours with Amelia. It would only be natural that he would grow fond of his aunt. At such an impressionable age, he might even get confused . . .

As if to prove her point, he went to Suzie at Little Steps

wearing a grin, and didn't even look back at Jo. 'Will it be your sister doing pick-up again?' asked the carer.

'No,' said Jo firmly. 'It will be me.'

★ ★ ★

Heidi was already at her desk, face leaning close to the screen, a finger on her mouse. With every click, a new selection of images appeared in a three-by-four grid. As Jo approached she realised they were photos from the number-plate recognition database. 'What are you doing?'

'Searching for a needle in a haystack,' said Heidi. She leant back and flexed her neck. 'I contacted the DVLA and they gave me the licence plate that corresponds to the VIN number on the Ford Focus you found abandoned. I thought, if the Audi's wearing the Focus plates, I could track it using them. But it looks like he's still one step ahead. The Focus plates haven't been seen by any camera for three months, meaning he'd likely been using false plates on the Focus too and he transferred those to the Audi.'

'Okay . . .' said Jo.

'Luckily, I'm stubborn,' said Heidi. 'A patrol found the gate where our man drove the Ford Focus into that field. It's off a farm track and, depending on which end he entered, there are two cameras within quarter of a mile. I'm going over both in the three-hour window before the car-jacking of the Audi, looking for the Focus by sight rather than plates. Once I've found the plates it had on, then we *might* be able to find the Audi, if it's currently wearing the same ones.'

Jo looked at her with bewilderment. 'And if he didn't go past the cameras in the Focus?'

'Then I may throw this computer through the window,' said Heidi. 'Heck! I can't sit here doing nothing.'

Jo looked to Carrick's office. His door was open, and his jacket was on the back of his chair.

'Where's the gaffer?'

'Briefing room,' said Heidi, 'with Aiden Chalmers.'

Bailey's solicitor. 'What's he doing here?'

'Being nosy, probably. He only arrived a couple of minutes ago.'

Intrigued, Jo dumped her bag and went through.

Chalmers was sitting with Andy Carrick, nursing a hot drink. When she walked through the door, he looked at her with a doleful expression, his skin pale. Her first thought was that there'd been bad news from the hospital.

'Is Greg okay?'

'He's regained consciousness,' said Chalmers, 'but he's still heavily sedated.'

'Well, that's good news,' said Jo. 'So what are we doing for you?'

'Mr Chalmers was here for an update,' said Carrick. 'I've told him we still aren't sure who it is that carried out the attack.'

Chalmers cleared his throat. 'Actually, I may have some information.'

'Oh yes?' said Jo.

'It's strictly confidential.'

Jo wasn't sure what that meant in the context, but she slipped into a chair opposite. 'Go on.'

'I received a call, yesterday . . . after I spoke to you,' Chalmers began. 'Gregory had been into the local branch of Coutts. His parents banked there, as does he. He emptied his current account, and tried to withdraw funds from a secondary account also, but it would have required a co-signature from his father. They refused.'

'And they called you?'

'They found it suspicious, and they were trying to get hold

of Mr Bailey senior. I'm listed as a contact. They were unaware of his murder.'

Jo shared a look with Carrick. *That clarifies what was in the bag, then.*

'So why are you telling us this now?'

Chalmers sighed. 'Mark Bailey was my friend as well as my client. I've been looking after that family's interests since before that girl even came on the scene. They are – they were – good people. I don't want to see anyone else getting hurt. I owe Gregory's parents that much.'

'That's very noble,' said Jo, trying not to sound too scornful. 'But have you any idea why Greg might be paying off either his sister or the person who shot him?'

Chalmers shook his head and looked her right in the eye.

'I wish I did, detective. I wish I did.'

'At the moment,' Carrick said, 'Greg might be our only chance of a breakthrough. He could unlock the whole thing.'

Jo addressed the solicitor. 'You know we're going to need to talk to him, as soon as he's up to it?'

'So I understand. I'd like to be there when you do.'

To help or hinder? Jo wondered.

★ ★ ★

The breakthrough came a little after ten in the morning, but it wasn't from Greg Bailey. Heidi was still looking through thousands of vehicle images when her phone rang. She answered, then said, 'Hold on,' before putting the caller on speaker. 'Boss, Dimi's on.'

Carrick came out of his office. 'Go on, George. We're all listening.'

'We've found him,' said Dimitriou triumphantly. 'James Brown, D.O.B. oh-three, oh-six, ninety-eight. Brother of Megan Brown.'

'A brother?' said Jo. What did that make him? Twenty-two? It matched the description from Saskia Patel.

'That's right. Both children were removed from their mother in 2007 when Megan was three, and James was nine. The fostering agency where Putman worked decided it was in their interests to separate them. Alice is still working through the files, but we'll scan what we can and forward it.'

'That's great work, George,' said Carrick. 'Anything on his recent movements or place of abode?'

'Not yet,' said Dimi. 'Some of the materials are pre-digital, and the filing system here would bring Heidi come out in hives. James was placed in a number of foster homes, but it looks like none of them worked out. He was a messed-up kid. Finally went missing from the system in 2015, aged seventeen. He must have a record though – he was first arrested at thirteen for going after a female teaching assistant with a pair of scissors.'

'What about the birth parents?' said Jo.

'Mum died from an overdose the night the kids were taken in. We've got the report from the emergency team who responded. It's a grim read, trust me. The kids were known to social services already, because of mum's history as a sex worker. Dad wasn't recorded, but given her line of work, it's anyone's guess.'

'Send everything through,' said Carrick. 'We'll check records for James.'

'Gotcha, boss,' said Dimitriou, before ending the call.

'Nothing like a bit of misery to bring the best out of George,' said Heidi.

'Those poor bloody kids,' said Carrick. 'Jo, bring up the records.'

He stood at her back as she opened up the national computer database, searching by James Brown's name and date of birth. Unsurprisingly, there was only a single result.

'That's our guy,' muttered Carrick, as they looked at a mugshot from 2016. James Brown's face was gaunt and defiant, his eyes staring straight down the lens, as if he wanted to throw himself at the officer unfortunate enough to be taking his photo. His thick dark hair fell over one side of his forehead, and the pallid colour of his skin gave him an almost monochrome relief. Black and white. His lips were narrow, almost non-existent. Everything about him looked sharp, a blade ready to cut.

The record was surprisingly thin. The 2016 mugshot related to the most recent arrest, for assault. Jo perused the file quickly, taking in the salient details. A fight outside a pub in central Manchester, in which a man's jaw had been broken. James Brown had been released with a caution. Further back, there were a dozen other arrests, for a mixture of vandalism, petty theft, trespass, and two more aggravated assaults. As a juvenile, no DNA had been taken, and though charges were levied, he was released each time with a caution, or under supervision, back into the council's care. The attempted stabbing with the scissors was listed too, right back in 2011. Jo opened up the more detailed file on that case, which linked through to the court findings. There was no question, it seemed, that he was guilty, but the teaching assistant in question had actually appeared as a witness in James' defence, reporting him as a highly intelligent pupil, who could, with the right support, go far.

I bet she never had this in mind, thought Jo.

Chapter 23

'*We arrived to find Constables Sheldon and O'Neill at the premises. A team of paramedics were working on Ms Brown in one corner of the living room, where she lay on the ground beside a sofa. At this stage she was alive, but appeared to be convulsing and vomiting. There were several items of drug paraphernalia on a table. Cons. Sheldon directed me to a closed door at the end of the corridor. He said he believed there was at least two children inside, and asked if he should break down the door. I asked him to wait, as I thought I might be able to convince James to open it himself.*

It took several minutes before he acknowledged me. I could hear him talking to his sister Megan, telling her it was going to be okay. I introduced myself by my first name, and explained that we'd met before, during a visit the previous year. He said he couldn't remember, and asked if his mother was all right. He said he had called the ambulance. By then Ms Bailey was completely non-responsive and the paramedics were attempting to resuscitate her. I told James we were doing our best to make her better, and asked if he would open the door so we could talk face to face. He said his sister's nappy needed changing, that he had tried, but he thought it was on the wrong way. I said we could help with that too. He said he didn't need help from me. He wanted his mother. We continued to speak in this way for approximately ten minutes. He swore at me often, aggressively. His fear, I determined, was that we would take his sister away, and he'd promised his mother that would never happen.

It was during this period that Ms Brown was taken on a stretcher out of the flat. I believe she was already dead, though her death was not officially declared until she reached the hospital shortly after. Megan, aged three, had begun to cry loudly. James was becoming more agitated, repeatedly instructing her to be quiet and saying that he was doing everything he could. I tried a final time to persuade James to open the door, but Megan's shouts had risen in pitch, indicating that she was in pain. I gave Constable Sheldon an instruction to break down the door, and he did so. Inside the room, we found James in one corner, shielding his sister. She was partially clothed, and there was a strong smell of human waste, coming from a pile of soiled nappies in one corner of the room. There was more drug paraphernalia, as well as alcohol containers, dirty bedding and what appeared to be historic fire damage along one wall. Megan was struggling in James' grip, and I told him to let her go. When he refused, together with Constable Sheldon, we forcibly removed her. In the process, James bit me, drawing blood, and I was forced to use an approved palm strike to make him release me. Subsequently, James and Megan were removed from the premises and taken to hospital for examination . . .'

The report of the emergency duty team continued in the same dry language for a few hundred more words, detailing the initial medical findings, which included malnourishment, dehydration, lice, plus an advanced ear infection affecting Megan and severe conjunctivitis in James. All symptoms indicated a case of extreme neglect and emotional abuse, though no signs of physical abuse. Following this, the EDT officer found an emergency temporary residence for both children. At this stage, he recommended that they remain together.

Jo closed the file, and passed it across to Carrick. They were seated opposite each other in the briefing room, sharing the material as it came in.

'Dimitriou said it was grim, and he wasn't lying.'

Knowing something of the people in question in the present made it worse. And, in the previous few days, Jo felt she *had* been getting to know Megan, even though they'd never met.

There were reams of paperwork to get through, and Reeves was sending more through all the time, adding to the pile of print-outs to absorb. Council evaluations, efforts to find relatives, a procedural inquest relating to the previous monitoring of the family, and then placement details. It looked like the children were kept together for the first few months, moved from place to place as temporary carers tried and failed to deal with James' violent outbursts. A child psychologist's report made a tentative diagnosis of conduct disorder, as well as observing a raft of other disruptive behaviours including a lack of impulse control. Megan herself was believed to exhibit symptoms of foetal alcohol syndrome due to her hearing deficits, retarded verbalisation and co-ordination, and her relatively small size.

It was early 2008 – around seven months after their mother died – that the two children were separated, with James remaining in the care system, and his sister finding a new home in Oxfordshire. Jo couldn't find a justification explicitly stated anywhere on first pass, but it wasn't hard to read between the lines and see that Megan would be a lot easier to rehome than her significantly more damaged brother. What it must have done to him particularly was hard to fathom.

And now we're seeing the fallout.

'He's come to get her,' said Carrick, speaking for both of them.

'Looks like it,' said Jo. 'But what's with the four-year gap? Arrested in 2016, it looks like the next slip-up will get him jail-time. Then he vanishes.'

'Maybe he was abroad,' said Carrick.

'You think he had the wherewithal to apply for a passport?'

'Turned over a new leaf then?'

'Oh, happens all the time, boss.' Jo gave him her most sceptical look. 'No, somehow he kept his nose clean for four years.'

'And he came back a different person,' said Carrick. 'A ruthless killer. Maybe he was in with a gang?'

Through the window, Jo saw Nigel from the front desk plodding through the drizzle to empty a waste basket into the wheelie-bin outside. She remembered what Saskia had said about his footwear – the boots – and the oversized rucksack he was carrying on the CCTV.

'What about armed forces?' she said.

Carrick tilted his head as he considered. 'That would explain his acquaintance with firearms,' he said. 'And the level of planning and reconnaissance he would have needed.'

'And maybe the Banbury decoy,' said Jo. 'It was a neat trick.'

'You sound like you admire him.'

'I wouldn't go that far. Let's contact the Ministry of Defence and see what they can give us.'

Jo went back to her desk and found the general enquiries number quickly. As she dialled, her gaze fell on the mugshot of a sixteen-year-old James Brown, now pinned to the main board. *We're coming for you,* she thought. His eyes, dark and intense, answered her challenge.

* * *

258

Dealing with the MOD was almost the exact opposite experience of trying to wrangle information from a local council. In a series of transferrals, and without anyone trying to bullshit or bluster, she was passed from the enquiries desk, to army personnel, to the infantry training base in Dering Lines, Wales, and finally, after a wait of about five minutes, a voice came on the phone and introduced himself as Corporal Kinnear.

'You're asking about James Brown?'

Jo introduced herself. 'That's right. Did you know him?'

'Very well,' said Kinnear. 'Is he in trouble?'

'You could say that,' said Jo. 'Can you tell me about him?'

'A very effective soldier,' said Kinnear, 'but a very troubled young man. He came to me straight out of specialist mechanic training. Served two deployments in Afghanistan. Seven months ago, he went AWOL from Chepstow Barracks. I can't say it's a surprise. He'd been skating on thin ice for a while and we'd likely have kicked him out at some point.'

'Can you give me any more details?'

'He had an anger problem,' said Kinnear, 'but we work with a lot of kids like that. Normally it gets channelled as they bed into the team, or the team sorts it out, but Brown always kept his edge. Ready to kick off all the time, and it didn't matter how many guys he was up against. He did some good things overseas, became something of an expert in IEDs and counter-ambush. You couldn't question his courage. If we could have ironed out his kinks and sorted the discipline, he could've made special forces. He had that sort of drive. Tough, tough kid. Sadly it wasn't to be.'

It was useful information, but Jo didn't have high hopes when she asked the next question.

'We need to track him down. Can you think of anyone who might be able to help us?'

'If James wants to stay hidden, he will,' said Kinnear. 'He's a survivor, that boy.'

'He's killed several people,' said Jo.

'You're kidding me?'

'You sound surprised.'

'I am,' said Kinnear. 'For all his problems, it was always provoked. I got the impression he just wanted to be left alone.'

'There's family involved,' said Jo. 'Listen, thank you for your time. If anything else comes to mind, will you let us know?'

'Of course, detective,' said Kinnear. 'I can send you his file, if that would help?'

'It would.'

They shared direct contact details before finishing the call.

'Sounded interesting,' said Carrick.

'Worrying, more like,' said Jo, before repeating what Kinnear had told her.

'We've got a job on our hands then,' said Carrick.

It wasn't long before the file came through from the corporal. The photo accompanying it, dated the previous year, showed James Brown in uniform. He looked considerably older than the mugshot from 2016, his face and physique more bulky, with a crew-cut. It could have been a different person from the police file, but for the same, chin-up posture and the burning black eyes. He looked like a young man rather than a boy, and though Jo searched for signs of the poor kid from the child services reports, he simply wasn't there any more. There was no vulnerability – just defiance and anger.

The MOD material included a full chronological record of Brown's service, dating back to his initial enquiry at the recruitment centre in Manchester in 2016, followed by his periods of training at Sandhurst, and later Chepstow, before deployments in 2018 and 2019. He'd graduated top of his mechanic class and there were other highlights, including a commendation for bravery. His first-class physicals suggested an exemplary approach too.

However, there were also a number of citations for disciplinary problems, ranging from offences involving the possession and consumption of alcohol to fighting in the barracks. At one point he had been temporarily demoted for throwing a mess tray at a superior officer.

'Hey, guys,' said Heidi. 'I *might* have something. Come and see.'

'You've found your needle?' said Jo.

Heidi had a shot of a blue Ford Focus on the screen. There was only one person in the front seat, driving. Heidi zoomed the image. Definitely Brown, though his hair had grown back.

'It's him,' Jo said. 'You did it.'

'No sign of Megan,' said Carrick.

'Get the plates plugged into the ANPR for the last seven days,' said Jo.

Heidi switched windows, and copied the alphanumeric sequence. It took a few second before a satellite map came up on screen, populated by green triangles.

'Holy shit,' said Heidi.

It was all there. The plates from the Focus had pinged cameras all around Oxford. There were also several notifications on the roads around Stanton St John.

'Check that one,' said Jo, pointing to the closest of them.

Heidi hovered the mouse over the dot, bringing up a date, time, and direction of travel, and a thumbnail of the vehicle image. *April 13th, 06.12.*

'Morning,' said Jo. 'Not long before the Baileys' neighbour heard the shotgun blast.' Clicking through for the full details, a larger image of the Focus came up. Again, it was only Brown visible.

'Narrow it down to the last forty-eight hours,' said Carrick.

Most of the triangles disappeared as Heidi performed the action. All that remained were a constellation of points in and around Oxford that also stretched out towards the north-west, including near to the Woodstock car-jacking.

'What's out that way? said Jo. The triangles stopped around nine miles outside the city.

'Some of the cameras have pinged multiple times,' said Heidi. 'He was using the same route repeatedly. With a little time, we should be able to map out the chronology.'

She narrowed the search to the last twenty-four hours and the pattern was sparse. Eight triangles, all on the road from the north-west.

'He came in and went out,' said Jo. 'Where's the most recent sighting?'

In a few clicks, a single green dot remained, just beyond the village of Over Kidlington. It was timed at 20.04 the previous evening. Heidi pointed to a grey dot beyond the outer reaches of Brown's route. 'That's a camera location too, but he didn't get that far.'

Jo leant over her, and sketched a circle with her fingertip around the green dot. 'So he's likely in that vicinity.'

'The car is,' said Heidi. 'Whether he's with it or not is another matter.' Much of the land to the west of the road was forest, with a number of tracks cutting through, and occasional buildings too. Perfect for concealing a vehicle from prying eyes, even those in the sky.

'You think we need the armed response?' asked Jo.

'Let's recce first,' said Carrick. 'Heidi, if the ANPR picks him up, we need to know straight away.'

Chapter 24

They drove north without sirens, and with little in the way of conversation. Jo understood Carrick's decision not to deploy the AR team. Though no one would ever say it, the previous day's failure must have weighed heavily on him, and he likely didn't want to make the same embarrassing mistake twice unless they had better intelligence that James Brown was present. The worst thing in the world would be to remove the firearms officers from Oxford again only for him to turn up there bearing deadly force and bad intentions.

They passed through rural Oxfordshire, and Jo noted the discreet grey ANPR cameras mounted at occasional intervals above the road. She was struck by the uncanny feeling of seeing the world through Brown's eyes. Given his plate-switching, he couldn't have failed to notice the cameras too. But if he had pre-empted them before, was he still doing so now? Or perhaps he hadn't anticipated Heidi Tan's tenacity, feeling his tactics were foolproof against police intelligence, and hadn't realised they were about, finally, to catch up with him. Despite the lack of armed support, she noted that Carrick had silently tossed two bullet-proof vests into the back seat.

As they passed through Over Kidlington, he slowed and the atmosphere in the car took on a more serious edge. Soon they were passing thick trees to the left. They rounded a corner and Jo spotted a track on the left marked 'Chiltern Timber'. Carrick indicated, braked suddenly, and swung into it, earning a horn from the car behind, plus a raised middle finger. It didn't appear to bother her boss. A gate was closed across the track, and padlocked. The single track beyond was gouged with the dried-up ruts made by heavy-duty vehicles. A sign read: 'Site Traffic Only. Visitors please use main entrance.'

'You'd struggle to get an Audi coupé down there,' said Jo. She checked the map and saw there was another road a couple of hundred metres up.

Carrick reversed out, and they drove further along the road. The next entrance was tarmacked and ungated. As they drove down it, fir trees loomed on either side, light barely penetrating between them. They passed through occasional patches of wetter ground, where drainage channels crossed the road from left to right, down a slight slope. Jo thought of the mud spatters on the sides of the Ford Focus and the repeated pings from the local ANPR cameras. James Bailey had been using this place as a base for some time.

After a minute or so, they came to an open space occupied by a large warehouse, several temporary buildings, some earth-moving equipment, and an industrial log-cutting apparatus. There were off-cuts of timber scattered around, and some piles too. The site had the feel of a place that hadn't been frequented for a long time. As they drove into the yard, there were signs indicating danger from machinery, alongside an arrow pointing to the office reception. Jo eyed the buildings and trees as the car crawled alongside the warehouse.

'Doesn't look like anyone's working today,' said Jo.

Carrick pulled up at the office door in the side of the warehouse, but kept the engine running. A sign on the door read, 'We are closed until April 1st.' An enquiry number was listed, and a further sign informed them 'This site is monitored by CCTV.' There was indeed a camera above the door, with a spider's web spun across the lens. It didn't appear to be operational.

'Can't see anyone,' said Carrick. 'Let's do a circuit then go.'

He set off again, around to the rear of the warehouse, keeping below 10mph. The buildings looked thoroughly locked-up. They drifted over ground covered in sawdust, and Jo wound down her window to let in some fresher air. The smell of the forest, rich and earthy, filled the car. There was something else too.

'Boss, can you smell smoke?'

Carrick lifted his nostrils, and said, 'I think so,' just as they passed the edge of a large half-covered structure with two trailers and a tractor parked up. Alongside them, looking completely incongruous, was a black Audi.

'Oh fuck . . .' said Jo. A fraction of a second later, she heard a crack that sounded like a splintering trunk, and the rear window of their car exploded inwards. She ducked instinctively, and Carrick must've stepped on the accelerator because they lurched forwards. James Brown came walking slowly from the trees, dressed in black, the gun held in both hands, thrust out in front of him, arms locked straight. A second shot pinged loudly off the metal of the car's chassis.

'Go!' cried Jo, though she needn't have bothered, because Carrick careered off in the direction of the exit. There was a third shot, making Jo flinch, but it must have missed. She looked back to see Brown now running towards them, still firing. Carrick skidded back out onto the narrow road and accelerated wildly away, shooting glances into the rear-view mirror. A hundred yards away, he slowed to a halt.

Eyes on the mirror, he asked, 'Are you all right?'

Jo nodded hurriedly, too shocked to speak. She looked back over her shoulder through the shattered rear window which now covered the back seat. As far as she was concerned, they still weren't clear of danger. She hadn't counted the shots to know if he'd emptied a magazine or not.

Carrick hit the transmit button on the car's radio.

'Shots fired at Chiltern Timber, A44, eight hundred metres north of Over Kidlington. Tactical response team required immediately. Suspect James Brown is armed. Two officers on scene in Red Toyota.'

The dispatcher asked him to confirm there were no casualties, which Carrick did with an unflappable calm, as well as giving details on the two entry points they knew of.

Jo heard an engine as he was still talking. Behind them, the Audi had reached the site entrance and stopped. She could see Megan in the passenger seat, and James Brown was looking right at them. A bolt of panic went through her gut. If he came now, he could probably catch them. But the fear quickly dissipated when he turned in the opposite direction, heading along the rough track used by the logging lorries.

He's gone the wrong way. He'll hit the gate.

Carrick saw it too.

'Suspect is exiting towards the A44. We are in pursuit.'

He gunned the engine, not after the Audi, but back towards the main road the way they'd come. If Brown got through the gate, he'd emerge just a couple of hundred yards from their own exit. Jo had no idea how they were going to stop him, but staying in contact was the main thing.

Carrick barely slowed as he swung out onto the A44, grinding through two gears and sending smoke from the rear wheels as he accelerated south to intercept the Audi. But there were other cars on the road too. He overtook one and slipped back behind a second – a Volvo estate.

Fifty yards short of the gated entrance, there was an almighty bang, and a vehicle on the opposite side of the road swerved violently as the gate itself slid across the tarmac with a shower of sparks. The Volvo ahead of them slammed on its brakes, and Carrick jerked the wheel clockwise to avoid it. It wasn't enough, and the front wing on Jo's side caught the Volvo's rear end. They went into a spin, and Jo's overriding impressions as the greenery swirled on every side were Carrick's gritted teeth and his hands fighting the wheel. All she thought of was Theo, and the instant tableaux of police at the nursery, her brother weeping, and her orphaned boy in Amelia's arms. Then something hit them with a horrible crunch, and future tragedy was forgotten as the pressurised airbag exploded in her face. Blinded, she felt the car tilting, almost weightless. Glass burst and scattered, and with an almost leisurely movement, they rolled upside down, coming to a stop.

Jo wasn't sure if she'd lost consciousness for a few seconds or if her brain was just playing catch-up. She was alive, Theo still had a mother, and radio traffic informed her that the armed response team and other patrols were on their way. Beside her, Carrick was upside down and blinking as the airbag deflated. 'Andy?' said Jo.

'That was annoying,' he said. 'You okay?'

Jo flexed her neck and took stock of her limbs. All present and correct. 'Nothing a double vodka won't fix.'

'My right arm hurts,' said Carrick.

'Hang in there,' she said. She managed to unclip herself, then him. Her door wouldn't open at first, jamming a little, but the window was still down. 'Don't move, boss,' she said. 'I'll come around.'

She scrambled through the window, and managed to get her hands on the tarmac. People from several other cars were gathering round. There was plastic debris and grass across the road.

Lowering herself inelegantly, she found her feet and staggered a little dizzily. A man caught her before she fell. 'Steady on, love. You've been in an accident.'

'You're telling me,' muttered Jo. The Toyota was on its roof, halfway into a ditch like an upended turtle. Other cars featuring a variety of dents were strewn at angles, and more were building up either side of the road. She scanned for the black Audi but it was nowhere to be seen. 'I've rung an ambulance!' said a more distant voice that seemed, like everything else, to be coming at Jo from underwater. She went around the front of the car, still unsteady on her legs, and clambered into the ditch to get to the driver's side. Carrick hadn't moved. His door was badly dented from an impact, but opened with a clanking sound.

'It's all right, Andy – I've got you.'

'Is it bad?' he said. 'It bloody hurts.'

His arm was tangled in the remains of an airbag, and the sleeve of his shirt was covered in blood. She held in the vomit when she saw where it was coming from. A four-inch shard of bone from his upper arm was jutting through the material, and the elbow was at completely the wrong angle.

'You're going to be all right, mate,' she said. 'Ambulance is coming.'

JAMES

TEN DAYS EARLIER

Stripped to the waist under the harsh light of the disabled toilet, he gingerly removed the pad from his neck. The flesh was still raw beneath where the shotgun blast had caught him. *Fuck* it hurt. It seemed likely a couple of pellets had torn a tendon. He could hardly turn his head without pain lancing from his shoulder to his ear. He supposed he was lucky the fat bastard was such a bad shot.

It might heal on its own, if there was no contaminant under the skin. Anyway, hospital was a non-starter; too many questions. He doused the wound gingerly with water, dabbed it dry with loo roll, then replaced the gauze pad with a fresh one, and pulled up his collar again. His sister didn't need to know he was suffering, and the less she knew about the disastrous visit to her parents' house, the better. It was her fault, really – all because she'd wanted a few supposedly 'important' things from her bedroom.

In the café she was drinking a milkshake through a straw, and he sat opposite her.

'You okay?' she asked. 'You were gone a long time.'

'Queue,' he said, doing his best to smile. Even that initiated a spasm of pain.

'I got the stuff you wanted from the house,' he said, then handed her back the key she'd loaned him. 'All in the car.' *Along with the shotgun he'd relieved from the fat prick who'd shot him.*

'Thanks,' she said. She looked a little uncertain.

'It was a nice place,' he said, 'but I can see why you want to leave. All those stuffed creatures. Bloodthirsty bastard, your old man. Probably better than your real one, though.'

'Did you leave the letter for them?'

'Right where you asked – on the kitchen table.'

Actually, he'd set fire to it by the side of the road. Though it hadn't contained anything that would directly lead someone after them, it would be better to leave the authorities entirely in the dark.

Megan looked a little distant as she played with her glass.

'What's the matter?' he asked.

'Still thinking about Xan,' she said. 'I can't believe he's dead. It's fucked up.'

James remembered the startled look on the kid's face when he understood it was a gun being pointed at his head. Had he processed what was about to happen before it did?

'If you mess with drugs, you're asking for it,' he said. 'Dangerous people.'

Megan drained the drink. 'I guess so. Do you think the police might want to talk to me though?'

'Probably,' said James. 'But we'll be long gone by then.'

'To your place in Manchester?'

'Eventually. We might need to lie low a bit first – I know a place.'

'Is it nice?'

'It'll do,' he said. He wondered what she'd say when she saw the camp. 'It's only temporary, until they stop looking for us.'

'And can I get a new phone then?'

She thought she'd lost her last one, didn't know he'd smashed it to bits with a hammer.

'Course.'

She was getting cold feet again. Sometimes it was easy to forget how young she was. How innocent, despite the tough face she showed the world. It made him love her even more.

'Look, Meg, there's nothing for you here. You've told me your folks don't give a fuck. We can start again. A new life, fresh chances.'

'I know, I know . . .'

'So what's wrong?'

She laid both hands over her stomach, as if cradling herself. 'It's just a big decision, you know?'

'It won't seem like that soon.'

'What about Harry?'

'What about him?'

'He helped me. He doesn't think I should . . .' She stopped.

James heart sank like a stone. 'You told him about me, didn't you?'

Her face said it all. He struggled to control himself. He wanted to grab the chair he was sitting on and hurl it through the window. He lowered his voice. 'I *told* you, didn't I? You *mustn't* mention me. If you do, they'll find us.'

'I didn't say you were from Manchester or anything,' she said. 'I didn't tell him your surname . . .'

He slowly regained his composure as the red mist faded. 'Okay. It's going to be fine. You can send him a postcard, when we get out of here.' Megan smiled. He could see she wanted desperately to believe. 'You want this, right?'

'Yeah, I think so.'

James reached across the table, and wrapped her hands in his. 'I promised I'd look after you, but you need to trust me. We're going to get out of this place, and it'll be the best thing you've ever done. Let me talk to Harry, okay?'

She nodded, slightly wary, like there was something she wanted to say but couldn't. In the end, she said simply, 'He's a good man.'

Chapter 25

Miraculously, Andy Carrick was the only serious casualty in the pile-up, though it looked like at least four cars had been written off. The first ambulance arrived in less than ten minutes, and they got an oxygen mask on Jo's boss straight away, along with an injection of painkillers. They treated him in the car for twenty minutes before they were satisfied the arm was the only injury. Once he was on a stretcher, he looked at it for the first time, and Jo saw genuine fear behind the spaced-out look in his eyes.

'You're in good hands,' she said, as they took him to the ambulance. She held an ice-pack against her cheek, which was swollen from a friction burn from the airbag.

'Alert the air support,' he said.

'It's done,' said Jo. 'We can handle things.'

Carrick nodded, head sagging back. 'I'm sorry. I should have got the firearms crew.'

'Shut it,' said Jo. 'I'll see you soon.'

The ambulance doors closed and Carrick was taken away.

Two other paramedic crews were dealing with the walking wounded, treating cuts and bruises. A fire engine had arrived as well though Jo wasn't sure what they could do other than perhaps move some of the stricken vehicles out of the highway. The gate that had once blocked the trucker's road lay on the tarmac, buckled. Together, a team of motorists gathered to shift it off the road. Jo sat by the side, and answered a call coming from Heidi.

'Tried to get you on the radio.'

'It's still in the car,' said Jo. She filled Heidi in, including Andy's injury.

'Jesus Christ,' was all she could say. 'Is he okay?'

'He will be. Tell me you've got the Audi.'

'We haven't picked it up,' said Heidi. 'So he's either ditched it somewhere, or he had a camera-free escape route.'

If Jo hadn't been feeling so beaten up already, she might have punched something.

'He fucking shot at us, the bastard.'

'You're lucky then.'

'I've got no car,' said Jo.

'Dimi's going to be with you any minute,' said Heidi.

'They're back?'

'On their way,' said Heidi. 'Detouring to your position. You sure you don't need to go to hospital?'

Jo flexed her neck. It was stiff, and tomorrow would be worse, but for now she could manage. 'I'm all good, Heidi, we need to catch him.'

'We will,' said Heidi. 'One way or another.'

Dimitriou and Reeves arrived within twenty minutes, both marvelling at the carnage and Jo's narration of the circumstances that led to it.

'Why didn't you have an ARU?' said Dimitriou. He looked almost angry, but Jo knew it came from legitimate and heart-felt concern.

'We were just having a recce,' she said. 'Brown came from nowhere, gun blazing.'

Dimitriou appeared incredulous, and about to push his point, but Jo cut him off. 'We need to get in there and inspect the site,' she said. 'They quit in a hurry, and they might have left clues.'

'No way,' said Dimitriou. 'You're going to hospital.'

'With all due respect, sergeant, you can kiss my arse.'

Dimitriou shot an appealing glance at Reeves. 'Alice, can you talk to her, woman to woman?'

Reeves looked like a deer in the headlights, and said nothing.

'Wise choice,' said Jo. 'Come on.'

★   ★   ★

Returning to the scene in the silence of the forest was a weird feeling. The dusty ground around the timber yard bore the evidence of the chase – tyre marks from both cars, as well as footprints, broken glass and spent rounds. Jo led Reeves and Dimitriou to the place where the Audi had been parked. The smell of smoke still lingered and it didn't take them long to find its source, the remains of a camp some fifty metres into the trees. A canvas tent was pitched in a small clearing and a fire still smouldered; cooking pots and a gas stove were strewn about, along with a carrier bag containing several cans of food. Inside the tent they found a magazine, some clothes, and a battered 1:25,000 Ordnance Survey map of the area. There was no sign of the large rucksack that Saskia Patel had reported Megan carrying, so Jo guessed they still had it with them. She inspected the map, which was covered in markings. Some, she intuited, were the road cameras, but others were written in a code she couldn't decipher.

He's well prepared . . .

'If the ANPR data is anything to go by, they were using this place for several days,' she said.

Reeves was picking down a bag hanging in a tree. 'Looks like trash,' she said, and tipped out the contents. Jo saw there were several bloody bandages.

'Hardly five-star comforts,' said Dimitriou, coming through the trees. 'I think I found the latrine out that way. I'd recommend holding it if you can manage.'

His phone rang, and Jo's pulse raced, despite her aches and pains. 'Okay, we're on our way.' He turned to Jo. 'We found the car.'

'Where?'

'Parked under a viaduct – two miles west of here outside Charlbury.'

'I'm surprised he got that far,' said Jo. She looked at the map, and sure enough saw Charlbury, with a spot marked by hand with the letters 'CP'. What did it stand for? *Concealed Point*?

In her head, she carried out some calculations. He might have reached the CP location in five minutes, so the car could have been there an hour already. Charlbury was in mostly open countryside, but there was more forest to its south-west. If he was on foot, that would provide the best cover. More likely though, he'd try to get another vehicle and put as much distance as possible between himself and them.

'Hey, is this what I think it is?' asked Reeves.

Both Dimitriou and Jo turned towards her. Reeves was holding something in a handkerchief – a white plastic object about five inches long, tapered at one end. As she carried it towards them, Jo knew exactly what she was looking at. A pregnancy testing device. And on closer inspection, one that had delivered a positive – a distinct cross motif in the results panel.

'Looks like congratulations are in order,' said Dimitriou, with a wry shake of the head.

But Jo was on a different page entirely as her mind worked through the implications. Whether or not it was a delayed reaction to the car accident, or the new thought that struck her suddenly, she had to place her hand against the trunk of a tree while she was sick over the ground.

'Right, no arguments,' said Dimitriou. 'We're taking you to hospital.'

This time, Jo put up no fight. If she was right about the test, the hospital was exactly the place she wanted to be.

★ ★ ★

Jo let them carry out their exam, shining lights in her eyes and ears, prodding and poking, and taking her blood pressure. They cleaned the wound on the side of her face, all while she tried to tell them she was okay. She refused the neck-brace they offered.

Andy, she learned, was in surgery. They couldn't tell her anything more, but she wouldn't forget that injury in a hurry. It was a lot worse than a standard break.

Though it was frustrating, and several times she considering discharging *herself*, there was also something quite pleasant about being looked after. She'd told Paul and Amelia not to come, and under no circumstances to bring Theo. She even sent them a selfie to show all was well. She got a video call thirty seconds later.

'This is becoming a habit,' said Paul.

'Woah!' said Will, crowding into shot behind his dad. 'Were you inside that car that flipped?'

'Uh-huh,' said Jo.

'He thinks it's like *Grand Theft Auto*,' said Emma, peering over Paul's other shoulder.

'Not that much fun,' said Jo. 'Is Theo okay?'

'Better than you, I reckon,' said Paul. 'Of course he is. When are you getting out? I'll come and grab you.'

'Really soon,' she said. 'I'll get a cab.'

'You'd better not,' said Paul. 'The bed's all set up here, and Amelia's going over to yours now to pick up some clothes and things.'

'You don't have to,' said Jo.

Paul smiled. 'We're not having this conversation again,' he said. 'And you're in no position to argue. Call me, whatever time it is.'

★　★　★

Throughout the time she was being treated, the pregnancy test rose intermittently into her thoughts, like a buoy amid rough seas rising on the crest of a wave. When she'd seen it in the forest camp, its meaning had been so clear, but after some time to reflect she wondered if she was jumping to conclusions. Heidi arrived, just after six pm, while Jo was awaiting a final sign-off. She brought some chocolates, and no good news from the front line.

'Brown's disappeared again,' she said. 'Like a bloody ghost.'

It's just like Corporal Kinnear said. If he doesn't want to be found . . .

'Have you seen Andy?'

'I popped up,' she said. 'His family are in with him. Didn't want to intrude. Doc said he's pretty out of it still. He almost lost that arm.'

'It was awful,' said Jo. She wondered if Heidi meant the *whole* family or just the kids.

'Dimi and Alice have ordered in a takeaway,' said Heidi. 'They're standing by at the station in case anything comes up tonight.'

'I should be with them,' said Jo.

'I don't think Dimi would appreciate that,' said Heidi, with a knowing tilt of the head.

'You think he's trying it on with her, don't you?'

Heidi nodded. 'Have you ever known George Dimitriou to pass up an opportunity?'

'She's getting married!' said Jo.

'*Getting*,' said Heidi. 'Not got.'

'You're being unfair,' said Jo. 'He often puts in overtime. I remember he worked loads of overtime on that case involving the model who was being stalked last year.'

'Oh yeah,' said Heidi. 'I take it all back.' They both laughed and enjoyed the moment, before the pregnancy bobbed up again in Jo's mind. Heidi looked at her watch. 'Speaking of overtime, I have to go. You need a lift somewhere?'

'It's okay – my brother's coming. I'll see you tomorrow.'

Jo waited for Heidi to go, then walked down to the main desk. Her clothes were a crumpled mess, with a bloodstain on her cuff, but she rolled down her sleeve to cover most of it. 'I need to speak to Greg Bailey,' she said to the receptionist. 'Do you know where I can find him?'

'He's in IC3,' said the receptionist, before looking Jo up and down. 'Are you family?'

'No,' said Jo. She took out her badge. 'I'm trying to find the person who shot him.'

'He's not really up to receiving visitors,' said the receptionist.

Jo nodded. 'Understood.'

She backed off, letting the next in line move up, then followed the signs to the intensive care unit.

* * *

There was a security door to IC3, but Jo waited until a harassed-looking orderly was heading in with a gurney, and tagged along behind, clutching her box of chocolates with a wan smile. The act probably wasn't necessary, as the orderly barely batted an eyelid as she followed him through.

279

Finding Bailey's room without asking one of the staff was going to be tough, but by chance she saw a familiar face emerging from a ward ahead. It was Father Tremayne, the priest from Stanton St John. Before he had chance to clock her, Jo backed into a small waiting area with beverage-making facilities, and let him pass. Once he'd done so, she quickly brewed two instant coffees. With the chocolates tucked her arm, the coffees in each hand, she strode confidently towards the ward, and used her backside to open the swinging doors.

The Venetian blinds at the far end were drawn across, casting the room in twilight. Of the six beds, only two were filled. Nearest the door, a middle-aged man lay on his side, asleep. She walked to the far end, where Greg Bailey was lying, half reclined. One arm above the sheets was heavily bandaged. He watched her approach, but neither his eyes nor his expression showed surprise. He was linked up to several monitors, including one that silently displayed his heart rate.

'What are you doing here?' he said.

'Brought you a coffee,' she said. 'How are you doing?'

'How do I look?' he said.

'Not great, if I'm honest. May I sit down?'

He looked away, towards the windows. 'Do you mind letting in some light?'

Jo set the coffees and the chocolates down, and pulled a chain to adjust the blinds. Outside, the evening sun was still strong, and its rays fell across the floor and bed. Bailey squinted, and rolled his head back again. The light picked out his pale lashes and added a pink, almost translucent glow to his eyelids. His previously clear skin looked blotchy, his lips dry.

'Would you like some water?' asked Jo.

'Yes, please.'

She offered him a cup, but rather than raise a hand, he merely craned his head. She held it to his lips, and he drank. 'Thank you.'

Jo set the cup down, and took the chair beside the bed.

'Greg, can I talk to you about what happened?'

'Someone shot me,' he said.

'We know that. Do you know why?'

He answered with an uninterested query of his own. 'What happened to your face?'

'I had a run-in with the same man. Do you know who he is?'

'Should I?'

'You had a lot of money for him,' said Jo.

His face twitched. 'It wasn't for him,' he said. 'It was for her. Like I told you, before – I wanted her gone.'

Jo blew on her coffee. With each second he lied, she was more sure of herself. In an interview room, she would have gone for the kill straight away, but it felt wrong in this context. There was no vying for power here. He was at her mercy, trapped under a tightly tucked hospital blanket, and tethered to machines.

'I remember that, Greg,' she said. 'But you knew we were looking for her. You should have called us.'

His heart rate was steadily creeping up through the eighties. He didn't speak for a while, then he spoke softly. 'Can you ring Chalmers please?'

'Why?'

'Because I want him here, if you're going to ask me questions.'

Jo sipped. 'You don't need a lawyer, Greg. We're on the same side, aren't we?'

He didn't answer at all, but he had crossed ninety beats per minute.

'Greg, Chalmers was the one who told us about the money. We saw the messages you sent. You were scared and anxious. Your friend Rohan said you were agitated. Why?'

'Because I wanted her gone,' said Bailey firmly. 'Are you deaf?'

His face was still, but the heart-rate monitor told another story. The beeping intensified to over 100bpm.

'Greg, did you have a sexual relationship with Megan?'

'Don't be fucking disgusting,' he said.

110.

'She was pregnant before, too – when she was at school. The identity of the father wasn't known.'

'Well it wasn't me! She's my sister, for Chrissakes.'

115.

'She's not though. Not really. And the law recognises it – it's not illegal to have sexual relations with an adoptive sibling.'

Though if she's twelve, that's a different kettle of fish entirely.

'I have no idea what you're talking about,' said Bailey. He looked firmly towards the door. 'I . . . I want you to leave.'

'I'm sure you do,' said Jo. 'Thing is, I've had a rough old day. My colleague and I have been chasing the guy who shot you, and we've both ended up in here. We thought he was some sort of drug dealer, ready to blast up a Jericho café just for some cash. But that never made any sense. I mean, if you were delivering the money, there was no reason to hurt you like that. But if it was *personal* . . . well, that makes all the difference. And what could be more personal than you fucking his underage sister. His *real, blood* sister.'

Bailey glanced at her, momentarily on guard.

'You didn't know that, did you?' she continued. 'But that's why he did it. She must have told him what you did to her.'

'I didn't *do* anything. It was her, every time.'

'Greg, she's pregnant again,' said Jo. 'And this time, a simple test is going to prove who the father is. But it's going to be okay.'

'Please, stop talking like that,' said Bailey. His lips had twisted.

'You're not going to be in trouble, Greg,' she lied. 'These

282

sorts of things happen all the time. If anything, it's your parents' fault. How old were you when they dumped her on you? Nine? I doubt you even wanted a sister, right? And you certainly never saw her as one.'

'You don't know what she's like,' said Bailey.

'But we do. We've got all the reports from the people who knew her. She uses sex to get what she wants. Just like when she sent those pictures to her teacher. She's *damaged*, Greg. Anyone can see that. I've no doubt at all that *she* came on to *you.*'

Greg didn't answer, because he'd begun to cry. Eyes sunken, he looked literally hollowed out – a shell of the young man who'd bossed the meeting at Chalmers' office. Not a man at all any more, but a boy. Jo felt something close to sympathy for him and thought about stopping. *Not yet. I've got to hear it. Got to work it all out.*

'Did your parents know?'

'Know what, for fuck's sake?' he sobbed.

'About what was happening. What Megan was like.' *What you were like*, she meant. *Their biological child. Their boy.*

He stared at her suddenly, fierce and defiant, but she could see it was a last stand. An act of outraged innocence. Like she'd seen hundreds of times in interview rooms over the years.

'Did they?' she pushed.

Sure enough, the fire in his eyes died and he turned away again. 'They knew,' he muttered.

And there he was again, in her thoughts unbidden. *Her* little boy. So innocent, so untouched by any of the horrors that lay in wait. Incorruptible, for now at least. She imagined what Mrs Bailey would have thought, what she had really known about the relationship between her two children, so unsuccessfully thrown together with only good intentions and Christian zeal. Had she still found it in her heart to love her son, even after all that? Of course she had. Perhaps Greg, beneath the contortions of his face, was thinking of the same thing.

'It's going to be all right,' she said. 'We can talk later, when you're better.'

In reality, an arrest for statutory rape and sex with a minor would follow, though if the case would ever see court was another question. Certainly he'd be listed on the sex offenders register for a lengthy period.

Bailey's upper body shook under the blankets as he wept.

His spiking heart rate must have alerted the staff, because a nurse walked in through the door. When she saw Jo and the state of Greg Bailey, she sped up. 'Who are you? You shouldn't be in here,' she said sternly.

Jo stood, leaving the box of chocolates, and showed her badge. 'I'm leaving,' she said.

As she left the room, and the nurse went to Bailey, Jo bumped into Dr Wilson Kim. He frowned to see her. 'Hello?' he said.

'I was just passing by, and needed to speak to Mr Bailey. I'm afraid he's distressed.'

Kim nodded. 'He took the news badly,' he said.

It was Jo's turn to frown. 'What news?'

'His coccygeal nerves were irreparably damaged,' said Dr Kim. 'We did what we could. He may get a little feeling back around the pelvis, but he won't ever walk again.'

* * *

She took a cab, rather than calling her brother. After all that happened, and all the help they had given to her unbidden, she couldn't ask for more, even though he'd insisted.

Will was in bed, and Emma was at her boyfriend's place. After Jo had been upstairs to check on a sleeping Theo, safely installed in an ancient cot, she returned downstairs to have a glass of wine thrust into her hand by Amelia. Around their kitchen table, she gave the barest details of her day, sparing the sordid facts that had recently emerged. Neither Paul nor her sister-in-law pressed for more, and they contented themselves instead with sharing Will's latest school report, with Amelia explaining what coded words such as 'spirited' and 'creative' really meant in the lingo of the teaching profession. The semblance of normality was a welcome distraction, even if Jo knew in the back of her mind it was only temporary.

Chapter 26

Just how temporary was highlighted when her phone rang at seven in the morning. She fumbled for it with her mind still booting up.

'Hello?'

'Sergeant Masters?'

'Speaking.'

'Hi, sorry to bother you so early, ma'am – you're listed as SIO on the Bailey case . . .'

Jo sat up quick enough to make her head spin, taking in the surroundings of her brother's guest room. Theo was still asleep.

'What's happened?'

'Probable sighting, ma'am. I'm Sergeant Wethers, Gloucestershire. We're responding to aggravated burglary at a vet's outside Kingham.'

Jo wondered if she'd misheard.

'As in, a veterinary practice?'

'That's right. A man and a woman held the place up at gunpoint. Descriptions match James Brown and Megan Bailey.'

Jo looked at Theo, blissfully unaware. Little Steps didn't open its door until eight am, but Amelia had already offered the night before to babysit while Jo 'rested'.

'I'll be right there,' she said guiltily.

She had only the barest details to go on as she sped towards the address DS Wethers had provided. They tried to speak on the phone a couple of times, but the signal kept cutting out as she drove through the Cotswold countryside. The break-in had happened around midnight, and a single member of staff had been injured, but hadn't been discovered until six am when his colleagues arrived. An off-road vehicle had also been stolen.

Jo found the place just after eight. It was half a mile from Kingham itself, remote and rural, and from the sign out front – showing the words 'Pegasus House' and a rearing horse – Jo guessed it was a specialist in equine care. She drove along a lane lined with fencing towards a row of stables beside a farmhouse. There were several cars parked in a yard, including a patrol vehicle.

A suited man walked to meet her as she switched off the engine.

'Ma'am, Hugh Wethers,' he said.

'Any sign of the vehicle?'

'No, ma'am. It was a 1992 Land Rover Defender. Safe to assume it's gone off-road.'

She followed him into the farmhouse, passing the stables. Several stalls were occupied with horses. The smell brought back memories of her youth – she'd once been a keen rider, and every year promised herself she'd take up the reins again. Now, with Theo on the scene, that seemed more unlikely than ever.

The farmhouse wasn't a residential building any more – it had been converted into a clinic and offices. In one such room, a slight young man of around twenty wearing pyjamas with a warm coat over the top was seated on a battered armchair, clutching a cup of tea. He had a deep cut on his lip, and his jaw was bruised. Beside him were an older couple, perhaps fifty. The man wore a tweed suit and wellington boots, and the woman a hacking coat and jodhpurs. Paintings and photos of horses covered every wall.

The woman patted the young man on the shoulder and approached Jo. 'No one will tell us *what* is going on,' she said.

'That's what I'm here to find out,' said Jo. 'Can you explain what happened?'

'What does it look like? They assaulted the poor boy! Stole our car too.'

'Do you work here then?' asked Jo.

'We own the practice,' said the woman. 'My husband and I.' She held out her hand and gripped Jo's with surprising force. 'Kat Spekeman. My husband is Roland – he handles the medical side of things.'

'And is this your son?' Jo gestured to the younger man.

'Good heavens, no. Poor Tim just mans the place at night. He's a stable-hand. We got here this morning and we found him downstairs, gagged and tied up. He said he'd been there all night.'

'Would it be okay if I spoke to him?'

'He's very shaken up . . .'

'But he saw the burglars?'

'Oh, yes. He saw them all right.'

Jo moved past her, and sat beside the young man. She introduced herself, and learned his full name was Tim Tucker.

'Tim, can you tell me what happened last night?'

His voice was soft and heavily accented with a West Country burr. 'I was asleep and I heard a noise. We've had a problem with badgers getting into the stores, and I thought it might be that. Came downstairs. The back door was wide open. Then he came out of nowhere and whacked me with a torch. I couldn't even shout out. He just kept hitting me.'

Roland Spekeman placed a comforting hand on Tim's shoulder. 'Bloody animals, some people,' he muttered.

'Then what?' asked Jo.

'I must have been knocked out. When I woke up I was on the ground, but he'd tied me up, and stuffed a rag in my mouth. There was a girl watching me. She had a gun.'

'What did she look like?'

'Blonde hair. A teenager, I'd say. And small. The gun looked massive in her hand.'

'Did she say anything?'

'Just to stay where I was, and if I did, he wouldn't hurt me.'

'The man?'

'Yes, he'd gone into the clinic. He was in there for about twenty minutes.'

'And all this time you were with the girl?'

Tim nodded. 'She just kept saying I'd be all right if I didn't move.'

'Did she seem scared?'

Tim frowned. 'Not then.'

'But she did later?'

'Afterwards, they were arguing. She said she didn't want to do it – I thought he wanted to kill me and she was trying to persuade him not to.'

Jo paused. Was Megan growing a conscience as the murderous rampage continued, or had it always been there? Just how much of a participant or a passenger was she?

'And her companion – what was he doing in the clinic?'

'He's torn the place apart,' said Mrs Spekeman.

'Do you keep drugs here?'

Roland Spekeman nodded. 'We're a treatment centre as well

as a vet. We take care of most equine ailments. A few years ago, we lost a lot of ketamine when some bright spark realised we had a lot on site. And believe it or not, horse thefts are on the rise.'

'The girl said the man was hurt,' said Tim. 'He needed something for his neck.'

Jo remembered the bandages in the forest, and the one on James Brown's neck that Saskia Patel had mentioned, presumably from the wound sustained at the Baileys' home.

'What would you have to treat an infection?' she asked Mr Spekeman.

'It would depend on the location and severity. Something like trimethoprim or metronidazole.'

'And would those be effective for humans?'

The vet frowned. 'In the right dose, but a doctor would be a far more sensible option. You think this person wanted antibiotics for personal use?'

'Possibly. He's not exactly thinking straight.'

The vet looked bemused. 'I suppose the cameras will tell us if he found what he was looking for.'

'Oh,' said Jo. 'You have footage?'

'After the ketamine went missing, we installed them in the yard and in the clinic,' he said.

Jo hadn't noticed one outside. It might help to examine the footage to be sure the culprits were Megan and James – not that there was much doubt.

'Would you be able to show me now?'

'I don't see why not,' said Spekeman.

'Can I go home?' said Tim.

'Of course,' said Jo. 'My colleague will take your details, but you've been a star.' She felt oddly protective of the boy. He'd been through quite an ordeal.

'Kat can drop you,' said Spekeman.

291

'It's okay, sir – I'll call my brother.'

'As you wish.' He turned to Jo. 'If you'd like to follow me?'

In an adjoining office, he switched on a laptop and wound back the footage. The screen was split into two halves, each showing the simultaneous external and internal views. At 00.19 a man wearing a balaclava approached the front of the property, with the gun clearly visible in his hands. He vanished around the rear. Nothing happened for almost ten minutes, before he reappeared at the front door and left the way he'd come. It must have been during that window that he overpowered the stable-hand. When he came into frame again, it was 00.43 and he'd removed the balaclava. Megan was with him, and he led her by the hand, with the gun tucked into his trousers. They both entered the front of the house. At 00.46 he was in the clinic, looking through the cupboards and drawers. It wasn't quite a rampage, because he did at least seem to be inspecting the items closely, but his actions were hurried.

'Those are the antibiotics,' said Spekeman, leaning over to pause the video as James Brown took a plastic drawer from a cupboard. 'Looks like you were right.'

'How do you think he knew what to look for?'

'Oh, a basic internet search would tell him that. The dose wouldn't be obvious though.'

Brown seemed to have found what he was hunting for, stuffing several boxes in his pockets. At the same time, his eyes drifted upwards and into the camera. He quickly picked up a broom from one corner, hefting it by the handle and walked across the room. Next moment, the footage shook, the room blurring. Another apparent blow made one half of the screen go black.

'Nice try,' said Spekeman, 'but we've seen you now, boyo.'

'What was it he took?' said Jo.

'Hard to tell from this, but we keep a thorough inventory. We can check while we're clearing up.'

Jo continued with the tape. Thirteen more minutes before Megan and James emerged. This time the body language was different altogether. He was pulling her and she seemed reluctant to follow. Perhaps not scared, but certainly wary. He practically forced her into the Land Rover, before climbing in himself and driving off.

'We'll need a copy of this footage,' said Jo.

'Of course,' said the vet. 'Anything we can do to help you catch them.'

Jo stood. In the first room, Wethers and Kat Spekeman were talking, and Tim was gathering a bag to leave.

'Just another question,' said Jo. 'After the man came out of the clinic, did he say anything?'

'He wanted keys to the Land Rover,' said Tim.

'And you gave them to him?'

'I told him they were on a peg in the other office.' Here he looked sheepish. 'I didn't know what else to do.'

'It's fine, lad,' said the vet. 'It's just a car.'

'And then what?' said Jo.

'Then they left.'

'Straight away?'

'Pretty much. Like I said, they argued. She just kept saying it wasn't right. She didn't want to. I think she must have got through to him, because they left me alone.'

Jo didn't tell him how lucky he was, given James' spree up until that point. She didn't want to freak the poor kid out.

But she thought back to the recording. Something about the timings didn't match. Getting a key didn't take nearly quarter of an hour, and nor did the argument he was telling her about. Either Tim was misremembering the sequence of events, which wouldn't be that surprising, or James and Megan hadn't left immediately after he found the antibiotics. What had they been doing for over ten minutes, inside the building?

'Do you keep any other valuables in the property?' she asked.

'In here?' said the vet. 'I suppose the computer might be worth something. The odd painting . . .'

'And none of that was touched.'

He shook his head.

Jo thanked them all, and Wethers, saying she'd be in touch. As she was leaving, Kat spoke up. 'What do you think the chances are of finding the Land Rover? Makes our job pretty hard without it.'

'Rest assured we're on the lookout,' said Jo.

'She's got my phone too,' said Tim.

Jo stopped in the doorway. 'Pardon me?'

'She took my phone, while the man was in the clinic.'

Jo held in her excitement. A phone meant GPS. It meant, if Megan had it on her, that they could find her. She could've kissed poor Tim right on the lips, but instead she kept her composure.

'I'll need the number, if you've got it?'

Chapter 27

Stow-on-the-Wold was a tourist trap of antique shops, country-clothing outlets, and restaurants to suit all tastes. Jo had visited with her family once as a girl and remembered only one aspect of the day. She had been dipping her feet in the river that babbled through the town, and eating an ice-cream. Paul had splashed her, and in the movement to get away, the cone had slipped from her hand. The memory of the scoop of raspberry ripple slowly melting into the water as it drifted away was still more vivid than seemed credible. That it should still be with her now, as she sat in the village police station with DS Hugh Wethers, seemed particularly odd given the stakes of the current investigation.

They were waiting on the telecoms team to come back with a location for Tim Tucker's phone. The question was, why on earth Megan would have taken it. James was surely aware of the police's tracking capabilities, which left the tantalising prospect that Megan did also, and this was part of her plan. Jo had struggled from the start to see how or why she had turned killer. Now it was beginning to look like she'd had enough of being an accomplice to murder. St Aldates was on standby, as were the armed response unit. This time there would be no mistakes. This time they were the ones with the advantage.

When Jo's phone rang, it was Heidi.

'You need to hear this,' she said. 'Emergency Comms Centre received a call twenty minutes ago from the number we're trying to trace. I think it's Megan.'

'What did she say?'

'It's not that simple,' said Heidi. 'Forwarding the audio now. You need to listen.'

★ ★ ★

'. . . *It's going to be okay . . .*' a man's voice, the accent thickly Mancunian.

'*I feel shit.*' A girl said. '*My stomach . . .*'

'*Here, drink this.*'

'*I don't want to.*'

'*Drink it – it'll help.*'

'*I think I need a hospital.*'

'*No hospitals. Told you that before. I'm doing this for you.*'

'*Did you give me something?*'

'*Meg, I'm looking out for you.*'

A prolonged groan. It reminded Jo of a contraction. '*There's something wrong. James, please . . . I'm cold. What did you give me?*'

'*Here, put this on. We'll be on our way soon. I'll find a car.*'

'*Then what? They'll find us.*'

'*No they won't. I know where we can go. Just the two of us.*'

Another groan. '*I don't want to come any more. I'm scared.*'

'*Nothing to be scared of. Come on, drink.*'

'*I said, no more!*'

'*Then shut the fuck up while— What's that?*'

'*What?*'

'*That noise. I heard a beep.*'

'*I didn't hear . . . Hey!*'

The sound of scuffling, maybe a struggle.

'*Get off!*'

A pause.

'*Meg, what the fuck?*'

'*Give it back! I want to go home. Please, just leave me. I want to go home.*'

'*Oh fuck. No, no, no! Why Meg? WHY?*'

The next groan was cut off as the clip ended. Jo and Wethers sat in silence for a moment. Heidi had said the ECC had tried to ring back, but no one had answered.

Then Jo pressed play again. Heidi had told her roughly what to expect, but hearing the voices of Megan and James Bailey for the first time was still astonishing, like they were in the room with her.

One question was answered at least. Megan had indeed kept the phone from her brother. She wanted out, as shown in the five seconds of footage as he tugged her towards the Land Rover. She had taken the phone because she *wanted* them to find her.

Jo stopped the clip after Megan's fearful question: '*What did you give me?*'

'Whatever it was, she's in trouble,' said Wethers. 'You think he's drugged her?'

Jo has a pretty good idea what with. She played the audio again.

'*Meg, I'm looking out for you.*'

A few seconds later.

'*. . . Just the two of us.*'

'Have you got the number for the vet's?' she said.

Wethers found it and the phone was answered by Kat Spekeman. Jo got straight to the point and asked if they'd had chance to run through the inventory yet to see what else might be missing.

297

'I'm sorry, we haven't. Roland's still out doing the morning rounds.'

'This is going to sound like an odd question, but do you ever carry out abortions on horses?'

Beside her, Wethers' eyebrows shot up.

'Frequently,' said Kat. 'Though we call it a termination. Normally in the case of abnormalities, or multiple gestation.'

'And is there a drug you use?'

'Yes, it's called prostaglandin. E2 Alpha if you want the full label. An oral medication. We have it here. I mean . . . You don't think he would have taken *that*?' Jo could almost hear the other woman's furrowed brow.

'Would you mind checking the stocks?'

'Right now?'

'Please.'

She took the phone from her ear.

'You've got to be kidding me,' said Wethers.

'*Two*,' Jo said. 'Not three. The *two* of us.' She realised the Gloucestershire detective likely didn't know about their discovery of the positive test in the woods near Over Kidlington. 'Megan's pregnant. I think James has given her something to get rid of it, something he didn't want the camera to see.'

'Why?'

Jo thought about the bullets fired at Gregory Bailey. And where they'd been aimed. Not the heart or the head, but the groin.

Let's just say he didn't like the father.

'James has been looking for his sister for years. I doubt a baby fits in with his plan.'

'Which is?'

'Like he said. To get away – them and no one else.'

Kat Spekeman returned to the phone. 'It looks like you're right. We're don't keep much prostaglandin on site, and what we had has gone. Why the hell would they steal it?'

Those groans sounded bad. Really bad. She was scared.

'Have you any idea what would happen if prostaglandin was administered to a human?'

'It is, all the time,' said Spekeman, 'normally in combination with other medications to induce abortion. Hang on – that girl hasn't taken some?'

'Possibly,' said Jo.

'Then she needs to get to a hospital very quickly indeed,' said Spekeman.

Chapter 28

Jo was on the phone to Vera Coyne when Wethers signalled to her that the phone had been traced. Once a practising physician herself, Coyne's prognosis was much the same as Spekeman's, only more dire.

'Her cardiovascular system won't be able to cope and she'll almost certainly die,' she said bluntly.

'How long has she got?' said Jo.

'I couldn't tell you without knowing the dose,' said Coyne. 'She may already be dead, to be honest.'

After Jo ended the call, she looked at the map on Wethers' computer pinpointing the co-ordinates from the service provider. It looked to be only four or five miles from the veterinary practice, and maybe seven from their own position. Zooming in in the satellite imagery showed a spot in sparse woodland, just south of a town called Hook Norton.

'I know the place,' said Wethers. 'There's a sealed rail tunnel nearby. It's part of the old line to Chipping Norton that closed in the fifties.'

Jo called Dimitriou at St Aldates who confirmed the spot was on the map they'd recovered from the forest.

'Is the phone still pinging towers?' she asked.

'Apparently so,' said Dimitriou. 'You're wondering why he hasn't destroyed it?'

'Not really,' said Jo. 'I guess he's on the move already.'

With Andy Carrick still in hospital, she liaised directly with Chief Constable Harden, who was based in Reading, to authorise the tactical response team. Meanwhile Dimitriou and Reeves were hightailing it from Oxford. Harden and Jo joined a call with a DCI in Gloucester by the name of Pettifer, and together put a plan in place. Patrol units would set up along the four main routes out of Hook Norton, all with an armed contingent. Jo, Wethers, Dimitriou and Reeves would meet the two remaining members of the tactical unit at a rendezvous point close to the phone's location – they selected a small crossroads around five hundred metres to the south. With no direct road access, it would be a case of moving in on foot. Or rather, letting the armed officers do so. Jo could observe their progress via their helmet cameras, but operational control would be in the hands of Gloucestershire, and DCI Pettifer. Harden made it clear that no one was to approach the scene until they had reconned by air.

Before she got in the car, Jo paused outside the station in Stow. She dialled the number of Little Steps.

'Hi, it's Josie, Theo's mum. I just wanted to check everything was okay? Bit of a rush this morning.'

The key worker assured her that Theo was absolutely fine. 'He's playing at the sandtable.'

'Oh . . . good.'

For some reason, the thought of it, of her little boy oblivious and happy, made Jo well up. Wethers emerged from the station with an urgent stride and headed towards her. She turned away to conceal her emotion.

'Is there anything else I can help with?' asked the voice on the phone.

Jo swallowed back her tears, and put on her game face as Wethers closed in. 'No,' she said. 'Just tell him mummy's thinking about him.'

★　★　★

Theo remained in her thoughts as she closed in on the location, with Hugh Wethers following in the car behind. It was a physical sensation, seesawing between pleasure and pain, not helped by the light-headedness caused by not eating that day. Something didn't feel right at all, and she had the uncanny urge to turn the wheel around in the middle of the road and drive back to Oxford, to simply forget James and Megan, or at least to run away from whatever awaited.

It was only when she heard the thud of the helicopter overhead that she began to shake away the doubts. She passed the first patrol unit, showing her badge, and was waved through onto a deserted road. She found the tactical response van was already waiting at the RV point, with two officers, wearing black gear, a helmet and visor, standing at the open rear doors. A second vehicle, a sleek, navy BMW, was parked in front. Jo pulled up and stepped out.

'Ma'am,' one of the rifle-carrying officers greeted her.

Jo recognised the face and the lowland Scottish burr from their previous encounter, back in Oxford more than a year before. 'How are you, Menzies?'

'Very good, ma'am. And you?'

'Getting there,' she said. 'Any sign of the Land Rover?'

'Negative,' he replied. 'But there's a lot of tree cover. If you'd follow me. DCI's in the van.'

She accompanied him to the back of the AR vehicle. Inside, as well as two rows of seating, there were equipment stores locked behind metal doors. A third officer, helmet-less, sat in one corner facing two heavy-duty computer screens mounted side by side on a bracket bolted directly to the van wall. Standing over him was a tall woman with cropped red hair, in tailored dark grey trousers and a black jacket, maybe a couple of years older than her, but a lot better groomed.

'DS Masters, I'm DCI Pettifer. Gloucester.'

'Ma'am.'

'Jeffries here can brief you,' said Pettifer. 'We're almost ready.'

She stepped past, and jumped to the ground outside. Jo approached the screens. Jeffries tapped one of the screens with a gloved fingertip, where two red dots flashed on an aerial satellite map.

'These dots are Constable Connor and Sergeant Menzies,' he said. 'The plan is to approach the target following this streambed, heading south-east.' He pointed to what looked like a line of trees. 'It's mostly depressed, so we should be out of sight.'

Jo took a second to get her bearings, stepping to the back of the van and looking east.

'If he's there, he'll be expecting us.'

Menzies and DCI Pettifer were standing below.

'We can hold at a safe distance,' said Menzies. 'We'll assess risk before engaging. If we can get within thirty metres or so with line of sight, that's all we need,' said Menzies.

'And the girl?' said Jo. 'She'll be close. He might try to use her as a shield.'

Menzies glanced at Pettifer. 'We're operating under the assumption the girl is a dangerous individual too.'

'She's being held against her will,' said Jo.

'That's speculation at this stage,' replied Pettifer.

Jo assumed she hadn't heard the truncated 999 call. 'Ma'am, with all due respect, Megan's scared. Under duress.'

'I don't doubt it,' said Pettifer. 'She's directly involved in the deaths of four people. And there are at least two firearms in their possession. Sergeant Menzies and his men are cleared to use lethal force, but only if they perceive their own lives directly threatened. As long as Megan doesn't do anything stupid, she'll be fine.'

Jo didn't hold great hopes after everything Megan had done so far.

'She's sick,' she said. 'We need to get her to a hospital.'

'And we will do,' said Pettifer, steely-eyed, 'once any threat is neutralised.' She could obviously see the disquiet on Jo's face, because she lowered her voice. 'Sergeant, you've done fantastic work on this case so far, but we've reached the endgame. I won't risk any officer's life for that girl. Do you understand?'

'Yes, ma'am,' said Jo.

From the van, Jeffries called out, 'Phone's still not moved.'

'Are you good to go?' Pettifer asked Menzies.

'My colleagues from Oxford are still en route,' said Jo.

'They're non-essential,' said Pettifer, climbing back into the van. 'This is our window. Sergeant Menzies, you're ready?'

'Yes, ma'am.'

★   ★   ★

Jo, Wethers and DCI Pettifer stood behind Jeffries and watched the first-person perspectives of the two officers move up the shallow stream. On the opposite screen, the digital representations of their bodies crept across the map towards a small black cross that marked the position of Tim Tucker's stolen phone.

Jo had a strong suspicion already what they'd find and was bracing herself for Megan's dead body, James Brown long gone. Dimitriou and Reeves were still fifteen minutes out, and Jo told herself not to worry. Pettifer had it right – neither of them were critical to the mission.

Menzies and Connor came to a halt under a bank, and the voice of the former crackled over the comms.

'We're in position, fifty metres.'

'Can you get a visual?' asked Pettifer.

Jo saw Menzies' hands extended in front of him and he scrambled up the bank, gripping an exposed tree root to pull himself up. All Jo could see were bushes and trees. 'Negative,' said Menzies. 'Too overgrown. Permission to approach closer.'

'Granted,' said Pettifer. She was gripping the back of the Jeffries' seat, eyes glued to the screens.

Menzies waited until Connor was alongside him, then made a hand signal. Crouching, the two of them proceeded on short bursts, one ahead of the other, before waving their partner on. Occasionally, a rifle butt swung into shot. Through their mics Jo heard the rustle of foliage and their laboured breathing. After half a minute, Connor's camera picked up a red metal door ahead through a wall of leaves. Menzies showed the same a moment later, but clearer. As Wethers had explained, it was a train tunnel shaft, blocked up over forty years ago when the railway shut down to stop local kids getting inside and causing mischief. The door gave access to the inside, should engineers ever need to enter. The other end of the tunnel, about three hundred metres north, had been filled with concrete, and the ventilation shafts built over. If Megan or James were in there, the red door was the only way out.

'Any visual on the suspects?' said Pettifer.

'Negative,' said Menzies. 'Permission to proceed.'

'With caution.'

Menzies hoisted his gun, and the rifle, steady and straight, appeared in the bottom of the camera's frame. The effect of the angle was to make it seem they were staring directly along the barrel at the target ahead. Connor was sweeping the area in arcs with his weapon, while Menzies, a few yards ahead, kept his gun trained on the red tunnel door. Jo was focused there too. If anyone burst through now, they'd be mown down in a hail of bullets.

Menzies closed in. Ten metres . . . eight . . . five . . .

Jo bit her lip hard enough to draw blood. *Megan, if you're in there, please stay put.*

The door was metal, with a yellow 'Keep Out' sign fastened to it, and another notice in text too small to read. It was fractionally ajar.

'Is anyone in there?' shouted Menzies, and through the monitor's speakers it was deafening. Jeffries, the operator, turned a dial.

'We are armed police officers!' yelled Menzies. 'If you have weapons, lay them on the floor now, and come out with your hands behind your heads.'

No sound came from the other side of the door as the seconds ticked by.

'This is a last warning,' said Menzies. 'We are armed police. If you are armed, we *will* shoot you!'

Still nothing.

They've gone, thought Jo. *Or James has, at least. Megan might be lying on the other side dead already.*

'Permission to enter?' said Menzies.

'Go,' said Pettifer.

'Targeting lights,' said Menzies, and he flicked a switch near the barrel of his gun. Connor did the same. Then Menzies stepped to the left of the door, turned sideways on to face Connor, and the camera bobbed as he nodded. Connor's hand reached out and gripped the rim of the door, pulled it open and moved to the right to remain shielded. Menzies dropped into a crouch, twisted, and pointed his rifle through the door. The camera took a moment to adjust as a wide arc illuminated the interior. The floor was bare earth, uneven, and the light only penetrated around twenty metres. She couldn't see anyone inside.

Menzies entered and the torch on his barrel threw flares of light over the interior.

'No visual on suspects,' he said. 'Wait, I see the phone.'

He stooped, and the image became confusing. Jo looked instead at Connor's POV. Menzies was crouching and holding the phone. 'Looks like they've gone,' he said.

As he stood, Jo's eyes caught a strange gleam near his feet – it looked like a wire.

'Holy shit,' she said, reaching over Jeffries to point it out. 'Is that a—'

Both screens went white, and a split-second later Jo heard a loud bang like the first shocking crack of thunder.

Chapter 29

'Serge?' said Jeffries.

'Sergeant Menzies?' repeated Pettifer.

Jo walked swiftly to the back of the van and looked outside. A cloud of smoke was rising above the trees to the east. She jumped out and dashed to her car, and fumbled with the radio through the open window.

'This is DS Masters, we need an ambulance and air evac. Suspected bomb detonation in the vicinity of Hook Norton. Two casualties, both armed officers. Use my car as position.'

As she left the car, more radio traffic was coming over, but she ignored it. She strode along the side of the road, looking for a place she could get over the hedge and into the field beyond. Any way she could get to them.

Pettifer appeared in the back of the van. 'Where are you going?' she called. 'It's not safe!'

Jo was about to shout back, when a vehicle appeared, heading their way. Her first instinct was that it was a member of the public who'd somehow slipped past the cordon, but then the horror dawned as she realised it was an old model Land Rover. It was steaming straight towards them, at speed.

'Move!' Jo bellowed at the DCI.

Pettifer froze.

'It's him!' Jo screamed. As he drew closer, James Brown extended the pistol out of his car door. Jo dived across her bonnet and slid over the far side, face first into the hedge. She heard a *Pop! Pop!* as bullets hit metal, then a brief pause, followed by 'No!'

Three more shots.

Jo scrambled upright and saw the Land Rover was parked a few metres up, alongside the van. The place where Pettifer had been standing was empty. James Brown climbed casually out of the front seat, and approached the van. He aimed downwards at the ground and fired one shot at something hidden between the front of Pettifer's car and the van.

Jo's stomach recoiled. She couldn't move. There was movement in the back of the Land Rover. A head resting on the glass.

Megan . . .

Suddenly, Brown spun around, red mist exploding from his right shoulder as a crack emanated from the van. He caught himself against Pettifer's bonnet, then swung round, swapped the gun into his left hand, and fired four times through the open rear doors. Jo heard a cry of pain. Brown's gun clicked empty, and he stuffed it in his trousers, climbed back into the Land Rover and pulled away. The whole incident had lasted around fifteen seconds.

Jo ran to the van, fearing the worst and finding it. Pettifer lay on her back, three gunshot wounds in close grouping on her chest, and a fourth, just a discreet red dot above her left eyebrow. She was completely still. Jeffries lay on his front, completely still, as blood pooled under his head. His gun lay on the ground beside his head. Wethers was slumped beside the monitor, clutching his thigh.

'Go after him!' he said.

'You need help,' said Jo, clambering in.

'I'll survive,' he said.

Jo shook her head. 'But . . .'

'Go! Now! Take the gun.'

Jo looked at the standard issue Glock beside Jeffries' inert fingers. Before she really had time to consider it properly, it was in her hand. She ran back to her car, jumped in. With the gun on the passenger seat, she sped off in pursuit of the Land Rover. She could only have been fifteen or twenty seconds behind, but already she feared she'd lost him. She came to a crossroads, choosing to stay on the same road. As she passed the junction, her eyes caught the fleeing Land Rover to her left. There wasn't room to turn, so she slammed on the brakes, put the car into reverse, and scooted backwards, engine whining. Yanking the wheel and accelerating, she almost lost the back end around the corner.

'DS Masters in pursuit of green Land Rover Defender, driven by James Brown. He is armed and dangerous. Ambulance required on Quiet Lane, Hook Norton, 800m south of the Chipping Norton Road. DCI Pettifer has been shot and killed. Sergeant Jeffries also. Sergeant Wethers has a gunshot wound to the leg. Repeat two dead, and one injured.'

'Confirm your position, DS Masters.'

She was gaining on the Land Rover, and checked her SatNav. 'I am driving north along Weavers Lane from Quiet Lane.'

The Land Rover swerved, then righted itself.

'Jo,' came a voice, 'this is Chief Constable Harden. You said DCI Pettifer has been killed?'

'Yes, ma'am,' said Jo and the cool voice sounded alien to her. 'James Brown shot her four times. Sergeant Jeffries is dead as well.'

A pause. 'Jo, discontinue pursuit.'

'I'm right behind him,' she said.

'We've got multiple patrols standing by,' said Harden. 'Let him go.'

'Ma'am, he's just shot three people. He's an active threat. He's armed.'

'And you're not, Masters!'

Jo glanced at the Glock.

'Masters, I gave you an order. Confirm you understand.'

'Yes, ma'am,' said Jo.

She pressed the accelerator, and closed the gap.

Brown braked hard, and swerved off the road, along a smaller lane. Jo reached the same spot and went after him. The distance between them was down to fifty metres.

Jo didn't know what she was going to do if and when they came to a halt. She didn't know what she was doing, *full stop.* Her firearms training had consisted of a single day, a 'taster' session more than twelve years ago. She'd been a good shot, better than her colleague Ben Coombs, much to his chagrin, but the whole thing had left her exhausted, mentally and physically. Maybe it was the stress of the day imprinting things on her memory, but she still recalled the instructions of the trainer all those years ago. *One hand on the grip, one supporting the wrist. Set your feet. Pull the trigger slowly – a bullet's fast enough on its own.*

It had seemed easy when the targets weren't firing back, when they were just making holes in paper. But Brown was a maniac, and his bullets were unforgiving. She thought of Pettifer, lifeless on the ground. Of Jeffries, a trained firearms operative himself. Of the blood-soaked pavement in Jericho. Of Xan Do, half his face destroyed.

She thought, among all the images of horror, about Theo, probably dozing off his lunch in the peaceful ambience of the Little Steps dormitory room.

What am I doing? What am I fucking thinking?

She almost stopped the car.

But she couldn't. James Brown wasn't going to hurt anyone else – *not on my watch . . .*

As they came around the next corner, Jo saw a building ahead. Her first thought was a farmhouse, and that meant civilians, but as they neared, she realised it was deserted. Just a ruin. And it wasn't a cottage, but some sort of industrial facility, from the turn of the last century, maybe, with crumbling brick walls but the remains of large doors at one end. There were windows at the top, at the height of a second storey, and just under a shallow-sloping roof. Tall arched windows in the walls had been bricked up, so she couldn't see inside. Outside was a large area of concrete, overgrown with patches of tall weeds, surrounded by a temporary metal fence that had collapsed in places.

The Land Rover braked, and Jo did the same, forty or fifty metres back. If he put the thing into reverse, and came at her, she wanted time to turn around. But instead of stopping he continued at low speed, drifting until the front of the Land Rover hit a fence and came to a halt. No one emerged from the vehicle.

Jo remained where she was for a few seconds, breathing hard. She pressed the radio button.

'This is DS Masters. He's stopped' She checked her SatNav, but the lane had no name. 'I took a track off Weaver's Lane.'

'*This is HS4. We have your position. Transmitting visual.*'

Jo looked up, and saw the helicopter above.

'Megan's in the Land Rover. Can you land?'

'Masters.' It was Harden, and she sounded beyond pissed off. 'Can you see Brown?'

'I think he's injured ma'am.'

'Can you see him?'

'No. But Jeffries shot him in the torso.'

'The chopper doesn't land until we have a visual.'

The left rear door of the Land Rover opened with a clatter, and Megan Brown tumbled out. Her hands were bound with a plastic tie. She tried to stand, but fell, and caught herself on her wrists and knees. Her ankles were tied too. She saw Jo's car, and scrambled to her feet, only to fall again. 'I see Megan.'

'*We have her too,*' said the helicopter.

Jo left the engine running, and cracked open her door.

'Stay in the car,' said Harden.

Jo realised the Chief Constable was seeing the footage from the chopper. She reached across, and took the Glock.

Megan looked up at her. Her hair was hanging in front of her face, and her skin was white.

She needs help.

Jo stepped from the car, and heard Harden swear over the comms. Through the back window of the Land Rover she couldn't see James Brown. Jo crouched behind her open door. 'Come on, Megan,' she said. 'Come to me.'

Jo had edged out a little, when the front door of the Land Rover opened. Brown stepped down. Jo saw the right side of his dark hoodie was saturated from shoulder to hip with blood. He carried the shotgun in his right hand, sawn off halfway along the barrel.

'Get back here!' he roared at Megan. She saw him, gave a wail, and redoubled her efforts, practically dragging herself towards Jo like a fish flopping back to the safety of water. Brown walked past her. Awkwardly, like the limb was almost a dead weight, he slung his right hand across his body, resting the shotgun over his forearm, and took aim at Jo. She ducked behind the door as the booming shot went off. Pellets thudded into the door, and the glass of the window showered over her head. She wasn't hit, but for a moment, she was paralysed in fear. Her mind screamed.

If you don't move, you're dead. Theo won't have a mother.

Her body didn't listen.

'You're not taking her!' Brown shouted.

A second shot went off, and the door shook.

She was lucky he wasn't using the pistol. A 9mm round would have cut through the door easily. She dared to look out. He was on one knee, barrel resting vertically on the ground, reloading shells.

Might not get another chance.

Jo levelled the Glock through the broken window, keeping the car door was a shield. 'Drop the gun, James!' she said.

Brown didn't look all that alarmed. He snarled, set the shotgun down, turned around and walked towards Megan. He grabbed her by the collar, and yanked her after him. She screamed and tried to fend him off as she was dragged along the ground on her bum and heels towards the building. Jo, unable to pull the trigger for fear of hitting Megan, watched them go. As soon as he was out of sight, she followed. Running across the ground, she saw metal tracks inlaid, and realised the building she was approaching must have once been an engine shed or something of that ilk. Like the tunnel earlier, this was a remnant of the old railway.

The helicopter circled overhead, keeping her in sight.

'James, please,' she shouted. 'Let Megan go. We can look after her.'

She didn't know if he could hear her, or if he would even care. Did he still have the pistol? Did he have ammo? The Glock felt heavy, cumbersome, her hand sweaty on the cross-hatched metal grip. She tried to loosen her fingers, but they seemed locked.

She edged along the wall until she reached the end. Taking a series of deep breaths, she spun around the perimeter, gun held out at eye level. There was no one there, but a metal set of double doors, flaking with rust, were open. Blood trailed inside. Jo walked towards them. Her legs felt like jelly. If he still had the Makarov, he'd be firing left-handed. But he'd killed Jeffries just fine.

'James, I don't want either of you to get hurt,' she said. 'There's no way out of here. Not this time. If you throw the gun out of the door, no one will harm either of you, I'll make sure of that.'

'Shut it, will you?' he said. The voice was angry, plaintive, almost childlike.

'James, Megan is going to die unless we get her to hospital,' said Jo. 'That stuff you gave her, it's going to kill her. They'll look after her.'

'I'll fucking look after her.' He sounded desperate. She wondered how much blood he'd lost. How compromised was he?

'Look at her, James! I know you love your sister, but *look* at her.'

There was no answer. She waited, listening to the rotors of the chopper and the distant, indistinct radio chatter coming from her car.

'James?' she called.

Another minute or so passed and she worried he might have slipped away somehow. She risked a peep around the door.

Inside the shed was almost empty, apart from the remains of a gantry around the upper half, collapsed in places. The roof was supported by exposed steel beams, and three sets of tracks ran through the centre. James Bailey was sitting against the wall, with Megan clutched in front of him between his splayed legs. He looked exhausted. He had one arm around her chest, holding her to him, and in his right hand, resting on the floor, he held the Makarov.

Jo moved inside, gun trained on him. Could he even lift that arm? Impossible to tell.

'Let her go, James.'

'She doesn't want to come with you,' he said.

'Why don't you ask her, James,' said Jo.

'What do you want?' he said, chin resting on top of his sister's head.

Megan's eyes were on the gun too.

Jo had a shot, but six inches off-target and it would be Megan who died. She set her feet, her hands rock solid on the gun. She couldn't do it. Not unless Megan put some distance between her and her brother.

'I asked what you want?' said James. 'You want to go with them, after everything I've done for you?'

'I don't know,' said Megan, her voice a whimper. She slumped forward, but he pulled her back against him.

'I did all this for you,' he said. 'So we could be happy, yeah?'

'I know,' said Megan. 'I know you did. But I don't feel right. I need to go to hospital.'

'I can make you better,' he said. 'When that thing's out of you, you'll feel better.'

'She needs a doctor, James,' said Jo. 'Let me take her. You can see each other after.'

It was the wrong thing to say.

'Fuck you!' he said, face twisting. 'You know how many fuckers like you said that to me before? Every time I asked, every *fucking* time I wanted to know where she was.'

'Okay, James,' said Jo. She took her supporting hand off the gun, spreading both to placate him. 'I won't lie to you. You're going to be arrested. But you will see Megan again, if she wants to. She can visit you. That's a promise. Isn't that right, Megan, love?'

'Yeah,' said Megan.

Brown banged the back of his head on the wall, hard enough to make a thud, and gnashed his teeth. 'Why couldn't you people just leave us alone?' he said. He lifted the Makarov and pointed it at Megan's head. His arm trembled with the effort.

His sister squirmed, wailing in fear, but he kept the barrel on her temple.

'James, no!' said Jo.

'You think I'm going to let you take her?' he shouted. 'She's my sister! You think I'd *ever* let *you* take her?'

Megan's hands went to his ankle, and before Jo understood what was happening, she pulled a long bowie knife from a hidden sheath. He saw it too, and lowered the gun, for just a second to make a grab. Megan thrust the knife into his leg just above his knee with considerable force.

Brown screamed, and shoved Megan away from him. For a second he looked at the knee in astonishment, then at Megan. He swapped the Makarov into his left hand and raised it towards his sister.

Jo pulled the trigger. Brown's body flinched, and the gun swayed in his hand. Jo took two steps forward and fired again, this time at his head. She thought she'd missed, but his arms fell suddenly limp. Blood began to trickle from the inside corner of his left eye.

'James?' said Megan, sitting a metre away.

Brown's head remained stationary but both of his eyes moved in his sister's direction, like they were the only living thing in his body. They watched her, black and fierce, for a second, then their focus shifted and he seemed to be looking into the distance.

Jo ran up and kicked the Makarov away. It clanked across the rails in the floor. Megan slumped onto her side.

'Hey!' said Jo, rushing to her. 'Don't give up now,' she said.

Megan didn't respond. Her own eyes were glassy, her breathing shallow. Bloody froth seeped from her lips.

'Hold on,' said Jo, placing her own gun on the ground. 'Help's coming.'

Though as she ran outside to wave the chopper down, she had little hope it would come in time.

Chapter 30

SATURDAY, 26TH APRIL

At the door of the ward, Constable Marquardt signed her in.

'You're looking smart, ma'am.'

Jo didn't know what to make of the compliment, or its implications. Was she really that sloppily presented normally?

'Got somewhere to be later,' she said. 'How's the patient?'

'Sprightly, considering,' he said. 'The solicitor was here earlier. For about thirty seconds until she told him he could sling his hook. Well, the equivalent, in rather choicer language.'

For security reasons, Megan Bailey had a private room. When she saw Jo, she sat up straighter in bed, as if a tiger had entered the room rather than a five-foot-six woman.

'It's all right,' said Jo. 'This isn't an official visit.'

With her hair tied back, Megan looked older. Or maybe that was the ordeal she had been through. Jo felt older too.

'Mind if I sit down?' said Jo.

The girl nodded.

Jo took a seat, and reached into her bag, bringing out the make-up bag she'd recovered from the girl's bedroom in Stanton

St John. 'Thought you might want something from home,' she said.

Megan watched in silence as Jo placed it beside the bed.

'How are you feeling?'

'Better,' said Megan. She didn't seem to know what to make of Jo's presence.

'I'm sorry about the baby,' she said.

Megan shrugged, not dismissively, but as if she didn't quite know what to make of that either. 'Probably for the best,' she added.

Jo didn't have any answers for her in that regard.

'My name is Josie,' she said. 'I'm a police officer with Thames Valley. In time, you'll be asked to give an official statement, but it can wait until you're stronger. I'm also a friend of Harry Ferman.'

Megan nodded, her skin pale. 'They told me he was dead.'

Jo blinked. 'Yes, he is. Being smashed on the head with a metal bar will do that to you.'

Megan had begun to cry. She shook her head. 'James told me they were just going to talk.'

'About what?' asked Jo. She didn't know whether to believe what she was hearing.

'About James and me going away,' said Megan.

Too many unanswered questions . . .

'You're telling me you didn't know what happened?'

Megan paused. 'If I had, I'd never have . . .' She looked at Jo angrily. 'Harry was my friend.'

Jo remained dispassionate. 'BFFs with a seventy-year-old bloke?'

'You said he was your friend too,' said Megan, through tear-filled eyes.

There were tissues on the stand nearby, but Jo let her cry. 'So how did you and Harry end up being mates?' she asked.

Megan looked at her, and Jo saw her mind going over options, wondering what version of the truth to tell.

'I know you broke in,' said Jo.

'He was kind,' said Megan. 'I'd hurt myself. Cut myself on some glass. He told me he wouldn't phone the police. I . . . I couldn't believe it.'

'And he just let you stay? Just like that.'

'He wanted to phone my parents. I told him I didn't have any family. I don't know if he even believed me or not. But he said he could help me.'

'Help you how?'

'I . . . I don't know.'

'And you just moved in?'

'Not then. He said I could come back, if I needed to talk. Things weren't good with Xan. He wouldn't leave me alone. But he didn't know about Harry's place.'

'So it was convenient?' said Jo, feeling her lip curl.

'It wasn't like that.'

'So how was it?'

'I dunno. We talked. He had problems too. Drinking. He said we could help each other. You know, get clean.'

Jo almost scoffed. Harry was a kind man, but he wasn't stupid, or romantic, especially when it came to drug addicts. No cop was. Yet the lack of booze bottles supported Megan's claims. And Harry hadn't been a cop for a long time. Was it possible that time off the job had softened him that much?

'The first few days were awful,' said Megan, 'but he looked after me. He said he could find people to help me, if I wanted. Fed me. Toast mostly.'

Jo smiled, despite herself. Now the girl wasn't lying.

'So how does James fit into all this?' she asked.

A long pause followed, with Megan's eyes darting like she couldn't make sense of it herself. 'I hardly even remembered

321

him. I guess that sounds stupid, but Mum and Dad never spoke about him. I don't know if they even knew I'd *had* a brother. None of the council lot mentioned him. It was easy to forget. Then he showed up, while I was staying with Harry. It was . . . *weird*. He said he'd been looking for me. That we could go away.'

'And what did you think of that?'

'I was excited, I s'pose. I *wanted* to leave. Harry was worried for me though.'

'And what about your mum and dad?'

'They were away. They wouldn't care.'

'I find that hard to believe.'

Megan's eyes flashed. 'You don't know anything about *them*.'

Jo sensed, if she pushed it, this weak and tiny girl was liable to leap out of bed and start swinging.

'Did you ever tell them about Greg?'

Megan shook her head. 'They knew though. I know they knew.'

Sometimes a thing could be right before your eyes, thought Jo, and you might still not see it. Sometimes it was easier to keep the truth at bay rather than deal with the consequences.

Megan's mouth twitched. 'Someone told me he was here.'

'He will be for a while,' said Jo. 'James hurt him badly.'

'Yes,' said Megan. 'He didn't deserve that.'

'He won't be able to come near you now,' Jo said.

There was no anger or bitterness in the girl's face, but Jo couldn't discern *what* the girl was feeling about the brother who'd slept with her, or what she thought herself. The courts might have a view, but whatever judgement ended up being passed down seemed an inadequate response to the messy lives of the adoptive siblings. Nothing could ever fix what had happened between them.

But, despite everything the girl had suffered, Jo wasn't ready to absolve her yet. How could James Brown ever have looked like a good option or a promising future?

Jo leant forward. 'Your brother killed eight people, including four police officers. Your mum and dad. Xan. Don't sit there and play innocent. You were on the run, holding people up at gunpoint, stealing things . . .'

'Not me. James . . .'

'But you were *with* him. You didn't stop him. You didn't run away.'

Megan threw a glance at the door, as if hoping to be rescued. When no one came, Jo pushed her.

'Tell me, please,' said Jo. 'I need to understand what happened.'

I need to understand you.

Megan took a deep breath. 'It was different, at first. James was different. He just wanted to help.'

'By killing Xan. And your mum and dad? And Harry?'

'I didn't *know* about any of it!'

'Or you didn't want to.'

Megan gave the tiniest of nods. In an interview room, Jo would have noted it for the recording. Not a confession as such, but an acknowledgement, as if the enormity of James' crimes, and her own part, was still sinking in. 'You have to believe me.'

It doesn't matter what I believe, thought Jo. Andy Carrick had told her the day after James Brown's death that the Chief Constable wanted her nowhere near the interrogation of Megan Bailey.

'James said they would be looking for us, and our only chance was to hide. If they found us, they'd separate us again, and maybe even put us in prison. He took my phone – said we could get a new one later. He'd planned it all.'

'Did he know you were pregnant?'

'No one did. I'd done tests at Harry's. I hoped it would go away like last time, but it didn't. I was feeling sick all the time, so I told James. We got another test, and he completely changed. It was like he was disgusted with me. I shouldn't have told him about Greg, but I wanted to explain that it wasn't simple. It wasn't my fault . . .'

'He took it badly?'

She blew out her cheeks. 'Yes. I told him we could use it; that Greg might give us money to get away. I knew he had loads, and that he'd do anything to keep it all from Mum and Dad.' The faraway look returned to Megan's eyes. 'I honestly didn't know they were dead.'

'And then James gave you drugs?' said Jo.

Megan touched her stomach inadvertently. 'His neck was really bad. He said he needed medicine, and any doctor would turn us both in. But when we were at the horse vet's, he said he had something that could help me too. He said it was the same stuff they give women who want to get rid of babies.'

'It is,' said Jo, 'just not in those sorts of doses.'

'I tried to get away that night, but he just flipped completely. I thought he was going to kill me. He said I was an ungrateful bitch, and everything he'd done was for me. After that, it's all mixed up . . .'

Megan looked up sharply towards the door, and Jo saw Annabelle Pritchard and another woman standing on the other side of the glass, speaking to Constable Marquardt. He let them pass.

'Sergeant,' said Pritchard formally.

Jo remained seated. 'Lots of visitors today, Megan.'

'Would you mind if we spoke to Megan in private?' asked Pritchard.

'I was just leaving,' said Jo. 'Goodbye, Megan. And good luck.'

She picked up her bag and walked past the bed, past the council workers, reflecting on the hollowness of her own words. The girl would need a lot more than luck.

'Hey,' said Megan. Jo turned by the doors. Megan lifted the make-up bag and gave a small smile.

Jo nodded in acknowledgement, and left. As she signed Marquardt's register, she glanced back through the glass partition as the two council workers moved to the end of the bed. They'd had a dozen years to fix the broken parts, and they were still trying.

Maybe I shouldn't be so cynical.

JAMES

NINE DAYS EARLIER

He scanned up and down the street. A fat woman walking a Jack Russell, but not paying him any attention. He knocked at the door to number 21.

'Hang on a mo,' came a voice. A few seconds later, the door opened, and the old man was standing there. 'Can I help you?'

'Mr Ferman, I'm Megan's brother.'

He nodded. 'Aye, she mentioned you. Not seen her for a few days.'

James didn't like his tone. 'Can we talk?'

Ferman took in a deep breath through his nose, then stood aside. 'Come in.'

James entered, wiping his feet on the doormat. No need to be impolite. Yet.

The house smelled musty. The carpet brought back memories of one of his first foster places. Ferman led him into a living room. Fireplace, crappy TV, a sofa that looked as knackered as its owner. Nothing worth nicking.

'So where is the young lass?' said the old man.

None of your fucking business.

'Hotel,' lied James. In fact, he'd told her to wait at the camp while he fetched a few bits. He trusted her to stay put. She seemed to find the outdoor living quite exciting, bless her.

'Can I get you a cuppa?'

'Coffee. Ta.'

Ferman traipsed through to the small kitchen, leaving James standing awkwardly. After a couple of seconds, he followed. He watched the old man's back as he set the kettle to boil.

'Do you take sugar?'

'Two.'

'Have a seat, please,' said Ferman.

James pulled out a chair from under the small Formica table.

'She's a good girl, Megan,' said Ferman, as he fetched two mugs from a cupboard.

'Yeah,' said James. 'It's great to see her again.'

Silence fell over the kitchen as the old man poured steaming water into the cups. As he fetched milk from the fridge, he shot a glance at James.

'She told me you two had a difficult time when you were younger.'

What was this? Some sort of counselling session? 'Did she now?'

Ferman placed a mug in front of James, and eased his frame into the chair opposite. 'I don't mean to pry. She's had a hard time ever since, by the sounds of it.'

Nervous, James sipped the drink too fast, and scalded the roof of his mouth. 'That's why I'm taking her away.'

'What happened to your neck?'

James shrugged. It hadn't healed well and he was almost certain it was infected. 'Cut myself shaving.'

'Ouch,' said the old man. 'You should go electric.'

James nodded.

Ferman folded his arms and leant his weight on them over the table, closer than James would've liked. 'She told me you served in the army.'

'That's right.'

'Whereabouts?'

'Afghanistan.'

'Must've been tough.'

'It was okay.' James didn't feel like any more chat. 'Listen, I only came by to grab her stuff and thank you for looking out for her.'

Ferman continued as if he hadn't heard. 'And you've got a place, back in Manchester? Big enough for the both of you?'

'Sure.'

The old man sipped his own drink thoughtfully.

'And have you spoken to her parents?'

'They're not her parents,' said James. 'I'm her family.'

'I understand that, but they raised her,' said Ferman. 'Don't you think they deserve to know?'

James felt the blood rising to his face as he thought back to the disaster of five days earlier. He'd only gone to the posh house to get a few of Megan's things. She'd told him they were away. It was her fault what had happened, really. After they'd seen his face, there was only one possible outcome. He hadn't told Megan, of course – didn't want to freak her out. The sooner they were away from Oxford, the sooner they could put it all behind them.

'It's up to her,' said James.

'Is it?' said Ferman, staring at him hard.

James pushed his seat back. 'I've just come to get her things.'

'Finish your coffee first, lad,' said Ferman. 'There's no rush.'

It didn't sound much of a friendly offer, and James suddenly had a good idea what this old geezer once did for a living. If he was right, it was time to leave.

'Tell you what, keep the stuff,' said James. He stood.

Harry stood too. He looked a bit taller now, his back a little straighter. 'If you give me your address, your full name, I could post them on,' said the old man. He was standing in the doorway, blocking the way out. Yep, definitely police. He had that way about him.

'I've got to go,' said James. He held out his hand. 'Nice to have met you.'

Ferman looked at the hand, but didn't take it. 'Was that your car, James?'

'You what?'

'The blue one you've been driving around?'

'Course it is.'

'So have you got kids?'

Fuck. He'd seen the child seat.

'No, but I sometimes drive my nephew.' He squeezed past, out into the living room. His nerves were fizzing.

'I didn't know you had another sibling.'

'Step.'

'What's the lad's name?'

James turned around to face Ferman.

'You ask a lot of questions.'

Ferman shrugged. 'I'm just curious.'

'Nosy, more like.'

Ferman nodded. 'Maybe. Thing is, James – I don't believe a word of what you're saying to me.'

'Don't you now? And why exactly should I care?'

Ferman cocked his head. 'Why don't we all sit down together – you, me, and Megan?'

'She won't be coming back,' said James. 'She doesn't need you any more.'

'Because she has you?'

James took three quick breaths, but none of them seemed to calm him.

'What is it with you, anyway? You some sort of perv? You like having a young girl in your house?'

Ferman shook his head, a little sadly. 'There's no need to get angry, lad.'

'Stop fucking calling me that.' His heart was beating its way out of his chest. No stopping now. 'You couldn't just leave it, could you?'

'Leave what? I'm just worried about Megan.'

James crouched, and took the knife out of his boot.

At the sight of the blade, Ferman moved to the other side of the sofa. 'Now, now,' he said. His voice remained surprisingly calm. 'You don't have to do anything silly, James. Walk away. I won't stop you.'

'And you won't phone your pig friends?'

'If you go now, and leave Megan alone, I won't tell anyone. You have my word.'

'You don't get it, do you?' said James. His tongue played over the blister forming on the roof of his mouth. 'You think I'd just walk away now, after everything I've done for her?' He moved to intercept Ferman, who kept the sofa between them.

'What is it you've done?' asked Ferman.

James thought of the parents, wriggling and wailing in the cellar as they realised what was coming, and of Xan Do and the surprised look as James had shone the torch into his car window. He probably hadn't even seen the gun before the bullet entered his brain. He thought of Christopher Putman, begging for his life, promising he'd told James everything, everything he knew, *everything . . . I promise, I swear, please . . .*

Ferman's arm came up suddenly. James dodged back instinctively as the metal poker winded past his face.

'You fucking cunt,' he said. As Ferman advanced and swung again, he overbalanced and fell across the end of the sofa. James reached forward and snatched the poker from him. Ferman looked afraid as he approached. His foot caught the edge of an occasional table, and spilled over a small vase of flowers.

'You don't have to do this,' said the old man, holding up his arms to defend himself. 'It's not too late.'

James swung the poker, and felt an arm bone give. Ferman cried out and dropped to his knees, cradling his wrist. When he looked up, though, there was no fear. His gaze was filled with disgust.

'She's not stupid. She'll find out what you are, lad.'

'I told you not to fucking call me that,' said James.

He lifted the poker over the bowed grey head.

Chapter 31

The turnout at the funeral was better than Jo had expected. In addition to half a dozen folk from the Three Crowns, there were uniforms aplenty in the aisles at the crematorium chapel, as well as several grizzled faces, almost all male, who must have been former colleagues. Mrs Milner from the house two down on Canterbury Road had made the trip, and several other residents too. As Jo milled around before the service, she heard of the many small kindnesses that Harry had performed over the years, simple things like fixing a leak under a sink, or helping to find a runaway dog. It made her realise that the street where Harry had lived wasn't such an unfriendly place after all. They might not have been a community, but neither did they shun one another.

Jessica Granger and her step-son stood near the back for the duration of the service, despite that the organisation was their doing. Jo had contacted them to offer her help, but they had rejected any financial contribution. Jessica, however, had made a far more daunting suggestion, and Jo had been moved to accept. So it was, after a few words from the minister presiding, that she stepped up to the podium, just as Vera Coyne, alongside a shabbily dressed Mel Cropper, entered late at the back of the chapel.

Harry's coffin lay off to one side on a raised dais – it had seemed too small to hold his body as the pallbearers carried it in, and she tried not to imagine him inside it now. On a trestle table were three framed photos: two that bookended his police career, and at the forefront, Lindsay and Harry on the beach. Jo looked up at the expectant gathering. In the silence, she fancied Harry himself speaking to her over a glass of something peaty.

They're not getting any younger, Josie. Get on with it.

She took a deep breath.

'Some of you will have known Harry longer than me. You'll have your own stories, about good and bad times on the job. I met him only a couple of years ago, but sometimes that's all you need. And time – real quality time, anyway – isn't measured in minutes and hours. So I'll keep this short . . .' She pulled out her pocket book, which drew a few muted chuckles, and opened it to the allotted page. 'In the time we spent together, I've estimated Harry drank one hundred and seventy pints of ale, and fourteen bottles of Irish whiskey. That's a conservative number, by the way. Later, when I was pregnant and on the wagon, he occasionally switched to ginger beer in my presence, though I expect he was laying a drop of something else in the glass too. When I talked, he always listened, and when I wanted advice, he gave it graciously. And even when I didn't think I needed advice, he managed to give it anyway. He would have hated to be called wise, but that's what he was. I remember going through a proposed list of names for my son, and he could say a great deal with just his eyebrows.

'We laughed a lot, even when life wasn't funny. And much

334

of the time, as my colleagues will know, it *really* isn't.' She looked down at her feet for a moment, thinking about the other funerals that would be taking place today, or soon. 'We lost more of our number last week. Sergeant Alan Menzies, Constable Fred Connor, Chief Inspector Amanda Pettifer, Sergeant Simon Jeffries. They all put their lives on the line to protect the innocent; they were willing to pay the ultimate price. Harry would want us to remember them today as well, his brothers and sisters.'

She left a few moments of silence, before continuing.

'We deal with the worst, and Harry was no stranger to those realities. He served his community for over thirty years, and it took its toll. And all of us, even those who aren't police officers, can understand that. It would be all too easy to let life's horrors overwhelm us. To think the worst of the world. But not Harry.' She paused, wondering how long it would take her to get over the horrors. If she ever could. Maybe it was more about living with them. 'For Harry, the glass was always half full, and he lived his life in the belief that people, even ones who behaved badly, could do better. It would serve us well to follow in his footsteps.' She glanced at the coffin. 'Safe travels, Harry.'

* * *

Outside, in the ornamental gardens at the back of the crematorium, she joined Andy and Heidi as they lay a wreath from the CID team at St Aldates among the amassed floral tributes. Heidi had to leave promptly to attend a PTA meeting at her child's school, and gave Jo a long hug. 'He'd have been bloody proud of you, you know?'

Jo didn't know what to say to that.

She spoke to Mel Cropper for a while, who revealed he had known Harry since the days when smoking on a crime scene was not only acceptable, but positively obligatory. He'd once been charged with trying to explain the intricacies of DNA profiling to a class of investigators, some newly qualified as detectives, others dyed-in-the-wool and nearing the ends of their careers. Harry had got it immediately, but there was one old geezer near retirement age who muttered the immortal line, 'It'll never catch on.'

After half an hour or so, Jo was thinking about taking her leave – Theo was with her brother – when Andy Carrick arrived at her side and offered his good arm. 'Fancy a walk, sergeant?'

Jo smiled, and linked her arm through his, and they set off together along one of the paths that wound through the crematorium grounds.

'How's the other one healing?' she asked.

'There are bad days, and flippin' bad days,' he said. 'Apparently, I'll need physio for three to six months. My tennis game isn't going to be what it was for a while.'

'I didn't know you played tennis.'

'It's more Jasmillah's thing to be honest.'

The present tense caught her attention, and she glanced at his face, searching for the emotion behind the words. He looked far from the bereft man she'd spoken to before. 'Does this mean you two are . . . ?'

'Not exactly,' he said. 'But we're doing some counselling. It might be the start of a long road.'

They walked on in silence, under an arched trellis, and out into the cemetery. Jo had always found such places oddly comforting.

'I've been thinking about work,' she said. 'I reckon I might have come back too soon.'

'Undoubtedly,' he said.

She smiled. 'Be serious.'

'I am,' he said bluntly. 'I'm glad you've worked it out before it's too late.'

She stopped and broke from his side. 'So you'd approve of me taking a break?'

'Very much so,' he said.

'Oh . . . right.' It wasn't quite the reaction she'd imagined.

She'd made the decision the night after she'd shot James Brown. The moment when she'd come through the door of her brother's house, Theo had shuffled towards her on all fours from the living room, his movements malcoordinated and jerky, but pure concentration on his face. Amelia had followed, exclaiming. 'You didn't tell us he'd started to crawl!' and Jo replied, 'He hadn't this morning.' She'd picked him up with a whoop of delight, and let his smell fill her chest.

The day's awful events were still a jumble in her mind, but the one that struck her most as she held her son was when she'd been ordered to discontinue the pursuit, and had disobeyed. At the time, she'd thought she'd made the decision as a matter of course, weighing up the pros and cons. Megan was in danger, and she was the only one who could help save the girl's life. And she might have been right, but that didn't make the decision the correct one. The only thing that mattered was in her arms in that moment, and if she couldn't trust herself to put him first *every single time*, then the choice was sort of obvious.

'I was sort of hoping you'd try to convince me to change my mind,' she said to Carrick.

'I know it's hopeless to try and convince you of anything. I'll miss you, of course. We all will.'

'Even George.'

'Especially George,' said Carrick. 'He respects you a great deal.'

Jo chortled. 'He has a funny way of showing it.'

'Can I let you into a secret?' he said.

'Always.'

'When you went off on maternity leave, *no one* thought you'd be back. The whole Jack Pryce thing, on top of Ben Coombs – we thought you'd have Theo and never darken the doors of St Aldates again. Dimi actually put in for a transfer to London. Said he wanted to *expand his horizons*. But then, when you announced you were returning after six months, guess who withdrew his request.'

'Okay,' said Jo. 'You're confusing causation and correlation. He could have had a hundred reasons. Where is he anyway?'

'He had some good news this morning. From Riley Matthis.'

'Blake's older brother?'

Carrick nodded. 'Seems he took a beating in prison the same night his mum's house got torched. He's willing to talk to us – name names. Dimi's gone there to squeeze the juice out of him.'

A bigger fish . . . thought Jo.

They'd done a circuit, and arrived back where the guests were milling. Many, though, were moving off. The wake, with no dissenting voices, was being informally held at the Three Crowns, and Jo promised she'd be along shortly, with Theo.

'Talk to me next week about work,' said Carrick. 'We'll go through the options.'

She kissed him on the cheek. 'Thanks, Andy.'

She was walking towards her car when Jessica Granger approached from the other direction, alone. Beyond her, her step-son stood just inside the chapel, in conversation with the funeral director.

'I was worried you'd already left,' she said, 'and I hadn't thanked you for delivering such a lovely speech.'

'It was my pleasure,' said Jo. 'I'm flattered you asked me.'

Jessica spread her gloved hands. 'You know, I think I never

really knew him all that well. I thought I did, but it's my belief now that the job shaped him more than I realised. It shapes you all, I expect.'

And rarely for the better, Jo thought.

'You're probably right,' she said.

Jessica smiled, and her gaze lingered on Jo quizzically. 'You know, I hope you don't mind me saying this, but you remind me very much of my daughter Lindsay.'

Jo flushed, with no idea how to respond.

'Oh, I've embarrassed you,' continued Jessica. 'I'm sorry. You don't look alike, but you have something in common. A sort of strength. I imagine that's why Harry liked you so much.'

Once Jo would have laughed, to deflect the compliment, but the earnest look in Jessica Granger's eyes stopped her.

'I don't feel strong most of the time,' she said.

'We'd better go, Mum,' called her step-son.

Jessica rolled her eyes, and took off one of her gloves, reaching out to lay a bare hand on Jo's cheek. Her skin was cool and smooth as satin.

'Dear,' she said, 'the really strong never do. Look after yourself, my girl.'

Her hand slipped off, and Jo watched as Harry Ferman's ex-wife walked away. Her son put his arm around her, and she leant on him a little.

Back in the car, she called her brother and told them she was on the way to get Theo. Then, before she started the engine, she dialled one more number.

'Hello?' said Lucas.

'Hey, it's me.'

'Jo?' he said. He sounded surprised, and thankfully sober.

'The one and only. Listen, we never got round to that walk around the gardens, did we?'

'I didn't think you'd want to,' he said.

It's not about what I want, thought Jo. 'I'm sorry – it's been mad at work. But if you've got time . . .

'Of course! Yes. When?'

'How does this afternoon sound? I think we need to talk, don't you? Properly.'

He didn't answer for a second or two. 'I'm not sure I'd know where to start.'

Me neither, to be honest.

'We'll muddle through,' she said. 'Three o'clock, main gate? I'm the knackered-looking woman with the pushchair.'

'I'll find you,' he said.

Acknowledgements

All characters and scenarios in these pages are entirely fictional, but I was influenced by many stories in the news, and from acquaintances, regarding the care system in this country for vulnerable children. I would like to thank Julie Lewis for answering my questions regarding the procedural elements of that system and the plausibility of certain scenarios within the novel. Factual inaccuracies are all my own, and have been introduced as the story required.

If you enjoyed *Watch Over You* then why not go back to where it all began in the first Josie Masters book.

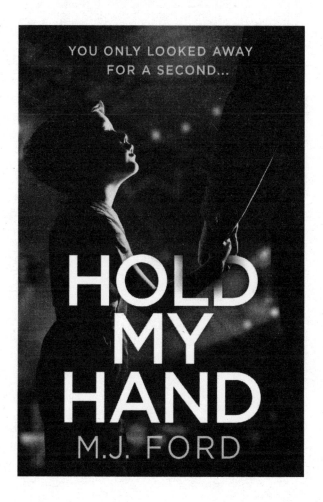

Josie Masters is in a desperate race against the clock to find the killer . . .

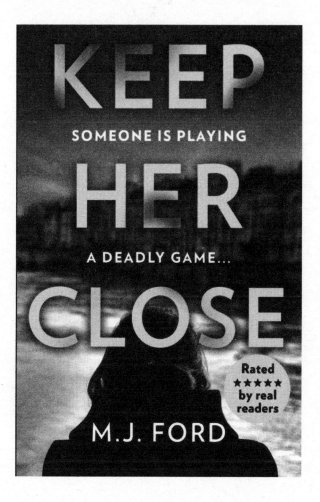